Praise for Mark C

The Draken

'Drakenfeld is a flawed yet appealing hero and Newton has wrought a fast-paced fantasy thriller which should appeal to readers of C. J. Sansom'   *Independent on Sunday*

'A richly written and always engaging work'   *SciFiNow*

'*Game of Thrones* fans will find plenty to enjoy in the story's sharply played political skullduggery, and this first book in the series stands as an intriguing introduction to a world that's challenging and provocative without falling into Grimdark clichés'   *SFX*

'A compelling novel that wouldn't be out of place in the modern thriller genre . . . Charan Newton's new novel *Drakenfeld* shares more with historical fiction and detective fiction novels than it does with traditional epic fantasy, but there's just enough to his world that will make this feel just at home with most epic fantasy readers. The result is a deliberate, interesting novel that grows in scale from beginning to end . . . a smart, interesting thriller'
                                                        io9.com

'*Drakenfeld* is an interesting blend of historical fantasy and crime fiction, set in a beautifully imagined world that seems to have been inspired by Ancient Rome . . . *Drakenfeld* is a novel that became more and more interesting as the depths of its groundwork became clear'   thebooksmugglers.com

'Not every story has to have its own completely unique and original world. Sometimes taking inspiration from a past era works out better than creating a new world, and Mark Charan Newton proves that he can do both' www.fantasyliterature.com

Mark Charan Newton was born in 1981, and holds a degree in Environmental Science. After working in bookselling, he moved into editorial positions at imprints covering film and media tie-in fiction, and later, science fiction and fantasy. He currently lives and works in Nottingham. He is the author of the Legends of the Red Sun series and the Lucan Drakenfeld novels.

For more information and updates, visit his website
www.markcnewton.com

By Mark Charan Newton

Legends of the Red Sun

Nights of Villjamur
City of Ruin
The Book of Transformations
The Broken Isles

The Lucan Drakenfeld novels

Drakenfeld
Retribution

Retribution

MARK CHARAN
NEWTON

PAN BOOKS

First published 2014 by Macmillan

This edition published 2015 by Pan Books
an imprint of Pan Macmillan, a division of Macmillan Publishers Limited
Pan Macmillan, 20 New Wharf Road, London N1 9RR
Basingstoke and Oxford
Associated companies throughout the world
www.panmacmillan.com

ISBN 978-1-4472-1931-6

1 3 5 7 9 8 6 4 2

A CIP catalogue record for this book is available from the British Library.

Typeset by Ellipsis Digital Limited, Glasgow
Printed and bound by CPI Group (UK) Ltd, Croydon, CR0 4YY

Visit **www.panmacmillan.com** to read more about all our books
and to buy them. You will also find features, author interviews and
news of any author events, and you can sign up for e-newsletters
so that you're always first to hear about our new releases.

'*If only nations would realise that they have certain natural characteristics, if only they could understand and agree to each other's particular nature, how simpler it would all be.*'

—D. H. Lawrence, 'The Crucifix Across the Mountains'

In memory of
Laurie Blanshard

Acknowledgements

Novels are never solo efforts. So I'd like to thank my editor, Julie Crisp, for helping to make this book a much better one than before, and to the wider team at Pan Macmillan for their work on the physical book in your hands (or on your e-reader), from cover design to typography. Thanks to Jared Shurin for his reliably robust and entertainingly abusive comments as a reader. And finally yet another hat-tip to my agent, John Jarrold, for his essential advice throughout the journey.

Nations of the Vispasian Royal Union c.201

Tryum

DETRATA

Drobeta

THERAN

MARISTAN

Polonda

FREE STATE
Free City, the City of Gods

Zephron Ocean

KUVASH
POPULATION 350,000

SORGHATA
PREFECTUR

KUVASH
PREFECTURE

Waiting

Standing perfectly still, I listened to the patter of the rain, mesmerized by its cadence as it brushed the leaves of the forest. Ahead of me four children from Bathylan, each of them wearing only a pair of short trousers and a ragged old shirt, played a game around the trees. One couldn't help but smile at the way they endured the rain. Most adults tend to view the rain as a nuisance that soaks our clothes or delays our plans. We seek shelter under arches or loiter in taverns, scowling at the sky. But not these children. For them the rain brought a wonderful new dimension to their day. The sudden deluge delighted them and their faces creased in innocent delight.

Sometimes I long to have such a view of the world again, and wonder what it might take to reclaim that perspective. But in over thirty years of life, a decade of which has been spent as an Officer of the Sun Chamber, the world has long since robbed me of my *limitless* optimism.

This was a beautiful forest and my time here among the low, damp branches of hazel and ash was pleasant indeed, but I needed to head back to the settlement of Bathylan before the rain gathered momentum and really drenched me.

Leaving the children to their games, I walked back towards the chasm. Standing at this precipice, my breath caught in my throat. Great heights were not an issue for me, but this enormous gap took even my breath away. A scar right through the forests and grasslands on the border of Koton and Detrata, it was a mile long and eight hundred feet wide, and an imposing sight. Down the cliff faces, birds spiralled towards their nests among the nooks, and at the very bottom, barely seen, were the white tips of a river in full flow.

The wind began to pick up, offering relief from the humidity, as I strode across one of the four wooden bridges leading to the central village, which stood atop a single island of rock in the centre of the chasm. The bridge shifted this way and that under the pressure of my steps.

Bathylan was a settlement no bigger in size than the largest and most sprawling of villas, but it had developed into an important diplomatic exchange point for trade and information. Situated on the border of Koton and Detrata, it owed allegiance to neither, though both flags could be seen on the rooftops: the black bird in profile on a yellow background for my home nation of Detrata, and the raised red stag on bold blue for Koton. Truth be told Bathylan had become an administrative island of its own, with tiny embassies and aged diplomats looking for a quiet life.

One did not settle in a place like this. It was the sort of settlement that attracted travellers, a handful of well-established traders seeking to avoid tax, or spies, for it was well plugged in to the political scene. It was always easy to tell who the agents were. They always discussed, in a nonchalant manner full of casual hand gestures, that they were travelling on business, 'researching properties' or 'investment opportunities' on behalf of someone else. Imports and exports; the old trade. I made a point of smiling and revealing my Sun Chamber brooch to them, the flaming sun.

It silenced some. Others thought it an opportune moment to pick my brain on various political agendas, showing no shame in their effort to glean information from me. Despite their presence, Bathylan, with its regular thoroughfare, and a gateway to the rest of the continent, was the perfect hub to rest for a few days while waiting for further orders.

On the twenty-first day of our stay I peered out from the shelter of the balcony and sighed at the continual dreary weather. At the opposite end of the garden the blue of the flag of Koton could just about be made out. Beyond the Kotonese flag were the towering, forested and fortified hills – the rolling green vista of the high country – almost lost in the incessant drizzle.

Upon discovery of a small library within the settlement, I had used its resources to brush up on my history of the nation before me. The current ruler, Queen Dokuz Sorghatan, had inherited the throne from her father, King Vehan Sorghatan, who had seized the throne in a military coup. For decades powerful rival factions had bickered over power within Koton, with no one clan ever maintaining overall control. The king's bloody siege, known as the Night of Plunging Blades, had put an end to the matter once and for all and established him as the sole ruler. He had spent his final years in deep paranoia that someone would return the deadly favour to him. But he died peacefully two decades ago, and his only daughter, the young Dokuz Sorghatan, ascended the throne. It was claimed by the scholars who wrote lengthy pieces on Koton that the queen had since worked miracles with the nation and dragged it into the modern age, attempting to bury and rewrite the crude ways of the nation's past – but I noted that the scribes themselves were of Kotonese origin, and were hardly likely to claim otherwise.

A figure tramped quickly up through the swamp-like gardens

of the station post. As she marched along the deck her boots thudded on the wet wood. It was my companion Leana. She took the steps up towards me two at a time. Her wax coat was sodden, even though the journey to the gatehouse to check for any new messages was short. A thick leather cylinder was clutched in her hand.

'Next time,' she said, the water pooling by her feet, 'you can fetch your own post.'

'Oh come on,' I replied, 'it's not that bad out there.'

As if the gods themselves willed it, a jagged line of lightning split the skies. It was followed shortly by a stomach-rocking boom.

'Anyway,' I continued, 'let's take a look at this. Hopefully, we'll have orders to move on.'

I took the dripping tube from her and noted the flaming sun in the wax seal – an icon of the Sun Chamber.

At last.

I hastily opened it and pulled out a rolled-up letter.

'What does it say?' Leana asked impatiently, every bit as eager as me to have a new job.

'At least let me finish it first. It's from Commissioner Tibus herself.'

Lucan Drakenfeld,

I do not like to leave our officers without purpose for long. With this in mind I am sending you to look into what may be a trivial matter, but it is local to your current position. We received a request from Sulma Tan, the Second Secretary to Queen Dokuz Sorghatan of Koton, to help locate the whereabouts of a senior bishop of the main temple of Koton. His name is Bishop Tahn Valin, and he has been missing for five days at the time of sending.

You are to head to the capital city of Kuvash and you will liaise with

Sulma Tan directly. Please note: <u>only liaise with Sulma Tan</u>. Koton is not a nation that looks often for external assistance. Its people are proud and Sulma Tan may have contacted us by mistake, for a second message followed immediately after, declaring that we were no longer required. We will disregard this message — use your discretion and send word as soon as you discover what is happening. The city has an exceptional messenger service, so I shall expect frequent updates.

Finally, recent events in Tryum have, as we suspected, led to plans to press for a republic and continue without a king. The Senate is already conducting a radical overhaul of trade routes and distribution of the military. Be warned: things are not shaping up well in Detrata. The tensions are getting worse and could, potentially, represent a threat to the Union itself.

On a lighter note, of the four proposed consuls elect for the first year, one suggestion is your friend Senator Veron. I hope this amuses you as much as it does me.

Commissioner Tibus.

I conveyed our orders to Leana.

'About time,' Leana replied. 'Was there any news from Detrata?'

'Yes, as it happens. Tibus mentioned Senator Veron.'

Leana's expression soured. 'Has he drowned in a sea of his own debauchery?'

'Not yet,' I smiled, recalling my friend's hedonistic lifestyle. 'It turns out he's a candidate for consul of Tryum this year.'

'Spirits save us,' Leana said, incredulous. 'How does he do it? Can you imagine *him* in charge of a nation?'

'In good times, perhaps, but not in the disarray we left it.'

A royal nation without a king, heading deliberately towards becoming a republic, with a warmongering senate in control who were ready to break free from the united continent — the Vispasian Royal Union — and relive the 'good old days' of a conquering Detratan Empire. No, that was not a good state in which to have seen Detrata. I could only hope that Veron would be a voice of reason.

We had been involved in creating the current upheaval and unrest, an act that was still playing on my conscience. We had acted in good faith and brought justice where needed – but this had been the unforeseen result. A political nightmare.

There was little we could do about it so it was best to concentrate on the job ahead.

We packed our few belongings, and I purchased a long wax coat – similar to Leana's – from the village store. After settling our bill with the guest house, we set out towards Koton and a city that may – or may not – need our help.

Kuvash, Capital of Koton

We spent four days on the road, sleeping in basic hillside taverns. We ate freshly hunted meat by the dwindling flames of ancient hearths. Between the major cities of Detrata and Koton was a harsh landscape. People did not *live* here, they survived. What wasn't forest was scrubland, populated by those hardy and determined enough to make the best of terrible conditions. Farmers had long been forced to create terraces to grow their crops and we could see them working in the fields from dusk till dawn. Goats, with their remarkable balance, were navigating the steep hillsides and fists of granite that pushed through the scrub. Boar clattered through the undergrowth of copses.

The human company out here was nothing like the relative conviviality of Bathylan. In taverns men and women stared silently into their drinks. When they did talk, they discussed things such as sickening horses and failing crops. The disparity between this and my birthplace of Tryum, a city of high culture, where politics and art were discussed as frequently as the weather, was noticeable. Here people did not have the luxury to discuss intellectual matters – but were mainly concerned with getting through each day alive. This was how communities had existed for thousands of years. It made Tryum look rather petty.

People regarded Leana with a predictable caution. No matter where we travelled in the less cosmopolitan regions of Vispasia, there would always be a second glance her way because of her dark-brown skin. Even I, who possessed some of the colours of the desert inherited from my Locconese mother, did not seem especially welcome judging by the glances. So we kept a low profile. We ate quietly, away from others, and contemplated the journey ahead. Our silence served to help us fit in with the stoic community.

Only on one night did I suffer a seizure. It had been mild – perhaps a few heartbeats long at the most. 'No more than a severely disturbed dream,' Leana related to me in the morning. Thankfully I still had a small supply of the tisane I had bought from an apothecary in Tryum, a concoction that was supposed to help with such things. If anywhere the wilds of Koton were perhaps the ideal place for me to suffer an episode – away from prying eyes, away from somewhere word could spread that I had been cursed by the gods.

If it were known that I suffered these fits my reputation would be tainted; even my compatriots within the Sun Chamber wouldn't trust me. It was better that it remained a secret for as long as possible. Only Leana knew and, because of her different beliefs, she did not care about them. If only I could think the same way.

Eventually we neared the sprawling, hilltop city of Kuvash, the capital of Koton. Though there was a central settlement of large stone structures, out towards the fringes were sprawling tented areas.

To the east, dozens of horses were roaming freely on the grassy slopes and running across the plains – the whole herd flowing together like flocks of starlings in a late spring sky.

Closer to us herds of white cattle – in spectacular numbers – were being driven by young boys on horseback, whooping and hollering to keep their charges moving. Like Leana, they rode without a saddle and she looked at them approvingly then threw a mocking glance at my well-padded Detratan saddle.

The road took us through the tented settlements. Woodsmoke spiralled up from within the homes, only to be taken away by the wind. Men and women stood outside wearing more primitive clothing than I'd imagined. Rows of vegetables had been planted all around the area. Severed animal heads stood on poles as decorations. There was no order and it had a temporary feel to it, as if the smiling faces could pack up their homes and leave at any time. Nearby stood what I took to be a crude temple; outside the structure was positioned a straw ox or bull. A woman in black robes began to set fire to the straw, and a solemn congregation trudged in a circle around it.

There was no outer wall to Kuvash. It was common knowledge that no Kotonese city had protective walls around its limits. If the Kotonese had an empire, and Kuvash was at the centre, the lack of walls might have suggested that these people had no need to fear invaders, that their empire's military might was unsurpassed.

No, Kuvash's lack of walls was symptomatic of something else: it was a sign of a nomadic people attempting to adjust to urbanization. It had been two hundred years since the start of the Vispasian Royal Union, two centuries since the people of Koton had been allocated their nation. Even after all that time, there were still signs of a culture in the process of settling down, and the products of instability. Old ways died slowly.

The more solid buildings of Kuvash were comprised of low structures spread over a steeply sloped area of the landscape.

There were a few buildings of note that we could see: temples, of course, as well as old Detratan-style law courts that had survived the days of the Detratan Empire and since fallen into disrepair. Most notable of all, in the distance, was an immense white wall that contained a large area. It might have been the royal grounds, though it looked far too big for that.

Sulma Tan would probably be found there. We headed in that direction.

Urine from leather tanneries gave off a potent tang, even at this distance. The reek then mixed with horse manure and wood-smoke, gaining in intensity as we moved into the city. Dirt tracks eventually transitioned to firm stone roads, which were not as smooth as some cities I'd been in, but by no means the worst. The further inward we travelled, the sturdier the structures became – stone buildings of a practical design, without much care for ornamentation. Here and there were more formal, decorative structures, but they had fallen into disrepair, as if the more feral elements of civilization had reclaimed them and used the stone elsewhere.

Eventually the place began to appear more like a typical city. Its streets became straighter and more sensible, unlike those in Detrata which often curved and twisted randomly. Washing was strung up between windows, and children ran up and down lanes playing games. There were many cats on the streets, too, clustering together in bewildering numbers – some with scraps of food in their mouths, others padding along the walls above and peering down on passers-by. Despite the dreary shades of buildings and clothing, there was the occasional spark of colour: a strip of blue cloth for decorating horses, or a red prayer flag. And of course everywhere was the banner of Koton, a red stag upon blue. No variation in theme or texture, simply this same bold flag, in an array of sizes, as if they had been imposed rather than arranged naturally.

People stared at us as we rode by, so much so that I was beginning to wonder if we had breached some local etiquette. Due to their relative isolation, the people of Koton – or at least Kuvash – possessed a distinctive look. Their faces were generally broader, their hair darker than was usual in Tryum. It was unsurprising to see so few foreigners, since the place was away from major trade routes. The locals wore dreary clothing in shades of brown, grey and black, and some wore necklaces of animal bones. Others, perhaps of a different status, wore either leather or metal cuirasses, which had been crafted to look like snakeskin. In the centre of their breasts was a medallion featuring the stag from the nation's banner.

People I took to be members of the City Watch carried bows, much like the famous mounted archers of Koton. Their horses, too, had decorative bridle fittings. In addition to a red cloak and blue tunic, the soldiers wore scaled leather cuirasses. However, their shields were some of the most elaborate I had ever seen, crafted to display some carved and painted face. Presumably this was once to frighten enemies on the battlefield, and had now become ornamentation.

We made our way through the complex, spiralling lanes of the city and arrived at the main gates of a white-walled compound. Its crenellated top must have been a good twenty feet high. After we dismounted, I had a quick conversation with some armed and helmeted soldiers. Dressed in the same reds and blues, they were manning the thick iron double gate that towered above us. Initially I tried speaking to them in broken Kotonese, but they gauged that Detratan was my natural tongue and, surprisingly, they preferred to use that language. And used it well.

'It is a more cultured speech,' one said. He had nervous

mannerisms and bright eyes that couldn't quite meet mine. He was too busy staring at my Sun Chamber brooch of a hollow, flaming sun. 'So our queen *tells* us,' added the other, much older one. He wore a ring fashioned as a small silver snake, and his beard was long and grey.

'Does she indeed?' I asked.

The two guards shared a glance. They didn't reply to that question.

'So is this where she lives?' I continued. 'Beyond these gates.'

'Sort of — this is the Sorghatan Prefecture,' the old guard replied. 'Queen Dokuz Sorghatan lives further in, in her own palace. This is a rich district, and a lot nicer. Much safer than out there. Food's better and you can drink the water without fear.'

People, horses and carts continued to roll by behind us, and the guards looked fiercely over our shoulders as if they were about to be besieged by invaders. A few people, curious as to what was inside, stepped closer to get a look at the gates, but the guards moved them on with sharp prods from their weapons.

'They should know their place,' the younger guard said.

'Are the people not permitted entry?'

'Only on certain days according to the Astran calendar, and even then we've been told to use our discretion and filter out the real riff-raff. There's a lot of them, mind you. Only reputable traders and the like are allowed in. The queen keeps finding more and more reason to allow them in, but they're better off out there, aye.'

My brooch was sufficient proof of my status as an Officer of the Sun Chamber. It was part of the myth that preceded us wherever we were despatched. Although I had other papers should it have been required, we were permitted in, and we walked our horses through the gates.

My breath was taken away by the sight before me.

Here was a new city entirely. Gaudy, golden colonnades stretched into the distance on each side. Lanes were paved with precision and the people who strolled along them wore resplendently coloured cloaks, fine boots and tunics. The smell of sweet incense came from large brass braziers that stood burning at street junctions. The buildings were made entirely of bright, clean stone, with barely a wooden beam in sight. A solitary man was brushing the spotless street.

This region reminded me of Regallum, the wealthiest district of Tryum, except – and I found it hard to believe – everything here was *even more* ornate. There were temples with garish bronze statues standing outside of a god I didn't recognize.

Not too far away a palace loomed up on a higher level than the rest of the city. It was more impressive than even Prince Bassim's ziggurat in Venyn City, where Leana and I had spent so many years honing our street skills. Could it have matched the royal residence in Tryum? From here it appeared white-walled with a flat, black roof, and featuring elaborate golden gargoyles and other decorations, the details of which I could only guess at from where I stood.

It was turning into a warm day, not unpleasantly hot. A few clouds scudded above the hills in the distance, but otherwise the sun was out, causing the golden statues to shimmer like other-worldly beings.

I asked a young boy for directions to the entrance to the royal palace, and he guided us politely to the main avenue.

'It's at the end,' he said, and I spent a moment following his instruction.

As I tried to thank him he dashed away along the road.

'He did not even ask for money,' Leana observed. 'What strange children they have here.'

A wide straight road guided us towards the gate of the palace.

Stalls lined one side of the road and on the other side was a gap, which opened down onto a large river. The water had been used to form a moat around one half of the palace. Down below barges moved along the water, others unloading their cargo, while up here among the stalls people were bargaining furiously. It looked as though there was a healthy trade in goods such as silverware, rugs, leatherwear and tack for horses. I turned back to look at the river. Some way away was a bustling inland port, possibly another settlement entirely.

After walking our horses up the hill and along the busy thoroughfare, navigating the eddies of customers and traders cajoling and haggling, we turned a corner and arrived at the palace. Enormous walls rose up. At the top, forty feet above, four soldiers in ceremonial clothing walked up and down behind the crenellations. We stood looking up, assessing what looked to be a largely decorative structure with no real capability of withstanding a siege. Only then did I notice that we stood alone – none of the locals dared to come within twenty feet of the palace walls.

'Well, this is it,' I announced to Leana, 'now we just have to find a way inside.'

The soldiers on the walls were looking down at us and, shortly, a small doorway opened and several guards marched out and surrounded us. They were wearing different colours from the City Watch, purple and gold, and carried highly polished glaives.

Leaning towards Leana, I whispered, 'They're certainly a *colourful* lot.'

'State your purpose for being here, foreigners,' came the command.

Foreigners, indeed. We were representatives of the whole *continent*. Our badge of office should have been enough to permit us into the most sacred of spaces. No sooner had I revealed it to him than his countenance changed entirely. 'My name is Lucan Drakenfeld,' I began, 'and I'm an Officer of the Sun Chamber . . .'

Sulma Tan

Leana and I had been waiting in a small, well-lit antechamber at the front of the queen's magnificent palace for at least two hours. It was a wood-panelled room with tall candles in sconces and vibrant red rugs. A stag's head of considerable size was positioned on the wall to one side, one of many hunting trophies we had seen. While I looked at the colourful portraits of those I took to be of the queen's family – one of whom appeared to be her militant father – we continued to wait by a splendid fire. Every few moments we were reassured by guards that Sulma Tan would 'soon be here'. More periods of waiting and looking at the paintings followed.

At last a voice addressed me: 'Are you Officer Drakenfeld? I've received no official notification of your visit – am I correct?'

The woman who entered the room spoke in a remarkably clear form of Detratan, without a hint of a local accent – in a way that was far too *precise* to be truly associated with someone from my home nation.

'Good morning.' Rising to meet her, I began to introduce myself formally, but she held up a hand.

'I am Sulma Tan,' the woman continued, 'second secretary to the queen.'

Her black hair, with a heavy fringe, was worn down unlike many of the other ladies I'd seen in the corridors, who wore theirs pinned up or tied back decoratively, almost artistically. Framed between curls was her broad face, with delicate features. She wore a necklace of silver and emerald and heavy black boots, while her long, tunic-style dress was made of heavy blue silk. She was about my age – perhaps a couple of years younger. In complete contrast to the nervous guards, her hazel eyes met mine with confidence and intensity. There was an intelligence and analytical mind behind that gaze, with almost a sense of impatience with the rest of the world. Right now she was assessing me, processing why a stranger was here interrupting her busy schedule.

'I know who you are,' she said. 'Or at least, who you represent. You are both from the Sun Chamber, yes?'

'That's right. We've just now travelled up from Detrata, after stopping off along the way. This is my colleague, Leana.'

'Colleague?' Sulma Tan asked, scrutinizing Leana, though without showing a sneer as the guards had done as they escorted us inside.

'It's a more preferable word to use than bodyguard,' I said. 'And I don't know what the word is to describe someone who tries to keep me from taking myself too seriously.'

Sulma Tan once again weighed up my words, and chose not to follow my light-hearted introductions with anything like the same tone.

'Though I note your brooch, I would like to see your papers. You must understand that to us a man travelling from Detrata may be on the business of espionage.'

'Yes, of course.' I rummaged in my satchel and produced documents stating my name, my station, and a list of honours within the Sun Chamber. 'As you can see,' I continued as she shuffled through them assiduously, 'I am no spy.'

'You are as you say, Officer Drakenfeld.'

'Yes,' I replied, 'and any ambassadors here from Detrata may vouch for me.'

'The Detratan ambassador, Carrus Mineus, has returned to your country,' Sulma Tan declared. 'He was recalled by your Senate.'

She noted the look of surprise, which must have shown on my face, with obvious interest. Admittedly I was confused as to why the Senate would withdraw its ambassadors. It was no good omen when a country withdrew its diplomacy. 'Did Mineus reveal why he was leaving?'

'He said only that he had been recalled.'

'Did he indeed,' I replied. There was no tension in her voice. She was very matter of fact about it. 'Perhaps his departure has something to do with having so many soldiers around the palace?'

'That is not the reason.' She paused slightly, and studied me for a little longer. 'You may as well hear it from me rather than some exaggerated rumour. There has been an attempt on the life of Princess Nambu Sorghatan.'

'I'm sorry to hear that. Was she harmed?'

'No. The intruder came close, but could not get through to her chamber. He fled out of one of the windows, with a surprising athleticism. It is why we are being extra cautious right now. But to matters more pertinent to your arrival. Am I to understand, then,' she added firmly, 'that my second message did not come through?'

'Your second message?' I pretended to have no idea what she was talking about, but knew full well what she meant.

'Ah.' A smile accentuated the lines of her face. Though this was not a warm expression at all, more of a knowing realization.

Perhaps she suspected that the message had been received, but the Sun Chamber had decided to ignore it. There was something about her manner that suggested she was constantly one step ahead of me. 'This will explain your . . . *presence*. Well, for your information we have, it seems, resolved the issue of Bishop Tahn Valin.'

'Is he well?'

'The matter is resolved.' She regarded me as if to say, *why are you still here?*

'I would very much like it if you could introduce me to him, so that I might record the matter as *resolved* to my superiors. You must know how the Sun Chamber can be. We're very thorough and I must report this case to be closed in a satisfactory manner, lest more officers be sent to investigate.'

'If you insist.'

'I get the impression you don't appreciate outside influence,' I asked as the three of us walked along the corridors of the palace.

'Please, try not to take my actions personally,' she said, then her voice softened. 'It's difficult for outsiders to understand what a proud culture this is. Though we're openly part of Vispasia, we are people who like to do things ourselves. Or, at least, that is how it used to be. But Queen Dokuz Sorghatan is a lady of high culture and she welcomes ideas from the outside. The finest philosophers, poets and engineers from the surrounding nations are now often to be found in our court. Her donations and large salaries attract a great deal of interest from great minds and scholars.'

'But when it comes to your bishops,' I said, 'you'd rather sort out your own mess.'

'I would argue that it is not a mess, as you put it. But I see your point.' Her words came slowly – not out of any difficulty in speaking Detratan, but because she was considering them carefully, like a diplomat or politician.

The corridors were much plainer than the rest of the building promised. There was little in the way of ornamentation, just one dark passageway after another, with bare stone broken by the occasional cresset or narrow window, some of which made a pattern of light across the floor and I could smell . . .

I came round slowly and looked up from my position on the floor. I had obviously suffered a seizure.

Leana was peering over me and, to her side, stood Sulma Tan, with a deeply analytical expression upon her face. Leana was making excuses on my behalf, but my embarrassment was overwhelming. I had no control over these matters – they seemed to strike at will – but to do so immediately upon having met someone from this nation was humiliating, to say the least.

Leana helped me to my feet. I stared sheepishly towards Sulma Tan to make my apologies, weighing up if I should tell her the truth that the gods were punishing me for some misdemeanour.

'Interesting,' was all she said. 'I have seen such things before. How long have you suffered?'

'Most of my adult life,' I replied tentatively.

She began to probe me with questions, as if a physician rather than a secretary to the queen, but my almost monosyllabic responses should have given her an indication of my discomfort. Yes, they were mainly in my sleep. There were sometimes headaches. No, they did not happen all the time, just on average every few days. No, I can't remember what happened. The gods caused them. And so on.

'I would be grateful,' I concluded, truly worried for my safety now, 'if you could keep this event quiet. Just between us. Only Leana knows I suffer such seizures, and it would make my job very difficult if people knew about it – they would not trust me. They would think me cursed by the gods – and they would refuse to work with me.'

Sulma Tan snorted. 'Ridiculous superstition. I do not believe this is some affliction of the gods.'

It was remarkable that she could be so matter of fact about it. I was certain that I would be treated differently if anyone knew of my seizures. Yet Sulma Tan continued to regard me with as much indifference as previously.

'I do not think you are *tainted*, no.' She looked pleased with herself.

And with that she turned and beckoned us onwards. Leana simply shrugged, but her angry glare said much. I vowed discreetly to her that if we came upon an apothecary, we would get some more herbs. Together, the panic over, we moved on.

We eventually reached a large, brick chamber with several desks and wall-to-wall shelves that were rammed with old scrolls. There was one window that overlooked a sunny courtyard garden containing numerous rose bushes. However warm and pleasant it was out there, it was very cold in this old room.

'This is one of our many copying chambers,' Sulma Tan said. 'The queen is very keen on creating copies of core Vispasian texts in both Kotonese and Detratan. We keep copies of each in our very large library elsewhere in the city.'

'A very industrious process you have here,' I replied.

'There is much knowledge to be passed on.'

'What texts are they?' Leana asked.

'Everything from plays to scientific observation, laws and discussions of moral rights,' Sulma Tan replied. 'Queen Dokuz wants *everything* from all over Vispasia – she wishes it to be copied and stored in Kuvash, to be discussed by our people so that we may be enhanced as a culture.' For a moment she glanced out of the window, the sunlight catching her in profile. That last sentence almost sounded as if she had committed it to memory like an actor. 'People may think it ambitious, but I'm truly glad that we now have a queen who appreciates these things. It is much easier to be a woman in Kuvash these days.'

'Such developments are very recent,' I suggested. 'You were once a more *primitive* country?' I immediately wished I had not used the word.

Sulma Tan gave me another patronizing stare. 'When I was a child, we were living in a *primitive* country, as you say. This is not to say that women were never powerful. We were made up of tribes — and two tribes were made up entirely of women. They would hunt and fight, every bit as ferocious as men. Once a year, as the days grew shorter, they received the visits of males from surrounding tribes for the purposes of breeding. The babies would be born in the warmer months so they would be able to survive better. Any male children were cast from a cliff or sold into slavery, while the females were cherished and raised as part of the tribe. But eventually these two tribes were absorbed into others, and such practices petered out. That was centuries ago. There was no sophistication back then. Even when our nation became part of Vispasia, the results were mere lines drawn on a map to herd our tribes together, and we were very much of the old culture. We had little understanding of the outside world for decades because our kings and queens have always wanted to remain isolated.

'But ever since Queen Dokuz took the throne — which was some twenty years ago now — she has been working hard to bring the arts and sciences to Kuvash. One can see the results in our buildings and our trade. Even our towns and cities — they may not *appear* much, but they are better than what was there before.

And a woman can walk through the streets of the prefecture and not expect harassment all the time. Can your culture claim the same?'

'If you speak of Detrata, then probably not,' I replied. It was difficult for me to *understand* – and she was someone who I wanted to understand. Being a man I had no experience of what it was like to be a woman in normal society, to be hassled as I walked down the street, to feel threatened, or leered at, or debased in some way every day by the opposite sex, to have limited rights, or to be treated like a commodity.

I had engaged in such discussions before, with Leana, and knew there was no debate to be *won*. Everyone lost.

Sulma Tan glanced between me and Leana. 'Though you employ a woman as your bodyguard. That suggests you are not quite as *primitive* as many men in our country.'

There was an awkward silence.

'Are we to wait here to meet Bishop Tahn Valin?' Leana asked impatiently.

Sulma Tan walked over to the large table near the front of the room, and reached under it. With a sigh she lifted out a heavy wooden box, which she then placed on top of the table and beckoned us forward.

'There is no need,' Sulma Tan replied with the same cool expression, and lifted open the lid of the box.

Inside it lay two pieces of a human arm.

The limb had been severed just above the elbow and was caked in dried blood. Despite the stain and decay, I could perceive faint tattoos and religious inscriptions. The limb still bore a slender silver bangle with strange symbols carved upon it.

'This belonged to Tahn Valin,' Sulma Tan announced.

'You're certain it belongs to him?' I asked.

'We are, yes. His religious tattoo indicates that it is him, the bangle that he's wearing was of a bishop's rank, the only decoration they wear, and we have verified this with a priest who worked at the same temple. This is all that remains of him and, in this state, we are confident that the bishop has not survived his ordeal. So it seems, Officer Drakenfeld, you have wasted your journey.'

'I don't know.' I met her gaze. 'You haven't found the rest of him yet. And this . . . well this could easily be the remains of another priest.'

'We have not found any other parts of a corpse, and we strongly believe this to be the bishop. He is the only bishop we know to have disappeared – no others have been reported missing.'

'I must ask the obvious, but I take it you don't know who did this?'

Sulma Tan shook her head and I could tell from her expression she was still trying to work out what my plan of action might be, but she was at least far more open in her manner than before.

'Since I've come so far,' I said, 'perhaps I can assist in locating the rest of him? The rest of him might still be alive, for all we know. He'd be in a bad state, of course, but it is worth considering.'

Sulma Tan let out a long breath and regarded the remains in the box.

Leana leaned over to get a closer look. 'This is curious. Why has the bangle not been taken?'

'Yes. It was not a thief that killed this man,' I agreed, 'else why leave such a precious item? And we're assuming that this man is actually dead. Even if it had been part of a robbery, which seems unlikely, what kind of thief would go to the trouble of butchering him in such a way?' I turned my attention once again to Sulma Tan. 'Where did you find these pieces?'

'They had been thrown over the walls to the Sorghatan Prefecture,' she replied coolly. 'A soldier found them while on patrol, though the arm had been thrown into a rather public area. It was not necessarily for a soldier to find.'

'And you keep the remains here, because it's cool?'

'I thought it wise to preserve them until we knew more, and since we have studied them this has become their temporary home.'

It was impressive that a queen's secretary knew about the decay of flesh in warm temperatures. 'Who's been looking into this matter for you so far?'

'We asked a soldier from the City Watch to investigate, but he has not been successful. Now his rotation has sent him to patrol further out of the city, the matter has ... slipped, admittedly. The staff here are very busy. Being the queen's second secretary, I have little time to dedicate to this issue. We also have a large segment of the army returning from their posting on the border, which is an administrative headache, and I have plenty of work to be done. So yes, this has not received the dedication that perhaps it should have done. It was why I sent my first letter.'

'And your second because you did not want the outside world prying too greatly?'

'If you wish to believe that.'

This was a intriguing situation. It wasn't merely my orders that were keeping me here. It was strange that someone would kill a bishop, not take his bangle, and then throw his body parts over a wall to be found by others.

'If you'll permit me, then, I'll look into the matter for you,' I said. 'That will leave you free for whatever state business you were originally tasked with.'

Sulma Tan never relinquished eye contact during the ensuing silence, but eventually she said, 'I will need to discuss it with the queen, though I see no problem with such a commission. Please return here tomorrow morning. Make sure to ask for me.'

'Will we have to wait as long to see you tomorrow?'

'That depends on how busy I am,' she replied, choosing not to note my sarcasm.

A Place to Stay

It was an interesting state of affairs. Why would someone sever the bishop's arm? And, as Leana had pointed out, why had they not taken the bangle? We had established that whoever killed him did not care for such trinkets, which suggested they were of a status not in need of the money the bangle might bring. If that was the case, it limited our search to a small stratum of the city, though I was cautious about jumping to any conclusions at this point.

What intrigued me in particular was the notion of throwing the pieces of his arm over the wall. Such a gesture was deliberate and not a discreet way of doing things. Yet, if a relatively wealthy person had been responsible, they would not necessarily have thrown the pieces from the poorer side of the wall, in the Kuvash Prefecture – the pieces of the arm might simply have been left there, waiting to be found. They might even have been dropped in a curious accident.

During my conversation with Leana we speculated on the possible reasons for placing the pieces there. It was a signal, perhaps. It was just as likely that it could have been a warning to someone on the other side – a threatening gesture to the temple.

The next step would be to visit the bishop's temple and find out as much as we could about him, but not today – the hour was late and we needed to find lodgings for our time in Kuvash.

Sulma Tan had issued us with a piece of paper that declared we were permitted to stay within the Sorghatan Prefecture. It suggested that people were not free to move between the two prefectures. The queen's second secretary advised us to head to a guest house for wealthy businessmen who passed through Kuvash. A few streets away, she told us, it was one of the more pleasant places in the city for a traveller to spend time.

It was run by Jejal, a rotund man in his fifties. He walked with a limp and his left eye was a different colour to his right. His grey hair was long yet frizzy, and he wore a very bright tunic, much in the Detratan style, though it was a somewhat cheaper variation. He was paler than the average person of Koton and his gaze was perpetually wild and promising, as if he was someone who knew secrets but wasn't particularly good at keeping them.

'They ask me if I want someone from the Sun Chamber here, and I say to them, yes please.'

'Who's them?' I asked.

'You know.' Jejal gave a shrug. 'Authorities. Clerics. Administrators.'

Sulma Tan's influence, I thought.

Jejal continued saying, 'I know they pay you people well and trustworthy coin is hard to come by.'

We carried our own bags up the narrow, wooden stairway. Ink portraits had been arranged up the wall following the ascent, and there was a strange smell coming from the kitchens. 'Do you not have many trustworthy people stay here? I was under the impression this establishment attracted honourable people.'

'Oh yes! I like to keep my guest list full of honourable people, sure, but you can never tell, eh? Merchants can be unscrupulous bastards at the best of times. Give me coin that isn't pure gold or silver. Melted down.' He paused and shook his head. 'This prefecture is a respectable place these days. So you are most welcome here, both you and your wife.'

I smirked knowingly at Jejal's common assumption, which Leana had long since ceased to find amusing. 'She's not my wife.'

'Ah, your lover – don't worry, I do not ask questions on such matters – I know better! There's trustworthy and *trustworthy*, eh.'

'No,' I said as we paused on the corner of the next floor. 'She's not my lover either.'

'Your slave?' He squinted one eye, as if attempting to comprehend a piece of art. 'Where's she from?'

Leana snapped, 'I am slave to no one.'

'Your bodyguard?' Jejal asked.

'That's as close as you're going to get,' I replied. 'And she's from Atrewe.'

'Good artists from Atrewe, so they say,' Jejal said. 'I had a dealer here once trying to make a payment in original paintings and vases, but such things are wasted on me. I enjoy basic necessities – good money, good food, good wine and good . . . well, bad women. Balance is everything.'

'I'm sure your wife wouldn't agree,' I said.

He stared at me incredulously. 'How could you know I was married?'

'Your recent guest-house plaque – a local licence of sorts, I suppose – was nailed to the wall downstairs above the door, bearing both your names and last year's date. You might want to renew it, by the way, if the authorities come to check.'

Jejal grunted and turned away. He kept on muttering to himself as we walked along the corridor, deciding not to pursue the conversation any further.

Eventually he stopped at a door and showed us to our room. 'This is all I have for you,' he announced. 'It is, I hope, enough to please such people of high culture, eh? Please, step inside.'

It was much larger than expected – there was a large four-poster bed, with sumptuous green and red silk cloth, large oil lamps, a desk where I could work, a large couch under a small shelf full of books, and a window overlooking a quiet part of the city. The floorboards were polished and there was a wonderful citrus scent coming from somewhere.

Jejal was not going to offer this room cheaply, and as soon as he saw my signs of happiness he quoted something a little more than the amount I'd anticipated. But given that I'd recently sold my property in Tryum, I had enough money for now, so I readily accepted. The Sun Chamber would presently forward on my wages and any interim expenses in the form of a credit note, so the situation was comfortable enough for the time being.

'You honour me with your decision to stay in our humble guest house,' Jejal said, walking to the door. 'A small deposit of a small gold coin worth seventy kron is all that is required – the rest we can settle upon departure. Food is not included.'

'Thank you.' Placing my bags down by the window, I casually regarded the wide street below. Seventy kron was about ten pecullas in Detratan money, which wasn't unreasonable, so I reached into my pocket and handed over the money. Jejal scrutinized the coin in the light of the window.

After he appeared satisfied, I asked, 'I don't suppose you've heard of a man called Tahn Valin, have you?'

'The missing bishop?' Jejal looked up at me without surprise. 'Yes, who has not heard of him?'

'Who was he exactly?'

Jejal gave a shrug. 'I cannot tell you who he was as a person – I don't know priests in that way. But he was a much admired man.

I saw him preach once. He was calm and intelligent and I liked his delivery. Not one of the great orators of our time, but he got inside people's heads – that's what a bishop is supposed to do, isn't it? But he did a lot of work with those more unfortunate than us. When he wasn't preaching he was giving alms to the poor. He was not involved in corruption like priests you might find elsewhere. That is all I can tell you about him. I can't understand where he has gone and why he would abandon his temple.' He paused as if recalling what it was that the Sun Chamber did. 'That what you're here for? Have you come to find him?'

'I'm interested in his whereabouts,' I admitted – which wasn't entirely untrue.

'Say no more!' Jejal whispered with some urgency, and proceeded out of the room.

Listening to his steps fading downstairs, I turned to regard the room. 'Well, we seem to have done rather well. Not as good as my home in Detrata, but not as bad as our small dwelling in Venyn City, that's for sure.'

Leana made for the large couch and placed her belongings on the floor beside it.

'If you want, you can take the bed instead,' I said, 'you're more than welcome to.'

'You know how I feel about comfort,' she replied. 'It dulls the senses. Blunts your wits.'

'I'm only being polite,' I replied.

'So you believe what he said, about the bishop?'

'I see no reason why not. It was interesting that his death has not been formally announced to the city. Sulma Tan was convinced the man was dead, so surely the issue must have been mentioned to the people by now.'

'As she reminds us, she is a busy woman.'

'She is. Well, we should first find the bishop's temple and take a look around there.'

Out of the window, down below, a couple of carts were being drawn by hand from the marketplace, which was starting to pack up for the night. It was going to be a clear evening. The last of the day's sunlight glimmered on the red roof tiles, which were of a similar sloping style to those found in Tryum. In fact, a lot of the buildings here appeared to be familiar – as if the designers had constantly looked to Tryum for inspiration when they constructed this city. There were even long colonnades and column-fronted buildings just like at home. Statues and busts adorned the fronts of buildings. More than once a fresco could be perceived through an open doorway. The temples were Detratan styled, too, and not like the tall, wooden, spired structures we saw throughout the Kotonese countryside on our way here.

'This city is trying too hard to impress,' I commented out loud.

'Those on the other side of the wall would see things differently,' Leana replied bluntly. 'For them it does not seem so impressive.'

Two Gods

The last few rays of the day's sun skimmed across the low slate rooftops of the prefecture, and the hills in the distance were now dark shadows. We walked through the streets, navigating by the answers of locals towards Bishop Tahn Valin's temple. A gong was struck several times a few streets away, the sound carrying along the quiet lanes amidst the scent of woodsmoke from the evening fires.

The bishop's home and place of worship was like those dedicated to Polla that I had seen in Tryum recently, a fact that unsettled me at first. I had expected a different religion – different gods in a different country – for it to have its own identity. Set back from a busy street, it was a large rectangular building made from stone, with reliefs along the top and a triangular pediment at the front, with two columns on each side of a large wooden door. I stared up at it, and for a moment it felt as if I were back at home.

As we climbed the steps towards the door, we were presented with small statues of two very different gods. A woman's torso blended into the legs of a horse; a male god's muscular torso met with the lower half of a fish. Both of them carried glaives and directed them to the heavens.

'Can I help you?'

A man marched towards us, a stern look upon his aged face. He wore layers of claret-coloured cloth – from tunic to cloak – though there was no emblem or markings on his clothing. He was a stout individual, with grey hair and tired-looking, but very searching eyes. He had the air of someone who had been through a great deal of stress.

Turning towards him, I made sure he could see the brooch of the Sun Chamber on my chest.

'My name's Lucan Drakenfeld, and this is my colleague, Leana,' I began in Kotonese. 'We've been asked to investigate the matter of Bishop Tahn Valin.'

'Ah. My name is Priest Damsak. We should talk somewhere more discreet.' He held my elbow gently and steered me into the temple, all the time looking about him as if he had reason to be worried.

Inside, statues of the strange animalistic man and woman were repeated, and in every instance they maintained the same half-horse, half-fish representation. Rows of cushions and small rugs were arranged for the congregation to sit or kneel upon. Thick tapestries hung from the walls, each one depicting strange scenes featuring the same male and female gods, some versions with them in armour, some naked.

'Which gods are these?' I asked.

'Astran and Nastra.' For a moment he lost his sense of fear. 'The two split aspects of heaven. Astran, she is the goddess of the land, while Nastra is the god of the seas.'

'On our way here I saw a straw ox on the fringes of Kuvash. There seemed to be some sort of ceremony going on.'

Damsak glared at me. 'Those are the old gods. The old ways. Such practices ought to be forbidden.'

'That was nothing to do with your gods then?'

'It was certainly not. There are unfortunate remnants of a more primitive time. Several old cults use ceremonial sacrifices of livestock where they cannot afford to waste real animals. It is a barbaric practice. It is a commune with the dead rather than the correct way of venerating their spirits.'

I had seen similar religious offerings across Vispasia, particularly Detrata. It didn't seem so primitive to me, but I put the priest's disgust down to the fact that it was not something his own gods agreed with.

Damsak let out a sigh and muttered something in a much older version of the language, which sounded very respectful.

'If I may say, you seem rather concerned.'

'Why shouldn't I be after what happened to Tahn,' he snapped. 'The man had done nothing to deserve such evil treatment. What if it is someone who dislikes our gods? What if I'm to be next, sliced up in such a manner?'

'You're aware of his fate, then?'

He nodded his acknowledgement.

'What have you been told?'

Changing languages to Detratan, probably so only the learned might eavesdrop, he said, 'I know only what the authorities have shown me. I believe it is him who has been found – those parts of his arm.' The priest held out a bony arm, and I could see a similar bangle to the one worn by the bishop. 'What else can you tell me so far?'

'I'm afraid I don't know much else,' I replied. 'That's why I'm here. I've come to find out more about the bishop and I was hoping you could help the start of my investigation. And the more you tell me, the more I'll be able to help you in finding who did this to him. I can put your mind at ease. That is,' I added, now he appeared less on edge, 'if you yourself had nothing to do with his death?'

'How could you say such a thing?'

'Quite easily,' I replied. 'We must eliminate all possibilities. You might stand to gain from his death.'

'On the contrary,' he replied, a bitter sneer upon his face. 'With the bishop going, I have no idea what will happen to this temple. I'm certainly not in line to follow someone as grand as a bishop. I have my place and it was by his side. We had plans, next year, to venture from the city on a pilgrimage so Nastra-knows what I'll do now.'

'You were going to leave the city?' I asked. 'Who else knew about this?'

'It was common knowledge, as of the last new moon a couple of months ago, when we announced it to our congregation. We said we were going to leave for about a year, taking the practical aspects of our gods further afield, and living in more humble circumstances than this – by the side of the road, or in the houses of whoever would welcome us on our path. The bishop was very keen on this – in his later years he grew increasingly concerned that people needed rescuing from other foul gods. He wanted to help people. He wanted to bring them the comforts of Astran and Nastra.'

The hierarchy of this religion would be easy enough to research to confirm his statement. I made a mental note to send for confirmation of the facts via Sulma Tan.

'Could someone have wanted to prevent the bishop from leaving the city?'

Damsak looked dumbfounded by the question. 'If they wanted him to remain, why send him to a different spiritual realm altogether?'

'He may have been smuggling secrets with him. Documents important to the state.'

'This is very fanciful.' Damsak's expression made it clear he felt the idea absurd. 'The bishop barely left the temple other than to help the poor from time to time. There were certainly no business affairs.'

'How *well* did you know him?'

'We were as brothers.' Damsak paused for a moment, and his head turned as if he was listening to something in the distance. 'Of the priestly kind. We spoke very little about our personal lives, but in our religious community we do not especially have personal lives to speak of. We are known only by our work.'

'Your work being . . . ?'

'In many ways I was learning from Tahn. There are many rituals to perfect, and a common priest like myself only has the authority to conduct a certain number, lest they go wrong. I studied our main texts under Tahn.'

'You seem rather old to be studying,' I said.

The priest smiled in a way that suggested he had heard that comment many times before. 'One does not get access to higher strata of society easily in Koton. My family is from a far lower caste, and related to the Yesui clan, who were not looked upon favourably by our queen's father.'

'The Night of the Plunging Blades?'

'Thankfully not then, which is why they are still here. No. A family name can mean a lot in Koton. Things are easier than they used to be, thanks to the queen. But some of the old ways are still prevalent, and authority is reluctant to give up power.'

'Even in the house of your gods?'

'It is perhaps more forgivable in such circumstances. Only appropriate people should be allowed to channel such gods.'

Very convenient for a priest to speak in favour of being a

gatekeeper, I thought, no matter how low his rank. 'How long ago was it that the bishop went missing?'

'About twenty days ago. It was just after the Service of Remembrance, a day for all fallen soldiers. He conducted a most memorable service.'

'What were his last known movements? I'd like to know where he went, if he decided to meet with anyone. No detail will be too small for us.'

'You ask for much.' The priest gave a sad sigh and sat down on one of the cushions. He gestured for us to do the same, and we obliged – facing opposite him. Only then did I notice the amazingly detailed fresco on the ceiling of the temple – the swirling patterns of the heavens and yet more scenes featuring the two gods.

Then the priest began to provide his verbal portrait of Bishop Tahn Valin.

The bishop had lived in the city of Kuvash for all of his fifty-seven years, Damsak told us. Like all city priests, he lived alone in a room at the back of his temple, so that someone was present even when there was no congregation. He had led a simple life; he was a bookish man who did not eat meat – something that was a sharp contradiction to the rest of Kotonese culture, which thrived on meat. The queen was an admirer of his work and even of his religious and mythological poetry – sometimes she would invite him to her personal court to read it aloud at banquets.

'He was well loved by the community,' Damsak said with a sigh. 'People would often leave food offerings at his door – though he never asked for such things – and sometimes he even spent the following hours handing those donations to the poor outside the main gates to the prefecture.'

'And his final moments,' I asked. 'Do you recall them *precisely*?'

'The last time that anyone saw him was at the end of his last daily, dusk sermon — on the remembrance evening. People left one by one and he went alone to the back of the building — as he had always done. I heard him go into his quarters and I left him to it while I went to mine.'

'And he just vanished?' I said.

Damsak nodded. 'When I knocked on the door later that evening, to ask if he would like a cup of wine to help him sleep, he gave no reply. I went in, and his room was empty.'

'You heard nothing?'

'No. Though my quarters are on the other side of the temple, and I liked to leave the bishop to his quiet contemplation. He was due to rise early, you see, to take alms to the poor. And so . . . I really cannot see why someone would be so . . . vicious as to butcher him in this way.' The priest paused to make a circle with his hand above his head. 'What ill times we live in . . .'

Damsak's face once again exhibited the distress of someone who felt like he was being hunted.

'What did you do when you didn't find him?'

'I did little that night. He might have gone for walking meditation about the city. It was only in the morning, when he still had not returned, that I contacted the City Watch.'

'Is it possible he left his quarters willingly, then?' I suggested, leaning back on my hands. 'To meet someone else?'

'Very much so, though he'd have no reason to,' Damsak replied, somewhat confused. 'Anyway, as I say, I contacted the Watch and they must have notified the various authorities within the queen's palace. I heard very little. I maintained everything as it was here and wrote to the elders within our organization, to keep them informed. After that matters were kept out of my reach — they were not for me to know. The bishop had gone, and that was that.'

Only to be later returned in pieces. If the priest's account was completely true, then there was only a small window of time that night in which the bishop could have been taken. It was possible that the killer invited the bishop outside, but that sounded unlikely. What was more probable is that the killer was all too aware of the bishop's movements. He knew exactly when to strike so as to cause minimal fuss – it had all the hallmarks of a well-planned assassination, by a killer who was familiar with the bishop's routines, and who had easy access to this prefecture. The idea that someone would send an assassin to kill a simple bishop did not make sense, unless the priest was only giving us part of the picture. He might not have known all of it himself.

'May we see his room?' I asked.

'Of course.' Damsak rose with ease from the cushions, and I followed with a grunt.

Despite being far younger than the priest, I was going to find it difficult getting used to the Kotonese custom of sitting on the floor and getting up again.

I could almost hear Leana's thoughts: *You're too soft.*

We were led into the small living quarters at the back of the temple, and Priest Damsak lit the candles on the wall mounts. Frugality did not seem to adequately describe this place – in comparison, my current rented accommodation was fit for a queen. Here was just a small bed in one corner, an old oak table at which he must have dined and worked – judging by the ink pots, candle and plates – and a rug across the flagstones. The handful of books on a shelf beside his bed were theological texts.

'He wasn't much one for furnishings or ornaments,' I said, thinking how the room was too dark at this hour for a thorough search. I glanced up to a simple leaded window above the bed.

'We do not encourage trinkets,' Damsak replied. 'Tahn always said that one cannot take trinkets to the heavens. Other than for purposes of identification, generally speaking our organization does not approve of such things.'

'What about lovers?' I asked, wondering if the priests were celibate like some other religions. 'Was there any woman or man in the bishop's life we should know about?'

The glare I received was expected. 'No. We do not socialize in such a way. There is too much work to be done and lovers can be something of a distraction from our cause. They are *frowned* upon.'

'What exactly is your cause?' Leana asked.

'The work of Astran and Nastra, of course,' he replied with a peaceful expression.

I followed up Leana's line of approach. 'That work being . . . ?'

'Guiding souls to the heavenly realms, ensuring that their lives are led in the appropriate way so that they may attain as fine a position in the next world as possible, and divining from the texts what people's right course of action should be. We have a focus on helping farmers to nurture the land and occasionally we go out to bless their fields.'

'No, the day-to-day work,' I replied. 'What did the bishop actually *do* as a priest?'

'Sermons, administration for the temple, alms for the poor – though much of that was conducted in Tahn's private time. Generally we ensure that Koton's spiritual needs are met.'

Vagaries. This was all I was going to get for the time being, so I let the matter pass. Perhaps Damsak would warm to the matter over time and divulge something that was out of character for the bishop, but at the moment these descriptions of habits weren't helpful.

'Who came to this temple?' I asked. 'Just those from this prefecture?'

'Oh no. Those who can prove themselves honourable are

permitted at certain times to attend religious services. The gates are opened and individuals vetted. Occasionally we might take our teachings to the street in the hope that we can steer one or two less fortunate souls onto a firmer, more divine path.'

'And he was the only bishop in the city – no rivals tucked away elsewhere?'

Damsak gave a gentle shake of his head. 'No rivals, no other bishop.'

Looking around, the place was too bare. I could perceive no blood on the floor or walls, nothing to suggest a struggle. I casually tested some of the walls for a loose block, though there were none, and the flagstones were sound underfoot.

'Has anything been touched since the bishop's disappearance?'

'Not at all,' Damsak replied. 'This is the first time I have really set foot in Tahn's quarters since the incident. It *still* does not feel right for me to do so.'

Judging by his tentative movements, the fact that he loitered in the doorway, and the concerned look upon his face, he was probably telling the truth. The bishop really did live in such a pure way.

'If you could see to it that this room continues untouched for a few days, we'd be most grateful. It is likely we will want to return.'

'Of course. I shall see to it that it is not disturbed.'

It is not as though I'm inclined to distrust a priest on instinct, but I thought it prudent for the rest of the day to interview people around the temple – metal traders who were going about their business, bread merchants, weavers – and visit any other place of interest I saw nearby.

The surrounding lanes were well maintained, just as the rest of the prefecture. Walls displayed occasionally decorative frescos, but the colours of the street were simple and bold – red, blue and dark-green paint covered columns and walls alike. It was gaudy compared to the austere surroundings of the temple. Animal motifs had been painted in gold, each one a sublime representation of that creature in a noble pose – a far cry from the severed heads we sighted as we entered the city. It was remarkable how little graffiti there was, too – barely an insult or curse to be seen anywhere. Leana remarked to me how unusual it was to keep two sides of a city apart from each other. Even in Detrata, where the contrast in wealth between rich and poor could be enormous, there was no such barrier.

By going door to door I was able to confirm some of what the priest had told me. The people I spoke to were generally welcoming, offering us tisanes as they went about their business in shop-fronted houses or under awnings. As I had hoped, a few of the traders frequented the temple for various religious festivals and to make donations for quiet contemplation. Everyone here knew of the bishop's disappearance, but not everyone knew of his death. Those I informed of the news appeared distraught at first, and made signs in the air as they attempted to stifle their emotions.

The much-admired bishop had indeed declared his plans to leave the temple, much to the community's disappointment. He had been a kind and gentle soul who, unlike other bishops they had known, always took the time to explain some nuance of the gods Astran and Nastra, whether to an old veteran who had recently converted from one of the old gods, or a curious young child. He came across as a very pure being, had never said a bad word, possessed inspirational oratorical skills and ensured that any donated food – once offered to the gods for the first bite – was then distributed among the poor of the external prefecture. The bishop had hoped, so everyone said, to live to a great old age so he could dedicate many more years of service to Astran and Nastra. It was even why he wanted to go on the road – to bring more people into the fold of the enlightened religion, to do *more* good.

This had not been a wasted afternoon by any means, but as Leana and I walked away from the streets surrounding the temple and we watched the last rays of the sun vanish over the prefecture walls, I felt vaguely dissatisfied with what everyone had told us. The bishop appeared very pure, too pure, and not one of his neighbours could give me any insight into why anyone would want him dead.

A Night Mission

Night descended fully over Kuvash and the humidity and close air of the day remained. But the *mood* of the city – or at least in this prefecture – had changed entirely. It was likely that all cities were essentially the same in that each showed two distinct, jarring personalities for the day and night respectively. Unfamiliar cities tended to exaggerate these differences, as one looked with more focus at the details: the erratic behaviour of the locals and how social dynamics might alter after sunset, the different scents of street cuisine, or the noises of religious ritual. As we walked through these clean, well-behaved streets, with the occasional glimmer of a City Watch glaive here and there, all I could tell about Kuvash was that it was incredibly restrained. Anything slightly remiss remained hidden just out of sight – a contrast to Tryum where everything and anything happened on the streets in front of you.

'I do not understand why someone who lives such a pure life would be killed in such a way,' Leana said.

'If he's dead, that is,' I commented. 'He might well be out there still.'

'He is dead,' Leana snapped. 'Just look at those pieces of his body. If they are an indication of his condition . . .'

'I'm inclined to believe you,' I replied. 'Maybe someone took exception to his sermons.'

'So what are our next steps?'

'We've only seen the pleasant side of the city so far,' I said. 'Suppose the pieces of the arm of the bishop really were thrown over the wall. We might be able to find the rest of his remains. Besides, I'd quite like to see the *real* people – I bet some of them might give us another perspective.'

We walked down-city from the temple towards the wall that separated the two prefectures, and headed to the huge gate. The guards at the station point were perplexed that we would want to leave at this hour; but I stressed that I was on official business.

'You'll not find much out there but madmen who worship savage gods,' one said, tipping up the brim of his helmet. 'All the sanity is this side.'

'Even a madman thinks he sees the truth,' I replied.

Without response they shuffled over to the gates and began to haul back the double doors. 'We've had more soldiers return, and there are more coming back later, so the place will be busier – just to warn you. At least you'll be more secure though.'

'Where are they returning from?' I asked, hoping to get a glimpse into the military procedures. All I knew was that these people had a strong military tradition, especially their cavalry, and that their warriors were proud and noble people – even if there were not many excuses to fight these days.

'They're coming back from all over,' one replied. 'By all accounts the border with Detrata is going to get livelier.'

'Why do you think that is?' I asked, somewhat surprised. 'No one's at war.'

He gave a short laugh. 'Not yet. But we hear all sorts of strange talk about troop movements on the border.'

'Nothing will happen,' I declared. 'We're a continent in union. We have been for two centuries.'

'Aye. Tell that to the soldiers at the border.'

We were ushered through the small gap they made in the gate, and the gate shut behind us. For a moment we stood outside the door, and I felt a little numb at what had been said.

'You do not think that it is serious?' Leana asked.

'It is difficult to say anything on the subject knowing so little about it. I'd wager that Sulma Tan can let us know what is happening from a Kotonese perspective, but what on earth is happening in Detrata? Has the Senate gone mad to start military operations of this kind? Then again, it could just be a skirmish over a trade route – a mere tension between nations that will be settled diplomatically, as happens so often. I will ask for more information from the Sun Chamber when I write to them in the morning. But for now, we have our case to resolve.'

Moonlight caught the angles of the buildings in a particularly sinister manner, which might have explained why few people were around at this hour. Unusual, animalistic utterances were coming from beyond the edges of the streets; unfamiliar dialects and strange-sounding words highlighted the sense of alienation.

A soothsayer collared us in the streets, her rancid breath carrying portentous omens – that we would find nought but death in the city. 'There'll be bodies and bodies,' she muttered. 'Bodies and bodies everywhere.'

'Thank you, lady,' I said, excusing myself, but to no avail.

Leana was a little more forceful with her request to be left alone and at the sight of the blade, the soothsayer bowed and retreated into the darkness.

'That people believe such nonsense only encourages sooth-sayers like that,' I remarked.

'People will believe anything,' Leana muttered.

This was not the time for me to bring up Leana's own strange beliefs concerning living among spirits, so I maintained a diplomatic silence.

A fine mist had worked its way up from the river, leaving only our immediate surroundings fully visible. There was no sign of any soldiers as yet. The place was eerily quiet.

'So what is your plan?' Leana asked. 'Do we walk around here until we get stabbed?'

Looking around, it wasn't likely that anyone would try to hassle the two of us other than the soothsayer.

'We should find a tavern,' I concluded. 'The nearest one.'

'You want a drink?'

'Not exactly.'

We continued walking through the dingy, twisting lanes until we spotted a whitewashed building with timber frames and a brazier burning outside. The smell of spilt wine and urine was strong.

'This seems to be appropriate enough. And to answer your original point – no, we've not come to drink. This place is within a quick walk of the bishop's temple. Someone in here might well have attended one of his daily sessions, if they had been permitted into the other prefecture. They might have a useful word or two to say about the priest. We're only ever going to get the clean-living version from officials. It is what inappropriate acts the bishop has committed – if any – that I'm interested in.'

Inside, the tavern was dreary – barely any brighter than the night. A few candles burned on the tables and bar, sitting in holders that had swelled up with years of dripping wax, but their light was absorbed by the darkness. A dozen customers were scattered about the place, tucked into alcoves or sitting alone on benches, staring into their tankards. Sprigs of herbs had been nailed to the walls for scent. Four skinny cats were asleep near to the stove for warmth, but far enough away from any customers who might disturb their peace.

I asked for wine from the young man behind the bar, a lad as slender as the cats and with a face to match. His head was a fraction too large for his frame, his face was broad, his eyes green and almost lifeless. Surprised that anyone else had come in tonight, he served us wine with a jug of water, and placed down two wooden cups. His gaze caught my brooch and when he made eye contact with me again I asked in Kotonese: 'Did the Bishop Tahn Valin ever come in here?'

A smile grew on his face, just a slight one. 'Hardly. People of his sort don't tend to come down these parts.'

'Do people like you go up to those parts?'

'Some do, some don't. I'm too busy. As for religion, my mother has a shrine out the back and we hope for the best. Invite the gods in when we have dinners, that sort of thing. That'll do for me. Others take their business with the gods more seriously.'

'Could you point me in the direction of someone who has attended any of his services?'

'Sure.' He nodded to a woman sat at a table behind me. She looked a little older than me, and was dressed more smartly than the others in the tavern. 'Lady there, she goes up quite a bit. One of those who thinks getting involved with people like that will see her right in the next world. Or this one, if she can get her way.'

'Thanks for your help,' I replied.

Leana and I walked into the small alcove where the woman was drinking alone. 'May we join you?' I asked.

She was wearing a black lace shawl and black dress, with

chestnut hair now slightly greying and must have been in her early forties. Her eyes were a pale shade of green. She had a nervous face so I tried to put her at ease.

I explained why we were there, and our business with the bishop, but without letting on that he had been murdered. 'So you see,' I added, 'we merely wanted to know if you knew the bishop so we can find out what's happened. Many people are deeply worried about him.'

After a moment's silence, she spoke in calm, clear words. 'He's dead. It's nothing to do with me.'

'Ah, dead,' I replied.

She glanced repeatedly between Leana and me, as if uncertain of knowing how to act or what to say. She clearly wanted to be anywhere but talking to me, but I let the silence linger hoping she would fill it with detail.

She did not.

'Did you attend his temple?' I asked eventually. 'The gentleman behind the bar believes you did.'

'What's it to you?' She glanced over my shoulder briefly, at the bar, then back down to the table.

'If he's dead,' I said, 'it might help me find the killer – if you could share some of your knowledge.'

She continued to be evasive until I produced a silver coin. I hadn't changed any coin to the local currency, but Detratan silver was never to be sniffed at. She snatched it from my outstretched hand.

'I went to his temple, that's right. Good man. Honest. Too few like him around.' She was obviously proud of the bishop. 'Helped people like me, too. Gave food when it was needed. Never asked for anything back.'

'Did he ever create trouble?'

50

'Never.' She almost laughed at the notion, but seemed too dour to comment fully. 'Not even with non-believers.'

'And you're convinced he's dead?' I asked.

'I am.'

'On what grounds do you believe this?'

Her sudden, feral stare almost startled me. 'Because I know who's keeping his *head*.'

Show Us the Head

'It's common knowledge down here,' she said. The woman led us out of the tavern and back into the lanes of the city. She still wouldn't give her name.

She pulled up her hood and relaxed at the sanctuary it offered her. After that I only ever caught a brief glimpse of the angles of her face. She appeared to thrive on the fact that she had knowledge of use to someone, that it gave her purpose, yet she didn't seem particularly comfortable in the company of others. The only response she gave to my incessant questions about herself were shrugs of indifference. For all I knew she could have been leading us into a trap – but no one knew why we were in the city, and we had not done anything to cause much trouble – *yet*.

She guided us through the winding, mystifying passageways. Wooden buildings leaned precariously out of the mist, though it might have been the angle of the poorly laid road creating an illusion. Bamboo had been used in the construction of buildings, as well as a damp, dark wood I couldn't identify, but it all went some way to give a sense of local identity. Little coloured lanterns glowed warmly from second- and third-floor windows, only heightening the isolation down on the ground. Though the night wasn't exactly cold, the wind was surprisingly strong and bringing wraiths of fog.

'How long ago was the head found?' Leana asked.

'Two days,' the woman muttered. 'Word spreads quickly around here. Everyone knows each other. That's why I know about it. And everyone in the taverns talks about the house with the blue door.'

'Did you not think to tell the authorities?' I asked.

The woman simply laughed at that. 'They live in their *own* world. A heaven and hell, that's this place. Two gods and two cities – that's what the bishop used to say, though he could do little about it. Besides, they must know themselves. They know everything else. This way now. Might not be here for all I know. People say that a strange man owns it. Loner, like.'

A left, right and left again and if it wasn't for our guide I would have been utterly lost. Leana had drawn her sword long ago and, judging by the shadows that were lingering in doorways or leaning out of alleys, I couldn't blame her. The strong winds had led to a mass of clouds obscuring the starlight above the city. A few flecks of rain began to fall.

'Here.' She stood rooted to the spot with her hands deep in her pockets.

We had arrived at a small wooden door, situated at the end of a cobbled lane. Though the light was bad, it looked as though it could have been blue paint that had been slowly peeling from it over the years.

'Thank you for bringing us,' I said.

'I'll leave you be.' She turned to leave with a sudden keenness to be away. She ran back into the fog, and soon there was only the sound of her footsteps leading away.

'Well, we might as well get on with it,' I said to Leana.

I knocked on the door and we waited patiently in the damp

evening. While I wondered just what type of person would claim the head of a dead bishop, Leana stepped cautiously around the building, examining the place for any traps. The rain became heavier, fat drops striking the cobbles and pinging off the door.

Eventually it opened. A man in his fifties, wearing only a pair of trousers, peered out at us from the gloom. In need of a good meal and a shave, and with long, straggly hair, he also wore several necklaces bearing symbols similar to ones I'd seen in the temple earlier.

'It has been made known to me that you have the head of Bishop Tahn Valin,' I said in Kotonese, but he didn't reply.

His eyes grew just a fraction wilder. He stumbled back inside. Leana shoved her foot in front of the door before he had the chance to close it.

I held out my hand in a gesture of peace. 'We want to see the head. No harm will come to you if you just let us in and show us where it is.'

Nothing. He stared at me with such intensity, but it wasn't until I produced a silver coin that he deigned to notice my presence. The rain hardened to the point where Leana finally lost her patience.

'Oh enough of this.' She barged past him and I followed her, before suddenly placing my hand to my nose.

His room reeked of decaying matter. Food remains were scattered everywhere, on the table, on the floor. Two ill-looking black dogs regarded me from next to the smouldering embers in the grate. There were bones, too, heaped in crates and upon the table – I took a step closer and was relieved to note that most of them had come from animals. The man nervously followed us as we navigated the islands of rubbish strewn across the floor. He came towards me with his hands outstretched, but Leana thumped his chest with the hilt of her blade and sent him crashing into the wall.

'I don't think he'll try to harm us,' I said to her. He certainly didn't look capable of causing any damage. Judging by his house, he didn't seem capable of anything other than festering in his own waste.

Leana shrugged. 'He will not harm you *now*, at least. A polite warning does some people good.'

I turned to him as he cowered against the wall, perhaps mystified at our Detratan conversation. 'The *head*,' I stressed, in as much Kotonese as I could manage. 'Show us the *head* of Bishop Tahn Valin.'

Nothing again. Leana directed her sword at his breast and he gave a coarse, guttural reply: 'Next room. Shrine.'

Leana lowered her blade and he scurried through a dark passageway. We followed him into an even darker room. With a match the man lit a candle and metal glimmered on one side. I could just about make out the formation of a shrine.

'Light more candles.'

He obliged, moving to light them around his room.

Each new glow confirmed my suspicions – it was indeed a shrine, upon which were small bronze statues of Astran and Nastra. They were adorned with dozens of small bones, trinkets and beads. But right in the centre of the display was a rotting head: its closed eyes had sunken into the sockets, it had changed colour, become darker, the lines of the face exaggerated, the fleshier parts, such as the lips, shrivelled and distorted. Though not entirely clear, through the small gap of the mouth it appeared that his tongue had been cut out.

'Is this really our friend the bishop?' I wondered out loud.

'Looks about the right level of decay,' Leana said. 'Not inconsistent with the other parts.'

'That is true. There's only one way to confirm it's genuinely the bishop's head and that's to take it back to Sulma Tan tomorrow morning.'

'And you propose to take this from the house, just like that?' Leana asked somewhat mischievously. 'Our friend here has become quite attached to it.'

'No, I'll pay him.'

'I knew you would. You cannot just take things.'

'But people are more useful when you're nice to them.' I turned to the man once again, who by now had wrapped his arms around himself, and was rubbing his skin for warmth. 'I'll give you two silver coins for the head.'

He looked to the head and back to me, visibly weighing up his options.

'Three coins,' I continued, 'if you can tell us where you found it.'

And to that he nodded eagerly.

'See,' I said to Leana. 'He has more use yet.'

'Of all the miserable places . . .'

'Of all the miserable places you have taken me,' Leana mumbled, 'this has to be the worst.'

'Which is indeed saying something,' I replied cheerfully.

In the dead of night, after the worst of the rain, we found ourselves trudging up a festering heap of Polla-knows-what that had been left behind by Kotonese society. With one hand I held a sack that contained a severed head, and with my other I pressed a handkerchief to my nose and mouth to cope with the odour. This was a gentle slope, though the terrain was soft and therefore hard going; occasionally things would crack and splinter, and I could only speculate as to what had been crushed under my feet.

The heap was about the area of the forum in Tryum. Built – if that was the right word – on the edge of the river, it was surrounded by high, thick wooden fences on the other three sides to stop it spreading.

All I could learn from our guide, the half-clothed man, was that this place had grown from an unofficial heap to something later accepted by the authorities – and then used for dumping by those living in the Sorghatan Prefecture. The poorer, Kuvash Prefecture, he claimed, was too thrifty to waste so much. Now the site possessed a culture of its own: there were numerous figures loitering around the perimeter of the site, but even more up on the heap, scouring the waste for anything they could use and storing their finds in sacks similar to the one I carried. They wore little in the way of clothing and had allowed the rain to wash them, leaving grimy streaks down their bodies. Like ghouls from another realm they looked up silently as we passed them.

My theory for such a place as this was simple. A civilization that once moved on regularly had no need to deal with its waste; it could simply leave its detritus and move on. A settled nation or growing empire, however, had long evolved projects to cope with the amount of rubbish that its population produced. But the once-nomadic people of Koton had only settled relatively recently. Despite having had their own territory for two hundred years, they had not yet found a productive way to deal with it all.

Leana was not at all interested in my ideas at this point.

'At least the view is good,' I offered facetiously, indicating all the lanterns of the city that could be seen in the middle and far distance. It was probably a good thing it was dark out here, as I could not observe the expression on her face as she muttered something about me in her native Atrewen tongue. She had never taught me the fouler words.

Our bone-hoarder friend scampered up ahead with a new-found enthusiasm. He was more talkative now we were out and about, away from the confines of his home. Even so, his conversation seemed to be largely between himself and some other, more distant region of his mind – it would have been a lie to say we were part of that discussion.

Eventually we arrived at a point near to the water's edge.

'Is my patch,' the man declared proudly.

The river glistened in the moonlight; it curved through the nooks and crannies of the city. There were little wooden shacks at the edge that blended in with the boats that had been crammed in along the banks. Further out, the river opened up considerably, carving up the rolling landscape. As for the man's 'patch', it was difficult to discern what exactly marked the boundary of this particular area — this was the same kind of refuse to be found elsewhere in the heap.

'Is still here,' the man said, before entering a coughing fit.

Pressing my handkerchief to my mouth a little firmer, I looked on as he scurried to a point nearest one of the wooden boards. There he crouched down, pulling some of the surface detritus away. The way he moved around this heap, with a slick agility, revealed his intimate knowledge of it.

A gust of wind groaned as it moved past us. Sharp flecks of rain came and went once again.

Presently he waved us over and pointed out what looked like a torso emerging from the refuse. Lowering myself to get a better look, I noted that it was missing both its arms and its head.

'What happened to the other arm?' Leana asked. 'Only one arm in two pieces has been found.'

'It might be here, somewhere.' I gestured to the detritus surrounding the torso.

What little clothing remained was sodden, smeared with grime. In this light and without a head it was difficult to tell who it might have been. The body's boots had been removed, too, though that could have been done by anyone. Anything that could be learned from this corpse was going to be highly dubious due to the nature of the scavenging culture here.

'If you think I am carrying this thing back, you can think again,' Leana said. 'Give your friend here another coin to do the hard work.'

'That might not be a bad idea,' I replied.

*

I didn't want to ruin the body as so much had been lost already through natural decay. So we wrapped the body up carefully, in several layers of hessian, which we'd bought from a woman who made her living scavenging the site. We never did find the other arm.

Our scavenger friend didn't seem to mind helping to drag back the remains of the bishop. In fact, the chore appeared to relax him somewhat, and he began to sing a surprisingly tuneful melody.

When I asked him how he had found out about the corpse in the first place, he replied only: 'People say his body here.'

'Which people?'

'Everyone. Tavern talk. They say someone left the body here, yes, so I follow, I follow. Always follow the talk. Some other find it first, but I fight, fight good. Got myself good offering for the shrine, yes. The best kind. A bishop himself!'

'There were people who got to the body before you?'

'Yes, but who wants a body? Some too scared to touch it, but I know I make a fine job of my shrine.'

'Was his head attached to the body when you found it?'

'No. Already separated. Clean cut. Relieved 'bout it. Heads very hard to remove. Very hard. Had to search nearby – nearly made its way into the river!'

The man, still half-clothed, exhibited surprising strength. He held the torso in front of him, like an offering, as we headed towards the gates to the Sorghatan Prefecture.

He laid down the sack and knelt next to it for a moment, an imploring expression upon his face. I paid him more than was strictly required, because he had been incredibly useful, and it was obvious he had tried to overcome his lack of conversational skills in order to help. Though they were not much to me, he was awed at the coins I placed in his palm. He continued stroking them and looking back and forth at the sack as he rose to his feet.

Soon he scurried away into the darkness.

Leana liaised with the guards through a hatch in the gate and, within a moment, the immense doors opened. Lantern light shone our way. The guards stepped forward and said, with great uncertainty, 'You were the two who left earlier, right?'

'Excellent observation,' I said, kneeling down and beckoning them closer. 'Now, can either of you help me out? Do you know who this fellow is?'

I opened the bag and let them see the severed head. One of the guards immediately turned to the wall and vomited against it. The other looked across at me and gave me the answer I was looking for.

'That's the bishop, aye,' he groaned. 'The missing one.'

'Well, there you go,' I said to Leana. 'A bit of perseverance does wonders.'

I turned to the guards, one of whom was still leaning against the wall. He realized suddenly what he'd done and a look of deep shame came over his face.

'Now,' I said, 'which of you brave fellows would like to give me a hand with this corpse?'

Morning in the City

We decided to store the fragments of the bishop in a couple of large sacks deep in Jejal's cellar, where the temperature was cold, and they were safely away from prying eyes. Curiously, Jejal did not seem to mind at all that we wanted to store human remains in his establishment. In fact he declared, with great insouciance, 'Of course I will oblige. Though you must know, I will be forced to add a small fee to the cost of the room. Just because they are dead does not mean I will not accept payment for their use of my facilities! It is a mistake to draw such matters to a close when life has departed. Who is this fellow anyway? Should I fear some sort of reprisal attacks in my humble dwelling?'

'For now,' I said, 'it's probably safer you don't know anything.'

'You sound like one of my former wives.'

'I mean we should tell the authorities first.'

'Agreed, agreed. Always the secrecy with the Sun Chamber! Alas, at least a few secrets make life interesting, do they not?'

At Jejal's insistence both Leana and myself washed thoroughly before we went to bed – it was only then that I realized just how much we must have reeked after our time in the refuse area.

I rested well that night – enjoying a deep and peaceful sleep that I had not known for a good while. When travelling on the road, working on a case, I always felt on edge, agitated to make progress lest I found my end thanks to some rogue agent or a criminal in the dark wilderness, leaving the case unresolved. Sleep didn't come easily when one spent most of the time with one eye peering into the shadows, wondering when an attack might come.

Even with Leana, a warrior of considerable talent guarding me, it was not easy to relax. I had not experienced soldiering since the token training we received in the Sun Chamber, almost a decade ago, and so I willingly accepted that I was someone who relied upon basic securities: safe lodgings, armed protection.

To be completely honest with myself, part of me suspected that my curse of seizures would somehow leave me more *vulnerable*, especially in the countryside. Sometimes I could shake uncontrollably in the night and know nothing of it – who knew what attention that might attract out in the wilds?

In the city there were any number of strange noises and events to distract from those of my own creation. Fortunately Leana said I had no episodes in the night. She reminded me that I needed to find an apothecary or herbalist who could recreate the mix I had bought in Tryum, in order to stabilize my seizures.

After a hearty breakfast of flatbreads and local fish, which we ate on a small bench beside a street vendor in the sparsely populated marketplace, we checked with Jejal about somewhere safe to stable our horses.

They had been kept overnight in Jejal's stables, but would need to be taken somewhere else, to better conditions. What Jejal owned wasn't much, frankly, and was generally for those who were just passing through. Even the boastful Jejal admitted that it could get crowded and uncomfortable for the animals.

He told us of better quality stables deeper in the Sorghatan

Prefecture, so we led our horses along the short journey there, with the body of the bishop in a sack slumped over the back of my mare, Kinder, and the head hanging in a bag over the neck of Manthwe, Leana's own horse.

Though I was glad of my black cloak, whatever gusty chill might have pervaded the streets at night had long since gone. The day promised something more sultry, and there was a fug of woodsmoke lingering as the city awoke. The comforting, symmetrical lanes of the prefecture were filling up with those heading towards the markets. Scrawny livestock were being driven past new stone buildings. Carts carrying bright cloth clattered along the roads. There were a lot of highly skilled craftsmen here: woodworkers through to silversmiths, and many of them were making equine equipment of the highest quality. But it was the animal-based industry that impressed me most: several small tanneries could be found alongside butchers and shops selling leather goods. The level of ingenuity on display in such a confined space was like nothing I had seen throughout Vispasia. And the stench of urine being used in the process was equally as staggering . . .

I was beginning to recognize just how important animals were to the Kotonese, not just in what was sold. Subtle symbols were rendered on many of the signs around. Then there was the raised stag on the nation's flag, the statues of horses and the creatures in stone reliefs on major buildings.

This idea was strengthened further when we arrived at the sumptuously decked-out stables, which were good enough for humans to inhabit let alone animals. A large pale stone quadrangle was framed with wooden chambers for horses, all of which looked out onto a wide cobbled courtyard. The site was huge, full of nooks and crannies, workshops and filled with the noise of industry. Everything here was clean and in good order; there was plenty of food and water for the animals, and a good number of workers to hand.

'Everything about the place looks good,' Leana said. 'Manthwe and Kinder will be happy while we remain.'

'Not too comfortable for them?' I asked wryly, but there was no smile in response.

'Comfort is good for animals,' she replied. 'But not for you. An animal will remain strong with a bed of straw. You go soft.'

I caught the gaze of a well-built farrier, who had cropped blond hair and bright-green eyes. After brief introductions he offered to take care of our mares for the duration of our time in the city. I started the conversation in Kotonese, but he continued it in gruff Detratan.

His name was Sojun and he came across as a kind-hearted man, not one for long sentences and small talk, but judging by how he was with the animals, our horses would be well looked after and they would not mind the lack of conversation.

There was an air of patience about him; he was someone who took pleasure from his job. Very quickly it became apparent that he cared more about the animals than humans; he was more natural with them than us. More skilled. If the animal themes I noticed earlier were anything to go by, it was possible that many people in Kuvash were the same.

We discussed rates as he rubbed the nose of another handsome mare. His suggestion was more than reasonable, and I told him so.

'Outside of the military stations,' he grunted, 'you can find several smaller stables, scattered about the city. We must remain competitive with them. It is not ideal, because they cut corners, but we have deals with the tanneries.'

'For the horses?' I tried my best not to look startled.

'No,' he muttered, shaking his head. 'For their piss.'

With that he took the reins of Manthwe, since we would still be using Kinder to carry the bishop's body up to the royal palace before dropping her off later. I began to lead her away when another three horses cantered by, with only the one rider on the foremost animal.

Dressed in military uniform was a young woman with a broad face and black hair that stretched down to her waist. I smiled to myself as she exchanged a lingering glance with Sojun, with startling blue eyes, and wondered at the relationship – if any – between them.

It reminded me of my brief moments with Titiana, in Tryum, and suddenly I couldn't summon the emotions to continue happily with my expression.

I wondered why army personnel would be here in a civilian stables – it was a sign of growing military activity elsewhere, but perhaps I was being overly suspicious. I asked Sojun.

'You like your questions,' he replied.

'Merely curious,' I added. 'I'm trying to build up a picture of this place. I'm a stranger in a strange city.'

Sojun's gaze followed the girl as she rode across the cobbles to the other side of the courtyard. 'She trains the queen's horses, and helps others from time to time.'

'What do your soldiers do here usually? What trouble do you get?'

'Some tribes have never accepted Koton and they carry out occasional raids around towns, villages and trade routes. Reckon the old clans have a hand in that. Sometimes we get ships landing. Bands of warriors come from abroad to take what they can. Women, children, young men to be sold or used as slaves. That's not as often as I remember. Our queen makes sure we're protected. It's damn good pay being in the military. She makes sure of that. And with soldiers being much better off than a tradesman, they'll make sure she's well looked after in return. Less likely to be open to corruption that way.'

'That would explain two decades of stability.'

He grunted something close to a laugh. 'That's what outsiders will think. Not everyone likes it. Couple of the clans think it's giving the masses too much power by training them as soldiers and giving them military coin. Reckon it's dangerous in the long run.'

'And what do you think?'

'Job's a job.'

'Either way, all that military coin flowing through the city can't be bad for tradesmen like yourself,' I commented.

But, with a shrug, Sojun made it clear that he was done talking, so I figured it was a good idea to move on.

Leana and I exited the stables and made our way back towards the royal palace.

In the distance stood the snowless mountains, which I hadn't been able to see in yesterday's murkier weather. The terrain of the city was flat, and the buildings rarely rising more than three storeys high, so it was impressive to see how far that mountain range stretched.

Little square flags of various different colours had been strung up between buildings, some of them containing writing that appeared religious. Two priests had set up on opposite sides of the street, and I wondered if that had any symbolism in relation to the two gods or if they were simply competing with each other on who could preach the loudest. Their words seemed to spar with each other, causing many passers-by to pause as if unsure which way to turn their attention.

Finally we arrived outside the front of the palace. Here it was styled like a white-walled citadel, though all the decorative flourishes indicated that this place saw little in the way of combat.

It was without doubt the largest building in the city, with narrow glass windows spaced at regular intervals and reaching five storeys in height – though it looked as if there were more layers to be found further in. Looking up, there were four turrets on this face, spaced about thirty paces apart; passing back and forth in between them was the glistening helmet of a soldier. All in all, given the number of royal palaces I'd seen – from King Licintius' residence in Tryum to the ziggurat of Prince Bassim in Venyn City, not to mention the palace of the Queen of Dalta – I was not much impressed. Here was a fairly basic structure that had been built long before the country had a taste for fine designs.

I spotted a large, arched black gate manned by four soldiers armed with bows, and that was where we headed. I informed the archers, who on closer inspection wore ornate green and white uniforms with brightly polished helmets, exactly what was in the sack.

After their own private, urgent conversation, we were led through the gate and into the royal compound, whereupon I lifted down the body and we were told to wait. Here, the entrance appeared to be an even less grand affair, with exposed red brickwork showing and a garden full of herbs.

'The staff entrance,' Leana muttered.

We watched a man come out of a small door to empty dirty water down the drains.

Eventually two soldiers returned and declared, 'Sulma Tan will see you now.'

Two other men in the red and blue of the City Watch helped us carry the body inside.

Knives and brutal barbed implements hung on racks along the wall, and I wondered where we had been brought. This brick chamber, Sulma Tan informed us after noting my suspicious looks, was used for training students of medicine. White paper lanterns glowed under the large arched ceiling. Sulma Tan moved one of the lanterns over beside a ledger before I had the chance to glimpse what was on it. As she did so, I told her about my discussion with Priest Damsak and of the bishop leaving the city.

'Was that true?' I asked. 'Or do you need to confirm it with the Astran officials?'

'It was true,' she said. 'The queen had already asked me to look into the process of adding a new bishop to that district. She is a great admirer of those gods, given they are not representative of the barbaric cults of our past. She is keen to see their forward-looking ways are continued in the city.'

'And do you believe in such progressive ways?'

'My beliefs are not important.' She then steered us to a central table positioned directly beneath a skylight made of clear glass. Around this thick wooden table were three curved rows of stone benches, much like a theatre, only on a far smaller scale.

Sulma Tan had brought with her two middle-aged male officials, who were clothed in red silk trousers, black silk jackets with high collars, and long white socks. They lingered by the ledger at the back, ready with a reed pen to make notes as she spoke. Myself, Leana and Sulma Tan gathered around the covered remains of the bishop.

'There's not much hope for a recovery with this fellow,' I said, pulling back the cloth.

One of the men gasped and muttered something incomprehensible as I uncovered the head carefully, before discarding the sack to one side.

'By Astran,' the other breathed. If these men had come here to study, they were clearly not that familiar with corpses.

'Ah, it is so.' Sulma Tan clasped the edge of the table. She asked one of the other men behind to run out to retrieve the other limb. In the meantime, we continued stripping back the fragments of cloth, exposing the body piece by bloodied piece.

'You have the stomach for this?' Sulma Tan asked us, and she was being sincere.

Leana gave a short laugh and said fiercely, 'Lady, we have seen worse. I first met Lucan wandering around a field of corpses.'

That was putting things lightly. Our paths met during the aftermath of a most bloody battle. Her friends and family – and her husband – had been wiped out in the war. In the intensely hot location of a massacre, she had asked me if I needed a worker. I was an excuse for her to leave those horrors behind, to try to forget what could not easily be forgotten.

Sulma Tan continued to cut away at the final fragments of the bishop's thick woollen clothing, until his flesh was fully exposed. Leana helped pull away the strips of material and discarded them in a metal bucket underneath the table. Sulma Tan retrieved a small metal tray, containing water and a cloth, and began to ever-so-gently wash away the detritus from the torso. The water soon took on the colour of the blood and dirt.

Now and then the queen's second secretary would lean away to avoid the stench, and eventually she ordered one of the note-taking officials to open the room's windows, allowing in a re-freshing salt-tang breeze and the absent-minded chatter from a nearby courtyard.

The skylight above created harsh shadows, so Sulma Tan asked for three lanterns to be moved in order to see the gruesome details from all angles.

'Most disturbing,' I muttered, as it became apparent what had happened to the bishop.

'A sick mind was at work here,' Sulma Tan added.

The bishop's body had not *just* been severed at his shoulders and neck, though that would have been a terrible enough way for him to have been killed. In addition to this, and though it was difficult to make out fully, there were well over a hundred cuts across the various surfaces of his skin, which had long since started to transform in colour to that of a green-tinted bruise.

There were a couple of skin blisters, too, but it was unlikely that these were related to the method of his murder. I tried to imagine the bishop's final moments, being slashed repeatedly – though not all that deeply. It was as if he had not been allowed to die straight away. The murderer wanted to inflict pain upon him before concluding the matter brutally.

Sulma Tan said something quietly in her native tongue, perhaps a prayer – I couldn't quite discern it – and she shook her head. She turned to one of the officials and asked him to bring in a physician. I noted how she asked for *a* physician, as if there were more than one – quite unlike the royal palace of Optryx in Detrata, where such individuals were generally rare.

After Leana placed the head alongside the body, we all stared at the reunited pieces for a little while longer. Sulma Tan asked how we came by the remains, so I told her of our evening escapades and just how we came to find the body so soon.

'I must confess,' I said, 'that the bishop seems to have rotted too much for me to glean anything useful from him. This is certainly beyond my level of skill.'

'Yes, the real expertise is on its way.' Sulma Tan nodded thoughtfully. 'It has been a long time since I've had training in dissecting the human form, especially since my tools tend to be a reed pen and ledger these days.'

'In my experience, it isn't often one finds such attention to detail in a murder,' I said. 'Usually a killing is done quickly – a cut throat in the dark, or a blade to the heart. Murderers want to get away, cover up their crime or flee the scene of the crime. Get the job done quickly in a back alley, if possible, and then get out. But here we have so many lacerations across the skin, not to mention the issue of dismemberment, which on its own would take a lot of time to complete. There was *consideration* here.'

'A butchering, of sorts,' she replied.

'A torture,' Leana added.

'Both,' I replied, and turned to Sulma Tan. 'Has anything like this ever happened before in the city, some archaic religious ritual perhaps?'

'Never.' She looked up and there was a flare of anger, as if I had judged her culture to be primitive. 'I have *never* seen anything quite like this. We are a peaceful, cultured city now. Especially in this prefecture. Even before, when we were a more savage culture . . . No, this bears no resemblance to the kinds of ritual killings thankfully consigned to history.' After a pause, she added, 'The kinds that all cultures are guilty of perpetrating. Even Detrata, am I correct?'

'I don't disagree with you on that matter.' The acts of the Detratan Empire of old were of course well known to me; our families would discuss them as if they were charming fables, conveniently forgetting about the cruelty and bloodshed involved. Within Detrata these events were considered to be acts of glory rather than sin.

'Do you think the killer will have fled the city by now?' she asked.

'Anything is possible,' I said, 'but something does not feel right about this. This feels *personal*. The bishop must have had an enemy — has he *always* lived in Kuvash?'

'His whole life, or so I believe, has been spent in the Sorghatan Prefecture.'

'Did he travel much?' I asked.

'Though I am not familiar with his schedule, I never knew him to leave the city for long periods. He was very committed to his temple and his community.'

'So, if that is the case, presumably whoever committed this atrocity,' I gestured to the body, 'whoever had such a grievance with him that they felt they needed to slice and dissect him in such a manner . . . I would say that they, too, must originate from Kuvash. Probably the Sorghatan Prefecture. Which means in turn that they might still be around. Or if they have left, then they may return at some point.'

'They could have hired the skill,' Leana said. 'This could have been a torture and assassination carried out for money.'

'True,' I concluded. 'It still seems probable that the person responsible for it dwells in the city.'

Sulma Tan gave a sigh of annoyance. 'I have far too many things on my mind without having to deal with this. The bishop's funeral will require organizing and there will be even more legal matters to attend to as a result.' She paused, cringing at her indelicacies, and gave me a look of embarrassment. 'You must think me heartless. Please understand that it is not the case. Merely, I have many duties . . .'

'The queen works you hard, I take it?'

'I work hard *for* the queen.' She made it perfectly clear this was a point of pride. 'There is a difference. Both the secretaries do. The other, my senior, will retire before long, which means even more responsibilities fall to me. I have a census to declare in the near future, as well as the monthly games to coordinate . . . You should know that we are a nation of great planning and organization. I have several subordinates who help in establishing how our city – how our nation – is to be run. The queen would not have it any other way, of course. As a secretary, one of my roles is to oversee various strategies and schemes in order to drag our nation from its past into a thriving cultural future, one that we can all be proud of. We have done so at speed. So, it does not take the intelligence of the Sun Chamber to work out that murder like this does our reputation no good, Officer Drakenfeld.'

There was something about her manner, her sheer determination to take on the weight of her nation and carry it forward that impressed me deeply.

'I'll do my very best to help you out,' I replied.

The physician entered the chamber. He was a slender, jovial man in his forties, who introduced himself as Carlon. Though he had long, greying hair, he also possessed a deeply receding hairline. Wearing a brown shirt with his sleeves rolled up, black trousers and a large leather apron, he carried with him the box containing the bishop's arm.

He bounded over towards me. He clutched my forearm and we shook in the Detratan style, before greeting Leana in the same way.

'People of culture, you Detratans,' he said to me. 'Good to know.'

'So I keep being told,' I replied, marvelling at how much my home nation was respected here. Its culture wasn't something I ever noticed until others pointed it out, as I'd long since understood the follies of bold patriotism in a continent like ours. Every nation was different, yet some possessed a gravitas that went beyond mere lines on a map. 'Your own people clearly don't do too badly yourselves – it's impressive to know that studies of the body are taken so seriously here.'

'We try, we try. And you're the Sun Chamber officer, right? We don't get many of you out here. I hope the corpse doesn't put you off Koton!'

'I tend to see them all over Vispasia.'

'Does death follow you, or do you follow death?'

'A little of both.'

'Well, while we're on that then . . .' He placed the box on the table with the reverence of a priest making an offering at an altar. 'We're just missing the other arm otherwise we'd have a full set!' He took a moment to glance over the body and head, crouching down low to get a better look. For a moment it looked as if he was actually sniffing it, and I wondered if this was some new form of science. 'This is definitely the bishop?' he asked.

Sulma Tan nodded.

'Fine,' Carlon said. 'How long since he's been missing?'

'Twenty days, give or take,' she replied.

'Yes, I'd agree he's been dead more or less that long, judging by his colour. Hard to tell precisely. Decay tends to vary so.' Carlon repositioned the arm on the bench where it would have naturally joined, then placed the head above the severed neck. He began to give his analysis aloud, as he moved around the body with some spirit and excitement. Occasionally he would try to moderate his behaviour out of respect, remembering that he was dealing with the dead. First he pointed out the obvious wounds that we all had seen, but then after a good while of careful examination, he made some more astute conclusions: that the tongue had indeed been removed; one leg had been broken; both of the eyes had been stabbed; and that there were also deep puncture wounds along with the cuts, as if from a very thin blade. Carlon said, with great authority, that judging by the coloration of the bishop's veins and arteries, the man was of mild temperament right up until the moment of his death. He added that such knowledge of moods during the process of death was a theory he had only recently begun to teach, and I confess to not entirely following his line of reasoning.

'A very thorough job, whoever did this,' he concluded. 'They probably wanted to make sure the man was very much dead, eh? These religious types might know something the rest of us don't about coming back from the dead.' He chuckled at his own joke.

'Have you any experience of this kind of incident before?' It was the same question I had put to Sulma Tan. 'Something you've seen in the past or on your travels?'

'Oh I've seen plenty of people chopped into pieces. Cuts here and there. Severed limbs aplenty! But nothing quite with this . . . *consideration*. Many, many cuts – a slow way to die. It's a barbaric masterpiece.'

'Was he tortured or dead before they did this?' Leana asked. 'That could say a lot about the murderer.'

'A fine point, which I was just about to raise,' the physician replied. 'Torture . . . execution. I can see signs of something around the neck – perhaps rope? – but nothing to suggest restraints around the legs and arms. Though when you've a broken leg you're not exactly going to be running very far, and you'd have little need to restrain him. The cuts, well . . . they could indeed come from a thin blade. So we could say that the murderer merely wanted to ensure that the bishop experienced pain. Also, the numerous puncture wounds in non-vital locations seem to support such a view – though that said, they each appear deep to me. Torture, yes. But you don't often torture people for the *sake* of it. Information is usually required, yet how can a cut tongue speak? Such an act has so little use. Perhaps information was not needed this time.

'So I would say – and the corpse isn't doing us any favours here, being so long gone – that whoever did this wanted to cause an excruciating amount of agony for the bishop. This may be stating the obvious, yes, but the murderer wished to cause a slow and painful death, but most importantly that it be one the bishop would have been all too aware of. He would have been conscious up until the last moment, most likely. That says a lot. Yet as I theorize, his mood was quite calm even in those last moments — which gives us something to be grateful for, yes.'

None of us could really speak at that point. We just stood there, dumbstruck by the seriousness of the injuries.

'As I suggest, he's too far gone for a more rigorous analysis, I'm afraid,' Carlon continued, wiping his hands on his apron, 'so you'll have to make do with my vagaries for now. Probably could have worked out the same conclusions yourselves.'

'Carlon, you've been immensely helpful,' I said. 'That gives us much to ponder.'

'Pleasure!' Carlon replied cheerfully, as if I'd made his day. 'If you find another corpse, just make sure it's a little fresher, eh? You'll find I'll be much more use with something decent to work with.'

He took off his apron and said goodbye to Sulma Tan with a fatherly kiss on her cheek. There was a history between these two, perhaps that of mentor and apprentice.

There was very little point in examining the bishop's body further, yet I insisted we try, just in case something came to light. A junior physician came in to cut open his torso with some more efficient tools, yet there was nothing there, for example, to indicate a weapon or something left inside him. Carlon had been correct when he said the bishop was too far gone to really tell us anything, and it was really my own stubbornness that was getting the better of me. No doubt Leana would remind me of that later, judging by the looks she gave.

It couldn't have been more than an hour later when a young messenger came into the room and whispered into Sulma Tan's ear. All the time he was speaking she glanced towards me with that neutral expression which was so difficult to read. The one that was assessing me.

When he finished she nodded and said to him in Kotonese, 'We will be there shortly.'

The messenger bowed and left.

Sulma Tan regarded me with consideration. 'Queen Dokuz has requested an audience with both of you. You and Leana.'

'Oh,' I replied.

'I suppose we had better wash our hands first,' Leana muttered.

Queen Dokuz Sorghatan

During my decade as a member of the Sun Chamber, I had set foot in only three royal courts – or the localized equivalent. My formative years, in a very junior position, were largely spent in some of the vilest holes of the continent, or some of the dullest. Any orders back then were usually to copy out papers into a coded or foreign language, or to head out to investigate the dregs of society: lowly thieves, pickpockets and petty criminals who were deemed above the remit of more experienced officers.

As my reputation grew over the years – or, as I suspected, I simply became more trusted – I was awarded the honour of access to higher levels of society. During my time in Venyn City I had worked with representatives of Prince Bassim and been permitted to stroll through his opulent halls. Also, I had been in the presence of the Queen of Dalta, who surrounded herself with so much gold and lived in a place with such intense sunlight that, at times, I had to shade my eyes as she addressed me.

Every one of these courts was unique in its own way. Not so much the design, though that was certainly true, but more for the *atmosphere* – and it was the atmosphere that I was most interested in. In the expressions of those gathered at the court, a learned woman or man could read the state of the nation. From concern at local political upheaval, to jubilance at the growth of trade, everything was on display in the faces of those gathered there.

Rumours were always more interesting than facts in places like this, and I had never seen any of the truly scandalous events reported by my peers. Some told of executions in front of one king, drunken orgies in the presence of others, many forms of debauchery that only the rich could afford to enjoy with impunity. I occasionally wondered if they ever happened, or if the stories that came from such lives would always be more interesting than truth.

As we walked through the wood-panelled corridors and rooms towards the palace's main hall, soldiers stood in line on either side. In the gaps between them I could see incredible statues, busts and paintings, ornaments made of gold and silver. What struck me as unusual was that many of these items were replicas of famous ones I'd seen in collections elsewhere. This was more of a museum than a place to live, though if one lingered no doubt the soldiers would soon usher the viewer outside.

The central hall was situated under a dome that appeared so large it was almost structurally impossible. Ornate images were painted upon the inside of its curved surface. Remarkably there were tiny windows, which allowed a curious light to fall down directly on the throne below, in the centre of the room. The floor was made up of large, black slate pieces, and only the hundreds of lanterns saved the place from seeming too dour.

A good seventy or eighty soldiers lined the hall, spaced so that it never looked too crowded. A handful of courtiers loitered within this protective enclosure, wearing resplendent cloaks of green, red and blue silk. Today being a religious day, we were requested to wear a hood-like strip of bright-blue cotton over our heads and down over our ears, the lengths reaching to waist level. Sulma Tan said that it was out of respect to Astran and Nastra, though she did not say what was the purpose of the gesture. Not wanting to cause any offence by disregarding local customs, we willingly obliged.

Sulma Tan now had a nervous energy about her, and a sudden air of subservience that didn't seem in keeping with her character. The defiant woman who had greeted me, if *greeted* was the right word, had become a different person entirely in the queen's presence.

All sorts of people had come to the court. A couple of poets could be overheard reciting aloud nearby, and I was reasonably certain there were astronomers present: one man had unrolled a chart of some sort, which appeared to show the orbits of other worlds around the sun – a relatively recent way of thinking, as was my limited understanding on the subject. There were even actors, or dancers, waiting at the far end. This collection of individuals again showed the diversity of cultures in the city of Kuvash – or, at least, within the royal palace.

Out of those standing within the throng, just how many of them knew the bishop? I wondered if he had dealings with the court as well as seeing to religious matters. As an outsider, and a newcomer to the court, it was natural that many treated me with suspicion, which could easily be perceived in their glances. It was important not to read too much into that.

Sulma Tan steered us to one side of the chamber, not too far from the sumptuous throne. On closer inspection, I noted that it was built around a centre of luscious red cushioning. The throne itself was crafted from silver, with elaborate decorative features of what looked like planets and the sun, echoing the kind of things I'd seen on the astronomer's chart. The level of detail was staggering and it glimmered with the brightness of newly cast or highly polished metal.

Suddenly I realized what had been niggling me ever since I'd set foot in the chamber: whereas in Detrata, for example, there would be antique items, crumbling statues that indicated a long history, here absolutely everything was so very *new*. The statues were bright and had clearly been carved within the last couple of years; none of the metalwork had lost its newly cast vibrancy. Even the academics brought here were ready to discuss the very latest observations. Queen Dokuz was clearly a progressive monarch – or at the very least a woman who was fond of high culture. She wanted to be surrounded by the best, for people to walk among the finest offerings of Vispasia.

How, then, would she take to our details of the dismembered bishop?

I became alert to the approach of footsteps – slow, heavy boots from dozens of soldiers striking the stone floor. The rhythm was mesmeric, with at least three seconds between steps. The blue-hooded crowd turned almost in unison as men and women, garbed in red shirts with slitted puffed sleeves and white trousers, marched into the room two by two. There were ten of these ceremonial soldiers in all, though the sound of their passage suggested a far greater number.

At the rear of the entourage came four intriguing figures: two men in what I took to be flowing feminine versions of the national dress in pastel blue. They might have been the queen's eunuchs.

But the true focus of the room was on the two ladies.

One stood much shorter than the other, and was clearly in her teens. She was surely to transform into a woman of great presence one day, though currently her demeanour suggested that she would rather be anywhere but here. She must have been

Nambu Sorghatan, daughter of the queen, who strode alongside her as the vision of what her daughter would one day become. On our way here Sulma Tan had mentioned that her father, the queen's former husband, had died a long time ago of a coughing sickness, and that his name was now rarely brought up.

The woman led the nation; one day so would the girl.

Queen Dokuz Sorghatan and her daughter each wore a gown of exquisite silk – the mother's colour was a rich shade of purple with daedal gold stitching and bright silver buttons, while her daughter's was an exact replica, but a few sizes smaller and in crimson. The queen was heavily made up, lending her face a pale, almost ethereal sheen, and her black hair was arranged in an elaborate, if somewhat improbable, style. A large silver crown, more like a silver laurel wreath, rested upon her head. Her daughter's hair was much more conservatively arranged, and merely tied at the nape of her neck. I noticed that her eyes were an incredible bright-blue.

The queen broke from the group and led her daughter to the throne. With slow, measured movements, a point of ceremony rather than effort, the queen turned to sit on the throne. She did so in a manner that suggested the throne caused her some discomfort, and she raised both hands to alter the crown that appeared to sit awkwardly.

Her daughter moved around to stand on her right and the figures I'd taken to be eunuchs then moved to their position behind the throne, before turning to face the rest of the crowd.

Everyone visibly relaxed at that moment, though the tension remained thick, the room full of uncertainty. A few more people then filed into the court, until there were around sixty of us standing within the perimeter of soldiers. One of the eunuchs leaned forward to whisper something into the queen's ear. After she nodded, he then beckoned Sulma Tan forward.

She motioned for us to follow her through the crowd and only then did I realize I had not been briefed on the correct royal etiquette. There was little need to tell Leana what to do – we were experienced enough to know that we should keep a close eye on Sulma Tan's behaviour, and mimic her gestures where appropriate. However, it did not stop my anxiousness growing with every step.

The second secretary fell to one knee before the queen, and lowered her head, placing her forearm horizontally in front of herself. We did the same, rising only when Sulma Tan rose. These gestures seemed to please the queen.

The queen spoke without hesitation, her voice full of authority: 'Please, to your feet. You are Detratan?' She spoke in my native language.

'I am,' I replied. 'My name is Lucan Drakenfeld, Officer of the Sun Chamber. This is Leana, my assistant.'

The queen's gaze settled on my companion. 'Astran's mercy, such beautiful dark skin. How wonderful to see such variety in our humble city.'

'I am from Atrewe,' Leana said.

'You are both from places of high culture.' The queen gave a grin that almost started to crack her make-up. She possessed a wide, animated face and bright bold eyes. I estimated her age to be somewhere around fifty – her white make-up, with vibrant azure areas around her eyes, made it difficult to be certain, or indeed to read her emotions clearly.

'We like to think so, at least,' I replied, more to break the silence that lingered rather than to converse in a casual manner. From my experience, it often pays to let people in high positions speak first, and at some length.

If the young Nambu Sorghatan had made eye contact with

me, I would have acknowledged it, but she did not. Sulma Tan extended no ceremonial greeting towards her specifically.

Queen Dokuz simply sat there, letting it be known she was watching us, for a long, drawn-out moment. I had no doubt that her spies had been discussing me, that she had sent her menials to verify the events in which I had participated. To me, it was reassuring.

'We do not often get visitors from the Sun Chamber,' she said eventually. 'What a fine institution that is. I have always supported them when we queens and kings meet. Though not everyone can see it, Vispasia depends upon people like you. I understand not even every royal thinks that, but I appreciate the contribution in terms of justice. Stability leads to prosperity, yet often in times of comfort people forget that luxury of peace.'

'Your words are kind and wise,' I replied, somewhat relieved. 'I'm only sad that my arrival – as it tends to be *wherever* I visit these days – comes under such circumstances.'

'I have been informed about Bishop Tahn Valin,' she replied. 'Is it as bad as they say?'

'If not worse.'

One of the eunuchs behind, who possessed thick brown hair and striking blue eyes, made an expression that suggested he thought I was making more dramatic conclusions than were necessary.

'And you are the man who found his remains?' the queen asked.

'I'm afraid so. Last night I ventured outside of this prefecture and soon came upon a trail.' I wanted to suggest that it was a simple enough investigation, but I felt the statement might have undermined Sulma Tan in some way – so I left it at that.

'Report to me, Officer Drakenfeld, what you have so far discovered,' she declared. 'My child,' she gestured to her right, 'will one day be queen and need to deal with such matters. Leave out no detail, no matter how disturbing you think it might be.'

Carefully, and at length, I revealed the events leading up to the discovery of his remains, and of the work we had done so far with Sulma Tan, who was slightly embarrassed at the mention of her name in this context. It was understandable that being associated with the dead in any capacity was not well thought of throughout Vispasia. The dead brought with them bad omens. During my revelations, such as they were, I was all too aware that the entire court could hear what was being said. The queen made no effort to ensure the information was kept secret and I decided that was probably no bad thing, since I considered this to be a thoroughly *controlled* culture.

After I finished my report, I awaited a response.

'What are your conclusions?' Queen Dokuz demanded.

'It is too early to tell. All we know is that the damage to his body was *profound*. As your physician Carlon reported, this was not some simple backstreet murder. Or an attempt to settle a score or steal a purse. But a calculated effort to inflict the maximum amount of pain on another human. This sort of thing happens so rarely.'

I heard gasps from one or two members of the gathered throng, who had remained silent during our discussion and could not contain their disbelief.

'We are all such busy people,' the queen replied.

As ever when among the decadent quarters of society, I resisted the urge to gesture at all those people standing idly nearby.

'Sulma Tan, too, is too busy as a secretary. We are in the process of undergoing a great survey of our nation – the very first of its kind for a generation. Every member of my staff is stretched to their limits. What is more, we are constantly striving to better ourselves and our minds and our people. This murder in the

Sorghatan Prefecture will be a distraction from matters of enlightenment.'

I noticed the younger Sorghatan scoffed at her mother's comments, before she looked away in the opposite direction.

The queen gazed contemplatively, not angrily, across to the girl. 'You disapprove of something, Nambu?'

'Someone has just been killed,' she said quietly, in perfectly formed Detratan, 'and all you can think of is that it's a *distraction*?'

It was difficult not to smile, as there was much to be commended in the young lady's pithy sentiment. There was an obvious tension between the two, and it was as though they had reached an uneasy tolerance of one another. What battles there may have been were probably fought a good while ago. Having a queen for a mother would have made victory very unlikely for the young Nambu Sorghatan.

'A dead man will not halt our progress, Nambu,' her mother said softly, placing a hand on her daughter's arm. 'You *will* understand what that means one day.'

The young girl did not flinch; she barely noticed the gesture.

'Children,' the queen said, shaking her head.

'They have such wonderful minds,' I replied.

'You think so?'

'Absolutely I do,' I said, trying to maintain a gentle tone. 'Younger people look at the world with such innocence and have open minds as a result. They're not blinded by our more adult prejudices. They still have wonder. They still know how to dream.'

'Some have had the luxuries in which to dream,' she said, gazing at her daughter again. 'Some do not realize quite how lucky they are. That said, young Nambu here was the victim of an attack.' She explained briefly what had occurred. I assume she wanted people to know that her daughter's security was of great importance. It was possible she had suspicions of someone present, and wanted to make them uncomfortable. 'I am thinking of handing her to someone such as Grendor of the Cape. A friend of mine who I can trust.'

'He is a good man, majesty,' the blue-eyed eunuch added.

'Yes. Here she is a sitting target, a doe waiting to receive an arrow. Like all royals who remain still, we make easy sport for others.'

The queen snapped her attention back to me in a way that made me feel as sheepish as her daughter *ought to* have looked. 'Anyway, real life has not had the chance to wear down children. I still dream, Officer Drakenfeld, though those dreams take more pragmatic forms these days. They are my visions for this nation. My dreams, if the gods smile on us, become reality. Now, to the business of the bishop. If you have so far been employed in the process of understanding the cause of the bishop's death, I will grant you permission to ask whoever you wish. But I would like the matter to be resolved with some urgency and without too much distraction. We are undergoing our latest census, a great inventory, which is to be marked by an especially large festival of games towards the latter half of this month.'

She was half addressing me, half addressing the rest of the court. The eunuchs behind her glanced towards the rest of the room now, like some extension of the queen's arrogance and dominance. I wondered if she had taught them the nuances of her expressions so they worked together as a collective.

'It is a moment to celebrate our proud Kotonese heritage, with the monthly Kotonese Games and a feast, and from there we will as always look to the future.' The queen became calmer, and spoke subtly. 'You will understand that I would not like such momentum and happy times to be *ruined* by some vile character.'

'If the murderer remains within the city, I will do my best to find them and to bring them before your courts, for you to issue whatever justice you see fit.'

'Very good,' she said. 'I am glad that you will use our court. I do not like rogue operators.'

'I am not here to get in the way, but to help the wheels of justice move more smoothly. To help you find this murderer. The Sun Chamber works with each nation's laws, quite willingly . . .'

'How very diplomatic,' she replied, 'given that the Sun Chamber helped define our laws in the first place.'

The queen was making reference to over two hundred years ago, when the Sun Chamber was formed during the foundation of the Vispasian Royal Union. It wasn't quite that we dictated the laws. The founding principles of the continent were forged at the same time as the Sun Chamber itself. They were one and the same. Without the Sun Chamber there would be no independent organization to bind the nations together. There would be no fairness, no independence, and no accountability. If she was trying to test me, to see if her sardonic comment could annoy me in some way, then I would not give her any such pleasure. It was always the way with royals as they attempted to assert their authority, yet we both knew that if I failed to make my reports, then more officers would come and an army could follow.

'We are ever the diplomats,' I replied.

'In the meantime,' she continued, 'I ask that you both join me at an event I am holding later tonight. It is a gathering of great minds from across the arts and sciences, fields that I actively encourage to flourish in our nation. Both of you,' she indicated Leana, 'are welcome to join us and converse with others. There will be some of the finest food available, and rare wines from Dalta – a present from their queen.'

We probably didn't have much choice in the matter. I bowed. 'We'd be delighted to attend.'

'Sulma Tan will accompany you both to the event.'

'As you wish, your highness,' the second secretary replied, with a deferential nod of her head.

'I will be most pleased to have a Detratan and an Atrewen as guests. Those old countries . . . we in Koton envy them greatly. Our history is too undeveloped, so we must take our heritage from others.'

Her craving for prestige was obvious, matching up perfectly with what I had seen of her tastes in art, and I was very curious to see what the evening would entail.

The queen was about to dismiss us from her company when she suddenly stared at me and asked a question that appeared out of context. 'How are you with protection?'

I briefly explained Leana's talents, how they had served us in the past, and admitted I wasn't too bad with a blade myself. 'We won't need any of your guard to accompany us, let's put it that way.'

Queen Dokuz nodded, but said nothing else on the matter. She leaned back in the throne, her unsettling gaze lingering on me for longer than was comfortable, before she dismissed us.

On our way back out of the hall, passing through the on-lookers, I wondered if I had misunderstood that last question. It appeared as if the queen had made a simple mistake in a language that wasn't her native tongue, or had deliberately veiled her words – but had she in fact been assessing *our* ability to protect someone else?

Schooling

Sulma Tan guided us around the other side of the royal palace and eventually through the busy streets of the prefecture, heading on a much shorter route back to Jejal's establishment.

Sulma Tan appeared to be annoyed with me, but I couldn't place what I'd done wrong. I had casually been commenting upon how effective my investigations had been elsewhere in Vispasia, simply to build her trust. She might as well have been leading cattle down these roads for all the interest she showed in us.

'Have I offended you in any way?' I asked her.

'No,' she called back, striding past a vendor who sold various jars of oils.

'Are you sure?'

'Yes.'

'OK.'

Leana merely shrugged, but it was enough of a gesture to know that I wasn't imagining her attitude towards us.

'Only I was wondering,' I continued more firmly, 'why your conversational skills have taken a turn for the worse. My commissioner suggested you would be a good point of contact.'

It was never easy to tell whether or not such a comment would go down badly, yet this time it was enough to shake Sulma Tan from whatever mood she was in.

She stopped in the middle of the street, people bustling by around her, and turned to face me. It was obvious from her expression that I'd hit a nerve. 'I apologize,' she said. 'It was rude of me to behave in such a way. You've done nothing to vex me – I am unused to outsiders talking about the wider continent.'

'Let me guess,' I ventured. 'You've much work on your hands, and you do not really want to deal with a dead body?'

'Perhaps that is so.' She gave me an intense, concerned look.

'Then let us do all the hard work,' I replied. 'I represent the Sun Chamber. We really don't need much help – just a map, somewhere to base our investigation. And suggestions on where to find decent food.'

There was a smile – or at least a relaxation of her frown. 'I can arrange those things for you, but can I ask why you are so keen to find the killer?'

'It's my job to do that,' I replied. 'I was sent here to investigate the matter, and that is precisely what I'm doing.'

'Fine.'

'For some reason you seem suspicious of my answer.'

'Of course. You are a man. A man like every other, who blunders into a situation and thinks that I am incompetent. I have dealt with men many times before you came, and probably will many times after. So far they have all proven to be the same. Those who have worked with me in the past grab me in some dark corner and lift up my dress.' She jabbed a finger towards Leana. 'She will know what I mean, am I correct?'

'I do know,' Leana replied. 'Though I have my own effective methods for dealing with such cretins.'

I was honestly shocked at Sulma Tan's response, but there was little point in protesting about the ways of crude men and the fact that I was associated with them.

Leana interrupted. 'As much as I like to see him suffer, he has lived with me for years without so much as making one single inappropriate gesture. Nor has he undermined me. We are like brother and sister. Lucan is annoying for many other reasons, sometimes pompous and sometimes he bores me, but this subject is not a flaw for him.'

'Thank you for that heavily disguised compliment.' I turned to Sulma Tan. 'So when I say to you I want to help, it is not out of chivalry, nor is it the patronizing view of a Detratan who is looking down on your culture. I have orders, strict orders, and I will be following them. No matter what work you have on. You have the option to help me out or not. It is up to you.'

Sulma Tan looked up as a flock of geese shot across the sky above the narrow street. 'You remember that census the queen mentioned, the one by which our nation will assess itself and celebrate afterwards?'

A change of subject, an alteration in the tone of the conversation and the tension vanished swiftly in the afternoon heat.

'I am the one who is organizing it all,' she continued. 'Every single detail is mine to arrange, command and record.'

'Ah,' I said, contemplating whether or not the information might be of use to the case. 'Quite a project.'

'Ah indeed. It is an ambitious project and, though worthy intellectually, it is time-consuming. On top of that there are petty issues such as the monthly games and . . . It is no excuse. Better not to let the daily tasks overwhelm oneself.'

'Understood,' I replied. 'We'll keep out of your way. You can even head back now – we'll find our own way to Jejal's establishment.'

'You are perhaps a kind man,' she concluded firmly. With a

faint but detectable smile she added: 'But a hand out of place and I will castrate you myself.'

My tongue firmly in my mouth, I watched her vanish through the crowds.

'And so ends your first lesson in Kotonese culture,' Leana added.

On the Rooftop

Back in our room, with the low evening sunlight casting a bright-red glow on the walls and a fresh breeze coming in through the open window, I sat on the bed and contemplated the logistic puzzle that a census must have presented to Sulma Tan.

It was not merely counting the official number of women, men and children, or amount of land and goods, but the act of compiling the information too, surveying, interviewing, and presenting it in a way that the queen would find beneficial for her to make informed choices about the direction she wished to take Koton. There would be no end of liars and cheats seeing this as an exercise in tax collecting, or simply boasting, not to mention trying to make sense of the numbers of people migrating back and forth across borders like air through an open mouth. No doubt there would be many interfering, so that the census did not highlight any untoward business within the nation. There were thousands of people who lived in tribes across Vispasia, too, and who claimed no nation as their own.

The Sun Chamber always approved of official efforts to monitor a country like this. It went some way to analysing the large and fluid cultures of the Vispasian Royal Union so that strategies could be formed when the kings and queens met in Free State. They also went some way to keeping the rogue propaganda of a royal in check: artificial tensions would so often be used as a method of funnelling resources in a more favourable manner, and the more official data there was, then the more resources could be allocated evenly.

I didn't envy Sulma Tan in her efforts to assemble such vast quantities of information. What were her other roles, once the census had been dealt with? Dealing with people like me, arranging the Kotonese Games, generally overseeing matters of the court perhaps. She mentioned another secretary, which implied there was a great deal of business to arrange on the queen's behalf. Leana and I began to change into more formal clothing for the evening's event, both of us utterly oblivious to the dress code. Smiling to myself, I guessed that the queen would admire something that suggested 'high culture', and made a remark to Leana along those lines.

'She is a snob,' Leana muttered. 'This queen. There's something about her I do not like.'

'She's a queen, what did you expect? They're all snobbish to some extent. Some can be humble, some can be grotesque in their enjoyment of splendour. Royals, and many in their circles, can't help but view themselves as apart from normal society – because they live unlike anyone else. If people treat them like gods how can they be expected to behave differently? People don't simply become royals: they're sculpted by the acts of others. They have no *reference* to empathize with the people they lead after years of such god-like reverence. Is it any wonder we hear why so many went mad or committed bizarre deeds?'

'It seems more than that in this case. People – do not seem to matter to her at all. Her people. Any people, in fact. Even her own daughter.'

Leana had a point. There was a tension between mother and daughter that I couldn't quite pick apart. 'I'd be amazed if her rule was as progressive as she was making it out to be. But, that said, I do get the impression the old days of Koton are generally shunned in some way, that there's a keenness to separate themselves from the old country. Quite the opposite of Detrata.'

'Has Koton ever had an empire like Detrata though?'

'No, never. The people here – the tribes and families – have forever been nomadic. It's a shame she's hiding from the past – theirs is still a dignified history, as far as histories go. No great genocides. No great wars for centuries. Simply various powerful families jostling for control. Maybe it's too dull for her extravagant tastes.'

Leana reacted in a subtle but clear way that suggested something wasn't right – but her concern was not with my words. She gestured for me to keep talking so I continued, speaking about the queen's impressive residence and the wonderful ornaments on display, and I focused my attention on where Leana had originally been standing. Meanwhile, Leana stepped cautiously around the room, only to then move along the wall with her back pressed against it, heading towards the window. I continued addressing her previous position, my gaze following her movements, all the while wondering what it was that she had spotted.

Arcing her body, she dashed for the window. She leapt out through the open gap, feet first, and landed on the rooftop just the other side. I ran after her, climbing outside with caution as she skimmed across the angled plane with her arms held out wide for balance.

She stopped, placed her hands on her hips and sighed, peering back and forth across the adjacent rooftops. I followed her gaze but couldn't see anyone up here, only the lovely sunset.

Down below people drifted around the streets. In the distance, beyond the rooftops, were the dark peaks of mountains, which would soon be lost to the night. Only now, examining the vista, did I realize quite how beautiful this place was.

'What did you see?' I asked.

'A person,' Leana replied. 'A figure.'

'You're quite certain?'

'I definitely saw someone,' she snapped. 'A cloaked figure, at a distance. Just out of the corner of my eye. We were being watched.'

'No other details?' I asked. 'What clothing did they have on? The colour of their hair?'

'I could not tell, I had too little time and the light was behind them. It was probably a brown robe.'

We both crouched and sat tentatively on the sloping roof, eyeing the city below for unusual movements. An occasional, sharp gust of wind reminded me of the drop below, only a couple of storeys, but enough to remind me to be vigilant.

'Very few people know we're even here,' I said. 'Why would anyone be watching us?'

'Sulma Tan,' Leana said. 'She knows. She may have told others.'

'She'd be too busy,' I remarked.

'Or she does not trust us and wants us watched.'

That didn't seem either in or out of character. I knew too little about the woman. For someone who frequently conducted surveys and interviews, I imagined she would have a large number of suitable people to hand for such a task. It was possible that word had been spread about the court that the Sun Chamber was investigating the death of the bishop, and that someone else had put a spy to watch – in case I came too close. That was every bit as likely as it being an agent controlled by Sulma Tan.

While I peered over the edge, I noted several potential routes down for our visitor to have made an escape: a series of smaller rooftops or a ladder. Even the drop down was a manageable jump for a skilled individual. Whoever had been here was likely long gone – their escape route calculated well in advance.

We spent a little while sat absorbing the sights, sounds and smells of the prefecture. Though I had spent my days in many different cities, I often wondered what it was that made each of them unique, and what made Kuvash so . . . strange. A city's identity was born from its inhabitants: they created the mood and the design of the streets. The buildings were symptoms of a culture's art and, ultimately, its political or religious decisions. But from here I could see the mishmash of styles that weren't the expressions of its own people: these were buildings put up to satisfy the demands of a queen who admired other cultures. Though most of the motifs on the surrounding buildings were Detratan, I noted designs from Maristan, Theran, Dalta – even from the deserts of Locco.

There was little of Koton's identity to be found here. Little soul. In a way, then, that was Koton's expression: it had absorbed the various styles of Vispasia without developing one of its own. A borrowed culture, a denied heritage – a country unsure of its own roots and ashamed of its past.

Eventually Leana traced her steps back along the rooftop, while I continued to consider the streets. After a moment she called me over, and I went to meet her.

'What have you found?' I stepped carefully along the gently angled roof to her side.

Leana was crouching down by one of the tiles that had slipped out of line and jutted out at an awkward angle. She carefully picked off it a piece of brown fabric.

'It is just some cloth. A small piece.' She handed it up to me. 'What do you make of it?'

Tilting it this way and that, there were no discernible markings, no unusual stitching, nothing to really mark it out. 'Judging by the reasonably fine quality, I'd say that it could have come from a cloak. It's not wet, and there had been a brief shower not all that long ago. If it was fixed here, it was very recent.'

'There was no need to doubt me then,' Leana observed.

'I never did, not for a moment,' I replied, walking back to the window. 'Though it could have come from anyone. Could you tell from your brief glimpse if they were a threat to us?'

'I do not believe we were in any danger from this incident. I have no idea how long they had been standing there, but if it was someone who *had* been sent to kill us, they could so easily have fired an arrow or bolt through the open window, into your chest or face. There was plenty of time to make a mess of you.'

That was a sobering notion. 'Maybe we should see if we can move somewhere safer.'

'That might be wise,' Leana agreed.

No Party Tonight

Evening parties were something that, generally, I could do without. Yet because of my status I often received many invites to grand affairs, and due to my vaguely diplomatic position, it was usually unwise to decline such offers.

To my mind, from Detrata to Venyn, these social gatherings of the elite were nothing more than opportunities for cliques of people to show off their wealth to one another. Excitement only ever came from the thinly veiled power struggles in the alcoves. From my experience, such parties seemed to encourage grudges between the socially aspiring. They could exacerbate a family feud, manifesting in public fight, or even start a new political row between rivals.

But with all that considered, I was ever curious to observe some of the local customs at close-hand. These events always provided an excellent way to discover things about a culture.

So with a certain degree of reluctance, and with Leana moaning about having to come along as well, we made our way once again to the royal residence of Queen Dokuz Sorghatan.

There, beside the tall white walls, staring up at the brass beacons that raged with light against the indigo sky, and watching well-to-do groups of people saunter in through the open gate, we waited for Sulma Tan.

She joined us a little while later, apologizing sincerely for her late arrival. I was impressed at her new attire – a deep-red, high-collar dress, dark cloak – and her hair was pinned up in a way that mimicked the royal fashion. She was deeply uncomfortable at being dressed up like this. Leana, who hated these events even more than myself, would probably identify with that.

'Let me guess,' I said, 'you were busy?'

She gave an awkward smile. 'You must think me highly disorganized. I can assure you I am not.'

'Given you're in charge of a census, I would've been surprised if you were.'

'The queen had purchased some busts taken from a ruined house in Maristan, but I could tell they were forgeries, which led to a minor diplomatic issue.'

'Let's hope a war doesn't break out over art,' I replied.

Sulma Tan led us through to where the main event was being held, an enormous room that rivalled some of those in the king's residence in Tryum. I was quietly impressed. Enormous red and green frescos detailing battles covered the walls, while the ceiling displayed a map of the constellations, quite a recent depiction if I understood the latest studies correctly.

The room was almost two hundred feet long, so I could barely discern the paintings at the far end. Tall braziers stood in widely spaced rows, casting a warm glow upon the bronze statues that stood at regular intervals along the walls of the room. There must have been two hundred people in here, each of them wearing fine dresses, tunics, cloaks and boots, drinking wine from silver cups. People almost appeared to be in various groups, speaking to each other as if they were at a meeting rather than chattering together. Particularly unusual, compared with things I was more used to, was that many people were seated on the floor. Some were positioned on cushions, dozens of which were scattered about the place, but there were no chairs or benches to lounge on.

'Is this traditional?' I put my observation to Sulma Tan.

'Our people never really used chairs in large gatherings like this,' she replied. 'We had no need of them in our yurts. It is a custom that has followed us into cities.'

'No?' Perhaps the curious methods of polite debate were also leftovers from tribal culture.

'Chairs seem so wasteful, so bad for the body, and besides the floor is much . . .' Something caught her eye.

'What's the matter?'

Her gaze was directed at a group of men who were standing in a nearby corner of the room. I couldn't quite discern who they were from their clothing, but they didn't look like the other guests and they didn't seem to be guards – unless they were private operators or bodyguards, something I suspected was common in Kuvash.

'I will find out what is going on,' she replied. 'Please, wait here.'

With that she carved her way through the crowd with some efficiency, being careful not to tread on anyone's cloak or out-stretched hand.

'Your instructions for tonight?' Leana asked. 'I need something to take my mind off this nonsense.'

'For now, keep an eye out for our friend from the rooftop – or anyone regarding us for longer than seems necessary.'

'That happens all the time.'

'Well then, just memorize any faces that stand out – we know too few people in this city. Otherwise, it would be prudent to soak up something of the mood, and the concerns of these people. Eavesdrop here and there – you never know what might help us. Perhaps the bishop was killed due to some reason of state importance that we're so far unaware of? I'll be putting a few questions to the guests and . . .'

Sulma Tan returned quickly. Her distressed expression suggested our plans for the evening were about to change: 'You must come quickly, please. There will be no party for any of us tonight.'

We followed her back out the way we came, then along a wood-panelled corridor, but took a sharp left through a doorway that barely seemed different from the panelling.

She guided us through another series of rooms that, if we had not been with Sulma Tan, we would never have known existed. It suggested we were entering some secret part of the palace, and that was enough to tell me something serious had occurred. Sulma Tan said nothing.

Soon we found ourselves tucked away in a small brick chamber with a curved ceiling, and lit only by cressets on the walls and two storm lanterns on a table. The same four figures I'd seen a moment ago, during the social gathering, were standing here and each of them possessed a similar, sombre expression.

A tall, gaunt-looking man with long grey hair looked at me with a fierce stare. He wore the dark-blue silk robe I believe was associated with the Kotonese navy.

'This the fellow?' he snapped.

'Lucan Drakenfeld,' I began, 'Officer of the Sun Chamber. This is my assistant Leana.'

'Duktan, sea marshal – leader of the Koton Navy.' He sat on a long oak bench beside the table, and there was an air of nervousness about him now, as if despite his seniority the necessary procedure had escaped him.

The other three, a mix of ages, each wore similar robes, though in different hues of purple and green. They remained silent and in their own private thoughts.

'What's happened?' I asked, assuming the worst.

'There has been another murder,' Sulma Tan said quietly.

She did not say a thing after that and, for a while, no one else did either. My impatience was getting the better of me, but it was as if no one knew who should divulge the rest of the information. Perhaps Sulma Tan was waiting for one of the others to do so. The room was full of uncertain gestures and uneasy glances. Two of the men were visibly dumbfounded. They stood there shaking their heads. Another looked as if he would slit the throat of the next man who made eye contact with him. Each had the air of the military about them: strong posture, good, well-polished boots, military trinkets on their tunics, wristbands, brooches, badges of honour. Though there was no armour today, not even the colours of their regiment; they had not been looking for a battle tonight.

'Was the victim a friend or colleague?' I asked, to no one specifically.

'Stood alongside him for thirty years,' Duktan muttered eventually, though he expressed far more about his profound feelings during his ensuing silence. 'He saved my life once, on a ship off the coast of Venyn. Pirates. Said I'd return the honour and I waited another twenty years. I'll never get the chance now.'

Sulma Tan seemed either uncertain of the etiquette or merely content to allow others to speak.

A blonde-haired soldier entered the chamber through a large door wearing the blue and black of the city's equestrian troops. She beckoned us all to follow.

Leana and I waited respectfully, and still a little impatiently, at the back of the line as everyone filed out, back through the corridor. It was as if we would never find out what was going on.

We only had to wait a few minutes, until we arrived in another chamber, one that was similar to the medical room where we had examined the corpse of the bishop. Laid out before us on a table lit by paper lanterns was another body, this time in one piece. So far as I could tell, anyway, as a flag of Koton had been stretched across him, the red stag directly above his chest. However, a significant amount of blood had seeped through onto the surrounding bold-blue material, staining it a far darker shade. As I stood at one end of the outstretched corpse, I noticed his boots poking out from under the sheets. Though they were mostly clean, there was a significant accumulation of scuffing, dirt and mud on the heels, which suggested that the body had been dragged at some point.

Sulma Tan stepped to one side of the corpse with her head bowed, unable to hide her distress. She did not cry though. She merely clenched the side of the table and stared down with an unnerving vacancy.

'Grendor,' she breathed, and added something else I couldn't hear. The others crowded around the corpse. Their faces showed nothing but despair — whoever lay there was extremely well respected by them.

'He was like an uncle to me,' Sulma Tan said.

'Who was Grendor?' The only reference I had heard of him so far was that he was a friend of the queen, and that she was thinking of trusting him to look after her daughter. He was obviously someone of importance.

'Grendor of the Cape, that was his full title,' she replied. 'He was one of the queen's oldest friends — she will be horrified by this. Moreover he was one of our greatest ever naval officers. He helped build a fleet so big that we were no longer laughed at by other nations — as we once were, being a nation more accustomed to horse travel. He led the very first surveys of our difficult coastline, and charted the thousand islands. Grendor was sixty summers old and retired from the navy long ago. He advised the queen on wider military strategy, though spent some of his time managing a shipping company. He cheered her up with jokes. Everyone loved his wide smiles. I'll miss his laughter, and the way he'd diffuse our serious talk.' She smiled. 'He never could take me seriously – he said such seriousness was an affliction of younger people. When we got to his age, he said, hopefully we'd have learned to let go and laugh more.'

'He'll still be laughing up there when he faces Astran and Nastra,' Duktan added. 'Aye, still laughing.'

I waited a brief moment for everyone to pay their respects. It didn't seem right to blunder in with my questions until everyone had had their chance to grieve. Leana and I stood back, waiting as the others peeled away one by one, until only Sulma Tan remained.

'Where was Grendor's body found?' I asked.

'Near to his house,' she replied.

'Could you describe the location for me?'

'He lived in a large house near the centre of this prefecture,' she said, 'overlooking the new forum. It had only been constructed in the past year. It's a very nice place. His wife, Borta—'

'Nastra bless her,' Duktan interrupted.

'. . . found his body at the bottom of the stairwell,' Sulma Tan continued. 'It's a public space, a very visible part of the prefecture. In fact it was Borta who sent an urgent message to us. One can only imagine what she's going through.'

'I'll see to it that she's looked after,' Duktan said. 'And his sons.'

'I'd like to visit his home as soon as possible, but for now, if no one would be offended, I would like to see exactly what we are dealing with . . .' I gestured to the flag that had been draped across him.

Duktan moved his arms forward, then paused – glancing at those around him. 'Who will join me?'

I waited for them to reach their decisions, keen that my respect be noticed. Eventually all of them in unison peeled back the banner.

'Blessings of both Astran and Nastra . . .' Duktan breathed.

The body didn't look like it was sixty years of age. Instead Grendor of the Cape had the build of a man far younger – in his forties perhaps. Had it been neatly combed, his greying hair would have reached his shoulders, but instead it was tousled and covered in blood. Grendor had received a head wound above his right ear, but that didn't look severe enough to have killed him – it was more the kind of blow meant to knock him out. His finely made brown tunic had also become stained, though the cause of that was much more difficult to tell. It might have been blood, or muddied water. A quick sniff suggested the former.

Sulma Tan walked over to the side of the room to fetch a blade, then she handed it to Duktan to cut away his clothing. 'I have done this once already recently,' Sulma Tan said to him. 'I do not possess the will to do it to Grendor.'

Slowly, methodically, Duktan cut away Grendor's clothing, first revealing a bruised and bloodied torso. Then Duktan commenced cutting around the britches, down towards the dead man's boots. The group gave off the occasional groan as more and more of his ruined and battered body was exposed. When Duktan had finally finished and revealed the hideous wounds in full, Leana and I moved in closer to get a better look.

It was at that moment I realized our stay in Koton would probably be a lengthy one.

A spectacular number of cuts and puncture wounds covered Grendor's pale skin, much in the same way as had befallen the bishop – though the bishop's body was too decomposed for a true comparison. Grendor had only recently died. Given the stiffness of the limbs and the colouring of his face, I guessed no more than a day. None of his limbs had been visibly broken and the bruises had not yet grown so bad that they would obscure a lot of the injuries.

When his mouth was opened for examination, it was obvious that the tongue had been cut out.

'What do you think?' one of the men asked, looking up at me as if I might divine a prophecy from these wounds.

Sulma Tan nodded for me to go on, so I addressed the others.

'We examined Bishop Tahn Valin's body earlier today and found wounds similar to those we can see here on Grendor. The bishop's tongue had also been removed.'

'The same person did this then.' Duktan closed his eyes, grasping the end of the table, leaning over his dead friend, fighting back either tears or rage. Eventually he stepped away to compose himself.

Sulma Tan had a worried look, even though she couldn't quite bring herself to make eye contact with me, but she must have been thinking the same thing. The notion was probably more profound to her. This was happening in her home city after all.

'I can't say for certain that it was the same person who did this,' I continued, 'merely that the wounds share certain *characteristics*. Both men, I think it is fair to say, suffered cruel and unusual deaths. However, there was no dismemberment in this particular case, whereas the bishop had pieces of his body discarded around the city. No, it's too early to start making the assumption that we are definitely dealing with the same murderer. Not without more information. With that in mind, I would very much like to see the scene of the incident.'

'Oh come on, officer,' Duktan snapped. 'You're a man of the

world. Tell us what you think. Give us a hunch. Something to go on.'

People rarely wanted to dwell on what may be complicated facts. They wanted easily digestible answers, almost always right away. When emotions were involved, especially, there was little headroom for quiet contemplation on such matters.

'Well, here's what *might* have happened — but this is purely speculation and shouldn't leave this room as an official theory.' The others nodded their approval. 'Grendor was struck down with the blow to the head, which was just behind his ear.' I indicated the wound. 'That suggests it was not done in combat. Maybe he did not even come face to face with his killer at this stage.'

'At this *stage*?' Duktan muttered. 'What's that supposed to mean?'

'Please, bear with me,' I replied. 'Grendor's body was then taken somewhere, perhaps dragged, which caused the dirt and scuff marks to the heels of his boots. Then all these wounds were then inflicted upon him. Such wounds take time to inflict, and they are not done lightly, nor are they the sort of thing that can be done in the street without anyone noticing. Given this was torture, it is possible — though we cannot be certain — that he was awake to endure much of this. At that point he was face to face with his killer.'

A couple of the men muttered something inaudible to each other, as if in fear of their lives or planning some form of revenge.

'After this,' I continued, 'his body was returned to a very public place. It's likely his body was left to be discovered. Whoever did this wanted Grendor to be seen in this state.'

'Like the dismembered limb of the bishop,' Leana said. 'You do not do such a thing unless you are making a statement.'

While the others were lost in their own contemplation of the matter, Sulma Tan moved over and steered me to one side, out of earshot of Duktan. 'You are suggesting that two very high-profile and respected men could have been killed in the same manner, by the same people. That officials of our country are being deliberately targeted.'

'It is only speculation so far,' I replied. 'We need more evidence and I don't like to jump to conclusions. But I'm only describing what's obvious. You were probably thinking the same, too.'

Her eyes flickered minutely from left to right, from one of my eyes to the other, as she was trying to read my expression. She folded her arms and peered back at the corpse. 'What do you suggest we do now? I know perfectly well how the queen will react to this. There will be chaos in the court if this is made public knowledge, and I imagine rumours will spread. She will ensure more soldiers patrol the prefecture instead of being directed further afield. What's more, the gates will be monitored in such a way that it will make life difficult for traders to come and go. The rivers will be policed heavily too. The queen can put a tight grip on the city if she wishes . . .'

'I don't yet believe there's a need for such actions and I'll back you up if you think them unwise. Anyway, the queen might not jump to such conclusions. It's just as likely she'll simply be distraught at what has happened to a dear old friend. One can never quite tell how people will react to the loss of a loved one.'

'She will not approve of this display of barbarism in the Sorghatan Prefecture one bit,' Sulma Tan replied. 'She is . . . *sensitive* to such things. She prefers order to be maintained at all times.'

'I'm sure the loved ones of the deceased aren't too keen on this barbarism either,' I sighed.

Sulma Tan's posture softened. 'Please don't misjudge my tone. I'm not heartless – I mean to suggest that the queen will want this resolved quickly. You do not know her like I do. This is an embarrassment to her. Soldiers will make life difficult around here for everyone if she brings them inside this prefecture.'

I shook my head. 'Not if she wants to keep the news quiet. Soldiers, in their dozens, are rarely subtle in the art of investigation. It will attract too much attention – attention I'm sure she does not want. She can be persuaded on this argument.'

Sulma Tan turned to face me; all the pressures of life were in that one gaze. 'So, Officer Drakenfeld, tell me what you want our next steps to be.'

'Two things,' I replied, with confidence. 'The physician Carlon said he'd be more help with a fresher victim – well here, in unfortunate circumstances, we now have one. We should see that he makes a thorough assessment of Grendor and have him compare his findings to the limited information regarding the bishop. The comparison could prove important and I'm immensely grateful we have such a learned figure among us.'

'It will be done,' she replied, 'though that will only confirm our current suspicions and bring us no closer to finding who did this.'

'That brings me to the other matter: Grendor's wife, Borta. Maybe she can help me establish a profile of her husband, his movements, where he was last seen, and so on. If I can find a connection between her husband and the bishop, then that may bring us a step closer to finding the killer. We could have the matter resolved quickly and without too many other lives being affected. Order will be restored and the queen need not panic.'

'Then, please, make it happen,' she sighed, before walking back to join the others.

Borta

The street was unnervingly dark and quiet, and low clouds had long since conspired to bring about a warm drizzle. Leana, myself and Sulma Tan walked hastily across the slick cobbles of the prefecture towards the scene of the murder.

We had endured an awkward conversation earlier with the friends and comrades of Grendor of the Cape. They had all wanted to come, to offer their support; but I advised them that tonight might be too soon, and too much, for the wife of the deceased to cope with so many people all at once.

I could understand their urge to be there, to offer their help or advice to the loved one of a friend, but all of that could wait until tomorrow. Thankfully they were in agreement with me or rather Sulma Tan who spoke very persuasively to them. I conducted a very casual conversation in which I slyly probed them for knowledge about Grendor's final movements, but it appeared that none of them had seen him for several days. He was a sociable man, they told me, with a lot of friends, and he liked to make the most of his time, ever conscious of his age.

Leana's torch created a golden puddle of light that was reflected in the wet stone. Whitewashed buildings, mostly three storeys high, leaned into the street either side of us, dogs trotted alone, rummaging for scraps of food along alleyways. The area looked well-to-do, much like anywhere else in this prefecture, and the buildings well maintained. Private soldiers, or guards from the City Watch, were marching in pairs down the wide, main thoroughfare. I was curious, then, that it wasn't one of them who had found Grendor's body. Either the guards were slack, or the murder was thoroughly organized. Eventually we reached a stone building decorated with sculptures of numerous animals, especially horses and stags, carved into wood. The quality of the work was breathtaking. The theme repeated in stone reliefs high up, or had been painted as insignia on doors. It was a house constructed with great taste and a subtle show of wealth and power. I'd noticed how the nation's art used various elements of hunting, perhaps an echo of the people's history of a life roaming the plains in codependence with animal herds.

Grendor's apartment was on the upper floors and overlooked one of the two main forums of Kuvash. Here in the daytime, Sulma Tan explained, people would gather not just to trade, but to read out news and give political speeches. I found the latter difficult to believe, given that I'd seen no signs of a parliament, which all nations in Vispasia were meant to possess. The queen's rule looked to be a firm one, and if her government existed at all it was barely mentioned.

That aside, as this area was meant to be a thriving place in the daytime it was a good place to live to keep up with the city's affairs. Thousands of people would have passed by when the sun was up. Maybe that was how Grendor liked things – busy, hectic, full of activity. Then again, given the nature of his death, was he a fearful man, desiring to be close to others at all times, knowing that someone might come for him? I was perhaps letting my imagination get the better of me.

Access to the apartment was up a neat stairway. While Sulma Tan knocked on the door at the top of the stairs to call on Grendor's wife, Leana moved her torch along the walls of the stairwell. Blood had been smeared on otherwise-clean walls, especially down near the bottom. Because it hadn't rained hard, we could still see scratch marks between the pavement and the stairs.

'We saw that he had dirty heels,' I said to Leana. 'He may have been dragged here, from the road.'

'Brought by a cart?'

'It's hard to say. He might have been dragged all along the road for all we know. Although a cart would be more discreet.'

Leana crouched down by the marks with her torch. 'The marks seem wide enough – hip-width apart – to have come from boots.'

'There was mud on them, which suggests his body had been somewhere else at some point. We probably knew that anyway.'

A new voice interrupted us.

'Good evening.' A woman of around thirty summers came down the stairs to greet us and stepped into the flickering light of the torch. She wore her dark hair tied back; her bright eyes, green maybe, were soft and her expression, understandably, haunted by grief. She wore a black shawl bordered with crimson lace.

'My name is Borta,' she began in perfect Detratan. 'I'm Grendor's wife. You must be Officer Drakenfeld and Leana. I received your messenger, Sulma Tan, to say you would be coming.'

Only then did I think she was surprisingly young to be the wife of someone so old, and I wondered at what age she had married him. She must have been in her teens. Sulma Tan had told me that Borta was well connected, through powerful families such as the Rukrid clan. Like so many marriages in Koton, she explained, theirs had been arranged between two families – and it had grown into love.

After a few cordial exchanges, with great dignity, and without any encouragement from me, Borta explained the events that had led to her discovery of her husband's body.

Occasionally her speech was hard to follow and her words descended into an inaudible whisper, and at times she was fighting back tears. Her willingness to involve herself so quickly in the investigation was impressive, so much so that at first I thought it suspicious, but her body language appeared genuine. I did not think she was lying. Many of my older colleagues would have used a firmer hand, and been more blunt in seeking information, but I preferred a more gentle approach. In my experience, the truth was always more forthcoming with empathy rather than bullying.

'The last I saw of him was two days ago, late in the afternoon,' she said. 'Later that evening he went out for a supper with his five friends. All elder statesmen of the city, one might say. He was often out late at night.' She listed their names and I looked to Sulma Tan for guidance — she nodded a confirmation, suggesting these were all people she knew.

'They were all gentlemen of our armed forces,' she continued. 'Not the navy, with whom he often socialized, but the army. All of them friends of the queen. Good people. They always treated me with respect.'

'Why was he meeting with the army?' I asked.

'It wasn't anything official,' she replied. 'He has friends everywhere. He says it's good for business.'

Business. This must have been the shipping company that Sulma Tan mentioned earlier. To my mind Borta was describing a man whose social connections were simply ways to make more money. Grendor was a shrewd individual. To have friends in the army could make various trade routes more secure from raids, should he have money invested in certain quarters, or be importing from difficult regions. Though the nations of Vispasia were not at war, there were often tensions with factions and nomads who chose not to submit to any particular royal.

Borta continued to talk, occasionally wrapping her arms around herself and staring at the ground. The sentences were coming more slowly now and when I asked her once again about his final movements, it was an effort for her to speak.

'I've known them for many years. Each of those friends of his have visited me this afternoon to offer their condolences. They said he came to visit, ate well, drank a little too well, but showed no signs of uneasiness. There was no reason to think he knew he was in any trouble. I am sure no one ever does show such obvious signs, Officer Drakenfeld. You must hear all this nonsense so frequently.'

'You'd be surprised,' I replied softly. 'It's useful to know that he didn't *feel* he was in any trouble, at least. That might tell us much.'

A polite half-smile faded from her lips. 'That was the last anyone knows of his whereabouts. He left the supper late at night and started back here on his own. He never came home.'

A gust of unseasonably cold wind passed along the road, beating down the flame of Leana's torch. The night sky was now cloudless, the bad weather had moved away, and starlight defined the rooftops of the city. The scorching Detratan summer suddenly felt a lifetime ago.

'Why were you not invited to the dinner?' Leana asked, bringing her torch a little closer to Borta. Only then did I notice the woman's classical attractiveness: a beautiful face, surely, in any of the nations of Vispasia.

Leana had asked the difficult question and I was curious as to what the reaction would be. If Borta was hiding something, such as the couple having an argument beforehand, she was betraying nothing.

'He sometimes wished to dine alone with his friends, as do I,' she said sincerely. 'It's perfectly normal for us to enjoy the company of our own friends as individuals. We women should not be bound to our husbands like a trained dog just because we're married.'

Leana seem satisfied with that. Later I would have to ask Sulma Tan for the addresses of those men who had dined with Grendor in his final moments, so we could verify what Borta had told us.

'So to be absolutely clear, he never made it home,' I said, 'and that was two nights ago?'

'I only knew about his absence the following morning when I woke up and he was not lying next to me. I do not wait up for him to return and I am a heavy sleeper.'

'You presumably raised the alarm immediately?'

'Not . . . immediately, no.'

My neutral expression must have made her suspect I was thinking the worst.

'It's not for any bad reason. I thought then that he might have come back and left early to attend to trade, as he so often did.'

'Hadn't he retired?' I asked, hoping she would expand upon his business affairs.

'From the navy, yes,' Borta said. 'Though he often advised importers and exporters on trade routes and so on. His company kept his mind occupied.'

Imports and exports, I smiled inwardly. The business of spies and agents throughout the continent – there was no escaping them. There might have been more to Grendor's life than even Borta knew about.

'And so,' Borta continued, 'when he did not return *yesterday* evening, and I had received no message, I began contacting people. I grew increasingly concerned. Last night, nothing. I began to panic and fear the worst . . .' She trailed off, her eyes welling up, but she didn't let herself go fully. We waited patiently until she was ready to continue. 'Then, earlier this afternoon, I came back and found him . . . here . . .'

Sulma Tan placed a hand on Borta's shoulder and Grendor's wife turned into her, no longer able to hold back the tears.

No matter how many times I did this, one of the worst parts of the job was witnessing the impact on those left behind – their own world shattered by such exits. Many of my colleagues in the Sun Chamber did not concern themselves with emotions – either out of their own belligerence or simply because they found it easier to work this way. However, I couldn't help but feel sorry for Borta. My own father having recently passed away, I was perhaps even more sensitive to this than usual. It helped me to remember that each body was more than just a case to solve. They had been a person who had loved and been loved and left a hole in someone's life that would last forever.

Giving them a moment alone, I stepped away to get another look up the stairs, noting the blood once again, before peering along the street. It was possible that Grendor had been kidnapped on his way home and tortured for a whole day before his corpse was dumped on his own doorstep.

But what could Grendor have to do with the bishop? What connected these two men, if anything? If Grendor alone had been killed, I might have wondered if the murder had a military underpinning. Though I did not know of all the secretive ways of governments and armies, it was possible he had been killed as part of a military operation. Did that have anything to do with the tensions with Detrata? But then again, what could a bishop possibly have done to invoke the wrath of a military assassin?

I'd have so many more questions for Borta and tonight was not the best time to conduct a thorough interview.

I consulted Leana briefly on my thoughts, and she agreed that it would be better if we started afresh the next day.

'If the murderer is the same person,' Leana concluded in hushed tones, 'he is unlikely to have gone far. We may yet find him.'

After consulting with Borta and Sulma Tan, we agreed that Leana and I would return first thing in the morning, once Borta had taken the opportunity to sleep and gather her thoughts. Borta was grateful for the gesture and walked slowly, with heavy steps, up back through the darkness to her front door. Would she be alone tonight, or would any relatives come to comfort her? By the time I'd thought of this she'd already locked herself in for the night.

The three of us remained in the area a little longer, doing our best in the poor light to examine the streets for signs of the incident, for something that could give us a trail. For an hour at least we combed the cobbles and knocked on the doors of neighbours, but few people answered strangers at this hour and no clues turned up. At least, none that we could see in the dark.

Sulma Tan had been studying the stairs for further evidence. Not wanting to disturb Borta I said quietly: 'Have you found anything?'

Stepping back down towards me she shook her head. She stood on the edge of the kerb regarding the buildings opposite. 'Nothing at all, and it is getting late – I really ought to be back soon.'

'You don't have to help us find evidence, you know that?'

'I can't seem to leave such matters alone,' she said. 'I like to do things myself as I am so often surrounded by people who are useless. It is a habit I cannot shake easily.'

'What a compliment,' I replied, smiling.

'I didn't mean you,' she said. 'You both seem very capable – I meant the administrators in the palace.'

'I knew what you meant. Thank you for your help here. May we escort you back to the palace?'

'No, I'll be fine – I know my way around the prefecture well enough. You can presumably find your way back. Will you need me in the morning?'

'We'll not hold you up any more than we have already.'

'I would appreciate regular updates, so that I may keep the queen informed. Please use our messenger service – it is highly commendable.' She began to leave and then stopped herself. Her shoulders relaxed a little more, and now she spoke in a softer tone. 'Of course, should you need help and advice about the city or its people, you know where to find me and I will be happy to help you. In the meantime, I'll get the names and addresses of Grendor's dinner companions and get them sent to you. Goodnight.' She gave a discreet bow to us before walking gracefully into the darkness.

I sat back on the kerb and watched her until she was out of sight, then listened to her heavy boots for a few moments. It was then that I realized I'd forgotten to ask her if we could find a more secure place to stay.

Leana perched next to me, moving her scabbard out of the way, and I could sense she was about to impart some of her wisdom.

'I would have thought by now,' she began, 'that you would be less obvious in your approaches to women. Besides, you never get to the point with them. You . . . dither too much in such matters. In Atrewe, we do not mess about. If there is attraction, people act upon those sensations – women and men speak their minds. So, for once why not do things the Atrewen way and spare yourself the agony?'

Laughing, I shook my head. 'No, not that.'

'No attraction?'

I shrugged. 'I can't think of anyone but Titiana . . .' As soon as I spoke her name I could see her again: dead, hanging in my garden, blood pooling underneath her feet. Killed in such a way because of my investigations. I couldn't even imagine my own home any more, not without evoking her image. Titiana was an old love, one who I rediscovered; our renewed acquaintance never really had the chance to breathe and develop fully in those few days. Now it never would.

It was funny how closed paths were the ones we often wished to walk the most.

'You must let her go, Lucan.' Leana's tone was neither cold nor warm; it was never easy to perceive her intentions.

You can talk, I wanted to say. Leana, who lost her husband years ago during war, who was still bound even in death, wanted to lecture me in the art of letting go of a loved one. Perhaps she was aware of her mistake, for she gave as close as she normally gets to an apology. 'It is not my business, I know. Come, let us return to our room. We will not be solving much tonight.'

Leana held out her hand and picked me up from the pavement – a gesture I appreciated. Together we walked home through the darkness, her torch still a beacon, my Sun Chamber brooch still glinting in its light.

All around us, the nightlife in the Sorghatan Prefecture continued its quiet flow, every bit as strange and alluring as it was in Tryum, every bit as feral-sounding as it was in Venyn City, where I had spent so many years. But somehow these sounds were far more subtle, and distant, no matter the direction we travelled in. It was as if Koton deliberately kept its forbidden taverns and illicit nightlife well away from conventional thoroughfares, as if the city's streets were conscious and fluid, steering us away from what we were not meant to see. In Tryum such things were thrust in one's face, here I had the sense that you had to make an effort to find a wild evening.

But such notions rarely affected me. This wasn't the first time that Leana and I ignored enticing events due to our work, and it wouldn't be the last, so we continued on our way. And all the way back, amidst these strange, out-of-reach sounds, I kept an eye out, wondering vaguely if our friend from the rooftops would pay us another visit. Or if they were watching us right at this very moment from some hidden doorway.

Morning Analysis

The new day's sun rose through the gap in the buildings opposite our room, casting a warm glow across my face. Somewhere in the distance a priestess began to chant a lovely, pentatonic melody, which was rudely interrupted by the noise of geese being transported along the street outside, the cart rocking heavily on the cobbles. A breeze came in through the half-open window; it promised to be another warm and humid day, but at least last night's rain had cleansed the air.

Leana was up already, fully engaged in her morning exercises – it looked too much like hard work so I decided to lie in bed, allowing the sounds of the morning markets to rise up to my ears, and wallowing in contemplation.

As ever, I found it easier to work over cases during this hazy, calm hour. The relative stillness of my mind allowed me to process the events of the last couple of days, and this time I was attempting to find connections and differences between the incidents, rather than look at each in isolation.

Two murders.

Two high-profile victims.

A bishop, his body discovered many days after his disappearance.

Cut hundreds of times before being dismembered, a piece of him possibly thrown over the wall to the Sorghatan Prefecture – a public show, perhaps – and his tongue removed.

A retired naval officer, taken somewhere after a night with his friends. His body, too, covered in cuts before being dragged to a very public place where he could be found. His tongue also removed.

But he had not been dismembered. And he had not been hidden.

A point really niggled, if both men had been tortured. The usual reason for such brutal treatment while someone was alive was to gain information or a confession. It was odd that they'd had their tongues cut out. The tongue was very necessary to divulging information in the first place.

Another reason for the barbarous act crossed my mind. It might, in fact, have been to *silence* the men from screaming rather than let them talk. That Grendor was involved in imports and exports made me suspect that he might have been involved in something dangerous. Had both of these men stumbled across some dreaded secret and needed to be silenced? Had they both witnessed something they shouldn't have? It did not seem all that likely, since they led very different lives. One was quiet and contemplative, the other outgoing.

Yet there were more differences, too, and I wondered if the differences themselves were telling.

One body had been left fully intact, the other in pieces. One body had been dumped for others to find, the other had been returned home, for his wife or others to discover. Though it could be said, as Leana did last night, that both were very public settings. The murderer clearly had no concerns over the bodies being found.

Indeed, the incredible similarities couldn't be ignored and it was likely we were dealing with the same murderer. That fact offered up a worrying possibility: that the killer was still in the city and would strike again. Who was to say that this all stopped with Grendor?

I was not in the business of relying upon coincidences where patterns or connections could be perceived. I needed much more information about the bishop and Grendor. Hopefully an examination of Borta's house this morning, and a thorough interview with her, might bring me closer to that.

It continued to be a pleasant morning. Flower sellers were out with their carts, and in surprising numbers. People crowded them, buying huge quantities of bright-red flowers or digging into boxes of petals to scatter about the pavements, transforming them into shades of pink, white and yellow. It left a wonderful fragrance about the city. I wondered if it was a religious holiday, for priests were also walking the streets in brightly coloured robes chanting the wonders of Astran and Nastra, their censers swinging back and forth adding to the heady scents of the flowers. Today certainly contrasted with the usual woodsmoke and horse manure one could normally expect from any city in Vispasia. Some of the citizens laid petals at the feet of an enormous old man, who wore a large double-horned helmet and a loincloth, which only just showed beneath his rolls of fat. Blue spirals had been painted on his flesh and he sat cross-legged and rather serenely on the steps of a temple, seemingly oblivious to the gestures of the people around him.

The main forum of the prefecture, a stone's throw from Grendor's house, was packed. The crowds moved fluidly between the islands of stalls, which were not in rows but of a circular design without awnings. People gathered around them buying various vegetables, spices, leather goods, cookware and hunting

126

equipment. The wares of the most popular stall by far would have eluded me, so big were the crowds, had it not been for the carcasses strung up behind on large, sturdy poles. The meat glistened in the morning sunlight.

We arrived once again at the newly built street where Grendor of the Cape lived and slowly made our way towards the bottom of the stairway, casually examining the scene to see if daylight could give us more clues. A few stains could be perceived by the lower steps and that was all. Sheltered from the evening rain, the blood was clearer now, but suggested there had not been a struggle. Grendor would have already been dead by this point.

We continued up the stairs and knocked on the door. Borta in a long, high-collared blue dress answered almost immediately and urged us to step inside. She peered back down the stairs nervously before closing the door firmly.

'Does your family have enemies?' I asked.

'My family?' she said.

'Yes.'

'No . . . I'm not aware of any.'

I indicated the child's woollen sock lying on the floorboards behind her feet. 'Just the one, or do you have more?'

She took the sock and added it to a pile of washing. She seemed vaguely embarrassed. 'They can be quite a handful. I have two, by the way. Two boys. Would either of you like a drink? We have a good selection of tisanes. Grendor was always bringing me home new varieties.'

Leana asked for a cup of water and I agreed to try one of the tisanes. Borta left us momentarily.

This place was certainly impressive. Though I generally admired age and heritage in my houses, for homes to feel *lived in*, this was filled with a freshness of style. There were fabrics on display that had travelled far; the designs were not merely the natural, animalistic motifs found around the rest of Koton, many were from further afield – the gold star and red crescent of Locco, the white wings on blue of Theran. Much of this was consistent with a man who had travelled widely in the navy, or worked in a trade that dealt with imports and exports. There must have been some stories behind these – were they simply traded goods or had they been gifts from foreign ambassadors?

The apartment, all on one level, was a large complex of rooms and long corridors, and must have occupied all the space above the shops below. From just a casual glance down the corridors drapes hung from the walls and there was an eclectic display of ornaments. There was a lot of wealth on show.

The sound of children playing drifted in from another room – it suddenly occurred to me that they would now be fatherless.

The thought brought back memories of my own childhood. My mother, a loving, kind woman, died when I was very young and remained a notable absence despite my privileged upbringing. How much do these events during our youth go on to define us when we are older? Luckily I had taken on some of my mother's more considered, perhaps tender ways, and was not as stern as my father had been. But her absence affected me greatly, and so I understood what the two children might be going through – or about to go through – if their mother had not yet told them.

Borta returned with our drinks and guided us to the orange and purple cushions, which were arranged around a low oak table. The window beside it faced directly down onto the busy forum, and I marvelled at the number of people who were already milling about the stalls and tables.

'One can lose an entire day staring from that window,' she said. 'Grendor would often sit where you are, Officer Drakenfeld.'

We sat down on the cushions and I hoped that she might

continue a casual discussion of Grendor, something to set the scene of his personal life, but she didn't reveal anything else. Instead her bright-green eyes were focusing on the table. Her hands were in her lap, her shoulders slumped. It was understandable, of course, that she would not be all that forthcoming.

'Was he a religious man?' I asked, a question that surprised her.

'Not at all, no.' She paused, as if contemplating her initial reaction, thinking hard. 'Well, he *believed* in things, of course. Who doesn't have their own religious superstitions? But he never really went to a temple as long as I've known him.'

'What were his superstitions?'

'They were mainly based around the sea or the weather. He claimed he had seen all the wonders he'd needed to see in life as it is, though he never spoke ill of religion. Why do you ask?'

'You have no religious items around the house, is all. There are no statues. I could not see a family shrine. It's rather unusual when a home doesn't invite the gods inside.'

'No,' she replied. 'He said that the gods blessed him continually, without him needing to make the effort.'

'So he felt he was a lucky man?'

'I guess you could say that. Despite his age, he kept in very good health.'

There was a commotion outside where, in the streets below, a farmer was trying to drive cattle through the crowds with limited success. 'This is a busy street. Do you get much peace and quiet?'

A smile came to her lips. 'Many think that, but we always loved it here — to see the world passing by. It made us feel part of something bigger.'

'I have to ask some questions that may seem a little strange at first, Borta, but they will all help. All I ask is that you answer truthfully. If you need secrecy or feel in danger, we can ensure your safety. I have no previous connections with Koton, so revealing any secrets to me will not cause problems in the same way it might were a local person involved.'

She gave a nod, but didn't reply.

'Was Grendor in any financial trouble?'

'Not at all. His pension from the royal court was very high, and due to the advice he sometimes gave on trade routes he secured us an additional income. Not to mention that merchants, too, often sought advice from him.'

'Was his business in trouble?'

'Not at all.'

'Did he conduct business in this house with other merchants?'

'Sometimes. Or in taverns throughout the prefecture. It depended on his mood really.'

'Were you ever worried about the people he was dealing with? Did they ever seem to threaten him in any way? Was there ever a conversation you can recollect where things became tense?'

Borta was incredulous at my suggestion. 'They were all merchants of good standing. They were gentlemen and fine women, all of whom could be trusted. They spoke openly in front of me whenever I was in the room.'

'And you're certain there were no questionable deals he might have been doing behind anyone's back?'

'That wasn't in his character.'

It could have been behind *her* back, of course, but I did not reveal the thought. 'So he never showed concern when he returned from his meetings.'

'He didn't have to worry about business.'

'So what *did* he worry about?' I asked.

She gave a sigh, and a sad smile. 'Getting old mostly. He was sixty-one years old and very conscious of it – with young children around. He wanted to see them grow up. I think that brought a sadness of sorts. He had so much energy about him, you see. He bought good meat and fresh vegetables, so we ate well. He would often talk about what he was like as a younger man and tried to stay young. As I said, he was very active, even for his age. Each morning he would jog about the city and stretch his limbs.'

Now that it had cooled I sipped the tisane, a wonderfully minty and invigorating drink. She must have noticed the surprise on my face and smiled knowingly.

'I'd like you to tell me what sort of person he was — his manners and so on — so that I might build up a picture. I appreciate if it's difficult right now, but it will help me.'

'Oh he was very kind and thoughtful,' she replied eagerly. 'You might wonder about our age difference, but he was so gentle with me, never condescending, often seeking my opinion on matters. He had never married before me, never having a need to, but he craved a family later in his life, children to continue his legacy. He was gracious with others too and very generous with his money. Though this house is wonderful, if it wasn't for all Grendor's donations to the needy, such as the large orphanage not too far from here, then we could probably have afforded to live in a much bigger property. But neither of us needed it, Officer Drakenfeld. This place is more than enough for us . . .' She paused for a brief moment and glanced out of the window. 'It is more than enough for *me*, I should say.'

There again was a similarity between Grendor and Bishop Tahn Valin, though it appeared superficial. They were not merely high-profile individuals in the city, they were also men *of fine reputations* in the eyes of others. Both were well respected by those close to them and admired for their good nature. From what I'd heard, these were fundamentally *kind* people, too — so much so that the notion didn't sit well with me. Kind people can be murdered, of course. But two kind people who were entering their later years butchered in such a cruel way, in a manner that was usually reserved for unkind people? Of course, we were dealing with the words of those closest to them – perhaps blinded out of love or admiration. Who Borta was describing was not necessarily the real Grendor of the Cape.

'Did he ever cross paths with Bishop Tahn Valin?' I asked.

Borta thought about the question for a moment, glancing out of the window, though clearly searching her mind instead of paying attention to what was going on below.

'Never. As I said, Grendor wasn't a man for such things. But even in a social setting, or a ceremonial event, I can't think of a time when the two of them would have met. I mean, it is possible that they were both at the royal court at the same time, but I wasn't aware of a friendship, no matter how small. Grendor does tend to tell me everything.'

There was a silence, then Borta said, 'May I see my husband's body again?'

'That can certainly be arranged, if you wish it,' I replied.

'I do,' she sighed.

'I'll see if I can arrange it for the afternoon.'

Another silence lingered, which was interrupted by one of the children giggling in another room. Borta cocked her head in that way mothers of young children do, somehow connected to two rooms at once, fully focused on each.

Eventually she looked back and whispered, 'You think the person who killed my husband killed the bishop as well?'

'There remains a chance that we are dealing with two separate murderers,' I replied, 'but the details are a little too similar for comfort, I must admit. From the evidence we have so far, I believe your husband's killer had already struck once, a little earlier. There is no reason to say that this person is still within the confines of the prefecture.'

A look of alarm came over her.

'But this would not be a bad thing,' I replied, 'since it means we would be able to find them. They might not have escaped yet.'

Borta permitted us to take a look around her house — I reassured her that it was just in case we saw something that might be useful to the investigation, not that we were accusing her of anything. She grew relaxed at my sensitive negotiation of the matter.

While she tended to her children, Leana and I spent a good hour inspecting the other eight rooms. Each room was large, and each had shelves of exotic ornaments, statues, paintings or trinkets. Grendor was a man of fine tastes. Some of the Detratan amphorae on display were among the finest that the country had ever manufactured.

His study was bright, clean and well organized, and though I was allowed to sift through all the drawers and ledgers, there appeared to be nothing out of place for someone who was an expert in shipping and trade. There were dozens of maps of Koton, and quite a few that focused on the coastal region north of Kuvash, the estuary through which all ships would have passed. There were several beautifully bound books on maritime law and a stunningly illustrated bestiary on the various many-limbed sea creatures rumoured to inhabit the oceans. I tested the room for hidden compartments, loose panels in which he might have kept a secret or two from Borta, but there was nothing to be found.

Leana investigated other rooms independently and when she returned concluded that she had found little of interest. All of this suggested that Borta had nothing to hide. She remained in the dining room with her two young children, and I could hear her singing to them, an act that reminded me of my own mother. The melody was interrupted after the older one asked, 'When's

Father coming back from his business meeting? He was supposed to take us out riding today.'

We left quietly.

Outside, Leana and I were able to talk about the interview, but neither of us raised any concerns.

'Simply a rich and good man, and now a dead man,' Leana said. 'Was the bishop rich too? Were these killings to do with money?'

'That might be worth looking into, but surely there are more efficient and less time-consuming methods to relieve two men of their money. Why go to the trouble of all those cuts? Why remove their *tongues*?'

'The strongest possibility remains that the act was to silence them, that perhaps they both knew something independently, and whatever that knowledge was had been too much of a threat to the murderer. This also bears hallmarks of a revenge killing – and if that is the case, then we need to consider just what type of person would commit such a bloody revenge.'

'Someone needs to look at the bodies together,' she concluded. 'Similarities and differences will help establish what these hallmarks are.'

'I've asked that the physician, Carlon, give them a thorough examination.'

'Good,' Leana replied. 'Those cuts were not easy to make. I would say that the torture required a room away from people in which to work. It is important to know if these men died first or experienced the cuts as torture.'

'A physician,' I muttered. 'Koton, it seems, has quite a few good physicians. People with familiarity of working with bodies.'

'Even Sulma Tan,' Leana said.

'Even her,' I replied.

But Leana had prompted another train of thought: a killer

knocking the men out, dragging them back to a room, before later returning the body. If that was the case, then presumably there would be some place to carry out the torture. If both murders were within the prefecture, then that room would probably be close by. It would have been difficult to drag a corpse outside to the Kuvash Prefecture and back in again to the Sorghatan Prefecture. Therefore it was likely we were looking for someone based *inside* this part of the city.

Mentally I began to sketch out a profile of our killer. It was a human reaction to assume those who carried out such brutal acts were of the barbaric sort — ex-soldiers, street fighters and the like. These were *considered* crimes, and thus were probably committed by or at the request of someone with more deviance. A meticulous planner who possessed a suppressed rage, one which was only now coming to the surface. Moreover, if the killer was based inside this prefecture, it meant they must have a decent job, or had inherited enough money to be able to get by in the richer part of the city. I was put in mind of a physician, or a courtier, or a wealthy tradesman.

A different class of butcher altogether.

A Ring

It was time to make an unannounced visit to the former bishop's temple.

It took Leana and me, still largely unfamiliar with these streets, a good hour to locate the right way. We must have doubled back on ourselves twice, losing ourselves amidst the unrecognizable buildings and strange lanes, pausing to reflect upon examples of unique architecture or compelling faces among the crowds.

Priest Damsak, enveloped by a thick crimson cloak, was standing at the top of the steps of the temple. He was speaking quietly with two refined ladies, each of whom was carrying a basket of food, presumably offerings for the temple.

Distracted by our presence, he soon walked over to us with a calm demeanour and a soft gaze. 'Greetings to both of you. How can I be of assistance today?'

It wasn't easy to tell if his warmth was staged to hide his discomfort, or if he was being genuine. 'We're here to inspect the bishop's room more thoroughly.'

'Of course, as you wish.' He guided us through the temple, past those who knelt before the bronze statues of Astran and Nastra, to the rooms at the back of the building. Sunlight flooded in directly through the doors behind, extending our own shadows in front of us.

'It would be better if you attended to any other duties you have,' I said as we reached the door to the bishop's room. 'We will be some time and I'm sure you have so much to do. We'll come and find you when we've finished.'

'Please call if I can be of service.' He maintained the same expression that couldn't be read, and then closed the door behind him.

'What do you hope to find this time?' Leana asked. 'We know there's nothing here.'

'I'm not sure,' I said. 'There must be something that can connect the bishop to Grendor. Now there are two bodies, we need to find that connection. We need to check for every loose floorboard or brick. There's a pretty good chance that Grendor and Tahn Valin had *something* in common, so that might well be here. Perhaps there's a piece of paper with the name of a boat belonging to Grendor. That's the kind of connection we're looking for. There must be *something*.'

The room remained exactly as we had left it from our last visit – there was just a bed, a table and a few basic necessities. Not even the books on the bedside shelf had changed their position.

On hands and knees we pulled back the rug and tested for any loose floor tiles. Leana tapped each individual tile with the hilt of her blade, yet they all possessed the same resonance. For some time we examined the grey stone blocks that made up the walls, testing every one high and low, but again we found nothing.

The room was sound. The bishop had not hidden anything.

'We should be honest,' Leana muttered, 'there is nothing here. The priest was a pure and simple man.'

'We're not done yet,' I replied. 'Try the books again, there might be some code or a note within them.'

The books were all pure and immaculate tomes of religious scripture and advice, each one beautiful with charming ink drawings and elegant calligraphy. We turned every page of every enormous leather-bound volume to make sure there was no hidden document, nothing concealed, no messages inscribed, but there was nothing. The bishop obviously treated his books with respect, too, for they were in splendid condition.

Leana gently kicked the leg of the bed. 'Help me move this.'

We dragged the bed out from against the wall, and investigated the stonework around it, but again there was nothing to suggest anything had been hidden.

Then we pulled back the sheets of the bed and lifted up a straw-cushioned layer resting on top of the wooden frame. Leana took her blade and slashed through the material, emptying out the straw on the floor.

I heard a muffled *clunk* on the stone.

'Wait.' Leaning over I began to part the mess of straw.

Right in the centre of the pile was a small square envelope, which looked as if it contained something bulky. Leana reached in to grab it and as we stood up she opened the envelope.

'What is it?' I asked.

After scrutinizing it for just a moment, she eventually shrugged and handed it over. 'See for yourself.'

Inside was an exquisite silver ring set with a vibrant red gemstone. I couldn't work out what the stone was – it was too light and almost too imperfect to be a ruby, with a strange translucency. A white mineral vein could be discerned faintly within it, like a bolt of lightning in a crimson sky. Whatever this gemstone was, it had been cut square into the size of a small thumbnail and set with remarkable skill in a four-claw setting.

'For a simple man who doesn't do trinkets,' I muttered, 'I'd say this was something unusual.'

'Why keep it hidden?' Leana asked. 'Surely rings are for wearing.'

'Clearly this was not meant to be seen by anyone. Whether or not that's because of some arcane rules within the temple that forbade decoration, or he was enforcing this secrecy himself, remains to be seen.'

'Remember the bangle on the remains of his wrist?' Leana said. 'They allow *some* ornamentation.'

'Then perhaps this was a personal gift,' I replied. 'A token from a loved one.'

'He went to some lengths to conceal a gift.'

Leana was right. This had been deliberately kept secure. The bishop did not want it found. There were no discernible markings on the ring, nothing to suggest the name of the jeweller in question. The envelope itself was heavily worn.

'Any idea what this stone is?' I asked.

Leana held the ring up to the light of the window, then quickly handed it back to me. 'It is ugly, but I cannot speak of its quality. But then I make a point of not being familiar with trinkets. These precious stones cannot follow us through when we become spirits.'

'Quite. Well, we'll just have to find an expert in the city,' I said. 'This is the most interesting development so far – it could be important.'

Damsak knocked on the door and called through to see how we were getting on, and it was only then that I realized just how long we had been there. I invited him in to join us.

'Have you found anything to help?' he asked.

'We may well have.' Showing him the ring, I kept a close eye on his expression as I revealed where it was found. He came across as particularly disappointed that Bishop Tahn Valin could keep such an item hidden there.

'Look at my fingers, Officer Drakenfeld,' he snapped. 'Do you see a ring?'

I admitted I didn't.

'Exactly. We do not wear unofficial ornamentation – especially ornamentation that does not display any of our symbols, or is devoid of the markings of Astran and Nastra. Only simple pieces that are to display our rank. This is a personal trinket and we disapprove of such things.'

'I'd say that the bishop knew all too well that you don't wear such things either, which is why he was hiding it under his mattress. To keep it from people like you.'

'But it makes no sense.' The priest ran a hand through his thinning hair. 'This is against his entire character. I never saw the bishop wearing anything like this. He was a man of simple tastes. And, for example, he even became angry when people wore fine, bright silks and jewellery in our temple. He would often make remarks to me afterwards. He himself did not like such things, you see, as it distracted from our glorious gods. All he ever wanted was to serve our gods for as long as he could.'

'We'll look into the matter further, rest assured,' I said, placing the ring back in its envelope and firmly in my pocket, 'and we'll return with an answer soon enough. I suppose it's pointless asking you where we might find a jeweller?'

The look on the priest's face told me it was.

We stepped outside into the muggy warmth. Two fragrant censers had been lit and were chained up on the columns either side of us, the smoke wafting gently down the street. We went down a street to where the lanes opened out in many directions and I stood there wondering where we should go next.

As if reading my thoughts, Leana said, 'We could just ask someone where—'

Whoosh . . . In a heartbeat I felt a rapid displacement of air followed by a thud in the door behind us. We turned to see an arrow buried deep in the wood, the white fletching still visibly vibrating, but in the same instant Leana shoved me down some steps and under an archway nearby.

The arrow was still visible from where we were, and it was *angled down* – it was a good thing Leana had reacted so quickly, as our assailant clearly had the advantage of height.

'They might not be so unlucky with their next arrow,' she snapped. 'That went straight between us. We should wait here until they have moved on.'

'Was that an accurate warning or an inaccurate attempt at killing us?'

'Who can tell now?'

'I wonder if it was the same person as the one spying on us from the rooftop yesterday afternoon?'

'Let us look at that arrow and then we might know something more.'

We waited a few minutes before walking cautiously back up the steps to the temple. The crowds around us meandered on, seemingly oblivious to the arrow and our own furtive movements.

Leana removed a dagger from her boot and began to ease out the arrow from the wood. Meanwhile I examined our surroundings to see where the arrow would have been fired from. There were any number of rooftops, but following the line of the arrow's assumed path, it led directly towards a large building about sixty feet away, at the end of the lane. A precarious greystone construct with timber beams. Washing strung up across the rooftop fluttered in the gentle breeze.

'Here.' Leana handed me the arrow. 'It looks common enough. There is nothing remarkable about it – not even the craftsmanship is that good.'

'If it's cheap and mass produced, it might be one that the military use.'

Leana shrugged and pointed to the same building I'd been eyeing up. 'You think it came from there.'

'I do,' I replied.

'Then why are we still here?'

On the Rooftop

We were standing in one of the city's largest brothels.

It was a fact that surprised me somewhat. Throughout Detrata – and particularly in the city of Tryum – prostitutes of both sexes and of all sizes could be found calling out to potential clients as they walked by in the street. Sometimes the transaction was even shamelessly *completed* on the street itself. Even in far corners of Vispasia there were taverns or bordellos with not-so-subtle insignia outside to notify passers-by of what could be found inside.

But in Kuvash there seemed to be a peculiar absence of such things. It might have been yet another sign that the city was trying to keep up appearances. I assumed they preferred to keep things like the business of paid-for sex indoors, out of sight, though whether for religious reasons or some social policy dictated by the queen remained to be seen.

There were no signs at first on the inside to indicate the building was a brothel. It was only after an awkward conversation with an old lady in charge, who was called Charka, and noticing the stink of sweat mixed with sweet incense, that I realized where we had ended up.

A large woman with angry eyes, Charka wore a light-green, almost translucent dress and not much else. That was, other than an elaborate headdress that looked not unlike a crown. Queen of this compact domain, she clearly didn't have time for anyone who was not here to pay for time with her young men and women. Which, of course, we were not. She sat there in her throne room, a red-tiled chamber with dark, minimalist frescoes of geometric patterns on the wall. Two men were slouching, potentially unconscious after ingesting Polla-knows what substance, against the far wall, a strip of sunlight across their faces.

I explained who we were and that we needed to get access to the top of the building. Our urgency didn't seem to register with her, but eventually after listening to my incessant demands, and with reluctance, she gestured in the general direction that we needed to go.

'Stairs are at the end, but you watch out for my girls!' she shouted. 'No one likes being interrupted at work.'

Each room was only separated by a thick red curtain, and it was difficult not to overhear the exertions of the clients. Occasionally a face caked in make-up would peer out to regard us and ask if we were after any business. All I could do was smile back awkwardly as we continued on our way along the dimly lit corridors.

Three floors later, we made it to the stairs and headed straight up them. After pushing back a heavy hatch we stepped out into the brightness of daylight and a gust of refreshing air.

The roof was more or less flat, with huge stone gutters lining the perimeter. The washing we'd seen from the ground was bed sheets that rippled like banners in the wind. Presumably these were sheets that had been used by the brothel, and if so then the brothel was of a far higher quality than I imagined. But it occurred to me how they would have provided excellent cover for someone wanting to attack us earlier – as well as concealing their presence at this moment. So we remained on guard as we stepped about, looking this way and that in between flickers of coloured cotton.

With no sign of our attacker, we walked towards the crude stone balustrade. There, I stared down and noticed how there was a direct line of sight from here to the door where the arrow had impacted.

'This must have been the spot where the arrow was fired,' I said. 'There's a great view. This is an excellent position from which to rid the world of two members of the Sun Chamber. Given the vantage point, it makes me think they were trying to kill us rather than send a warning.'

'And yet we are not even close to solving the murders,' Leana added. 'So who could feel threatened?'

'We could be closer than we thought.'

'You are ever the optimist.'

Leana scanned around the surface of the rooftop for anything that may have been discarded by accident, something that might be a vital clue, while I decided to look for the escape route of our attacker. Given the size of the building, it was possible that they might not have come through the brothel but travelled over the rooftops. My suspicion was heightened as I saw other rooftops, each with some hatch that opened up to the level below. The attacker could have gone down any one of those to make their escape. They were probably long gone.

I strolled back to the balustrade where Leana was now standing, and for a moment we remained engaged in our own thoughts. The wind stirred. Birds skittered across the city. The outside walls of the prefecture were obvious at this height, and it was moving to see how the city was cut up into two large segments. Two cities, essentially. One for the rich, one for the poor, the hills in the distance belonging to everyone.

We had not been in the city all that long. On the assumption that someone wanted me dead, it was pretty obvious that whoever fired the arrow most likely did not approve of us investigating the two murders. That was the only reason I was here, after all. It was the only reason to have built up resentment.

Logically, it followed on that whoever released the arrow must then have known something about the killings. There was every chance they were involved in the crimes themselves and looking to stop me finding them.

Yet, that thought didn't sit well with me – if they sought discretion in this macabre business, then they were certainly going the wrong way about it by leaving corpses in public places. There was also the other possibility that they didn't want me to stop them because there were more people to kill.

I suggested this idea to Leana, who continued to stare across the city, the afternoon sun glowing warmly on her dark-brown face.

'A possibility,' she said. 'We can tell very little at the moment.'

'Come on, we're not going to find much else up here.'

We went back downstairs and I managed to get a moment to talk with the *delightful* Charka. She was a little more accommodating now that she had a cup of wine in her hands and a bowl of almonds by her side, which were quite a luxury in any city. I asked her if she'd seen anyone strange pass through and she scowled at me.

'Of course we get strange people passing through,' she grunted, and scooped up another handful of nuts. 'You will next be asking if people were behaving strangely! This is a brothel. We get everyone here, and most act strangely. We are Kuvash's guilty pleasure. People do not want to be seen here.'

'All right, let me rephrase that,' I continued. 'Have you seen anyone coming through here who *did not* seek the company of your staff?'

She spluttered a laugh and a gentle spray of wine came out of her mouth. 'Is he for real?' she asked Leana. '"Seek the company", he says. People come here to *fuck*, all right?'

'Oh really?' I replied, 'I had this down as a temple and mistook you for a saintly priestess of Polla.'

'Who the hell's Polla?'

'Never mind, just tell me if anyone came through who wasn't a customer and who went up on the roof.'

She shrugged. 'Not while I've been here, which has been all morning. Only people interested in that roof are those on the third floor staring up at its underside while bad lovers work away at them.'

'I doubt love is of any concern here,' I muttered.

Charka spoke to Leana as if I wasn't there. 'He's got a sense of humour after all.'

Messages

Sulma Tan was right. Kuvash, or at least the Sorghatan Prefecture, possessed an efficient messenger service. While the standard practice across Vispasia was that messengers did their business around a city for coin from individuals, here messengers were subsidized by the royal coffers. The queen thought that the flow of messages and information was necessary for the city to grow and prosper, and therefore worthy of her patronage.

Such a service was therefore free at the basic level to use for many hours of the day, and there were several messenger stations, no more than glorified shacks, to be found scattered around the city. Young men and women could be seen dashing about wearing a green tunic with a gold sash, heavy boots and a floppy velvet hat bearing the raised red stag of Koton.

I stood in one of the writing booths at a messenger station, a cold stone room on the edge of a small spice market. The building contained three private desks, made of good quality wood, at which I wrote two letters.

The first was to Sulma Tan, saying that I wished to meet her in the afternoon. I hoped that she could arrange for Borta to see Grendor's body, and could I be present while she was with her at the time. I concluded that I would like to arrange for a new place for Leana and myself to stay, suggesting that our safety was under threat. I didn't go into too much detail, but informed her of the attempt on our lives.

The second message would cost me a decent amount of money, since it was to be delivered across the nation's borders and I opted for the fastest possible messengers. This letter was an update to the Sun Chamber's headquarters within Free State, some way to the south of Vispasia, informing them of the case so far, my suspicions – there were none – and my future actions. I also sent a copy of this note to the Sun Chamber postal station located just to the south of the Kotonese border: along with a request that any return messages, or credit notes for me to cash in my wages with a reputable bank, should be sent to me via Sulma Tan.

Leana and I ate a dubious meat-based dish, in the shadow of an old statue of Astran, which overlooked a bubbling fountain. The cobbled plaza was much quieter as the afternoon came upon us and people avoided the heat. Morning trade had fizzled out. Now people filled the backstreet taverns instead and sat on the ground in the shaded alleyways, talking, always talking, as if it was some kind of sport.

After our lunch we headed through the streets to the royal palace, where Sulma Tan finally met us. She was clearly agitated, though not in her usual way. She wasn't unhappy, rather she was . . . *unsettled.*

We exchanged pleasantries and she informed me that Borta had been called in to see Grendor's body in two hours' time, as requested.

I pointed out to her that she appeared disturbed by something.

'You are right . . . though it is probably not what you think.' She glanced around as one of the administrators marched past carrying a ledger, his boots echoing along the hallway. 'I suspect it will be prudent to continue this conversation in a more discreet place.'

Very calmly she walked us to a quiet and pleasant chamber, away from prying eyes. The room possessed some lovely couches, shelves full of books, an empty fireplace and a large arched window overlooking a small courtyard garden. Sunlight fell across a red rug. We sat down on one of the couches while Sulma Tan stood with her back to the window, composing her thoughts.

'This might sound a little unusual,' she began, and fell into silence once again.

'Go on,' I urged.

'I am not one for believing fanciful explanations for the things in life that cannot easily be explained,' she said. 'Though I admire the gods, and acknowledge there are some wondrous things in the world, I have always preferred reason to the fear of the supernatural.'

'We share such a view,' I said. 'In fact, you walk in the path of my own goddess, Polla.'

'A fine woman.' She stepped around the room, her head slightly bowed in deep contemplation. 'That said, I cannot quite explain what I have seen recently. I have consulted some books in our library for an explanation, but nothing satisfies . . .'

I glanced across to Leana, who remained as cool as ever.

'What's happened?' I asked.

'Two things have happened.' There was a hesitancy with her every sentence, as if she was embarrassed by what she was about to tell us. If she would ever get around to telling us . . .

'Is it to do with the case?'

'In a manner of speaking. Well . . . I might as well just say it. First, I placed the pieces of the arm of the bishop back in the box where I have been keeping them, with the palm facing downward. I was quite sure of this. I then kept it hidden in a place that only

I knew about and locked it securely. However, when I went back earlier to prepare Grendor's body for Borta, I thought I heard . . .'

'Go on.'

'I thought I heard a *scratching* sound from the box. It could have been my imagination, but I decided to check anyway. When I opened it up I saw that the arm was there . . . however, the palm was now facing up instead of down.'

Nodding, I thought a rat might have caused the scratching sound, and that Sulma Tan might easily have placed the palm the other way around without realizing it. She was a busy person, and could easily have been distracted, no matter how adamant she was. Anyone could have imagined that.

'You mentioned there were two things,' I said. 'What was the other?'

'The bishop's head. This has never been kept in a box, not even since you brought it here, but stored separately alongside the body deep in the vaults with the sack still over it.'

'What of it?'

'It had managed to somehow . . . get out of the sack and roll onto the floor.'

After a moment's pause I said, 'Perhaps someone removed it and played a joke? They might even have done the same with the arm.'

'It is possible.' Sulma Tan nodded, clearly having examined the same thoughts herself. 'But that does not explain why there was saliva coming out of the bishop's mouth.'

'I'm sorry?' I leaned forward in my seat. Even Leana looked incredulous.

Sulma Tan repeated herself. 'There was saliva – just a little trail – coming from the corner of his mouth as if he was still alive. As if his body worked in the same way in death as in life. And yes, I am as surprised as you are – though perhaps a little more aghast at having seen it with my own eyes.'

'This is—'

'Impossible, of course. Ridiculous even. Yes, yes. I have analysed the matter in its entirety. The hand having turned over could, at a push, be put down to someone else doing that – though I stress no one knew where I kept it. The head rolling out of a sack could indeed be a freak occurrence. A joke. A small movement of the earth as can happen. But both happening at the same time, and with the addition of the saliva . . .'

Exasperated, she grinned, the corners of her mouth wrinkling wonderfully.

'No, Officer Drakenfeld. I have analysed it all. Something is amiss here, something outside of my areas of expertise, and I do not understand what is going on.'

Further Analysis

We locked ourselves in the medical chamber once again in order to study the head in detail. We brought lanterns around the bishop's head, its macabre decay even more hideous with the warm light, and leaned nervously over it. Leana had her blade in her hand — and I did not caution her that it was unnecessary. She must also have believed that this was a ridiculous way to behave, to be wary of something that was clearly untrue, yet neither of us mentioned this.

It is strange how we seem to absorb what other people say to us, even if it goes against our instincts. Anecdotes, even the convincing one provided by Sulma Tan, can be inserted into our heads without our being aware of the full effects. Here I was, glad that Leana was on standby in case this head would . . . what exactly? Bite my fingers? It was a severed head, one that had been removed for some time. It could do no harm. Yet my heart beat a little faster as Sulma Tan pointed out the trail of still-glistening saliva around what was left of the mouth and along the bruise-coloured, heavily wrinkled cheek.

'And so you can see for yourself,' Sulma Tan said, somewhat relieved that she could share the burden of knowledge, 'that I am not making this up. You may choose not to believe what I say about the moving hand, however, or indeed the fact that the head had rolled out of position. But at least this is evidence.'

Leana was impatient with both of us and leaned close, almost nose to rotting nose, to get a better look.

'It could be that some bug has left a trail,' she muttered. 'A slug. Something has sought nutrients from his decaying mouth. I have seen such things before. You worry needlessly.'

'You were holding your sword,' I replied. 'Don't think I didn't notice.'

'For your peace of mind only.' Leana leaned back with an air of satisfaction.

'Shall we dissect it to find out?' I asked.

Sulma Tan nodded. She commenced cutting around the lips to gain access to the mouth. She carved with all the delicacy of a fresco painter setting about applying colours to fresh plaster. There was an art to this, too, I realized, as she placed a piece of flesh to one side.

This process went on for some time, pulling layer after layer of skin and flesh away and placing the pieces on a metal dish, rooting down to see if there was anything of note. Minutes turned into an hour, maybe more. I was impressed at her skill. Here was a royal secretary, someone whose life had been spent on more important matters, cutting away at a corpse's face with a sound knowledge of science behind her.

Eventually, after some consideration, Sulma Tan concluded, 'There is nothing here. No creature of any kind, no trail left. The saliva was genuine. How do the two of you explain this now?'

We stared at each other for some time, the silence heightening our sense of confusion. Our contemplation was interrupted when a knocking came at the door, and a voice called in Kotonese for Sulma Tan.

'Please excuse me.' Sulma Tan washed her hands in the small bowl to one side before engaging in a short conversation at the door.

Leana whispered to me, 'The creature could have long gone.'

'Or it was never there in the first place,' I replied.

'Spirits save me, you believe the ghost stories instead?'

I was about to mutter something sarcastic, when Sulma Tan closed the door and marched back to the table. 'Borta has arrived to look at Grendor's body. Out of respect we should not keep her waiting, no?'

Where's the Amulet?

Another table, another body; this day was turning out to be gratuitous in its scientific rigour. However, Grendor of the Cape had not yet been cut open. He lay there with a cloth covering the lower half of his body, his brutally scarred, naked chest exposed to the room, his wife standing beside his resting form, while Leana and myself waited patiently in the adjacent chamber.

'Can she not hurry?' Leana whispered. 'It has been some time now. It is not as though she is the one looking for clues.'

A shake of my head was all that was required. Leana was used to my ways. Death was very businesslike to her, which was perhaps not a terrible way of dealing with the large quantities of it we had both seen. Treating it so matter-of-factly was a sound way to cope. However, I had my own way of dealing with things — as Polla, my goddess, would approve.

Respect. Dignity.

These were the very underpinnings of a *civilized* society, in life or death. They were also among the core values of the Sun Chamber. Without attitudes like these we would resort to being warring factions and savage people, much like the pale-skinned

Maulanders who had been subdued by Detratan troops so very recently.

No, we would be patient. We would allow Borta all the time she needed to mourn her husband. And, just as important, we would be *seen* to be patient and respectful, for we were also ambassadors for the Sun Chamber.

On a small side table behind us at the back of the room, and because of the lack of windows in this subterranean place, by lantern light Sulma Tan was busy making calculations in a ledger, presumably to do with her census.

'I'm sorry to interrupt,' I said, 'but I have a question related to the case and your census work.'

She looked up at me, her eyes glimmering in the light of the lantern. 'What is it?'

'Two bodies have been *worked upon* in some way,' I continued. 'Such work has been done from within this prefecture. And if not, at the very least close by it. We need to track down whether or not there could be such a building – say, a workshop – where this could be carried out. Even a disused shop might provide some valuable insight.'

'That is asking for quite a lot,' she replied.

'But you will surely have such information from the census?'

'Yes, but the volume of such information is enormous.' Sulma Tan was determined, however, and I knew that it wasn't in her character to say no to such challenges. 'But we can do this. I will task one of the other administrators with finding possible venues. Not merely workshops, but we will have a list of all disused buildings. Somewhere out of sight, perhaps?'

'That makes sense. Hidden discreetly away. Somewhere where there is not a large amount of footfall, I'd wager. It might all come to nothing, of course, but it's an avenue worth pursuing. If we do have the resources, we might as well use them.'

'Yes, yes. We have the resources.' Her answer came as if I had issued her some kind of challenge she could not refuse. Now that she was open to the suggestion, I pushed her further.

'It would be even better if you could map them out along with the locations of murder . . .' I realized that might have been asking a lot.

'This is simple enough, yes. We have plenty of maps, and so I can commission any necessary alterations. I will make it so.'

'While we can access this information, I'd like to build up a picture of who the killer might be, because I suspect it is someone within the prefecture.' I explained my earlier notions about the class of the killer. 'It is possible they have had connection with the military in some way, or with the bishop's organizations. If they have received medical training or instruction in the arts of butchery, then I would like to know of their existence.'

'That information,' Sulma Tan said, 'could be even more of a challenge . . . There could be thousands of names. The census is simply a broad list, though admittedly divided into current trades. As for people's former lives . . .'

'Even so, we have to try. You *can* do this, right?'

'Of course I can.' She was incredulous I had to ask.

The door opened and Borta was standing there, dressed soberly in a black gown. Several cressets burned brightly behind her. She looked indignant and I asked her what was wrong.

'His amulet is missing,' she snapped.

'I'm sorry?' I asked. The rest of us became suddenly focused on Borta.

She led us into the adjacent chamber and we all filed in around the resting body.

'I've looked through his belongings that you left over there,' she said, 'and everything was present – apart from an amulet.'

'Nothing has been removed,' Sulma Tan said. 'His possessions are exactly as we found them. I can assure you access has been restricted.'

'What kind of amulet was it?' I asked.

'One he wore around his neck. It was a circle of gold, decorated plainly, with occasional geometric shapes. With a gemstone the size of a coin set in the centre.'

'The gemstone,' I said, thinking of the ring we found hidden in the bishop's mattress. It was still in my pocket. 'What colour was it?'

'Red. A ruby.'

'Definitely a ruby?' I asked.

'I'm not completely sure.' A pause. Borta searched her memory. 'I always thought it a little ugly if I'm honest. It did not seem the thing one wore for ornamentation. I expected rubies to be . . . more refined?'

Leana glanced at me knowingly.

Sulma Tan said, 'You two know something, yes? Have you seen this missing amulet?'

'No.' I reached into my pocket and produced the envelope, opening it for her to look at.

Sulma Tan gestured for me to show Borta, though she was annoyed I had not shown her this piece of evidence.

'But was the stone the same colour as this?' I asked, offering her the envelope.

She peered inside, uncertain at first. 'It seems so. Yes. It has that curious cloudiness.'

'You need to be sure, because I do not think this is a ruby.' I plucked it out and handed it to her, while Leana brought a lantern over so that she could see it better. The stone glimmered in the light. 'Well it looks close enough,' Borta said, 'but sadly I have little expertise with precious stones. Grendor was very good with such things and he brought me home some lovely items.'

A connection, at last.

'I can assure you,' Sulma Tan stressed, 'that if the amulet has been taken by someone within this palace, they will be discovered and punished accordingly. I will send an urgent message to all senior staff within the building.'

'There's every chance it was taken by those who committed this wicked crime,' I said. 'I found this ring in the mattress at the bishop's temple. He had kept it very well hidden, so no one could have thought to take it. That said, he probably acted in this way since he could not wear such jewellery in his temple. Grendor, however, must have had no such problem with wearing an item like this.'

Borta shook her head and stared into a vacant corner of the room. 'He rarely took it off.'

'Do you know where he acquired it, Borta? Think hard, please, it could be very important.'

A shake of her head and I knew that a promising lead would be stalled. 'Gren always wore it, long before I met him. Once when I asked him about it, he said he bought it on his travels. That it brought him good luck. He often spoke of sailors and superstition.'

'How long have you known each other?'

'Eight years.'

'And he's worn it all that time . . . Thank you, Borta, you've been very helpful.' I exhaled deeply. 'Have you spent enough time with your husband?'

'I have,' she replied, staring at the ground. 'There is nothing else to say about it.' Then she gazed at me with a surprising moist-eyed anger. 'Please, Officer Drakenfeld. You *will* see to it that whoever did this will be caught, won't you?'

'I will do my very best,' I replied.

*

After Borta had left, Sulma Tan walked with me into the chamber to view the body of Grendor one more time. Concealed on a table nearby was the long wooden box, not quite a coffin, not quite a crate, that contained the body of the bishop.

'Carlon is going to be here shortly.' She pulled back the black cloth that covered the bishop's remains.

She gasped.

'What is it?' I couldn't see what had shocked her. Leana walked calmly over to the other side of the body.

'It has moved. This torso wasn't arranged like this. It was on its back and now it is different . . .'

'You're quite—'

'Certain!' she snapped. 'Yes, yes. I am certain. Stop questioning me.' A breath or two later and she apologized. 'I'm so sorry, Officer Drakenfeld. I didn't mean to shout at you like that.'

'It's quite all right. I deserved it.'

Leana chimed in, 'Yes. I get tired of him sometimes. Forgive him – he is a man, and does not know how heavily he treads.'

'Very kind of you, Leana,' I replied.

'But really,' Sulma Tan continued, 'I am not myself.'

'Please,' I replied. 'Think nothing of it.'

So it appeared either someone was playing tricks on us, or someone had got access to the body parts of the bishop and – somehow – had managed to give them a few last drops of life. Perhaps the bishop knew something we did not about the business of life and death.

A thick humid fug hung over the city. A few traces of rain seemed to hover over those far hills, but there was no sign it would ever come our way. It wasn't merely the weather that made the mood of the city different now. There was a strange ambience about the streets that I'd not seen so far: a sense of expectation, almost of excitement.

People began to surge through the wide streets. Merchants had brought their carts away from the markets and were selling items along the thoroughfares, an illegal act in many cities. It was all the more curious given the late hour of the afternoon, when trade was usually winding down.

We moved among the crowds, attempting to gauge what, if anything, was going on. Leana pointed out that the gates of the prefecture were starting to open, people grouping towards them. A horn blared somewhere beyond and soon I could see the tops of short, conical helmets, with crimson-coloured horsehair plumes drooping behind. Swords and bows were slung across the shoulders of the riders. They filed in, perhaps two hundred in all, absorbing the general cheers of the gathered throng. Up close I could see them wearing blue cloaks and black tunics of the equestrian ranks. They wore silver-scaled body armour, and raised above their mass was the banner of the red stag on blue.

They rode past us, taking many of the gathered crowd with them on their way. The bustle lingered for a while longer, before vanishing as if it had never been there.

'If the arrow that was fired at us turns out to be of a military type,' Leana commented, 'then matters have suddenly become far more confusing.'

'Ever the optimist,' I replied.

'I am the realist.'

When we arrived back at our temporary accommodation, we were considerably more cautious. Leana went into our room first, sword drawn, and I followed immediately after, heading towards the window. She scrutinized all our belongings before concluding, 'No one is here. Nothing has been taken.'

'There's no one outside either, from what I can see.'

No sooner had we sat down than Jejal rumbled up the stairs and burst into the room. His shirt was covered in sweat as well as some dubious food stains. 'Greetings, Officer Drakenfeld! A productive day, I hope?'

'It was, thank you.'

'Here.' He handed over a message tube before wiping his palms on his shirt. 'This was left with me but an hour ago. It has the royal seal! You must open it quickly, for it was sent with urgency.' He waited a moment more while I stared blankly at him, waiting for him to leave us in private. Eventually he understood my wish.

'My apologies. Such secretive people,' he muttered, before walking down the stairs.

I opened up the tube and read the rolled-up letter inside. It was an invitation to a private dinner with the queen tonight. My presence was 'expected'. No doubt the queen would be eager to note our progress, especially given the development with her friend, Grendor of the Cape.

Not a moment for quiet contemplation, I thought. Still, I felt rather alert given the long day.

Leana looked over the letter. 'At least we will eat better food than whatever Jejal had been preparing. Or, rather, has spilled down his front.'

Dinner

The room was not especially opulent. Not in the same way that the royal residence of Optryx in Tryum was. Or even any of the sumptuous rooms of the Queen of Dalta for that matter. But it was a very honest room, and I liked it all the more because of the fact, for it allowed me to see beyond the pomp of Queen Dokuz Sorghatan.

Here we could simply see a mother and her daughter, surrounded by good company, talking about the finer things in life. Or at least, that was the impression that the queen *intended* for me to take with me in my reports to the Sun Chamber. Humble and honest. Not, in fact, the secret dictator I suspected her of being.

'Do not judge me too harshly.' She smiled as if she possessed some mystical way of probing my thoughts.

'On the contrary,' I replied. 'I'm enjoying the evening immensely.'

The room was square, perhaps fifty paces wide, with hunting equipment lining the wood-panelled walls. Roasted meats along with thick slices of late-season fruits were distributed among the guests on simple silver trays. There were about twenty people in all invited to this private dinner, and they ate heartily. We were sitting on cushions, arranged so that we looked up at the queen, who reclined on a couch with one of her eunuchs seated to her right. She was wearing far less make-up than when I saw her before, revealing her to be in her late forties. She wore a dark-blue high-collar dress, with subtle gemstone detailing. To her left, her daughter Nambu was dressed similarly.

Leana had worn her smart outfit, a fine fitted black tunic and black britches, while I was happy to give an airing to my finest green cloak and crimson shirt. My brooch was always on display. Sulma Tan was sadly not present; apparently too busy working to join us.

This mellow, warm and sensuous atmosphere was a fine experience indeed. Philosophers, artists, poets, astronomers and physicians were among the guests, and they talked about their own lives and work. The wonders they discussed were fascinating: here was modern thinking, such a display of new theories; at times it was a little overwhelming. The philosophers descended into rhetorical problems, but it was the astronomers who engaged my mind the most – the way they talked about the night sky reinforced my belief that the stars, perhaps forty or fifty miles away from us if we could get to them, were not the domain of the gods, but something to be studied, to provide us with information about the movement of our own land and of the circles of the sun and moon.

This was radical theory indeed, as priests in Detrata – priests of Trymus in particular – would have the stars remain the business of gods and spirits. It was traditionally the domain of priests to read the stars, to discern their movement and understand their purpose in the world. At that point I noted there were in fact no priests or priestesses present. And only three soldiers were here, pacing quietly in the darkness around the edges of the room. I don't know why I expected there to be more. Perhaps they waited outside the doors. Perhaps they thought philosophers were no threat.

The queen later gestured for us to move forward to sit before her, so we shuffled into her immediate company. It was a position that reminded me of the relationship between a teacher and a young pupil.

'Please tell me how your investigation is going, Officer Drakenfeld,' she said matter-of-factly.

In a low voice — little more than a whisper, for I did not want too many people to hear my thoughts — I revealed my findings so far. I was careful not to divulge anything about the ring we had found in the bishop's room, nor of the body parts that had, supposedly, been moving of their own accord. Eventually I revealed that an arrow had been fired at us.

The queen's eyes widened at the statement. 'Astran's mercy. This is most extraordinary, and quite unbecoming of this prefecture.'

'It was probably a military arrow,' Leana said.

A murmur spread through our group. I knew the others had been listening in.

'You're quite certain of this?' the queen's eunuch replied, a remarkably engaging yet feminine timbre to his voice. The queen looked at him softly, as if a pet had done something charming. Only then did I get a thorough look at him and his striking blue eyes, slender face and tied-back long hair. He wore a red silk robe with beautiful silver ornamentation around his neck. It was interesting to see his confidence in speaking like this before the queen — almost interrupting a conversation — and yet she accepted it perfectly.

'It is a very strong possibility,' I continued, more loudly now as it seemed logical to have it well known that the queen wished us protected. 'We suspect that someone in the army — an archer, or some other warrior perhaps — may be keen to stop us doing our job. Are your soldiers under good discipline? I hope they do not bear some sort of grudge against us.' The soldiers pacing the edge of the room paused momentarily, but it was too dark to see if they were angry with my words.

'I will see to it that my senior officers are questioned thoroughly about the matter,' the queen said firmly.

'I'd like that,' I replied. 'This matter is serious enough as it is without there being an awkward new dimension.'

'Accusations about army discipline . . .' the eunuch muttered, almost smiling – it was difficult to tell. 'They won't appreciate talk of that kind. They're a *sensitive* lot.'

'These are troubling issues,' I added. 'Enough to warrant airing them.'

'Yes indeed,' she snapped, a sudden sparkle in her eye. 'This is terrifying news. Two men of good standing have been killed, one of whom was a very dear friend of mine, and it is of absolute importance that the killer be brought to justice. Why, such barbarism could spread through society. Anyone in this room,' she gestured to the seated crowd, speaking loudly, 'any of you could be next. Safety to us all is of great importance.'

In the sudden silence the eunuch leaned forward and picked an olive from a tray. 'You sound like you've one of your plans, my lady.'

'As it happens, Brell, I have.' She took on an altogether more haughty demeanour. 'The army has come in larger numbers to the city. It is no secret. It's also no secret that many of these soldiers are scheduled to move to the borders.'

'The borders?' I asked.

'Sadly, yes. The border with Detrata, if you must know, in the mountains. We hear all sorts of worrying news. Their king is dead. There is talk of war . . . In fact, you were there recently, were you not? What do *you* have to say about it?'

'The country is simply finding its feet after the loss of its king, is all,' I said, not entirely believing it myself.

I had left the country knowing full well what might happen. Without a king, or indeed any temporary leader, there would be many plays for power. Before his death, the king, it appeared, had been holding back warmongers in that ancient and proud nation. A nation that would happily reclaim its old imperial ways.

'That may be the case,' the queen replied, 'but it is of concern to other nations. When we do not work together we work against each other. And when we work against each other it leads, naturally, to a loss of life. But it is not merely us who are militarizing the borders. I understand encampments are being placed in Maristan as well as Theran. We are no different. We have interests to protect. But despite the fact that many of our warriors are moving to the border, the recent murders have led me to keep many of them here in the city. I have little choice. They will be patrolling the perimeter of the prefecture, as well as within it. I *will* ensure the safety of my people.'

Leana gave me a sarcastic look. She was probably thinking how curious it was that the queen did not deem the people *outside* of this prefecture as her people as well, but now was not the right moment to highlight the issue.

'I want to talk to the officer and his assistant alone,' the queen announced.

Without hesitation, as if used to such behaviour, everyone else in the room rose to their feet and shuffled out of the door at the far end. Only her daughter and the eunuch remained.

She waited until the room had emptied.

'I am not stupid,' she continued, 'I know what you're thinking – that moving soldiers into the area will protect no one.'

'We are dealing with a clever individual,' I explained. 'One who moves within the shadows . . . In fact, since the murders have occurred here, whoever is doing this is likely to live within the prefecture.'

'That may be so,' the queen said knowingly. 'But bringing in soldiers will offer *reassurance* to the people of the prefecture. However . . .' – her gaze settled on Leana – 'you are Atrewen.'

Leana nodded coolly.

'I have heard of you. My agents speak of the powerful woman carved from jet. They report that you are a fine warrior and that you rode in the stadium, with some success. And that you were the one who stopped King Licintius from fleeing in his final moments.'

Leana was nonplussed by the praise, though she was probably uncomfortable with the direction it was taking. I was simply impressed at the speed and accuracy of the queen's informants.

The queen added, 'And, Officer Drakenfeld. One might assume that an officer of the Sun Chamber, when choosing his own protection, chooses wisely?'

'Not a moment has gone by where I have regretted the decision to work with Leana.' I could have spoken of the time we met – when all she had known had been wiped out in a vicious war. I could have divulged information of the many times that Leana, a far better fighter than I could ever dream to be, had saved me, prevented a blade from ending my life. Or the numerous times she had helped 'persuade' – perhaps at times without direction – those stubborn individuals who were not forthcoming with information or who liked to make life difficult for us.

But none of this was appropriate because the queen had already made whatever decision she was about to divulge.

'Very well,' she said. 'Then I would like to trust you with the temporary custody of Nambu Sorghatan, princess of Koton, and heir to the throne.'

'Might I enquire as to why?' I tried desperately not to sound *too* incredulous at the request. Nambu merely looked at the ground as if embarrassed by the whole conversation. Even Brell raised an eyebrow.

'We are on a difficult case right now . . .' I suggested.

The queen waved me closer. 'This killer . . . could be among us. He knows his way around the prefecture and has taken – without anyone seeing – two fine men, one of whom I considered to look after Nambu.' She gave a brief, sardonic laugh. 'Our inner world is becoming vile, Officer Drakenfeld. Temples are no longer sacred. It is somewhat difficult for me to know who to trust.'

'And you can trust us, after so little time in our company?'

'I have received detailed reports from my agents about who you are and what you have done. You will suffice.'

It was as I had suspected.

'I even know how well respected you are within the Sun Chamber after your recent success in Detrata,' she continued. 'A queen can easily obtain such information. You are no Detratan spy. You have the whole of Vispasia in your heart. Besides, I am a good judge of character.'

I did not quite know what to say or do. Nambu was a girl of perhaps thirteen years, used to life around a palace. A comfortable life, no doubt, and so not exactly the sort of person one could drag around the city hunting murderers.

'We deal in somewhat macabre matters at times,' I said. 'We work around the dead. Sometimes we may even venture into the other prefecture.'

'I have negotiated this with her. It will be good for her to see a little of life's harsh realities.'

Leana was gazing at Nambu. And to my surprise Leana said, with utter confidence, 'We will look after her.'

'We will?' I asked.

Leana said more firmly: 'We will.'

'Oh that is excellent.' Queen Dokuz sat back on her couch with a sense of satisfaction. Her work had been done. She delicately ate a sweetmeat from the tray to one side.

Nambu still did not make eye contact with me, and there was a resigned look about her.

'She may have to dress down somewhat,' I added. 'Such fineries are all well and good here, but a little too elegant for asking questions in a dingy tavern.'

'We will have her outfitted in whatever way you think is suitable,' the queen said, her mouth full of food.

'Yes. We'll need more secure living quarters,' I continued, thinking it at least an opportunity to profit in some way from this unexpected predicament. 'We have already received unwanted visitors. For everyone's safety, this is an important matter that needs to be addressed. The most secure quarters you have available will be necessary.'

'The matter will be resolved this same evening. We will see that your requirements are met.'

'How old is Nambu Sorghatan?' I asked.

Nambu answered herself: 'I'm thirteen.'

I smiled and nodded my appreciation of her reply. Indeed, she could answer for herself and it was a mistake not to direct the question at her in the first place. But she focused instead on some distant corner of the room.

'If I may be so bold as to ask this question, my lady, is there any other reason that you think she should be kept away from the standard palace guards?'

'Other than it is good for the spirits of a growing girl to see something of the world, then no.'

She finished too firmly for my liking.

Leana looked across to the young princess. 'Nambu, do you know how to hold a sword?'

She called her Nambu. Not 'princess', not 'my lady'. I half expected the queen to berate us for the misdemeanour, but she did not.

The princess looked up, startled. 'I have never held one, no.'

'We will fix that soon enough.'

To my astonishment I saw a grin appear upon the young girl's face.

Depths

'Well,' I said, 'at least this place is more secure than our last room.'

'Being buried in a tomb would be just as secure,' Leana replied, finally dumping her bags on one of the couches, 'and that would still be preferable to this. Some kind of joke of Sulma Tan's, do you think?'

'At least no one can fire an arrow through a window.'

'It is very difficult admittedly,' Leana said, 'when there are no windows.'

Our new quarters were located somewhere under the royal palace. The stone walls, constructed from large limestone blocks, were little more than seven feet high. There were five rooms in all, each one of a similar size, yet decorated in a pleasant if garish local manner. Animal skins covered the couches and formed rugs, and crudely preserved heads had been mounted as trophies. There was a well-ventilated stove, wall hangings depicting scenes of the hunt, and a good dozen or so cressets lining the wall. When they had all been lit it wasn't that dark at all. Two rooms acted as bedchambers, one was for dining or entertaining guests, and another – equipped with a desk, ledgers and lanterns – could serve perfectly as a base for our operations. The only way in was through a thick, arch-shaped wooden door.

'It's a vault,' I said, 'and it's spacious. So there aren't any windows. What is this place anyway?'

Nambu Sorghatan, princess of Koton, and now – bizarrely – under our protection, answered in perfect Detratan. 'It's my mother's emergency quarters.'

'For use in . . . ?'

'Sieges,' Nambu said, sitting on one of the couches and leaning back on both hands. 'Or if she thinks people are out to kill her.'

'Does it happen often?'

'Only when she's paranoid.'

'She doesn't show much fear,' I replied.

'You get to see the queen. I get to see my *mother*,' Nambu replied. 'She also comes down here when she's taking lovers.'

Looking at Leana I raised an eyebrow.

Leana smirked. 'You wanted safety? You have found a love nest. A shame you never have anyone to romance.'

'That may well be,' I replied, 'but it's an improvement none-theless. I imagine, decades ago, this would have been some sort of storage facility.'

'Or a dungeon,' Leana muttered.

'Indeed.'

Nambu was standing with her shoulders slumped and a resigned look about her. She did not seem petulant – as the offspring of royals could so often be. She appeared to accept whatever direction she was steered in, and it occurred to me that a royal life may not be entirely blessed – though it was a thousandfold improvement on the existence of most young people. 'How many people know about this place?'

'No one,' Nambu said, 'other than her two secretaries and me. Maybe one or two close soldiers, if she can trust them. Her lovers are blindfolded on their way down here. Probably after they've arrived, too.'

'You take exception to your mother's . . .' I searched for the word, keeping in mind how young she was, 'entertainments?'

'Entertainments,' Nambu grunted, stifling a laugh. She looked across to Leana. 'Astran's mercy – did he grow up in a monastery?'

Leana addressed Nambu. 'You know, I think we will get along very well.'

'Well isn't that nice,' I said. 'I'm glad ridiculing me might provide a common interest for you both.'

'Relax, officer,' Nambu said, reclining on her side on the couch, and staring into the empty fire. 'Anyway, to answer your *delicate* question, I don't really care what she does with her lovers.'

'Well, she must care for you,' I continued, moving around the other side of the couch to see her face, 'in order to want you protected so badly.'

'Hmm . . . She's concerned that someone is going to take the throne. And I'm just something else for her to be worried about.'

I wondered if Nambu might open up on an issue that had niggled with me since I'd arrived. 'Do politicians thirst for greater glory?'

'They probably do, what few of them there are.'

'There are not many here?' I asked.

Nambu went on to reveal what I had suspected all along: that the political structure of the nation was anything but democratic. A handful of senators – mainly those with connections to the Sorghatan family – convened every new moon to discuss the affairs of the state. Mostly this conclave was made up of ranks of senators who were leading figures in rival clans – the Rukrid, Yesui, Tahtar and Jagats – and her mother had merely given them ceremonial roles to appease the embittered families. There was always the promise that one day they would receive more power, but it never came. Over the years the clans had become even more frustrated. Now and then these senators might put an issue or piece of policy forward to the queen, but she was someone who did things her own way and often ignored their requests. Those who sought any real power quickly disappeared.

It would explain why I had seen so few politicians around the city. Yet it was important to bear in mind that Nambu was possibly jaded, happy to exaggerate her mother's weaknesses to paint her in a bad light.

It was getting late in the evening and we decided to head to our respective chambers. Leana and I would share the larger room, allowing Nambu her own private quarters.

'Just so you know,' Leana said, 'at sunrise, we will be practising with the sword.'

Nambu peered from behind her half-closed door and replied, 'Sure. If you know when the sun has actually risen.' And she closed the door behind her.

Leana shrugged, turning to me. 'The girl has a point. I will light one of these candles on the side and estimate how long has passed. It can also provide enough brightness for us to light the cressets in the morning. You will start to miss windows soon enough, Lucan.'

Without the sounds of the city to disturb me, I suspected I would sleep well. There would be no carts grinding through the narrow streets. There would be no priests calling out through the night. There would be no fights breaking out. It would be blissful.

I had taken the bed and Leana, as ever, had wanted to sleep on the floor. We would probably repeat this arrangement wherever we were travelling, no matter how much I argued otherwise. Not that I ever argued too strongly.

'You have taken a bit of a shine to the young princess,' I suggested, lying there in the dull light of the candle. 'Forgive me for saying, but it doesn't seem like something you'd normally be happy to do, yet you seemed keen to look after her.'

Leana was silent in thought for a while, something which felt all the more profound down there, away from the hubbub of daily life.

'I do not mind so much,' Leana whispered in reply. 'Because I remember what it is like to be a young girl who is out of her depth.'

'You do?' I sat up in bed.

Leana looked uneasy, and then she said something surprising. 'I was not always a warrior.'

'How do you mean?'

Again, a lingering silence as Leana searched her mind for an answer. She was rarely in a rush to speak, but I could tell this was taking a lot of willpower. 'I was once in a much higher station than I have previously let on.'

'Go on . . .'

'Before the wars, this is. Before all the killings had begun.' She sighed. 'Spirits save me, when I was a girl I was in a position in society much like Nambu's. In fact, we are very similar. We *were* very similar, I mean to say.'

Leana had never even hinted at this before. I had always assumed she was trained to be a warrior — and remained of the warrior class in her own culture — because that's what I had inferred from her few statements on that period of her life.

'Are you telling me that you're Atrewen royalty?'

'Not the most senior royalty, no. But of . . . *significantly* noble birth, it is safe to say. I suppose at one point towards the end, as my people were killed one by one, I became senior royalty, but that does not seem appropriate to consider. That time has long since passed. The spirits wish for me to walk other roads, and I have taken them. I am not unhappy with their wishes.'

'But you always made fun of my relatively privileged upbringing,' I whispered. 'I just assumed you didn't like people of higher birth.'

'You never appreciated how lucky you were,' she replied bluntly.

'That isn't true, Leana.'

'I had my privilege destroyed. Not removed, but *destroyed*. Only when these things are gone do we appreciate them.'

I let out a long breath. 'You're correct.'

'What is more,' she continued calmly, without a trace of bitterness in her voice, 'I had to learn how to fight to get such privilege back. I had to train hard, and work hard, and commit myself to regain my dignity. Not that it mattered and not that I succeeded, but I did discover new things along the way and we must make the most of those discoveries. So yes, though Nambu has not been through any of what I have been through, I understand what it is like to be a young girl in a noble family, in a world where it is not so easy to be a woman as it is to be a man. Now, that is all I have to say on the matter. We must rest.'

I lay back down, stunned by the revelation.

Jewels

The following morning – or what I assumed to be morning, judging by how much the candle had burned down – Leana's confession still echoed in my mind. It was as if she had been living a lie to me all these years; though strictly speaking, she had not lied. She simply had not told me *all* the details. Instead, I had let my assumptions get the better of me, and allowed those errors to harden over time into a clay image of what I took to be the truth. I felt like some distant, secret admirer who, without truly knowing the subject of their desire, creates a story about them to fill the void of their longing.

I was very annoyed with myself.

Most of what I had known about her past was based on our first encounter. Understandably she had spoken little about it since then, and I had never thought it appropriate to enquire about such matters beyond what she was prepared to say. I would have liked to talk at great length and revisit her past – to understand who she really was before we met on that horrific day.

Though she was still the same Leana – someone I could depend upon with secrets about my god-cursed seizures, someone whose sarcastic ways prevented my station in life getting the better of me, and someone who had saved my life on many occasions.

I could not understand why she had not told me before. It was likely she was worried I would treat her differently. Just because she was not far from royalty did not make her any better or worse a person. It had no influence over her skills by my side, yet it had obviously shaped who she was today. There might be something else entirely behind her discretion, but it would probably take another few years until she decided to tell me.

Putting those thoughts to one side, I lit the cressets and the other candles, allowing the queen's 'love nest' to be seen in all its glory.

Leana woke Nambu and the two soon began to practise sword combat. It was the first time Nambu had done anything remotely like this. At first the fragile frame of the girl didn't seem to cope with even holding Leana's spare blade.

'What if I hurt someone?' Nambu said, holding the blade with uncertainty.

'A chance would be a fine thing,' I remarked dryly from one of the couches. The look Nambu gave me then suggested that there was some considerable spirit within her.

Leana was an incredible warrior and a superb teacher. She had helped refine my own skills over the years. Even after we battled petty criminals in the underworld of Venyn City, she would occasionally correct my technique and give me some inappropriately timed feedback. I watched her now in the light of last night's revelation. A royal warrior educating another royal.

Leana guided Nambu through some basic moves – how to hold the blade, footwork, posture and so on – and Nambu appeared to take to Leana's brisk instructions with considerable promise. I cringed the first time Nambu was knocked to the floor – this was a princess in our protection, after all – but the girl simply brushed herself down and got back on her feet again.

After the lesson I located suitable attire for Nambu from the belongings that the queen had sent down for her, in the end opting for a simple brown tunic, dark-grey cloak and military-style black boots – the garb of a boy. For the first time that she could remember, Nambu wore no make-up, did not style her hair as per the fashion and wore no jewellery.

She told us it was rather liberating.

We had managed to leave the palace at a decent hour. The sun had only just risen, so we had not yet lost much in the way of time. Being encouraged by the queen to not use the royal facilities, to keep Nambu's new situation discreet, we dined out on cheap street food.

In the shadow of a towering statue of Astran, the princess of Koton munched her way through a cheap pastry with remarkable gusto.

'This stuff is so much better than what we get in the palace,' she mumbled with her mouth full.

'It's probably not as good for your constitution,' I replied.

'Don't care. Can we eat this all the time?'

The three of us walked through the prefecture towards the market. I scrutinized the signs on the stores nearby, some of which were written in Detratan, others – which I had some trouble discerning – were written in Kotonese.

'What are you looking for?' Nambu asked, one of many questions that was about to come my way.

'I'd like to locate a jeweller,' I replied.

'Why's that?'

'Because . . .' I sighed. 'You heard me discussing the murders with your mother?'

'Of course.'

'So you think you know all the details?'

'Yes.'

'Well you don't. There's something we didn't tell her.'

She gave me a look of smug satisfaction. 'So this is a secret?'

'Not exactly. I was merely . . . managing the information.'

'It sounds a lot like a secret to me. What is it?'

I reached into my pocket and pulled out the envelope containing the ring we'd found in the bishop's mattress. I told her where we found it and of the similar stone in the missing amulet belonging to Grendor of the Cape. She examined it carefully before putting it back in the envelope.

'So, in conclusion, the jewel could be important. But we don't know what it is. And that's why we're here looking for a jeweller – to find out.'

'Oh. I thought you agents and spy types got to kill people to get information.'

'No. Well, sometimes she does,' I nodded towards Leana, 'but we generally try not to kill. Life is best preserved – there's almost always a loved one who will be affected by the death, a life to be ruined. Take poor Grendor – his death has now left a wife in mourning and two small children without a father. Such an act is not to be done casually. It can echo down the years.'

Nambu shrugged. 'You must worry about these things when you get to your age.'

'I'm not that old,' I spluttered. 'Besides, being young is important – you *should* be enjoying things at your age and not worrying about death.'

She made a noise of dissatisfaction. 'I don't get to enjoy all that much, not with my mother around.'

We followed the instructions of a passer-by to locate the nearest jeweller. Even though we kept to the woman's directions, it was still some time before we managed to find the place.

The shop was tucked down one of the older, more pleasant

lanes of the city, one with cobbled surfaces and raised pavements that reminded me somewhat of Tryum. The frontage possessed no windows — or awning, since it was shaded by the surrounding buildings — merely a faded green sign with *Vallamon's Gems* painted in a wonderfully esoteric script. Standing by the front door was a tall and muscular man, someone, by the look of him, who might have been familiar with military service. He wore a black tunic and heavy boots, and possessed a broad face, stubble and close-cropped black hair. The owner must have been doing rather well for himself if he could afford private security.

'Good day, sir. I'd like to meet with Vallamon.' I noted how the man stood with half his frame across the doorway, as if tempting people to try their luck.

'Who's calling?' he grunted.

'Lucan Drakenfeld, Officer of the Sun Chamber. We're on urgent business sanctioned by Queen Dokuz Sorghatan.'

'Who're these two?' With a tilt of his head he indicated Leana and Nambu.

'My assistants.'

'You need two assistants?'

'Yes, I'm a rather busy man. So I'd appreciate it all the more if you hurried along and asked Vallamon if he's free. This is the queen's business.'

His dark eyes were drawn to my Sun Chamber brooch, the gold star pinned to my breast. He nodded and turned inside. Muffled voices discussed our presence.

A moment later and he stepped outside once again. 'All right, you can go inside, one at a time. And you' — he pointed towards Nambu, who froze looking up along his outstretched finger — 'you keep your hands in your pockets at all times. We've had trouble with lads your age before. I broke the arm of the last one who tried to pinch something, then had their parents complaining afterwards. Law's the law – you steal, we take it back in whatever way necessary. Saves us the bother of courts and having to pay lawyers.'

I rested my hand upon his forearm and met his gaze. 'He won't be any trouble,' I said firmly, 'I give you my word.'

He peered down to where I'd touched his arm and made it perfectly clear he didn't appreciate the gesture, but he stepped aside and let us through.

Vallamon's Gems was extremely small inside – perhaps a twelve-foot-square room – and lit warmly by dozens of candles. There was a counter to our right, and to the left was a wooden wall containing hundreds of parchments, on which various ink sketches had been made. The remarkably intricate drawings were of different gemstones, ranging in shapes and sizes, as well as the silver or gold in which they had been set, and illegible writing surrounded them that may have been detailing the designs.

From the workshop behind, a small man with slick black hair parted to one side stepped forward into the light.

'Good morning,' I said. 'The jovial chap on the door said it was all right to enter.'

He nodded and said in rough Detratan, 'Allius is a trustworthy man. I have known him for many years and his judgement has mostly been sound. He informs me you are a man of some standing in society. I approve of men of good standing.' He grinned. 'They tend to pay for quality and with purer coin.'

Out of politeness, and given the poor nature of his Detratan, I continued in Kotonese, introducing myself and my assistants. 'You might be disappointed, but I'm not at the moment looking to purchase an item. However I would very much like your help.'

He was indifferent to me now he realized I wasn't going to give him much money, but I added, 'And, of course, I expect to pay for your assistance and expertise.'

'Then we have an understanding,' he replied, smiling on one side of his face, as if his other half did not function properly. 'What do you need help with?'

I reached into my pocket, produced the envelope containing the ring, and slid it across the counter to him. Suspecting him of possessing not a little arrogance, I said, 'No one in the city seems to know what the stone is in this ring. I'm hoping your knowledge is exceptional enough to discern what it might be.'

'Oh that it is,' he replied. 'I am the most experienced jeweller in the city.'

He immediately picked out the ring from the envelope and took it over to a corner where an ornate candelabrum stood. There he examined it at length, humming with confidence – or at least I hoped it was confidence.

'Very interesting indeed . . .' he muttered. Without removing his gaze he reached for a small tool from the side and began scratching at the stone in tiny, methodical strokes. He put down that tool only to pick up another and, as he continued working at it, said, 'Do you mind if I ask where you got this from?'

'It was taken from the premises of someone who's recently died,' I replied.

'Dead man, you say. Well . . . this item has history. Two dead people are tied to this little trinket already. The man who crafted the metal in which the stone is set died several years ago. Possibly a decade now, I can't quite remember. Oh, how time gets the better of us, Officer Drakenfeld!'

Nambu started to examine some of the images along the wall, under the watchful eye of Allius, the man on the door. Leana stepped in his line of sight, and let him see the blade on her waist. Though I didn't feel threatened by his presence, this was just one of hundreds of occasions where I was glad that Leana was close by.

I turned my attention to Vallamon once again. 'You're quite certain of who made it?'

'Oh yes, it's Harred all right,' Vallamon said, placing down the tools and once again holding up the ring, tilting it this way and that. 'You can tell from the way the silver is worked, the tiny leaf motifs. He was never that good – he liked to knock out these things quickly, to take the coin and forget about craftsmanship. You would not catch me working so casually.'

'Can you tell us anything about Harred?'

Vallamon turned around to face us, still holding the ring. 'No, just a very average jeweller. Nothing remarkable about him. He was a quiet man. I do not think he had a wife, and certainly there was no son or daughter to take on his business after he passed away. He used to do all sorts of jobs – he wasn't picky, couldn't say no, never asked questions. Just piled on the work. That's the mentality of a man who grew up in harder times, I'd say. The last two decades have been very prosperous for the jewellers, so there was not really any need for such an attitude.'

Didn't ask questions. Didn't say no. Perhaps just the right man to set a stone of questionable origin.

'So do you think this ring is interesting in any way,' I asked, 'or is it merely a piece of ornamentation? Only the man who'd worn this wasn't really one given to wearing rings – or any jewellery for that matter.'

'There's something interesting about this,' Vallamon said, holding up the ring but not handing it over. 'Yes indeed. I am sorry to say that the gemstone is one that I've never before seen, not in my forty years in the trade. An educated fellow might think it a poor quality ruby, but it really is not – it's far softer than a ruby. The *way* it's been cut reminds me of a diamond in many ways, but again the softness, and look at the shallowness of the colour. Very unusual. One assumes that something like this would be heavily polished as well, but ... No. A dullness. And, very faintly, an unusual coral-like texture. Remarkable stone. I've never seen anything like it.' Vallamon appeared to consider something for a moment and then said, 'I'll buy it off you. How much would you like for it?'

'It's not for sale,' I declared.

Vallamon tilted up his chin as if to look down at me – which was quite an effort given his lack of height. 'That is a great shame. I would like to present it to a few apprentices as a potential new discovery. The guild, of which I am in charge, would thrive with a good debate over this. We'd record it, of course, and speculate—'

'The ring is not for sale,' I repeated. 'But if you, an expert, seem so bamboozled by this stone, I would like to know where an *ordinary* man might acquire one. And why he would keep that hard-to-find stone hidden from view . . .'

'Was this the only example of the stone you have found?'

'Potentially another item had been made,' I replied. 'A small amulet.'

'A second specimen . . .' Vallamon breathed.

'We haven't got that – it was taken,' I replied. 'Possibly it was stolen, or maybe it has gone missing. But there is a strong chance that the stone was the same. I showed this one to the wife of the man who had worn the amulet, and she was of the impression it was the same colour.'

Vallamon had presented himself as someone potentially very useful in future. I reached into my pocket and drew out two gold coins, probably enough to purchase some of his cheapest wares. 'The first coin,' I said, 'is for your help and time today.'

'Much appreciated,' Vallamon replied stiffly.

'The second coin is if you could put out an information request in whatever circles you possess – networks that stretch from town to town, tradesmen, your guild, whatever it is – about such a gemstone. Especially where it might have come from. My full name is Officer Lucan Drakenfeld, and I can be found at the palace under the address of the queen's second secretary, Sulma Tan. Phrase your request in whatever technical terms you wish — I'm sure they'll be better than the words I have used to describe the stone.'

'You pay well for information,' Vallamon muttered.

'This information could be critical in solving two brutal murders,' I replied.

'Ah,' he said. 'So this is in connection with Bishop Tahn Valin and the famous Grendor of the Cape?'

'How did you know?'

'Nothing remains a secret in the prefecture for long. He was a good fellow, Grendor — he came in here from time to time, but he only ever bought for his lovely young wife. I never spotted any curious pieces of jewellery upon him. I will consider your request as a favour to Grendor's family.'

Vallamon slid the other gold coin back across to me and, as I met his proud gaze, my estimation of the businessman increased.

The Manuscript Hall

Horse dung and woodsmoke filled the air. A priest gave a sermon by a fountain nearby, though no one was listening to him. The three of us continued through the humid streets.

'Well?' Nambu asked.

'Well what?'

'Well, that was useless.'

'Was it?'

'Stop answering questions with questions,' she said.

'Why?' I replied, trying to hide my amusement at her impatience. 'OK, I'm sorry. But come now, Nambu, what makes you think that was a useless meeting? I'm serious.'

'He told you nothing. We got no information. Therefore it was useless.'

'Some might think so, but not me. Vallamon revealed a great many things that we needed to know. We know that the ring is special – that it is very rare, enough to puzzle an expert of his pedigree. It makes me think that the stone is significant to this case. If it's the same kind of stone as in the missing amulet owned by Grendor, then it's *incredibly* significant. The connection – and whatever it might throw up – could be the key. Indeed, one

189

might speculate that if anyone else wore a stone like this, they would have good cause to be worried.'

'It would be worth trying to send a message out to those citizens of the prefecture . . .' Leana added.

'Maybe. If we dressed up the message as one of public safety . . . It also means that those individuals might come forward, and give us more information.'

'Though I do not think they will come forward,' Leana said. 'These people will most likely have something to hide.'

'True,' I said. 'If they fear for their lives because of what happened to Grendor and the bishop then they might want protection or even to not draw attention to themselves.'

'They will have something to hide. Some secret.'

Nambu asked the question, before I could. 'Why would you think that?'

Leana addressed Nambu. 'Think. People do not die *horrible* deaths for no good reason. Thought has gone into them. There has to be something behind such killings – as with most killings. If the precious stone is the link, then those people who have the stone have probably done the same thing as those who have been killed. They will be in fear for their lives, yes, but if their past is so bad it gets them killed . . .'

'You make a good point,' I said. 'I hadn't thought of it quite like that.'

Nambu was quiet on the issue. Part of me wondered if she knew what she was letting herself in for, though I suspected her days were going to be more interesting than she originally thought, and more stimulating than shuffling to and fro down those echoing palace corridors. 'So where do we go now?' Nambu asked.

'Sulma Tan mentioned that there was a manuscript hall to be found within the prefecture.'

'Sure, I know where it is,' Nambu said.

It occurred to me how useful it would be to have someone who knew the prefecture well. 'Then lead the way.'

'OK. What do you want from there?'

'Information,' I replied. 'Knowledge.'

'What else would you go there for,' Nambu muttered.

'You asked.'

'What kind of information?'

I sighed, wondering just how many more questions the girl would ask. 'The manuscript hall contains information on key figures of the city. I would like to find specific details of naval movements – specifically of Grendor's past adventures. Sulma Tan also said there was a section on recorded deaths, as part of the previous national census. While considerably out of date, it may provide something of interest – on the subject of ritual killing. And before you ask why, it's to see if there have been any similar deaths in the past.'

'That all sounds pretty dull if you ask me,' Nambu said.

'The business of the Sun Chamber is not all sword fights in the dark,' I replied.

'Unfortunately,' Leana added.

As we continued through the streets, more than once I suspected that we were being followed. To an extent, I expected to be followed – if not by our friend from the previous days, then by one of the queen's agents keeping an eye on Nambu.

But this didn't feel subtle. At least three men gawked at us as we strode by. They were tall fellows with a simple though colourless military look about their clothing, and were loitering at different parts of the street. This common association between them was unnerving.

Later still, as we moved through an older part of the prefecture, not too far from the river, Leana casually informed me that there were five men following us in a group, all with that same, deliberately anonymous look.

We picked up our pace.

Luckily, we managed to make our way up the steps of the manuscript hall without being caught. The building itself would act as some kind of protection, and it was possible that those who were following would be put off now that we were inside an official royal property.

From the outside, the manuscript hall did not look all that impressive. Over the doorway was a large triangular pediment, the kind that might be seen in numerous secondary temples across Vispasia. From the doorway there was a view overlooking a small market area. Statues of unfamiliar warriors stood in pairs outside, their crumbling faces blighted by age, their stone swords dulled by time.

Inside, however, the place was remarkable. Well-kept green marble floors extended into the distance. A wide central passage-way led through row upon row of polished oak shelving. Each section of shelving was around twenty feet wide, six feet deep and went up to the ceiling. On each of the shelves lay dozens of rolls of paper, ranging in quality, age and size, but given the number of shelves there must have been thousands of elongated scrolls.

The ceiling featured good quality glass, allowing plenty of light to shine through – perhaps to minimize the risk of fire. I cast a wary eye on the metal cressets that were fixed to each unit, illuminating the path through the hall.

Attendants in plain white, almost monastic garb, proceeded slowly up and down the rows, making notes, carrying scrolls, or whispering in the alcoves. On one side of the hall stood a section containing impressively bound books; it had been a long time since I'd seen so many in one place.

We browsed through them, leisurely, almost forgetting that we had been followed on the way to the building. The books were written in many languages, though mainly Detratan – and using some of the old form, from when the Empire flourished centuries ago. There were letters from Lentus Magnus, one of the Three Noble Emperors. I was shocked to see theorems from the mad emperor Fingus Trentnor, who used to boil his prisoners and attempted, in his latter days, to boil his friends and family as well. Apart from his two sisters, of course, whom he married simultaneously. If there had been more time to read, I would have liked to spend some time with that entertainingly bizarre text, especially since I had thought them long-forgotten.

At my request Leana remained vigilant at all times, and prowled the hall for any signs of the men tailing us. She would no doubt look for potential escape routes should we be attacked – I had no need to ask her to do so.

Meanwhile Nambu and I headed deeper into this resplendent building. Nambu directed me to one of the attendants. I asked her where we might find information on shipping movements, trade and old census data – from before the time of Sulma Tan.

The attendant, a thin woman in her forties, suggested I give a donation to the upkeep of the manuscript hall if I wished to make use of the facilities. The royal blessing, she said, only went so far. It didn't seem an unreasonable request so, after I placed some silver coins in the donations box on the wall, we were directed to a dusty corner where there was a private desk and a candle to work by. Moments later, the attendant brought over some of the information we'd asked for before she wandered off and left us to it.

'You can read, I take it?' I asked Nambu.

'What do you take me for, a village fool?' She perched up on a stool alongside me. 'I've had some of the finest tutors in the country.'

'I merely thought I'd check,' I replied, sliding one of the tomes over to her. 'Read through that.'

'What is it?'

'A list of registered shipping companies.'

'Haven't you got something exciting? It is hardly an epic poem.'

'No, but right now this is more important than poetry. Please, scan through it.'

'Do I have to?'

'You could go back to your mother if you wanted.'

'Fine.' Nambu gave me a look of disdain before pulling open the heavy cover of the book. 'What am I looking for?'

'I'd like to know if any of these companies were registered in the name of Grendor of the Cape.'

'What are you going to do?'

'I'm going through these death records.'

We studied assiduously for a good two hours. Now and then Nambu would let out a gentle sigh, but I was impressed with her diligence. Meanwhile the census data provided a detailed and interesting reminder of the number of ways one could die, but I spotted no abnormal patterns. People died of lung diseases, accidental poisonings, horse tramplings and failures of the heart. With respect to recorded murders, many of which remained unsolved, there were stabbings, cut throats, objects being dropped from a great height, and a good number of deliberate poisonings using all kinds of substances. In rural districts there was more violence. But in the city of Kuvash it seemed that a lot of people had simply vanished, and over a space of about two decades. While in another era this might have been because of war, in times of peace I could only attribute it to a lack of information, or people falling between the gaps in society. Or a particularly rigorous purge by the queen, for there was a noticeably blank space alongside state-sanctioned executions. Simply it might be attributed to the wrong numbers in the wrong columns.

Leana cautiously made her way around the hall, peering this way and that, ever vigilant. Whenever she passed there were no signs of anxiousness on her part, which allowed me to relax into the research.

'Look at this,' Nambu breathed excitedly. 'I've found his name.'

She turned the book towards me and pointed to the page. The writing was not great, but there indeed was Grendor's name and that of a company called Naval Exports.

'Excellent work, Nambu.'

It was interesting that he had decided to use his military roots in the company name. From these accounts he had registered Naval Exports thirty years ago, though back then it had been known as Vispasian Exports. It was probably only when he retired that he changed the name, judging by the dates – unless, of course, there had been another reason to make the change.

'Did *you* find anything?' she asked.

'There are many gruesome ways to die,' I replied, 'as there always seem to be. However nothing that I've seen seems to share any characteristics with the recent murders.'

'That's a shame.'

'Perhaps,' I replied. 'It certainly makes things no easier. Right, we should go – I could do with reporting back to Sulma Tan.'

We stood to leave when Leana moved swiftly towards us. 'I have seen nothing out of the ordinary, which makes me suspect that whoever was following us is still waiting for us outside.'

'Have you found a more discreet exit?' I asked.

'Not from my surveillance. This place is a labyrinth, though. We should ask.'

After some furtive efforts, a helpful attendant directed us to another door that the staff themselves used, which was concealed behind a bookcase. We managed to pass through musty passage-ways and then stepped out into the afternoon.

No sooner had daylight covered us than I could see them: two of the men who had been following us earlier. Then came a third – a woman walking slowly with a baton of some description held behind her back. Only then did I realize how bad this route actually *was*. There were very few alleyways or paths where we could try to lose them again.

I whispered to Leana, 'Whatever you do, make sure Nambu is safe. She is our first priority.'

Leana nodded, and with her arm around her shoulder, steered the princess slightly to one side.

'What's going on?' Nambu was oblivious to the threat.

'For your safety,' I said firmly, 'you must follow Leana's instructions.'

We proceeded down the steps and onto the street. The road was busy, but not enough that we could lose ourselves in the throng. My heart skipping a beat, together we jogged towards the right, along the edge of a marketplace, and down one of two side streets.

'We should split up,' I urged in the tall shadows of the alleyway, 'but remember, take Nambu to safety.'

'No,' Leana said. 'We should wait until they do something. We can still fight them.'

'Not with the princess here. We've been instructed to keep her safe. If they come for me, I can handle them.'

'No you can't. Take her with you while I hold them off.'

'Protect *her*,' I repeated. Leana needed no further command.

We separated.

Dashing through the crowds, I ran down another road entirely, a much quieter street. I drew my short sword.

A large-set man suddenly blocked off my route, immediately stopping my momentum.

Another man slammed into me from behind, but I managed to stay on my feet.

'What do you want?' I asked, stepping backwards, now and then checking what was behind me so as not to trip.

No response came. Another three bodies filled the street. There were five of them in all. Two were holding cudgels. Another two stood at the far end, sealing me into the street. All wore scarves across their mouths. My blade was now firmly poised.

The surrounding buildings offered no escape routes: no open doorways, no passageways, no cellar, nothing that I could use to lever myself up over a wall – merely bland whitewashed buildings.

'Make your move. Let's get this over with.'

They advanced another step and I tried to take in the details: each one was garbed in *deliberately* poor and drab clothing, as if trying to disguise who they really were. Their boots were well made, their bodies well nourished. These people were not typical street thugs.

The first man came at me; I blocked his arm. I managed to scrape my blade across his ribs and, while he paused in pain, I slammed my head into his nose. He fell backwards, cudgel clattering to the ground; I kicked it to one side. Immediately another two came, simultaneously, slamming their clubs towards my legs. I managed to avoid the arc of one, but the other connected with my hamstring and I collapsed onto my knees, clawing at the cobbles. Two of them grabbed my arms and held them behind my back.

Blow after blow slammed into my stomach, and my face.

A punch to the neck and I could barely breathe. Pain pulsed through my body. I remained conscious for long enough to see my own blood splatter across the ground.

Bright colours passed through my eyelids.

Days Later

It was days later when Leana explained to me what had happened during that afternoon.

After she'd taken Nambu to a tavern, and left her there with strict instructions and a lot of local kron for the landlord to guarantee her protection, she had sprinted back through the streets to find me.

Leana had caught the tail end of the assault. She killed three of my attackers, leaving another injured with a broken leg, before the rest dispersed. After she had noted that I was not, in fact, dead she bound up the floored assailant before going back to find Nambu. She sent her back to the palace to bring a physician. Meanwhile, Leana waited with me, the other injured attacker, and the three corpses, until we were all taken to the palace.

On the queen's orders the individual with the broken leg was tortured, revealing that my attackers had come from a mounted division of the Kotonese army. After some time, close to death, he blabbered in great, heaving sobs the names of all of those who had come that afternoon, and upon whose orders they were acting.

It transpired that, because I had been accusing the military of firing an arrow at me, blaming them for something unproven, one of the senior officers had taken exception to the statement – and decided to dispense his own style of street justice.

That man, along with the others who had been named, was promptly executed. They were beheaded with no trial or ceremony in one of the cells deep under the palace. All of their bodies were then dumped into the river further away from the city. Their names were to be forgotten, expunged from the military records. The matter had been dealt with.

The queen, Leana explained, claimed there was no need to thank her, and she could only apologize for what had occurred.

All of this I discovered three days after the incident, and before breakfast.

During those lost days, I had been laid out in a comfortable bedchamber, wearing only my trousers, and covered with a thin sheet. My surroundings were plain – a red-brick roof and walls, an empty wood-burner, a couple of cressets, and some sweet-smelling incense. My cloak and boots had been placed on a table by my side.

The first thing I did on finding out what had happened was to apologize for the fact that Leana had killed three of the queen's men. I felt guilt that my initial accusations, with no proof, had set them on this path. My apology was not accepted. The queen declared, through Sulma Tan, that she would make a point of showing what would happen if anyone else tried to interfere with the investigation. It was important to set standards. The severed hand of one of the soldiers was retained and had been nailed to the door of the barracks as a warning to the others.

Solving these murders, Sulma Tan said, was the queen's main priority.

I was simply glad I was not her enemy.

*

By a quirk of fate, it turned out that it was the physician, Carlon, who had helped to reset my broken arm and patch up my wounds.

He visited again to see how I was coming along. He pottered into the room dressed in his brown shirt, though he wore no leather apron this time — something I took as a promising sign. After he greeted me he glanced at me with a great deal of curiosity.

'Thank you for looking after me,' I said.

'Well, we've worked together already,' he replied, 'so it seemed like the honourable thing to do! We don't want one of my apprentices tinkering with you — they can be a bit wild at times, and treat the place like a butcher's shop. Besides, I've been dealing with too many corpses of late, so it was nice to have fresh meat, so to speak. Anyway I am glad to have been involved as you have proven quite an interesting specimen.'

'How so?' I asked.

'Your wounds have healed up rather . . . quickly.'

'Have they?' Only then did I look along the muscles of my torso, surprised to find it *relatively* scar-free. The bruises were yellow-brown, and not dark at all. I flexed my arm, which still ached, but it was nothing compared with what it should have been, considering the beating I had taken.

'Splendidly so, it seems. *Ridiculously* so, others might claim. I would like to take some of the credit for the recovery, however it would be dishonest. Your chest, stomach, face and shoulders were all cut and bruised heavily when you first arrived on that table.' He gestured behind. 'Your wounds were caused by blunt instruments rather than anything neat and sharp, so you were quite a battered mess. And I expected things to look rather serious for another twenty days at least. In all honesty, I half expected you to die. But as you can see for yourself, you have not.

And your wounds, well . . . they have healed as if we are on day fifteen already.'

'But it has only been three days?' I asked, more concerned with how much time I had lost on the investigation.

'Three indeed,' Carlon declared. 'You are quite the mystery.'

'I need to get back to work,' I said, pushing myself up, but Carlon eased me back down again. Despite my having regained some energy, the physician's strong arms easily had me resting again.

'One more day at least,' Carlon said. 'Sulma Tan is very worried about you and wishes that you rest so you make a proper recovery.'

'Worried?' It was unlikely that the second secretary had the time to worry about me.

'You were close to death, Officer Drakenfeld. We should be more cautious until I'm satisfied you're healed. At least enough before you go gallivanting about the city.'

'Tomorrow then. I have a lot of matters that I must see to.'

'Your recovery has been impressive. You've not taken any suspicious elixirs, have you?' Carlon asked, as he inspected me again, checking underneath a bandage on my shoulder.

'Not unless you count the wine I consumed on the night before I was beaten.'

'The queen does serve a lovely drop, so it's said. But no – I do not think it was the wine. Think on, if you can, about anything you may have taken.'

'Honestly, Carlon, I don't think there's been a single thing.'

'Then this remains most intriguing. First Sulma Tan suggests we have corpses that seem to resist staying properly dead. Now you are healing so remarkably. Perhaps there is some strange magical property about this palace. Alas, I think not, judging by those soldiers who were executed here. No magic could have saved them.'

'Yes, I would rather such brutal justice wasn't done in my

name,' I commented. 'These aren't the hallmarks of a civilized society as the queen is keen on demonstrating.'

'No, but it is an efficient one. However, I do agree with you. We could do with as many soldiers as possible staying alive, given the current political climate.' He stopped and raised a hand to his chin. 'Anyhow, we still have the issue about your healing and the lively corpses. I wonder if there is anything in common between you all?'

'I hope not,' I replied.

'Well, think on, Drakenfeld! I'll leave you be now. Do rest, even though the gods are on your side right now. The gods change their minds as often as the weather.'

Smiling, Carlon exited the room. Only then did I notice Leana had taken up residence on a chair in the corner of the room. Her sheathed sword was hung up over the back of it. Her boots were raised upon the foot of my bed and she simply nodded her acknowledgement that I was alive.

There was something that niggled about what Carlon had said. There was, of course, one thing I had in common with the corpses; but it was something that I didn't wish to share with anyone of his stature just yet.

In my trouser pocket, the ring was still safely in its envelope.

'Leana.' I waved for her to come closer.

She pushed herself up from her chair and came over to my side.

'You heard what Carlon was saying,' I whispered. 'You don't suppose the bishop's jewel could be doing this, do you?'

'Doing what?' she asked.

'The recovery. *My* recovery. Perhaps there is something about this stone that helps *healing*? That whoever is close to it seems to absorb its properties?'

Leana leaned back, surprised at what I'd said. To be honest, I was surprised myself that I'd muttered such a thing.

'Really?' she said. 'Magic? After all you have to say on the subject?'

'Not magic, no,' I replied. 'Anyway, I'm open-minded to all possibilities, so long as we can apply some sort of logic. Say this ring – this item – did have particular medical properties? Perhaps this stone, one that few people know about, has other uses?'

'Spirits save us, now you are imagining things.' Leana turned back to the chair. 'You have lost your senses in the attack. A head wound. Rest. You will feel better soon.'

'You're probably right.' Smiling awkwardly, I lay back on my pillow and closed my eyes.

But I could think of little else other than my rapid recovery. In my travels I had come across stories of various substances that could affect the health of a person, but I rarely believed them. Going by logic, if a poison could very quickly remove life from someone, surely it was possible that an opposite substance could also heal, that it could give life?

It was frustrating to have to lie about for another day. I was eager to get back to work, but occasionally a dull ache would throb through my body, reminding me of what had happened. It made the need to discover the true nature of this stone all the more pressing.

Someone knocked on the door. I nodded to Leana who strode up and opened it. Nambu Sorghatan entered the room wearing a simple black hooded robe, with no ornamentation at all.

'Hello,' she said.

'Good morning,' I said. 'Or is it afternoon?'

'Afternoon.' She stepped close to the side of my bed. 'You should have stayed in the manuscript hall.'

I gave a quiet laugh, but despite the apparent rapid recovery, it still hurt to do so. 'You're probably right.'

'She *is* right,' Leana called from the corner of the room.

'It's a good thing you've got her,' Nambu said. 'She saved your life, you know?'

'I know.'

'If it hadn't been for her, you'd have been a corpse. Like those on that list you'd only just been reading.'

'I appreciate your clarity, Nambu,' I muttered, staring up at the ceiling once again.

'It is not the first time I have saved him,' Leana said. 'It is why I teach the sword lessons, not him. He thinks too much about the positions.'

'She's right.' I grinned at Leana. 'She just about earns her wages.'

'I only save you so I keep getting paid.'

'I trust you've been occupied while I've been lying here,' I said to Nambu.

'Yes. Leana's been teaching me to defend myself for the last three days solidly. I probably ache just as much as you do.'

'Well, maybe not quite as much,' I said. 'Still, I'm healing.'

The girl's face revealed some concern, but I waited for her to speak.

'There's something you should know,' Nambu said.

'What is it?'

'Well, two things. First, a letter came for you. You should read that first.' She reached into her pocket, picked out a small tube and handed it over. 'It arrived for you last night, but you weren't awake to receive it.'

Thanking her, I opened the tube and read the message, which was in Kotonese.

To Lucan Drakenfeld.

A young apprentice of mine has some information about the stone. He said that though he had not seen a substance quite as described (and it was difficult to describe it fully without the specimen) he believed he had heard that unusual items are often smuggled into the country among similar products, without complying with Vispasian law. The smugglers, however, are known to work closely with one company only. That company goes by the name of Naval Exports, and their 'loss rate' is said to be unusually high. This company can be found at the city docks.

I trust this is of some use.

Vallamon.

'Naval Exports,' I muttered. A company registered in the name of Grendor of the Cape. This was promising indeed.

'You mentioned there were two things?' I said.

'Yes.' Nambu hesitated.

'Go on.'

'Another body has been found.'

I pushed myself upright, ignoring the pain that flared across my torso. 'Who?'

'A woman this time. I don't know all the details, Sulma Tan has them. She said I shouldn't tell you until tomorrow because you needed to rest, but seeing as you're awake you should at least know about it.'

'Absolutely I should.' I eased my legs over the side and gently lowered myself onto the floor. The entire movement felt like I was trying to remember how to stand for the very first time. Eyes scrunched in agony, I used the bed for leverage. Looking up properly, I headed across the room towards the table, on which my boots and the rest of my clothes were piled.

'Do you need help putting those on?' Leana gestured to a clean shirt and cloak. My Sun Chamber brooch, a little dented by my beating, lay on top.

'If it isn't too much trouble,' I said.

'First I save your life,' she said, getting out of her chair. 'Then I must dress you.'

'I notice you don't seem quite as concerned as the others do about the fact that I have to heal,' I commented. 'Aren't you going to try to stop me as well?'

Leana shrugged. 'You have been lying around long enough. We have much to do.'

Innocent

Sulma Tan looked up from her desk as we entered. Her chamber was large, thirty-foot square, lined with polished wooden shelves. On them stood various objects of art, a scattering of scrolls and ledgers. An opaque, yellow-glass skylight above permitted daylight into the room, directly onto her desk, which faced the door. She was dressed casually in a simple white shirt, and with her dark hair pinned up. Her skin glimmered in the gentle light.

She immediately stood and came to greet us. I shambled towards her, with Leana's support.

'You should be resting but now you want to know who the victim is?'

'If you wouldn't mind,' I replied.

'Who told you?'

I tilted my head towards Nambu.

Sulma Tan brought over a small stool, and one other chair. 'Please, Princess, take my seat – it has more cushioning.'

As if this was as common an occurrence between the two as a greeting, Nambu walked around to the other side of the desk and sat down. Leana took the stool while Sulma Tan insisted I took the chair, and guided me gently to it.

'You haven't recovered properly,' she told me.

'You almost sound concerned for me,' I said, as I eased myself down, cringing under the strain on my torso. The agony soon became a gentle, manageable throb.

'It is of interest to this nation that you are well,' she said, after some consideration. She stepped around the side of the desk, searching for something on her shelves.

'I'm sure it is,' I replied.

She turned to face me, her gaze almost disabling me with its intensity. Her words came softly. 'Besides, you have a good heart, and there are too few people around with good hearts. It would be a shame to lose another.'

I didn't know what to make of this sudden display of kindness, so decided it was best to get straight to business. 'What can you tell me of the third victim?'

She glanced across to Nambu, hesitating, processing.

'It's all right,' I said. 'She's under our protection, so she'll do what we do, and hear what we hear. She's proving to be rather useful.'

There was a pause, then, though not an awkward one for me. It must have been strange for Sulma Tan to see someone speak so casually of her nation's princess.

She eventually continued. 'The victim, Lydia Marinus, was a lady in her fifties. For generations her family have owned large tracts of land along the coast, as well as salt mines further inland. I wouldn't say she was a public figure in the same way that Tahn Valin and Grendor were – she was content to live a quiet life. Her body is with us, and is to be inspected later by Carlon.'

'Are the wounds the same as the others?' I asked.

'She had been tortured, yes,' Sulma Tan said. 'There has been no dismemberment, but her body shares the characteristic small wounds as the two men.'

'Where was her body found?'

'It had been dumped in the street near one of the markets. Another busy place.'

'She lived in the city?'

'Not for the most part. She had a dwelling within this prefecture, but a much larger residence nearer the coast. That was where she spent most of her time.'

'We have another body deliberately left for the world to see,' I said. 'Has anyone looked into it so far?'

'Not yet. But there's more. There was a note with the body, addressed to you. We opened it.'

'Addressed to *me*?'

Sulma Tan opened up a book in which she'd stored the note to keep it protected. It was a small folded piece of paper, tied with string. She handed it over. 'As I say, this was attached to the victim.'

The note was grubby, though not stained with blood, and it was written on the cheapest type of parchment, which one might find anywhere. The handwriting was considered, and in capitals. DRAKENFELD was emblazoned on the top.

I opened the note, assuming the others had already read the message. It said simply:

REMEMBR, OFICER DRAKENFELD.
WE ARE INNOCENT.

We. Plural. More than one killer. A team of people, perhaps, or just a pair. Deliberate misspellings, maybe, or the results of partial education. Indeed, most people in a city could not write at all, so that indicated a level of sophistication consistent with someone who lived in this prefecture.

I tried to pick apart the meaning behind it. On the assumption it was written from the viewpoint of the murderers, it implied – with them being innocent – that they were attempting to *justify* what they had done. But then again, it could have been written on behalf of the victims. That they were innocent people, who had no reason to die. Or that it was an attempt to throw me off the scent entirely.

A more disturbing realization was not simply that whoever did this *knew* who I was, for a good deal of the court already knew. But that they knew I'd get to see the next victim – and had transformed it into a public spectacle, with me in the front row of the audience.

I revealed my thoughts to the others, before adding, 'And this note was definitely *attached* to the body of the corpse?'

'Tied to the collar of the victim,' Sulma Tan replied. 'Does it prompt any thoughts?'

'It prompts thoughts, all right,' I replied. 'But are any of them helpful? Probably not. It's vague enough to give nothing away from their point of view – other than the fact that we're not dealing with a single murderer. Then again, committing such crimes alone would have been very difficult. No, this note is the worst kind: cryptic, with no hard evidence, confession or lead. It can keep a mind bubbling over for days as a distraction. That might even have been the aim of it.'

'You have had notes like this in other cases, yes?' Sulma Tan enquired.

'Not all that many, but a couple. None of which were very helpful.'

A silence lingered, while I still looked at the note, each of us considering our own thoughts.

Eventually it was Sulma Tan who spoke: 'Leana gave me an update on what else you'd managed to find out before your attack, and I am impressed. Do you have anything else to add to those matters?'

As much for my own benefit as Sulma Tan's, we quickly went over the previous discoveries. I even mentioned the letter that the jeweller had just sent. As I spoke she moved over to examine a ledger on one of her shelves.

When I finished I asked, 'What have you got there?'

'I'm examining a list of our major importers and their goods . . .' She paused as if following a hunch. 'No, nothing. I had hoped we would have records. However, I do have an address for Naval Exports, which you may find useful.' Smiling, she made a quick copy of it and handed it over.

'Thank you,' I replied. 'Did you ever make a list of places where these people could have been tortured?'

Sulma Tan regarded me with a tired glance. 'Yes, yes, of course. However, such a request is ultimately futile – there are hundreds of buildings with workshops attached to them – this city is built upon such crafts as leather-working, tanneries, butchers to handle the meat, and so on. The more I looked, the more I found. That is, of course, if you limit yourself to merely workshops. Any room could be suitable for such grim deeds.'

'What about the list of people who are worth more detailed research?'

'There are seven hundred and forty-six people who are of a class you seek and who are of those trades you suspect interact with the victims.'

'Ah.'

'My sentiment was similar.'

'Do many individuals stand out as potential suspects?'

Sulma Tan gave a shake of her head.

'Do you think, from those names, there are some whose business connects with both the military and religion, or religion and trade?'

'I can whittle down the list, if you think it is necessary?'

'I do,' I said. 'Is the map coming along OK as well?'

Sulma Tan nodded. 'On it I have begun to plot locations of murders and those fitting the class profile within the prefecture.'

'And then we can search these places.'

'I will enlist good soldiers,' she added, 'ones I can trust.'

I resisted the opportunity to make known my opinion of the nation's soldiers, given my recent beating. 'But now, we still have much to do.' I pushed myself up, pressing my eyes shut as pain shot through my body.

'You should take things gently,' Sulma Tan said. 'You are no good to anyone if you're injured, am I correct?'

'If I should do anything,' I said, smiling, 'it will be to inspect the body.'

'Can I come?' Nambu asked.

'You think you can stomach the dead, young lady?' I replied.

She nodded, but I wasn't so sure. There was only one way to find out.

'Lead the way then,' I said to Sulma Tan.

As I made to move I stumbled; she dashed to my side and levered my arm around her shoulder. 'It seems I have little choice but to lead, unless you wish to crawl there.' .

'I have no desire for that,' I replied.

Lydia Marinus

Fifty-six years ago Lydia Marinus entered the world in my home city of Tryum, Detrata, born to an extremely wealthy family. When she was ten her father died suddenly and she moved to Koton with her mother. Her mother remarried quickly, linking the family company with the owner of a Kotonese salt mine. Their company grew and, thanks to the growing strength of the Vispasian Royal Union, trade flourished. They were able to make huge amounts of money in both Detrata and Koton, using old and new connections. Her mother died and, with no other siblings, the family business came to Lydia.

Tragedy struck again: when she was thirty Lydia's husband was killed in a riding accident. She did not remarry and with no children was more interested in her work. She set about building the biggest corporate empire in Koton, and one of the largest in the Vispasian Royal Union. Unlike most people with such status, however, she was not one for social gatherings and tended to lock herself away in her country property. She paid her taxes to the state of Koton regularly, always early, and always more than was expected. 'When someone makes as much money as I do,' she was said to have once announced, 'it all becomes rather abstract.'

And now her life had ended, Sulma Tan concluded, in the most brutal fashion. If there had been a family curse, it had been thorough.

Sulma Tan explained that Lydia's will would have to be examined to see who would benefit from her business empire. It was not likely to be someone desperate for an inheritance. As she had been generous with her money while she was alive, it was probable that she wouldn't have left anyone in the family in financial trouble.

Lydia Marinus' body was laid out in the same chamber where we inspected the other two corpses. She had been prepared: her skin cleaned, her clothing removed, and left with only a thin sheet covering her body. The hundreds of lacerations were painfully obvious. A thick red wound curved across her neck where the knife had ended her life. She was tall, slender, with youthful looks for her age, and brown hair that showed only a few strands of grey.

Her arm slipped off the side of the slab as if of its own accord and hung down to one side at a shallow angle.

Sulma Tan gasped. Even my heart skipped a beat, but I walked over and placed her arm firmly back in position, noting the stiffness of death had long since set in.

'Nothing out of the ordinary,' I reassured her.

Sulma Tan did not reply. Clearly convinced the body possessed strange properties in the same way as the bishop, she could not even make eye contact with me.

'Where was her body found?' I asked.

'A street that leads away from the marketplace.' Sulma Tan sighed and shook herself from dark thoughts. 'As it happens very near Grendor's house. It was in full view for everyone to see. Again without anyone actually seeing the body being brought there, which must have happened in the early hours of the morning.'

'You interviewed neighbours?'

'We disturbed every one of them from their slumber.'

'Good,' I replied. 'Was there anything with the body?'

'Only her clothes, and when we peeled them back we could see . . . well, the same cruel acts had been carried out.'

Carlon hadn't arrived yet, but Sulma Tan reminded me that the biggest difference between her death and Grendor's was the fact that her throat was cut. With the bishop's head being severed, it could not be said if that had been the act that killed him. She had suffered the same numerous cuts to her body as the others – hundreds of tiny wounds, including her eyes being stabbed. Her tongue had also been removed.

'Again, it is all very ritualistic.'

'Yes. The number of bruises present,' Sulma Tan concluded, 'suggest that she put up a fight.'

She looked at me for the first time with something resembling fear. Who could blame her? Three high-profile individuals had been killed in similar ways.

'What did Carlon have to say about it?' I asked.

'He concludes the obvious really – we're looking for the same killer, someone who has been tracking down individuals with one simple plan: to make them suffer immensely before killing them. Interestingly, he also theorizes that her mood was calm and relaxed – sanguine at the point of death. This is comfort, of a kind.'

'I know little of medicine but I suspect that comfort suggests she might have known her killers?'

'He has many theories,' Sulma Tan said. 'I don't know how much we can invest in this one.' There was a tiredness in her eyes now, raw compassion and humanity showing through her countenance.

Processing the sight before us, I could only agree with Carlon

– it was even more likely we were dealing with the same murderer, though I never liked to commit to a conclusion.

'Such incidents are rare across Vispasia,' I ventured. 'Those who strike more than once are usually paid killers, and like to make their kills cleanly and efficiently so as not to be caught. This is something different. The death is so inefficient, if you follow. The murderer had time.'

'And knowledge of the movements of the wealthy,' Sulma Tan added.

'Our killer's profile remains consistent at least,' I suggested. 'Access to higher circles. The luxury of time to commit atrocious acts. The care never to be seen by anyone nearby, which implies a rigorous plan in place . . .'

'A darker power at work, am I correct?'

I could only shrug.

REMEMBR, OFICER DRAKENFELD, the note had said. WE ARE INNOCENT.

Nambu stepped in beside Sulma Tan, looking over the body, her face catching the light of the nearby lanterns.

'And what does the Princess Nambu Sorghatan have to say for herself?' I asked, limping as I stepped alongside her.

'I don't know what to say.' Nambu's gaze drifted across the corpse. The expression on her face reminded me of when I was very young, looking at my mother's body laid out in a temple. My father then had encouraged me to touch her beautiful, dead face. And I did. I most recall the surprise at how cold her skin had become. Now I had grown used to such things, but that initial sensation brought home the fragility of life.

'Touch her skin,' I said to Nambu, and the princess did.

She snatched her hand away. 'It's so cold. She doesn't look *real*.'

'It's how we'll all end up,' I said. 'Well, hopefully not quite in this state.'

'How can you all talk about her so casually?' Nambu asked. 'She was a real person not so long ago.'

She had a point, though I didn't believe we were being disrespectful. 'In our business, one becomes familiar with the dead.'

'I've never really thought about dying,' Nambu muttered.

'You don't at such a young age, do you? The whole world extends before you – the options seem endless. Dying isn't really much of a concern.'

'I hope it comes quickly,' she said.

'You hope what does?'

'Death,' she replied. 'I hope mine comes quickly. I would not want too long to think about it.' Nambu stepped away – not out of fear, or upset, but because she had seen enough – and stood beside Leana, who remained as indifferent to the subject as always, in a way that I envied.

In the lingering silence, Sulma Tan took my arm and steered me into a corner of the room. 'People are now truly worried, Officer Drakenfeld,' she whispered.

'Lucan.'

She nodded. 'They've got a name for whoever did this. They're calling him the Koton Cutter.'

'They shouldn't attach a name to this individual. It creates a myth around them. Whoever did this could well be fuelled by their own success. We're dealing with a strange mind here, which doesn't need any more encouragement.'

'Well, you try persuading the masses then. They are uncontrollable.'

And I had few doubts that they had tried to do so ... 'I appreciate that wouldn't exactly be easy. Crowds behave differently in such situations. They have a mind of their own.'

'That is why the prefecture has now been locked down,' she

said. 'The gates are sealed and there are regular – and I mean almost all the time – military patrols.'

'What?'

'What else can the queen do?' she continued. 'She must be seen to act. This is about stilling the populace. Calming them.'

A pause, and she looked directly at me. 'Do you think there will be more victims, despite these measures?'

I eyed the corpse again. 'Without a doubt. To know such wealthy people, to then remove them from their premises or place of work, I'd say the killer's well and truly inside the prefecture.'

'Then we had better go to my offices,' Sulma Tan replied. 'I have procured for you the map you required and now we have another body to plot on it.'

A Cartography of Murder

It was an impressive piece of work, far beyond what I had asked for. Made from different rolls of parchment and affixed to the wall, the map was several feet wide. I could walk up and down the city in four steps. Sulma Tan explained that she had it commissioned as soon as I had asked for it, and that the city's foremost cartographers had come together, to scale up existing maps as accurately as possible. She was proud of her work and smiled at me as I marvelled at the detail.

'Naval Exports, Grendor's business premises, are here.' She leaned over the corner at the far end of the map, where the prefecture changed its rigid lines to meet the informality of the natural river.

My respect went further, as Sulma Tan had marked in red ink the location of the victims' dwellings. Where bodies had been found she marked with an 'X'. Then, in much smaller blue circles, she had plotted the location of several hundred people who had completed the census and matched the kinds of trades I thought might be of interest.

It was where my optimism came to a halt. There were so many people who fitted the profile of the killer, and there were no discernible patterns in their location. Though the murders were in the same prefecture, with allowances made for the bishop's dismembered body, they were far apart – potentially a mile or so. Their houses were not close to each other either. If I was going to force a solution from these details, it would not be easy.

'What does it take to murder someone?' There was an air of general curiosity about Sulma Tan's question, and it was not asked with intent. As if she wanted to expand her horizons.

'Money. Or status perhaps. A wish to gain more power or land, and a certain individual stands in the way of that wish.'

'So much desperation to climb life's ladders that the only solution was to have another's throat cut . . .'

'It is the way of things, I'm afraid. Rage is another factor. A fight that gets out of hand – too much alcohol with a sword close by. Sadly I'd seen too many men kill in their own homes, too – poor women cut down for senseless reasons by individuals who'd lost control, who were part of a culture that chose to ignore such brutality. Friends could fall out over a loved one and a casualty would result from the competition. Slipping poison in a husband's dinner to rid a family of a tyrant . . . I could go on.'

'Human emotions are fragile,' she replied. 'It is something I forget in my work. At times a whole society becomes numbers and columns on parchment. Or,' she gestured to the map, 'coloured markings.'

'Human emotions are why murders are commonplace. Though I must add that I have described *normal* murders. Normal people could commit them. Normal people could find themselves with blood on their hands. That does not forgive the crime, of course, but I've worked on hundreds of such cases and they are an every-day occurrence. But here we are dealing with something entirely different. Someone who makes a *ritual* out of the killing. We must ask ourselves: who would spend their time torturing not one but three bodies in such a way? And yet, it pays to remember that these victims have not been buried or hidden away. There's a certain confidence and almost pride in the placing of them. I suspect we are looking for someone who is not poor, who is educated, who has access to the routines of very influential people. They can kill these people and then leave their bodies in public, without themselves being seen.'

'It sounds as if these are very personal motivations,' Sulma Tan put forward.

'The murders *were* very personal,' I agreed. 'Whose clan were they aligned to?'

'None — save the Sorghatan family. But the clans do not engage in this kind of behaviour.'

'Well, it's certain this is no mere grudge over some spilt ale. From my experience ritual murders suggest a few things: cult sacrifices, revenge for a truly hideous deed — or a killer who enjoys their work and makes a game out of it.'

She frowned. 'There is nothing here I've seen that corresponds with religious rituals or cults, even in our own dark past. We have not seen strange symbols or offerings near the victims, am I correct?'

Rubbing my chin I glanced across the markings on the map once again, entranced by just how many there were. A breeze passed through the building, making the candles and the edges of the parchment flutter. 'Well that leaves the other options. How about revenge? Revenge for an unknown reason against some of the most powerful people.'

'It will be important to look into their affairs in more detail. There must be common ground. Where their lives intersect, we will find the reasons for the murders.'

'A bishop, a naval officer and a businesswoman,' Sulma Tan said. 'To my knowledge — and I can use the queen's diaries as reference – they had little interaction with each other at the palace. How had their lives crossed over?'

'They were all of similar age,' I suggested. 'They were all up-standing members of society. Unless the bishop has been quietly hiding a fortune, only two were wealthy. Grendor and Bishop Tahn Valin owned similar-looking stones, but there was no sign of such a gem with Lydia's belongings. But it is possible that these virtuous members of the Kotonese community were not as honourable as their image suggested . . .'

I left the question there for Sulma Tan to answer, but if she harboured secrets, she did not reveal them. In the ensuing silence I pinned the note from Lydia's body alongside the map.

REMEMBR, OFICER DRAKENFELD, WE ARE INNOCENT.

'Thank you for this arrangement,' I said to Sulma Tan, gestur-ing to her admirable work.

'So long as it helps. I trust it does?'

'Oh absolutely, yes.' I wasn't quite so sure about my answer though. Despite the census information, there were too many blue circles on the map. The killer, provided they were of the type I had imagined, could have been any one of several hundred people, and that excluded the hundreds of soldiers patrolling the prefecture.

These thoughts followed me as I returned down the corridor, back to my quarters. Cressets lined the way to the chamber. When I entered, I found Leana crawling on her knees in the semi-darkness but with a blindfold across her eyes.

'What are you doing, Leana?'

Leana stood up from the foot of the couch and brushed herself down. 'I am finding my way around this room without sight. We have no natural light. If all the candles go out, we will need to know our way around.'

'It pays to be prepared, I suppose.' I lay back down again as a throb of pain shot along my ribs. 'I never thanked you by the way.'

Leana continued to prod and touch her way around the room. 'For what?'

'Saving me. Again.'

'It is useful – such incidents allow me to refine my skills. Besides, you do not mind me killing people when it is to save your life and when you are unconscious you cannot warn me off. There is pleasure to be found in such work when you are not there on your high horse.'

'Glad I can be of help,' I muttered. 'Is Nambu all right on her own?'

'She is. I have been teaching her the basics of defence, and she has learned well.' Leana's countenance displayed pride, if only for a brief moment. 'She is a bright and attentive pupil and less of a liability than when we first met her. Of course, she complains of aches and pains from using muscles she did not know she had. This is to be expected. We progressed greatly during all that time you were lying around.'

'You know, I was actually recovering from life-threatening injuries, not merely lounging about like a decadent king.'

'Spirits save us. You were not exactly *active*, though,' Leana replied, tapping the floor with her hand.

'I'll give you that.' I smiled as she struck her knee on a table leg. 'But with Nambu, I really meant is she all right after the incidents earlier – after seeing a corpse for the first time? I'm not sure this is part of our "look after the princess" duties, but if she's going to be in our company, it is unavoidable.'

'She is a little put out by the body, admittedly, but it is important that she sees such things. There is no point shying away from them. Though it would be best if we did not tell her mother we are showing her dead bodies.'

I exhaled a gentle laugh, but it hurt to do so. 'A wise decision.'

Naval Exports

The purple sky was brightening to pink. A gentle, mild breeze rolled in from the south, bringing with it woodsmoke from the rest of the city. After a few days and nights of no rain, the prefecture's streets appeared to have changed colour – the stone becoming considerably paler, the mud sandier, and the place more attractive. My good mood was heightened by the fact that I was no longer limping from my injuries.

A couple of vendors were out selling food, but I couldn't understand why so few people were about.

'The place seems unusually quiet,' I remarked.

'People are scared,' Leana replied.

'Why?' Nambu asked, stifling a yawn.

'They are your people,' Leana said. 'Do you not know them? If you do not know them, how can you lead them?'

For me, Leana's comments were now in the context of knowing that she had once been destined to lead a nation. Nambu didn't seem to be put off by her stern words. In the few days I had been unconscious a new level of respect had grown between the two.

We continued through the empty lanes and decided to eat some street food for breakfast. Nambu said she wasn't hungry.

While Leana and I chewed on our flatbreads, a unit of a dozen soldiers marched past us in green and white, their bows slung across their shoulders.

Without expression or comment Nambu turned to watch them as they proceeded down the street. It couldn't have been more than a minute before we saw another unit marching by at the top of the road, turning into the distance.

'Well, I certainly feel safer,' I muttered. 'Don't you feel safer, Leana?'

'The killer will most definitely not strike again with soldiers rattling through the streets,' she replied dryly. 'After all, how could they concentrate with that noise?'

We went through the gates of the prefecture and around the main wall, a region with an entirely different atmosphere. Hundreds of people filled the uneven roads. Woodsmoke drifted up out of ramshackle buildings. To one side, a priest in a green cloak, bearing the symbol of a bull, brought a knife across the throat of a goat. He spilled its blood into the outstretched hands of his faithful, who knelt on the floor in front of him.

'Nambu, this hasn't anything to do with Astran and Nastra, has it?'

'No. That is the Cult of Hymound.' She gave a laugh of disbelief. 'That priest is mad to be doing that sort of thing so close to the Sorghatan Prefecture. Mother hates the cult. She hates all the old gods. Look how savage they are – the people are drinking blood!'

The people who knelt before the body of the goat brought their cupped hands to their lips as the priest gibbered in a much older form of Kotonese.

'Who is Hymound?'

'I do not know much, because it is forbidden to teach his ways, but his other name is the King of the Multitudes. Our people worshipped him when we roamed the plains. Well, when we roamed them a thousand years ago. He has a small but stubborn following.'

The priest fell to his knees and plunged his fingers into the open wound in the animal. Before long the act became obscured by the crowds.

'It frustrates Mother that she cannot reform out here as quickly as in the Sorghatan Prefecture,' Nambu continued. 'She wants to help people get better, eat better and live better. She wants them to have the same luxuries and rights as those in the Sorghatan Prefecture.'

'It cannot happen overnight,' I offered.

And indeed it had not in this part of the city. Everything was a shade more drab. The colour of the other prefecture had gone, and instead crude, dirtied furs and cheap leather were all around us. The decay of rotten fish and stench of manure was intense to the point of being overwhelming. In little passageways between wooden buildings and tents, men sat half-naked in the warm light insulting passers-by. Many of them wore animal horns around their necks. Weird, brutal-looking implements were strung up from windows. The main thoroughfares were packed, however, with people going about their business as best they could. I was almost certain we would not find the murderer among them. The killer was probably behind us, in the other prefecture, but for now our investigation carried us elsewhere.

It took us the better part of an hour to reach the dockyard walking down from the Kuvash Prefecture.

The dockyard was like a whole new city. Nestled along a wide, serpentine river, which went round part of the Sorghatan Prefecture, was a vibrant community. From the white walls separating the two prefectures, large and gleaming in the morning sun, the city descended gently, and then very suddenly down to the river. Shacks, timber houses, precarious constructions – only a few of which were crafted from stone – stretched as far as the eye could see. Long grasses stirred in the breeze. The river looped back and forth across the landscape, widening towards the sea, which stood as a thin grey-blue line on the horizon. The smell of marine food and dubious vegetation was intense and, combined with woodsmoke, horse-shit and the tang from a tannery, it made for an assault on the senses. Though there were hundreds of boats of all types in the river, people still managed to find gaps to wash themselves or their clothing – or to pour dubious-looking fluids away into the water.

'What is it that you're looking for exactly?' Nambu asked, pulling the top hem of her brown cloak around her mouth and nose.

'The office building of Naval Exports,' I replied.

'I know that. I mean when we get there.'

'If we are to investigate the affairs of Grendor of the Cape, then his offices are bound to give us a clearer picture of his businesses.'

'So . . . what are you hoping to find?'

'I don't know, if I'm honest. We'll have to wait and see. At the moment it is a case of sketching out the lives of those who have been killed, and identifying where there is any overlap.'

'There's a lot of uncertainty in your job, isn't there?'

'Of that, we *can* be certain.'

We passed a large, rectangular building, in notably better condition than the rest of the street, surrounded by a large perimeter fence made from wood. Between the posts I saw dozens of children dressed in rags, running around a courtyard and playing games with pebbles.

'Is that a school?' I asked Nambu.

'No, it's Kuvash's largest orphanage.'

Some of the children came forward to stand at the gates and held their arms out towards us. Only then did I notice how malnourished they were – and just how many had been crammed into this area. I felt a sudden guilt at my own upbringing – a relatively comfortable one, with the exception of my mother's death when I was a few years old. I had everything I needed and more. A stable family, good schooling, wealth and interaction with the higher ranks of Detratan life. And when I contemplated the day I could settle down and raise a family myself, safety and comfort were absolutely what I wanted to offer. That was on the assumption my life would ever get to that stage.

Nambu stood alongside me to regard the children.

'They are the same age as me,' she whispered in reflection.

'The gods have given you a good place in life,' I said. 'The question is, do you realize the fact?'

'I think I do,' she replied. 'I used to watch this place from the walls of the prefecture, from one of the viewing points. I had no idea that they were so . . .' She never finished her sentence.

A farmer called for his two oxen to control themselves, as they lumbered past, nearly knocking Nambu over before trudging on through the dusty streets. He shouted back an apology.

Once the hubbub had died down, we continued on our way.

The business end of the docks, the trading area beyond the long grasses, looked no less decrepit and sprawling than the residential areas. Wood yards, woodworkers and craft stores were doing a roaring business. Merchants wore gaudy costumes. Towards the banks of the river, men were mostly topless, their skin glistening with sweat. Some wore stained, ragged shirts as they hauled cargo aboard the boats.

The ships and boats were of all kinds. Curious figureheads

were fixed to each vessel: quasi-religious figures, dragons, naked men or women, half-human hybrids.

Various types of grain in sacks, wool and leather in bales, were being lugged aboard the ships. Gang-members loitered with little subtlety by some bales, suggesting there was even more precious cargo to be found passing through.

We passed along a line of faded business-fronts, which were as to be expected – little more than cheap wooden shacks with a painted sign to indicate the owner. Most of them featured the names of individuals, and presumably it was those individuals who were standing proudly with their hands in their jacket pockets regarding the workers. Some would shout orders or random insults now and then, before spitting on the ground. Others dozed in the sun.

Naval Exports was a considerably larger structure than the surrounding shacks, and of better quality. Its wooden walls had recently been constructed, or upgraded, and it was the only building to feature wooden shutters that faced out onto the vessels berthed a few yards in front. There was nothing on the sign to indicate that the property belonged to Grendor.

A stubbled young man who looked like he could do with a good meal shoved his head through the open shutters and leered at Nambu. 'What d'you lot want?' he drawled in a particularly coarse form of Kotonese. 'This is a place of work, not somewhere to pro-men-ade your wife.'

Leana grabbed the man by his collar and hauled him out from the other side of the window and onto the wooden decking with a thud. She placed a boot over his neck as he spluttered his apologies. 'I meant no harm, sir – m-madam.'

Leana eventually rolled her boot away and glanced casually at the surrounding labourers, who had stopped working to watch the spectacle. She unsheathed her short sword, but made no threatening gesture with it. It was a simple statement: *get back to work*. I wasn't so sure this lot would get back to work, though. They were huge men, a dozen or more, and many carried machetes. Eventually, after the scrawny man waved them away, they went on with their work.

'They're a lively lot, so you want to watch yer manners. They've killed stronger folk than you, madam.'

Leana remained indifferent to his comments.

The man picked himself up. Garbed in a scruffy white shirt and tattered black waistcoat, he looked far too weak to do any manual work. His eyes were cold, distant and bloodshot. His nose was thin and long, and he had the kind of facial hair that never got past a promising start. An insincere grin widened across his face. 'And how can I help sir and madam.'

'My name is Lucan Drakenfeld, Officer of the Sun Chamber.'

He raised his chin a little, his interest now piqued. 'Oh aye, Sun Chamber you say? Heard of them. Though many round here probably haven't. You're like lawyers, ain't you?'

'Some are, some aren't,' I replied. 'The three of us are here to investigate the murder of Grendor of the Cape. We're on the queen's business, as a matter of fact, so some prompt and honest answers would save us all some valuable time. And maybe even your life.'

'Grendor, eh.' The man rubbed his chin and considered his options. I still couldn't quite place his age – at first he had appeared so young, but on closer inspection his face appeared weathered. He looked like a worrier, too. There was a nervousness about him that was part of his being – the way he'd hunch slightly within himself, the way he'd hold his hands. He oozed subservience.

'You think I killed my boss?' he asked.

'No,' I replied. 'I don't think you've got it in you.'

'Well everyone pisses downwind when it comes to things like

this, don't they? Get some lackey's head on the block. Sign some papers. You walk off and take yer money. Job done.'

'If you didn't kill Grendor, there's no need to be worried about your head being removed,' I replied, ignoring his barbed comments on people of my station. They were probably well founded regarding local officials and those who did not serve in the Sun Chamber. But such an abuse of power would not be tolerated within our ranks.

'Sure. That's what the soldiers say before they rough someone up on the streets to keep order, or whatever their excuses are.' He looked down to the floor then, and back and forth between Leana and Nambu. 'So what can we do for you?'

'I'm here to find out a little more about Grendor's business interests.'

'He never bothered us all that much, if I'm honest. Did more important things than that. Come inside.'

We followed him into the building, which looked as if it doubled up as a warehouse. Crates and sacks filled one side of the single room, while on the other side stood a desk and shelves filled with ledgers. One wall was covered with remarkably detailed maps of the Vispasian continent, and there were more charts piled up on a table in the corner. Food remains sat on metal plates. Partially filled cups were scattered around on tables, chairs, on the floorboards. I noted two bone dice on the floor and could guess what people used these premises after hours.

'Naval Exports,' I said. 'The name sounds very official.'

'Grendor said the same thing when he employed me. Lends us an air of authority, he often said.'

'What's your name?'

'Dek. Dek Sunni.'

'Who do you do business with, Dek?'

'People here and there. We export a lot of animal skins —

leather in various grades for the most part. We ship out from the tanneries and sell along the coast down Venyn way, Gippoli, sometimes west to Detrata. We bring back grain and sell it on to the officials here, who then distribute it. That's where the official name comes in handy. Says we're trustworthy. Reflects Grendor's knowledge.'

'Aside from grain and leather,' I demanded, 'what else do you trade in?'

'We sometimes transport prisoners,' he muttered, his eyes betraying nervousness about discussing the topic. 'We don't do it all that often. Frowned upon, ain't it.'

Quite rightly – that was strange business indeed. 'Where do you take the prisoners?'

He shrugged. 'I'm not a sailor.'

Leana pressed the tip of her blade to his chest.

'Hey, I'm talking,' he spluttered with bulging eyes, 'we don't need torture.'

'It's OK, Leana. We can keep him alive for the moment.'

'I'm not worth killing,' Dek laughed awkwardly, but I didn't answer him – a little gentle pressure would be enough for his type. Sweat was visible on his shirt. As Leana lowered her arm, I walked around to examine the charts, noting the thick ink lines extending outward from the coast of Koton. 'You must know *where* they go.'

'I cross 'em off my list and they're gone, as far as I'm concerned. As I say, don't happen often.'

'What crimes had they committed to be disposed of at sea?' I snapped, assuming the worst. Given the queen's quiet, dictatorial regime, it didn't take much to assume these could have been political dissidents, removed to make her life more simple.

'I don't think they were dumped.' Again a shrug. 'No killings, like. Just human cargo. Same as wool, cloth or metal – something else to go from one country to another, to make a bit of coin.'

'Sounds like slavery to me.'

'Nah. Not legal, is it? Not any more.'

'No it isn't. Since the creation of the Vispasian Royal Union, slaves are not permitted to be taken internally – only from conquered lands abroad.'

'Yeah, well . . . It don't always work to plan, does it?' Dek scratched the back of his head. 'Besides, one of the first things the queen did when she became queen was to put a stop to all that business.'

'Dek, we're going to need to go through your books.' I indicated the shelves behind.

'Feel free. They're in order. I don't look like I'm bright, but I stay on top of the books. Grendor demanded efficiency.'

While my hand was in my pocket, I placed the ring of the bishop upon my middle finger and held it out towards the man. 'Recognize a stone like this?'

I saw the flicker of recognition in his eyes. He couldn't hide it. Now it was a question of whether he'd deny it or not.

'Aye, something like that,' he said eventually, much quieter now, much more unsure of himself. 'Not that I should have.'

'Go on.' I stood behind the desk now.

'Let me close the shutters. You never know who's listening in.' Outside stood five of the more menacing crew members, each looking in. One by one he closed the shutters, leaving only thin strips of light across the floorboards. One of which, I noticed, was loose.

When Dek returned he said, 'See, sometimes I catch things I'm not meant to see. It happens when I'm here all the time. Though I keep the books in shape, it ain't easy. Grendor don't mind turning a blind eye to the odd passenger that wants ferrying

discreetly out of the country, or to let in a few amphorae of wine
that's been siphoned off of some country duke. Things like that
happen all the time.'

'But gemstones?'

'We deal with the odd trinket, aye. We don't label them on the
books as such, because they're not really to be declared for tax
reasons, eh? You know how it is.'

My impatience was growing. 'So to be clear, you've definitely
seen a stone like this. Not another colour. This precise shade of
red.'

'Seen two come in, in small cases. To say they're rare don't do
'em justice.'

'Where do they come from?'

'No one knows. That's to say, a ship pulls alongside ours out
at sea and sometimes things like this come onto ours.'

The door snapped open suddenly and there were a couple
of bulky workers silhouetted in the doorway. Two more stood
behind them, their blades hidden discreetly. It was difficult to
discern their expressions, but it was a safe enough guess that they
didn't like people they did not recognize being here. 'You got
trouble, Dek?' one of them grunted.

He hesitated. 'Nah, nah – just potential business.' Then he
peered at me. 'We got no trouble, right?'

'Just business,' I said.

'Hmm.' They remained there for a few moments longer before
shuffling away again. Dek strolled towards the door and closed
it quietly. At that point I knew it wouldn't be wise to check the
loose floorboard just yet. If it was a place to keep secrets, Dek
would immediately shout for help.

'The ships,' I continued, 'where the exchange happens. Where
do these ships meet? Who sails the other vessels?'

'It varies, honestly.' He sighed. 'I'm not even supposed to know this much. Can tell you that it's happened twice since I've worked here, and that's been ten years this summer.'

'And how did you of all people see the gemstone? One suspects these little cases of highly precious stones are not left sitting open.'

'Definitely not. First time was during an accident and a load of cargo fell off the pulley. Second time was when the man carrying the case on board got in a fight with one of the other sailors.' Dek paused and smirked. 'That one didn't last long. Disappeared on the very next mission. Fell overboard, so they say. Too much to drink.'

'And you're certain it was the same type of stone.'

'Not *certain*, no, but pretty sure. Could've been a ruby I guess, but why go to all that trouble? Rubies get imported all the time on much better protected ships. Gangs get involved in that sort of thing. Messy business at times, bodies dumped in the river and the likes, but they get the job done effectively.'

We spent a good hour or two examining the ledgers and patrolling the property, all under the watchful eye of Dek and two of his well-built associates.

I inspected one of the ships that had been supplying grain, a large vessel that had only been sailing a year, and enquired with the captain about his routes and whether or not he had spent time with Grendor. The captain, who possessed a permanently philosophical gaze, told me that he had never met the famous Grendor of the Cape, though he would have liked to have shared a cup of wine with him.

'From what some of the other captains say, he was a good man. An honest man. Liked hard workers, and rewarded the best. Didn't stand for a bad culture, like some of the other owners round here. They'd see you sleeping on a bed of rats if it meant saving coin. Let their ships rot to the core, and they end up in trouble out at sea. Employ folk who haven't got a clue about reading the sea.'

The routes he described were nothing out of the ordinary. The names of destinations were nearly all large ports with a few fishing settlements around the local coast. There was a surprising amount of weaponry on board – swords, maces, bows and so forth – and when I enquired about them he told me of the piracy problems that plagued trade routes.

Dek, meanwhile, never left the office, and made a point of telling us so. He kept one eye on Leana and Nambu as they inspected his books. True to his word he had done a good job of maintaining a balance sheet. The goods he described to us were also present in ink – prisoners and dubious goods being omitted, of course. Grendor had, by and large, conducted exactly the kind of business I would expect: a fair and honest company, with a few unscrupulous side projects. I was inclined to believe most of what Dek had been saying.

It appeared as if Grendor was indeed the man who everyone said he was. The picture I had of him in my head transpired to be true here. Again it begged the question: why had such a good man been killed?

'Come over here,' Leana said. 'Look.' Her finger pointed to a page in one of the ledgers.

The line indicated regular exports for one 'L. Marinus' – Lydia, most probably, given that it was for salt. Every month a ship sailed to Detrata on behalf of the recently deceased.

Before we left, I asked Dek, 'Who's going to take over now he's dead?'

Dek shrugged. 'Haven't a clue. His wife presumably. Only saw her the once – lovely lass. Good kids. Can't see her selling up anytime soon – we make far too much coin for that.'

With that, we walked back towards the Kuvash Prefecture, in relative silence. That suited me fine as I was contemplating the day's discoveries. Once again I was waiting to discern the patterns, re-examining just what I'd seen.

'What next?' Nambu asked eventually.

'We go back after dark.'

'What?' Nambu said. 'Why would we want to do that?'

'There was a loose floorboard in that office that I never got a chance to look under. Dek never left the room during his questioning and he had men on standby, so that could indicate there's something important in that office. But I didn't want to create a scene with his machete-wielding workers around. I'm not yet in shape for a fight and we certainly don't want to get you involved in one.'

'Spirits save us. So we simply break in after dark and take whatever is under that floorboard?'

'Do you have a better plan?' I asked.

A Quiet Tavern

We waited in a quiet tavern on the edges of the docks. It was a stone building with a huge open fire at the centre. Several rooms sprawled out from it, some with discreet antechambers and rooms barely bigger than a cupboard. If ever there was to be a surreptitious meeting between agents, this would be the ideal place, and I speculated on the kind of conversations taking place around us.

Save for the curious antiquated maritime trinkets plastered across one of the walls, the place was not all that interesting. There were no fine frescos. The food appeared to be hearty, if a little simple, but it was enough to please Leana and myself. Though I was not so sure the princess felt the same. We took a table in an alcove while we waited for the sun to set, casually watching the tavern gradually fill up with customers who had finished a day's work. The odour of fish, dirt and sweat soon became heady.

Whoever had been tracking us previously, assuming they were unrelated to the incident with the arrow, appeared to have left us alone. During the day there had been no one following us, no uneasy glances from the shadows. Since no one in here was eyeing us up, at last we could relax. My aches from the morning had eased considerably, making my recovery very nearly complete, and I speculated again whether or not the ring had strange properties.

A young boy brought over our food and we tucked in. My fish-based broth wasn't going to possess any magical healing powers, but I ate eagerly nonetheless.

'Have you ever eaten in a place like this?' Leana asked Nambu, who looked distinctly uncomfortable. The young girl was pushing food around her metal plate and she sniffed every morsel, uncertain of its safety – or perhaps unsure of what it was meant to be. No doubt this was a change from the usual sumptuous meals served in the palace.

'If I am honest, no,' Nambu muttered, putting down her fork and instead seeming more interested in the people coming into the tavern.

'Relax,' Leana said. 'You will be fine. These are honest people. They are not here to bother you. They wish to eat and drink after a day of labour.'

'I know, it's just . . . I eat a lot of my sit-down meals in private, with the exception of banquets.'

'Then welcome to the rest of the world.' Continuing in a soft tone, I said, 'Imagine what it is like for the others – many of them will have to go home to crowded houses, sleeping four to a room and having to urinate in a bucket. This is luxury to them. Now, you should probably eat your food. We cannot have your mother accusing us of starving you.'

Nambu began to eat and soon began to devour the rest.

After a while I asked her, 'Nambu, you can trust the two of us now, can't you?'

'I believe I can, yes,' she replied. 'So much as anyone can be trusted.'

A cryptic answer for one so young. It sounded like words

inherited from her mother. 'Tell me, truthfully. Why does the queen want you out of the palace?'

'She wants me *protected*,' Nambu stressed. 'There was an attack on me. She wants me safe.'

'That's only part of it,' I replied. 'She could have you protected in any number of ways. She could lock you up. She could surround you by guards.'

'She's already done that before and that did not exactly work out too well.'

'Well,' I continued, 'she's hoping we *outsiders* will take you out of the royal court. Out of your usual routines. Why would she do that? Why would she want someone she hardly knows — though admittedly someone she can trust — to look after you, to keep you away from the court, to take you from her side?'

Nambu shrugged. 'We don't especially get on.'

'Rare are the youth and parent who do. Why else?'

'So she can carry on with her lovers.'

'She has a room for that. By Polla, we're living in those quarters now. Why else?'

'Her paranoia? I don't know. Maybe she's practising wrestling for the Kotonese Games.'

Smiling, I shook my head and leaned forward, taking a chunk of bread and dipping it in my soup. After I'd finished my mouthful, I continued. 'She's worried someone's likely to get to you, but from the court — someone *within* her inner circle. That's why she wants us — outsiders — to keep you out of there. She doesn't mind, after all, that we take you to some of the more questionable parts of the city, which are hardly the safest places in the world. So, who could she want to keep you away from?'

Nambu remained engrossed in her food. 'I know only a fraction of what she gets up to.'

'Are you worried?'

She regarded me with her bold blue eyes. 'Why should I be?'

'I guess you really aren't worried then.'

'Besides,' she continued, 'Leana has taught me the basics of swordplay. I will soon be able to defend myself.'

Maybe Nambu didn't even know herself why her mother would want her out of the way. From what little I'd seen of their relationship, it looked to me as if there was a strong bond between mother and daughter – if a little stiff and formal. So I didn't think it was merely out of spite, or simply wanting to keep her away, that Nambu had been placed with us.

I sat back casually, placing my arm around the chair next to me. 'Depending on how things go tonight, tomorrow I think it'll help us all if we split up to cover more ground. Since I've been out of action for a couple of days, I need you both to help me speed up this investigation. I'd like you two to visit Grendor's friends – the ones he was dining with on the night of his murder. Sulma Tan has provided their names.'

'And if they will not speak to me?' Leana said. 'You know how people can be.'

Nambu appeared confused, but I knew perfectly well what Leana meant: that they would not speak to her because of the dark hue of her skin, or for being a woman, or because she did not possess a certain rank in their society. 'I'm sure friends of Grendor will oblige if you show them something bearing the queen's seal. Here.' I reached into my pocket and handed over royal parchment, which featured a raised stag set within a crown.

'Ah, I see,' Leana replied, accepting the note. 'Though, spirits save me, I am not good at the questioning. That is your job.'

'You've coped all right before,' I replied.

'I am too quick to use the blade.'

'Then use it if you need to – just try not to kill anyone.'

'How many times have I heard you say that?'

'How many times have you ignored me?' I replied.

Leana lifted a heavy boot onto a stool and set about readjusting the laces. 'What will you want us to ask?'

'We need to know what was discussed, what he was like on the night, what he was shipping, anything notable he said. Ask them about his dealings with Naval Exports. See if you can establish links between Grendor and the other two victims. Find out more about Grendor's time in the navy, even. Perhaps the key to solving this mystery doesn't so much lie in the present as in the past.'

'Yet, if they had done something bad in the past,' Leana said, 'neither Grendor nor this bishop behaved in a way that said they were keeping themselves hidden from society. Trying to keep their heads down. The bishop was out in front of people all the time. Grendor as well – he kept himself busy running his business. He was not shy.'

'He was in the court often,' Nambu added. 'If he was trying to hide, that doesn't seem a good place to be.'

I let out a long breath as our conversation petered out. This was going to prove a complicated case. It struck me that our chances of knowing what was going on would be enhanced with each new body – but how many more would there be before we came close? Was it even possible to prevent more people from dying, given that we had no idea who would be next? I tried again to find patterns and similarities, other than the method of death.

'Grendor most likely was the one responsible for bringing the gemstone – which was found on the bishop, and a type of stone that he owned himself – into the country. It was a rare stone and well guarded upon entry.'

'If they knew each other,' Leana declared. 'They might have people trading between them.'

'This is not to say that Grendor and the bishop knew each other,' I replied, 'but that it is *possible* they met in some way to trade the stone. Grendor also worked with Lydia Marinus, in dealing with her salt business.'

'They were all of a similar age,' Leana said. 'Late fifties, early sixties.'

'If they had done something together in the past, how far back do we have to go? And what does any of this have to do with the mysterious stone in the present?'

I dipped another chunk of bread into my soup, half-heartedly listening to the local chatter to gauge the mood of the city. People spoke of work, mainly; of the weather or a particular haul of fish. Only one person muttered about the murders in the other prefecture, and it was wildly exaggerated.

Leana interrupted my train of thought. 'What will you be doing while we speak to Grendor's friends?'

Finishing my mouthful, I considered my answer. 'I need to look into the affairs of Lydia Marinus. Of the three victims so far, her case seems more unusual, given that she spent a lot of her time outside the city. For the reasons we've just discussed, her past intrigues me. We might have to head out into the country to see her other residence, but I believe she had a city dwelling, which I'll visit first and see if I can discover more about where her body was found, how far from her house it was, what the place is like, and so on. I'd also like to look into her business affairs, and to find out what she owned other than mining operations.'

Mining operations. While I had been largely thinking about mining in terms of her salt mines, only then did it strike me that precious stones *also* had to be dug up from the earth. The stone that the bishop wore on his ring would have come from a mine. Lydia Marinus owned a huge mining operation, but was it limited to just salt? Even if it was, then she would at least have the know-how to deal with a similar operation.

Grendor shipped to and from mines, and also – potentially –

transported the rare stone in question. Those were the connections so far, even though they were rather tenuous.

'And I suppose,' Leana added, 'there is also the hope that tonight's raid will yield something.'

'There is always hope,' I replied.

The Floorboard

With their manager now deceased, and business still in full flow, there was no reason for high levels of etiquette to be maintained by the staff of Naval Exports. As a result, the offices had been transformed into a gambling den and drinking hole. Raucous laughter echoed along the river, lost amidst the wilder sounds of the city – a marked difference from the Sorghatan Prefecture's relative silence and conservative ways. I should have realized that we could be in for a long wait.

Other than that, the night was calm. The water gently sloshed along the riverbanks, the boats occasionally banging against the makeshift decking. People drifted out of their homes or workhouses and headed towards the taverns. A priest was conducting some ceremony in a shallow part of the river, kneeling with his hands upraised – one of which contained a burning torch. We watched, entranced, as children swam precise circles around him, breaking up the reflection of the light in the water.

'Spirits save us, how long do we have to wait?' Leana asked as we strolled on another small circuit of the docks.

'As long as it takes,' I replied. 'We could burst in there now if you like and take our chances?'

'If it gets the job done quicker, then yes, I would prefer to do so.'

'No fighting. Not if we can help it. I'm not in any shape for combat and *I* would prefer it if we didn't cause a scene and draw attention to ourselves. We must maintain a high level of discretion.'

'You are almost recovered by now. Anyway, I could start a fire somewhere as distraction?'

'And have the whole docks go up in flames?' I replied.

Leana's glorious indifference returned. 'If it would speed matters up.'

In the ensuing pause in conversation, Nambu half-opened and closed her mouth several times, burning to ask something. She finally said to Leana, 'Why do you talk about the *spirits* saving you? Do you mean spirits as in ghosts? Surely they're not real?'

No such thing as ghosts, I would have once said. Only, not all that long ago in Detrata I had seen one for myself. The incident was not quite enough to wholly convince me of their existence, but I no longer dismissed the notion of ghosts as I had done. The image still lingered, an uncomfortable echo in my mind.

'It is a phrase,' Leana replied. 'That is all.'

'What does it mean?'

'That the spirits are all around us, in everything. The dead are closer to the living than we think, so I do not consider there to be much of a distinction between the two.'

'Does everything have a spirit?' Nambu asked. 'I'd like to know more.'

'Of course,' Leana said, giving a brief laugh. 'From the rivers to the sky. There is a spirit to be found in everything. It merely needs to be tapped, like sap from a tree. We can ask for their blessings or their help from time to time. They are ever-watchful of our actions. We have a spirit god, called Gudan, who is . . . an

amalgamation of spirits. A focus for our thoughts. Our priests –
though they are not really priests in the same way – channel the
spirits to give advice or instruction.'

'An Atrewen custom,' I added. 'Leana thinks me insane for
not believing the same as she does. It does somewhat explain her
indifference to killing people.'

Leana shrugged. 'I think you are insane for entirely different
reasons but, yes, the line between the living and the dead is barely
even there.'

'What do you believe, Lucan?' Nambu turned her attention
to me.

'I worship Polla,' I replied. 'The goddess of knowledge and
wisdom.'

'She was a real lady once, wasn't she?'

'You've been taught well.'

'Wasn't she killed for her beliefs?'

'Not quite for her beliefs, no. But she was killed by men
because it was deemed – among other things – improper for a
woman to enquire about the universe.'

I could see the annoyance, almost anger, in Nambu's expression.
'That isn't right.'

'It wasn't,' I agreed. 'Fortunately we live in better times. There
is nothing stopping women making their own way in society now.
You need look no further than your own mother as an example.'

For a moment the young princess paused. 'I never thought
about it like that.'

'In a forward-looking culture we tend to forget the comforts
of the present compared with the struggles of the past.'

'And if there are people who try to stop any such an ascent,'
Leana said, patting her sword, 'then there are women like me to
give them a gentle reminder.'

*

Eventually, as the night drew on, our final route approaching Naval Exports revealed that those who had been laughing and drinking had now left. Some were still making their way in separate directions – one to a boat, where he might possibly sleep on deck, and the others further inland. We waited until their footsteps became inaudible before we moved alongside the shutters to the offices.

Leana levered one of the shutters open with her sword and peered through, while I checked behind us in case we were being followed. A moment later and Leana whispered for me to follow her around the side of the building.

'Dek is asleep on one of the chairs,' she breathed.

'We could wake him if we're not careful.'

'I saw a jug of wine in there – I could smash it over his head, if you like.'

'Which would achieve what exactly?'

'Well, he would not wake up.'

There was a strange logic to much of what Leana suggested, but I saw no reason to harm an innocent man who had given us precious information, and who might be willing to do so in future.

'Nambu, you will stay out here and keep guard. Speak through the side shutter if anyone approaches the building. Leana and I will go inside and lever up the floorboard. I may need a candle for better vision.'

'There were two still burning inside when I looked. Dek had passed out. He was probably too drunk to remember to blow them out.'

'That's good. Right, let's get to it – the sooner we get this over with the sooner we can all rest.'

'Excuse me,' Nambu said. 'But should I not hold a weapon of some sort?'

Without hesitation, Leana reached into her boot and pulled out a small sheathed knife. 'Here, take this. I have another. The blade is only a handspan long, but it will cause some damage. Are you sure you are OK to use it?'

Frowning, she replied, 'Of course I am,' and, despite the fact that she clutched it firmly, I suspected otherwise.

'Remember, speak quietly when someone approaches,' I said.

She nodded and Leana and I turned our attention to the building. Leana led the way — she was the first to grab the frame, pull herself up and place a boot on the window ledge. Once she had got herself inside, she held out her hand.

I grabbed the wiry musculature of her wrist and with my other hand I took hold of the window frame. After some inelegant manoeuvring I managed to join her quietly inside the building.

The place reeked of spilt wine and pipe smoke. Half-a-dozen candles still burned in their holders, a fire hazard given that Dek was sound asleep and papers lay strewn everywhere. The man was not exactly snoring, but happily wheezing away. I proceeded through the murky light with agile steps.

Leana held up her hands as if to say, *Where did you see the loose board?*

With a tilt of my head I indicated the desk and together we walked cautiously towards it. Making small movements, I shuffled from left to right, testing the floor but not wanting to apply too much pressure. Leana repeated my actions nearby, and only then did I realize how ridiculous we would have looked should anyone have seen us.

The purpose to our madness revealed itself when an audible thud sounded under my left boot. Pausing, I motioned for Leana to bring the candles on the desk closer. I pulled a knife from my boot and proceeded to lever the loose floorboard upright, being careful not to make the slightest sound.

As the board came up, I wondered if we were wasting our time or if we would find anything of value. It was common enough to keep things hidden from public view in offices such as this – when a document needed to be kept from falling into the wrong hands, or needed hiding. I prayed to Polla that we would have luck.

On the other side of the room, Dek gave a significant enough utterance for my heart to skip a beat.

As Leana moved the candle closer, a small pang of relief hit me as I saw the warm yellow glow of paper. I reached down and pulled out the thin bundle, before resting it beside the loose board. No sooner had Leana lowered the board back down without making a sound, when we heard a stifled yelp from outside.

Wide-eyed, Leana whispered: 'Nambu.'

I clutched the documents firmly and followed Leana as she sprinted towards the window. She leapt out of it with a level of athleticism that astounded me and, while I perched a buttock on the frame trying to angle my legs out of the narrow gap, I saw that Dek was waking – though obviously groggy – behind us.

'What's going on?' he groaned, but I had already dropped down from the window and onto the ground by the time he would have been anywhere near approaching an alert state.

Neither Nambu nor Leana was anywhere to be seen.

Footsteps could be heard thumping at a rapid pace along the boards of the docks. I tucked the documents safely under my arm – still having no idea what they were, or if they were even useful to the case – and set off after them.

Who's After Nambu?

The feral sounds of the city were ever-present, but I could still hear the sounds of a pursuit. A moment later the noise of running footsteps vanished, only to be replaced by shouting. Darting along to where the boards changed direction, following the course of the river, I chased after the voices. It was not long before I caught up with them.

Leana had cornered a man against the edge of the docks.

He was tall and wore dark clothing, though his features were difficult to see in the darkness. Behind him was a deep point of the rancid river, while in front of him stood Leana, whose abilities he had presumably just witnessed.

He had no choice but to surrender himself.

Nambu was standing some distance behind Leana, and my first concern was her safety. We had been charged with her protection and we had not really followed our orders. I ran over to her, placed the stolen documents on the ground and put my arms around her. If there existed any etiquette that non-royals should not come into physical contact with royals, I ignored it. Right now the young princess clearly needed comfort. She pressed her face against me, shivering.

I eased her back and asked, 'Are you hurt?'

She shook her head. No matter how tough she believed herself to be, the night's events must have been quite a shock for her. I had the impression that the tall man had grabbed her and been chased by Leana to this point.

Her face showed no marks and she wasn't showing any signs of injury. The man must have carried her to have got this far, but with such an extra weight he did not stand a chance against Leana's speed.

Growing impatient with his indecision, Leana stepped towards him, her sword in one hand and a small dagger in the other. It appeared he had no weapon of his own so, while the stand-off continued, I looked around the walkway and found what must have been his sword, which lay some distance away.

'What did you want with a young girl?' Leana snarled again. 'To have her in your bed or for slavery?'

The man did not answer. He was simply evaluating his options, his gaze shifting this way and that to look for a way out of the situation.

'People like you,' Leana snapped, 'make me sick.'

As I stepped towards them, optimistic that I might get some answers, he turned to his left and jumped head first, arms out in front, into the water. During his dive, Leana whipped her dagger towards him – it clipped the back of his shoulder as he connected with the water, but the blade bounced off and sank without a trace.

Whoever this figure was he had now gone into the murky waters. We scoured the river for a break in the surface, and after a while I spotted him swimming towards the opposite riverbank.

'You wish me to follow?' Leana asked.

It would have been a waste of time. Though Leana was athletic on land, she wasn't the fastest swimmer. Neither was I. This attacker, however, was making considerable pace. He had clearly made his escape.

'No,' I replied. 'It's not worth it. The princess is unharmed.'

'I have lost a good dagger,' Leana muttered.

'But we have gained another,' I said, moving over to the man's discarded weapon. 'This weapon is not that of a common thug. Dockyard scum do not carry gold-studded blades.'

The figure was now clambering up the opposite bank, and soon lost himself among the wooden shacks and stone buildings. The moon glimmered on the calm surface of the river and somewhere in the distance a priest was calling out a prayer.

Leana grabbed the weapon and examined it closely. 'It is still too dark to tell much, but you are right. Though not exactly ornate, it is not a cheap blade.'

'Not the sort of thing you might find around a place like this.'

We both turned to Nambu and I knelt down in front of her. Her gaze was so distant and her young face full of worry. If she had not believed it before, the fact that her mother's paranoia might well be rooted in reality must have troubled her now. 'What happened, Nambu?'

'I was looking towards the river from the window,' she began in a whisper, 'as you requested of me. I looked at you now and then to see how you were getting on, since there was no one about. But he came from the darkness, as if he had been part of the shadows all along. Waiting for me.'

'Can you tell us much about him?' I asked. 'Did he say anything? What was his voice like? Was his accent local?'

'Nothing. He placed a hand to my mouth and twisted me so suddenly I had no idea what was going on. Then I found myself being shaken as he ran with me over his shoulder. I barely got a look at him. I was too surprised to even scream.'

'Leana, can you add anything?'

She shook her head. 'You probably saw as much as I did. He did not say anything. He dropped Nambu when he realized how close I was. I should have killed him when I had the chance, but I heard your voice in my head again. Do not kill, you would have said, get answers. And look where that nonsense gets us.'

'If he was dead he would still be unable to answer us,' I replied.

'The dead speak,' Leana muttered. 'As we have seen three times in Kuvash, the dead still tell us things.'

What could we tell from him so far? He was athletic and stealthy, which suggested that he could have been a skilled assassin. Yet he hadn't *killed* Nambu.

It was possible that it was an attempt to take the princess hostage and hold her to ransom – as happened so often across Vispasia with the daughters of wealthy families – but something did not sit right with me. Perhaps it was the fact that the queen might have anticipated someone coming after Nambu, yet she must have thought her safe enough with us. Whoever it was who had been sent after the princess was certainly good at tracking her down, and with some degree of professionalism. That did not bode well. Was this what the queen had been afraid of all along? A quality blade was consistent with someone whose status was one of the Sorghatan Prefecture.

'I think,' I said, 'that we have all earned our sleep tonight. Let's return to the palace and take as much rest as we need – even if the sun is high. I believe Nambu here could do with it after a day like this.'

'I will not disagree with you,' the princess breathed in reply. 'But I will be ready for whatever tasks you have tomorrow. I promise you.'

Her composure and sense of determination impressed me greatly.

And with that we set off back across the city, with the stolen documents under my arm. I knew for a fact that when I returned home Nambu would be the only one resting.

The Documents

Nambu lay fast asleep on her bed, a vision of tranquillity.

I felt guilty for what happened tonight. I never wanted her to feel as if we had been lumbered with her – even though that was, in all reality, a true fact. But how would the princess have felt if we were to make such disapproval obvious? She would have been miserable company, a heavy stone around our necks. Seeking to avoid that situation, I had treated her with equanimity, allowing her to see what we would see, to follow our steps through the city and so get a view she would not otherwise have. In a distant region of my mind, one that wished to avoid influencing future queens, I hoped she might see more of reality so that she would understand how difficult life was for people not born into grandeur.

Our routines were not typical. Though we were up with the sun, there was no guarantee we would rest our heads after it had set. We might walk for miles in a day with little success and we would, more often than not, find ourselves in a scrape or two. Clearly such events had taken their toll on the princess.

At least she did not have to do this for her entire life. Leana and I would move from city to city upon receiving an order and very often there would be too little time to settle into comfortable routines, to build up friendships, let alone start a family or direct affairs from the sanctuary of a court. Of course, many Sun Chamber officers could find themselves stationed in a city for years – decades even. My father was one such example. He settled in Tryum, Detrata, in his early twenties. He died there.

I tried not to let such distance from normal human affairs harden me like it had some of my colleagues. One could find grim souls working in various parts of the continent, enforcing Vispasian law through gritted teeth; jaded old officers and agents who had exchanged raising a family and watching their own young children play, only to handle corpses or ensure affairs of state were handled smoothly down on the streets.

Reminding myself of this sometimes saddened me. Was it the life I wanted indefinitely? Leana was a good companion, however, and stopped my path from being too lonely. In some ways, Leana had become a sister to me, and I would grieve deeply if she ever left my service.

Nambu stirred in her sleep and I moved from the doorway, pulling the door closed behind me. I couldn't blame the young princess if she was feeling scared and tired. It was justifiable, but she was made of tough stuff and would no doubt be eager to continue with Leana's combat lessons tomorrow. She was more than the child her mother believed her to be. There was a determination there, and a desire to learn not found in adults.

At what age did someone stop being a child, anyway? I had nothing on which to base a single thought on the matter. For some reason I found myself enjoying the princess's company: she had highlighted new qualities in both myself and Leana, which were difficult to realize at first. We had begun to care about someone else – no, to care *for* someone else.

Sighing, I poured myself a cup of water from an amphora and set to work.

Sitting at the desk under the light of several candles, I spread the stolen documents before me and, with a weary mind, proceeded to examine in detail just what Grendor of the Cape, or at least someone in Naval Exports, had wanted to keep hidden.

There were approximately fifty sheets in all – the paper being of the cheap variety, it tended to fray around the edges, so it was not easy to make out what I was seeing. Furthermore, it was written in Kotonese, a language whose angular script I found difficult, though I could speak it more or less fluently.

However certain words began to repeat themselves. And one of them I had never heard before.

Evum.

A shipment. Evum. Dates and times for the arrival. Evum.

Was that the strange stone? Were these documents describing how and when it had come into the city?

It looked to me as if there were numerous other companies written down, though it was not clear what they were, and I had not heard of them before. One thing that did strike me as odd though was the phrase:

More offers.

It cropped up a few times, seemingly without context. Was this food offerings for gods? Or was it offers of the kind that a business person might deal with?

Stifling a yawn, I investigated the pages more thoroughly, hoping that something else might present itself, or that I could spot more patterns. My thoughts were beginning to drift from tiredness.

The process felt incredibly isolating, especially given that these quarters were hidden away from the world. Few people knew we were here and no one else knew I had these documents. Sometimes these moments could be revelatory; other times I felt that I might die and no one would know or probably care. There would be some paperwork back in Free State, but usually the only people who were concerned about my business were connected to the cases we worked on, and therefore had an interest in my remaining alive.

Eventually, another name presented itself.

Marinus Mining.

Marinus as in Lydia Marinus.

Another connection – that was worth waiting for. Marinus Mining had been Lydia's company, then, with a quite legitimate trade, and which had been recorded in the other ledgers. However, in these hidden documents, her company was discussed in the same breath as the mysterious evum.

A gentle knock at the door startled me. I stood and cautiously walked towards it. A moment later a voice came. 'It's me, Sulma Tan.'

'One moment.' I slid the bolt back and opened the door.

Sulma Tan stood there, her hair pinned up though a few strands hung down across her face. She was wearing a white shirt tucked into black trousers. 'I hope I am not disturbing you.'

'Not at all,' I said, and stepped back for her to enter. She was such a heartening sight after staring at papers for so long.

'I was up late working.' She smiled knowingly. 'It seems you are too.'

'Yes, sometimes I long to work more in alignment with the sun,' I replied, taking a moment to scan the corridor and then closing the door.

'I came alone,' she said, her eyes glimmering in the candlelight. 'It's quite all right – there was no one following me. I walked past to see if you were still up. When I pressed my ear against the door I could hear you sliding papers across the desk. I know that sound well enough by now.'

'How goes the census?' I asked.

'It is almost finished. We will present to the queen in private before going through the motions in the court – she wishes to know these things well before the court in case there are any surprises. She will probably ask a thousand questions and expect them all to be answered in public. It will be a long morning, and then she will want to dwell on matters. More questions will come in the following weeks.'

'Well, it's nice of you to visit given how busy you are.'

'The work is done. I needed a distraction, and I was interested in seeing how you were healing.'

'Carlon sent you to check on me,' I muttered.

'No, I sent myself,' Sulma Tan replied. 'Besides, your Sun Chamber work offers more curiosities and a greater sense of adventure.'

'If that's what you wish for.'

'Sometimes I do wonder how long I can sit at a desk. My back aches sometimes from copying papers, and I am only thirty summers. I have to stretch and bend morning and night to ensure that I am not a cripple like some become in my trade.'

'The Sun Chamber isn't for everyone,' I said. 'Though you clearly have the mind for the job.'

She made a non-committal expression. It did not seem likely that she would leave her life's work to run around Vispasia – it was a more fanciful moment, perhaps, but the Sun Chamber could really make use of someone as knowledgeable as Sulma Tan.

'Not every culture allows women to flourish like Koton,' she said.

'For all the concerns about Koton being a backward nation,

it really is not so. You yourself are very driven, and you are in a position to change things.'

'You would be driven if you had my kind of upbringing.'

'Yours was a bad one?' I asked.

'Not a bad one; we were reasonably well off. My father died when I was very young and left us a good amount of money for years to come. But my mother filled the home with many strange men seeking to fill some kind of void. Many of those men were abusive, not so much striking her but belittling her, saying that she would remain worthless. I remember holding my sister close in bed as one of her lovers attempted to beat down our front door at some ungodly hour of the night. Yet, the next morning, my mother brought him in. She was vulnerable. I vowed to myself then to never be reliant on another man, to be in such a position.'

She said all this quite calmly. There was no bitterness, no anger, just a quiet determination. We continued our conversation for a little longer, she giving me some of the colour of her life, and asking the same of me, of my time in Detrata and some of the things I had seen in the Sun Chamber. She asked again about my seizures and I trusted her with talking more about them, though it was still uncomfortable for me. She was interested that I had not suffered a seizure for a while.

Eventually we focused on the case again, but not before she had berated me for leaving the lid off the pot of ink.

In hushed tones I told her all we had discovered so far, reminding her of the bodies and of their previous occupations; of the gemstone, who owned it and our information from the jeweller. Then I told her of Grendor's offices, our night-time raid and the documents we had taken.

'But it is only with these papers,' I gestured to the desk, 'that I can truly start to connect them all. Assuming this "evum" was indeed the strange gemstone, it highlights a direct connection between the three dead bodies. The bishop had worn evum on a ring, and so had Grendor, according to his wife, with his missing amulet. Lydia's company had possibly helped to bring the evum out of the ground and moved it, perhaps with shipments of her own legitimate goods – salt and the like. But ultimately Grendor's business had been responsible for the shipping of evum.'

'You think all three are related to it . . .' she breathed. 'But I have never heard of evum. In the records of the census, even the older ones within the manuscript hall, I don't remember the word evum. We have salt, copper, tin, coal, building materials such as slate and limestone, precious stones, and so on, but nothing like evum.'

'So evum remains a secret to all,' I whispered.

'Why do you think they are after this mineral? If it is indeed simply like a ruby, I can't believe there would be all this trouble over a decorative trinket.'

Because of its properties, I wanted to say, noting again how little I ached from my attack. But that made me feel foolish and little better than a street soothsayer. So instead I simply shrugged.

'It can't be simply for the money, either,' I said, 'since a precious stone or a mineral needs an active demand from people in order to create a decent business out of it. Should you come across emeralds and diamonds, there are enough wealthy individuals across Vispasia to pay a handsome sum for one. Should you come across iron, there are industries who need it. But evum has no such market. It has no clientele. It remains an unknown entity. All we know is that certain people have come into contact with it – and those individuals, or some of them, have been killed in a ritual manner.'

'Which implies *someone else* knows about evum,' Sulma Tan added. 'Enough to murder three people horribly.'

'This gives the investigation some hope at last,' I said.

'What is your plan now?' she asked.

'Tomorrow I wish to visit the city quarters of Lydia Marinus to see if there is anything there. Also I want to examine her other residence out of the city, and to look at her mining operations – wherever they are.'

'Yes, yes – I can have the route drawn up for you by noon,' Sulma Tan said keenly. 'I know of her properties.'

'That would be very kind. Could you bring them to her residence tomorrow morning?'

'Of course.'

'And . . . could you tell me where she lived? My knowledge of this city remains relatively poor for the moment.'

'It's an attractive property not too far from the palace. A quiet house on a wide street.' She added softly, 'One day, if I have a dwelling of my own, I would like it to be styled like this one – though a mere fraction of the size. Simple and pretty.'

'Like the old styles?'

'No, just uncluttered. My mind is cluttered enough.'

'I'll pay extra attention to how it looks in that case,' I replied, then tried to stifle a yawn – but was clearly failing.

Sulma Tan regarded me knowingly, ever-familiar with working late by candlelight. 'You should get some rest. Come and find me in my offices when you are ready – I'll only be reading over my reports for the queen – and I will show you the way to Lydia's house.'

With that she rose and walked to the door, turning just before she opened it. 'Officer Drakenfeld, thank you for keeping an eye on the princess. She is old for her years, and very smart – we often talk of natural sciences and art, and she has a thirst for knowledge. With her accompanying you about the city, it will help her to grow. That will be good for Koton in the future.'

'It's not a problem – we're finding her to be rather good company,' I replied honestly, which pleased Sulma Tan.

Chores

The following morning, one of the queen's private messengers arrived with a missive that had just been delivered to the palace.

'The messenger who gave this to Sulma Tan said it was urgent,' she announced, 'and the second secretary wanted to ensure it reached your hands quickly.'

'It has the Sun Chamber seal,' I noted. 'Please, thank Sulma Tan and tell her that I'll call on her office later.'

'She said that she will be an hour with the queen,' the messenger replied, 'no more.'

As she left, I headed back inside and opened the message while Leana started Nambu's morning practice session.

Inside the tube were my latest wages, in the form of a credit note from the Sun Chamber, with instructions to visit only the Crannan Family Bank in order to draw out the money. This came as something of a relief, as I was beginning to run low on coin. A shortage of funds also meant that I would be unable to bribe people should it be necessary – as it so often was in my line of work. Aside from giving Leana her allocation, the arrival of wages also meant that I could make a further payment at the stables, where our horses were still being kept. It was important that the animals were well exercised, especially as the following day I had plans to ride out of the city. So my morning was going to involve matters of housekeeping.

Nambu and Leana moved through some slightly more complicated moves. To correct Nambu's posture Leana guided her with a whisper, informing her exactly of what to look for in an attacker's movements, of what was left exposed. Leana's combat style had always been a bit of a mystery – and it certainly wasn't for the lack of my questions on the subject. She had rarely opened up about her time in Atrewe, even after all these years, and didn't comment about the skills she had learned there. It was as if she refused to acknowledge the existence of her own past, and committed her mind utterly to the present tasks at hand – which was no bad thing.

What little I had seen of Nambu could be seen in the sons and daughters of powerful people all over Vispasia – occasional bouts of defiance in their parents' presence, but with genuine uncertainty about their own position in the world, a tentativeness that could increase outside their normal circles.

Nambu was bringing out a more caring side of Leana, a side I hadn't seen before – she was helping Nambu grow and become more confident. The two of them finished their moves and Leana placed a hand on Nambu's shoulder. 'You learn quickly.' She turned to address me. 'Lucan, with your permission, before Nambu and I visit Grendor's friends, we will go for a run through the streets – she has been kept like a caged bird too long. She needs to be built up – stronger – and we will transform her with more speed.'

I'm sure such a rigorous exercise routine all went under the banner of 'caring', somehow. 'If that's fine with the princess?' I glanced towards her.

Nambu shrugged. 'If it is to make me better.'

'A strong body is as important as a strong mind,' Leana replied.

'Just make sure you cover yourselves so you're not identified,' I said. 'It pays to be cautious, especially after what happened last night.'

'Will you tell my mother about that?' Nambu asked.

'Do you want me to?' The thought had crossed my mind, but only because the queen wasn't being completely honest with me over why she had given her only daughter to strangers.

'I would rather you didn't.' Nambu had more than a hint of pride in her voice. 'I assure you, I have nothing to hide. I could just do without a fuss being made. Besides . . . I am enjoying being here and she might take me back to some awful cold room again, with nothing but books and a view across the city's rooftops for days on end.'

'Then there seems no need to let her know.'

Again, it occurred to me that the queen would not want her back – that she wanted Nambu out of the way. The queen might not be able to trust people in her court. I also considered that, if this was the case, she would not want any of her own *untrustworthy* guards placed on the door to a room that wasn't, in practical terms, supposed to exist. It bothered me that the queen might not trust her own people. Was that the simple paranoia of a royal holding on to power? The fear that someone would thirst for the crown so badly that they would not only kill the queen but her daughter too?

The queen might set great store by our abilities to protect her daughter but, considering our last few encounters, I wanted something a bit more physical. Our quarters were not half as well protected as I would have liked. So it was time to do something about it. If the official royal guards could not be trusted, so be it. There were other methods of security. And while I had every faith in Leana's skills – even she could be overwhelmed should numbers be brought to bear – it would do no harm to seek my own private protection to our door, as backup. It was another chore for the morning's list.

As Leana and Nambu set off for their exercise and to interview Grendor's friends, I donned my black cloak, pinned my Sun Chamber brooch to my chest, and made sure that the bishop's ring was deep in my pocket, before heading out into the warm morning air.

The spell of dreary weather Koton had been suffering from when we first arrived had well and truly moved on. Instead a wave of more sultry weather was hanging over the city, a stubborn, grubby heat that reminded me of the worst of Detratan summers.

The first stop was the Crannan Family Bank, which turned out to be a small, ornate stone building situated in the near corner of this prefecture. It looked much like a Detratan temple, with a triangular pediment and two small stone columns positioned either side of a narrow stairway. Its interiors were sumptuous, as one might expect from banks, with astrological frescos and numerous cressets reflecting on a well-polished marble floor.

I conversed with a large man who wore an elaborate crimson robe and who spoke with the authority and wisdom of some religious leader – though the only god he was channelling here was money. He spoke without an accent, like many of the most profound and legitimate moneylenders. Neutrality – visibly showing they possessed no fixed national allegiance – was everything. Bankers wanted powerful people and rulers to know that money was safe in their hands, that the bank could be trusted in any country. Noting I was a member of the Sun Chamber, he spoke to me as if I was his greatest friend, so it was with little trouble that I managed to exchange the credit note and leave with two large purses of money. I did not exchange all of the note's value, so I kept a leather tab for a smaller denomination on a chain around my neck.

As the day's temperature increased, I walked towards the large stables to check on our horses. Eventually, I found Sojun in a small workshop around the corner, struggling to repair a decorative saddle.

For a moment he didn't look up at me, even though he had registered my entrance to his dreary, cluttered workshop. Tools lay on workbenches and the air smelled of ash. The place was so small he seemed to be of even greater stature than I remembered, having to stoop as he went about his work. Eventually he rubbed his hand along the leather and said, 'A foreigner's saddle. You won't find many Kotonese with a need for this.'

'You ride without?' I asked.

'Before we can walk, we all ride without,' he replied. 'Though there are more and more who require one. Started with the rich. They insist on saddles for comfort. To me it is just as comfortable to use the bare horse. These things become fashionable. People want to look like the rich. An industry springs up out of nowhere and it pays well. But you'd never catch me on one.'

'My partner rides without,' I said, and he raised an eyebrow.

'I remember there was just the one saddle. Is your colleague local?'

'Atrewen,' I said, and he nodded approvingly.

'Good horse people.' He rose from his stool and stooped so that he would not bang his head on the ceiling. 'I always respect those who treat their animals with care and attention.'

'As do I.' I reached in my pocket to bring out more money, and handed over two large silver coins. 'Another payment. I'll need to use the horses tomorrow – just for the day, possibly the night.'

'They're fine animals,' he replied, taking the money. He walked past me and examined the coins in the light of the doorway.

There was something about his tone and mannerisms that made me think he respected the horses more than he respected me.

'The Sun Chamber wouldn't provide me with old hacks.' I tried something of a smile to raise his spirits, or at least the mood of the conversation, but it was difficult to tell if it had any effect on him.

'We will have both mares ready for you to collect in the morning. They've been exercised and given good food, but with the military passing through the prices have gone up somewhat . . .'

He looked at me in a different way then and so I knew to give him another coin. 'That should be enough to cover your costs.'

Sojun gave a short grunt of satisfaction before stepping through the doorway. Following him outside, I could hear the hammering of a blacksmith. Initially, I had to squint after being in the dreary workshop. Someone walked by and spoke loudly of a business meeting, which prompted something at the back of my mind. When I visited Borta, I overheard that Grendor was supposed to have taken his sons out riding, but Borta had told them that he was delayed at some business meeting.

'Sojun,' I said. 'I don't suppose you ever dealt with Grendor of the Cape?'

'Grendor of the Cape?' Sojun turned to face me. 'The rich man who ended up dead recently?'

'That's him. He was well known in the court of Queen Dokuz. A great naval officer.'

'Know little about things like the royal court,' Sojun said. 'Even less about the sea.'

'Grendor enjoyed going horse riding with his sons,' I ventured. 'I wondered if he may have passed through these stables at any point — if he kept his horses here. You might know of a stable that he dealt with.'

'These are among the finest stables in the city.' Sojun stood tall now, and radiated pride. 'Many a rich person wants to keep their horses here and he was a famous one all right. But I've never seen Grendor of the Cape around here, let alone groomed his horse. I can tell you where the other stables are if he stabled them elsewhere.'

'No, that's OK.' There was no need – I could get information on the other stables from Sulma Tan. But there was every chance that Borta had simply told a lie to her children, or perhaps it was the first time they were venturing out on horseback. There might have been friends in the military, too, who could have lent them a horse – any number of reasons came to mind.

'Well, I just thought I'd ask anyway,' I replied.

There was some hubbub in the courtyard as a group of twenty soldiers rode in, scaring some of the other animals, their horses' hooves thumping on the stone, strident orders echoing around the complex. Stablehands rushed out to subdue the animals with soothing gestures, and with impressive efficiency. Some of the soldiers dismounted and gave instruction to the stablehands and various bags of grain were soon brought out.

'Soldiers are taking all the city's spare horses,' Sojun said, and indicated a line of animals being led towards the new arrivals.

'Why's that?' I asked.

'Trouble on the border,' he replied. 'Trouble means reinforcements.'

'Have you heard what kind of trouble?' I knew approximately, of course.

Sojun shrugged. 'Detrata is posturing. Koton makes statements in retaliation. Heard that we brought back our ambassadors last week – that's closed off talk. It is the way of things. People will cling to their idea of borders – get fussed over lines on a map really. Maybe nothing will happen. Maybe blood will be spilled. It matters little.'

The intelligence behind Sojun's sudden statement was surprisingly accurate. Part of my fears about the lack of a Detratan king is that a power-hungry senate would glorify Detrata's lost imperial empire to the public and persuade them that those days could be recaptured – leading to war with the country's neighbours and destroying the fragile peace that the Sun Chamber had worked so hard to achieve.

We parted and, as I left him, I noticed the girl with whom he had been exchanging lingering glances the last time I was here. She emerged from the mass of soldiers and placed her arm around him; he kissed her back. It was heartening to note the romance that could blossom here, even in the midst of the clamour, and that even a seemingly pessimistic soul like Sojun could find pleasure in the world.

I walked with haste across the city towards the jeweller who had first advised me on the bishop's ring, and who had provided information on Naval Exports.

The streets were quieter. The sun banked higher.

I eventually arrived at the same green-fronted shop situated down the quiet lane. The shadows were now more emphasized in the better weather. A few cats trotted about the vacant cobbles, before gathering in numbers at the end of an alleyway, and there was a faint smell of rotting food.

As expected, still positioned by the door of Vallamon's shop was the same muscular guard with the shaven head. I greeted him in a jovial manner, but didn't expect much in return.

'You again,' he grunted. 'What's it today then?'

'How much money do you earn?' I asked.

He was taken aback by the question and he began to scrutinize me closely, weighing up my comment rather than barking out an instant response. 'I earn enough. What's it to you? You another rich man come to rub it in?'

'Not at all – I've a proposition for you,' I replied. 'When do you finish work here?'

'Sunset.' His eyes narrowed. 'What's all this about?'

'I'm in need of a man of your calibre, and I've plenty of money to pay you for the job in question.'

He eyed my outstretched palm, picked up the coin within it and began to scrutinize it.

'One of those every two days,' I added.

'What's the work?' he asked. 'Not many would flash a coin like this. Must be important.'

'I need a door protecting,' I said. 'You seem to be good at that.'

'I can do more than doors you know,' he snapped. 'I served in the Maristanian infantry for ten years. Proper fighting – not on horseback like this lot in Koton. On foot, right in the face of the enemy. And I can write, which is more than most in the army. So what's so special about this damn door of yours?'

It was only when he mentioned his country of origin that I could detect the long vowels in his accent; otherwise he was speaking perfect Kotonese. 'The door is located in the royal palace.'

'Surely they've got their own guards, so why bring me in?'

'They're not to be trusted.'

His eyes narrowed at the suggestion of the palace, but he remained cool and aloof. 'What makes you think you can trust me, stranger? We've had two conversations, including this one.'

'You stand outside of a store with Polla-knows how much valuable contents inside – enough to set *you* up for life, probably. It is run by an individual you could overwhelm in a heartbeat. That you've worked here for years without having taken anything tells me all I need to know.'

Again he gave nothing but an unreadable, stoic face. 'Have you got precious stones as well?'

'Of a kind, but it's not important you know too many details right now.'

'How do I know I'm not getting into trouble?'

'I can't be sure that you're not – not entirely anyway – but I'm an officer of the Sun Chamber and this is honest work. All that is important is the fact that the door remains well guarded and that no one disturbs us. Any goings-on during the night are reported in the morning.'

'Seems easy enough.'

'Will the lack of sleep be an issue? I've known many a guard fall asleep.'

'No. Vallamon only works a few hours each day, and takes his gemstones back to his home each afternoon. You don't need to do a full shift when you sell what he sells. Plenty of sleep can be taken around what shifts I do here. Besides, back in the day, in the army, we'd have to work during the night when out on a scouting campaign. An hour's kip at the most and I coped fine.'

'Good.'

'Only there's something I'm not all that keen on,' he said.

'If you can't do it, then I'd appreciate—'

'No one said I couldn't do it. You just don't come up to a man and offer a coin of that value if there's nothing . . . *dubious* attached.'

'Dubious?' I asked.

'Yeah. Extra services. You want me to come to your room – I *get* what that means. Guarding the inside. Then more . . . Rich ladies and men have made the same suggestion in the past. Handsome fellows like myself. A lot of stuff goes on behind closed doors in this country – propositions are subtle. Stranger like you might take a while to see that. People have this facade they need to keep and behave well in public. Not like Detrata, where you're from, where everything's out in the street. Nah, a man like me, you see, gets looks all the time.'

I did not think him particularly handsome, but I was interested that he held such a high opinion of his appearance. Also, he spotted my accent, which pleased me greatly – it confirmed his mind was sharp.

'No,' I said, smiling. 'I'm sorry to let you down, but I do not wish for you to join me on the other side of the door. I really do want you to stand on the *outside* and protect the *outside* of the door. You'll have no business coming inside the door unless it's of absolute importance.'

He held out his hand and we shook, clutching each other's fore-arm. 'Name's Allius. Allius Golt.'

'Lucan Drakenfeld, Officer of the Sun Chamber,' I said. 'You'll be getting paid by Free State coin, which means you'll need to be trustworthy and punctual.'

'Aye,' he said, and stiffened his posture as if on parade, as if the memories had returned to his body and a renewed sense of pride flowed into him. 'You'll not find a more trustworthy soldier in all of Koton.'

I gave Allius instructions on where to meet me later that evening, and left him standing back at his position guarding the doorway. Though he was merely going to be standing in front of a different door, he was visibly happy at the prospect of a door in the royal palace. I was simply glad of the extra protection.

Sulma Tan, true to her word, was in her office – surrounded by lanterns, her head lowered, parchment spread across her desk. She greeted me warmly, having completed her morning's task, while I regarded the census map she had made and once again marvelled at the assiduous level of detail. She pointed out where

Lydia Marinus' body had been discovered, and where her house was located. Certainly we could see no pattern to the murders in terms of the city's geography. They were scattered far and wide.

We spoke for a while about what that might mean, but concluded only that it ruled out further eccentricities in the killer. They were not leaving bodies in any pattern in the city, and the streets themselves were not significant – merely that they were all within the wealthy prefecture. I had hoped that we might, by now, be able to see that the murders were concentrated near to an area of potential workshops where the torture of the victims might have been carried out. Since the murderers were leaving the bodies in public places, it followed that there was a place where torture could be carried out. It hinted again that there was more than one killer. How else could the bodies be carried about the city so discreetly?

We moved the conversation on. I informed Sulma Tan about Allius Golt, that he was trustworthy and that he would soon start working for me.

'A good idea, though we may have to keep the issue quiet for the time being,' she said. 'The queen doesn't necessarily trust her staff as it is. Strangers? Who can say how she will react. But do not worry – I will ensure Allius receives the official passwords.'

'I've heard she can be distrustful of others. Tell me, why is that?'

Sulma Tan appeared uncertain for a moment, as if not wanting to open up. 'She won't say, but it is more than simply being worried the clans will one day get to her. She thinks them powerless for the most part, but . . . I can see her eyeing soldiers as they pass through her court. Yes, there is a look of disdain that I once thought was related to status, but recently I have considered that this has nothing to do with that. What she gives them is a look of fear, I believe, and it is genuine.'

'Fear?' I repeated. 'What does she have to be scared of?'

'Being dethroned. The same as any monarch, am I correct? Having read through passages of writings in other cultures, as well as our own, I have seen a common theme running through them all.'

'Which is?'

'Fear of losing a power granted to them by others. A queen or king is not merely born – they are *made* by others, they are maintained by others who give awed looks and arrange courtly rituals. We act around them as if they are gods on earth. Who can say what effect that will have on an individual's mind if all day long people behave in such a way? And the thing is, though people can make a queen, people can just as quickly *unmake* one. The queen perhaps realizes this fact and takes it to heart.'

Her statement reminded me of what had occurred in Tryum, how King Licintius had been dethroned and his own people had decided on his execution. Sulma Tan was right with respect to that case, too: the senators changed from championing their king to practically mobbing him in his final moments in the Senate gardens. They propped him up as monarch and, ultimately, they took away his powers – and his life, deserved or otherwise.

'We should probably proceed to Lydia's house now,' I said. 'Did you manage to get any maps of her wider estates?'

'I have them for you to study later.' She patted her leather satchel, which was hanging over the back of her chair. 'Though I knew Lydia owned a lot of land I didn't realize until compiling these documents how vast they were.'

'How much are we talking about?'

She rose from her chair to put on a cloak. 'About one twentieth of Koton. By and large, most falls under royal ownership or is the property of the temples. But the bulk of our country remains free for the people as common land. They have the rights to graze animals over most of this country. And as you have probably noticed, we have a *lot* of animals, so it is important to the people that the land remains in their custody – the people manage it themselves, see that it is not overgrazed and take only what is theirs, and this tradition has lasted for centuries. Yes, it was an essential part of our heritage.'

'So if most of the land is free, that means Lydia's huge wealth is actually more significant than it sounds.'

Sulma Tan nodded. 'She owns just under half of what the temples own, which is again just under half what Queen Dokuz owns. The Marinus estate controls the flow of nearly all metals and salt. Without Lydia's mines, there wouldn't be the same craft work you see in the city. The smiths would be quieter. There would be little decoration in the palace – or perhaps it would come from abroad.'

'I imagine she had quite a few enemies in that case,' I said, 'business associates, competitors . . .'

'Yes, yes, but there are so very few competitors,' she replied. 'Everyone was either a friend of hers or under her employment. Not even the Rukrid family at its height could claim to have as much influence. Even today, the rest of the clans combined are not as powerful as she was. The temples have no interest in these operations. The queen, I'm sure, would like to own them, but she never had any problems with Lydia. As far as I know, when Lydia came to the city, they were often in court together, speaking privately.'

'Do you know what about?'

'No, what the queen discusses in private, neither of her secretaries – nor her daughter, servants, eunuchs – ever hear what is said. From what I gather though the conversations were rare, but jovial.'

I must have made a curious expression, because Sulma Tan said, 'What is it?'

'Oh, I was merely curious as to why a second friend of the queen has been found dead. First Grendor and now Lydia . . .'

'You can't think the queen has anything to do with these deaths?' She looked incredulous. 'The murders were hideous. If she wanted to kill people, she would have them executed with dignity, not with barbarism.'

'Is any form of killing actually dignified?'

'Besides,' Sulma Tan ignored my comment, 'you saw for yourself just what it means to offend the queen. Those soldiers who attacked you? They were despatched while you were asleep.'

'I was actually *unconscious* . . .'

'Well, the queen does not harbour grudges for long periods. She gets things done.'

'You're right,' I replied, 'and you know her better than anybody. I merely wonder, though, why it is that two people – seemingly unconnected, other than through trade – who were friends with the queen have perished in such a way. You understand that I must look at patterns in these cases.'

'Yes, yes, I follow the line of thought.' The apology was there in Sulma Tan's eyes even if she could not bring herself to actually say it. 'We should go now. It is a hot day and the streets will start to smell by the afternoon.'

The City House

We proceeded along newly built roads and high pavements, across high stepping stones that were placed for when the heavy rains washed through. Again I marvelled at the symmetrical streets of the prefecture, quite unlike those found in Detrata, which wound about cities according to the whims of rulers. The stone here was recently cut and the statues were bright, and there was a gentler pace to everyday life.

Eventually we arrived at the street of Lydia Marinus' house. However, the word *house* did not really do the building justice. The property was immense, and took up most of the length of the street. Though relatively narrow, and two floors high, it stretched along for fifty yards, protected by a ten-foot-high perimeter wall standing only a few paces out from the building.

Constructed from pale stone and containing row upon row of arched windows, there was nothing to suggest much artistic licence taken by the architects. If anything, the place was surprisingly bland and spoke of a woman not concerned with art. It surprised me that Sulma Tan had commented on it with affection. There were no statues, no ornamentation, no decorative flourishes. Lydia had not spent money on extravagance. Perhaps that was why she remained so incredibly wealthy. Still, I was not here to judge the artistic tastes of a dead woman, or those of Sulma Tan. People liked what they liked.

The perimeter wall was broken up by a large, red, wooden gate, set in a brick arch. Sulma Tan banged on the gate with her hand and eventually a hatch slid open revealing a metal grille, partially obscuring the face beyond.

'State your business,' came a voice.

Sulma Tan explained who we were – declaring her role as second secretary to Queen Dokuz – and within a heartbeat the guard pulled open the gate.

A slender man in his forties stood there. With greying hair and a narrow, avian face, he wore contoured leather chest armour, black clothing, and stout boots, but looked weak, as if weighed down by it all. His expression was one of concern. If ever I needed to storm a palace, I would pray it was defended by men as easily cowed as this.

'Lydia Marinus is not at home,' he muttered quietly. 'She's uh . . .'

'She's dead,' I said. 'We know.'

'Ah. Right then. Well you'd, uh, better come through in that case.' He stepped aside and allowed us into a narrow garden that stretched around this side of the building. Ornamental flowers climbed decorative willow-frame archways; lavender hedges ran along by the house. The sounds of the city were suddenly very distant.

'Are you the only guard on duty?' I asked.

'There's another inside, but we weren't expecting her back in the city,' he muttered. 'She's got a private guard who follow her around. We're mainly here to deal with questions and send people away, tell them to mind their own business and the like.'

A private guard and yet still she had been murdered. I turned to Sulma Tan. 'Where did you say her body was found?'

'In the street,' she replied, 'not too far from here as it happens. A merchant who was setting up his cart for the day found her body and alerted the City Watch. We never had the opportunity to analyse the scene, but it was very public – again, we believe the murder had been committed elsewhere, the body dumped.'

'For all to see,' I added, and turned to the man. 'How did she manage to be abducted with a private guard protecting her?'

He shrugged and looked uneasy – well, more so than normal. 'No idea, honestly. She really shouldn't have been on her own. She makes enough demands to make sure one of us is with her most of the time, even if it's just in the next room. She's normally very insistent.'

'Did she seem scared of something or someone?'

'I don't know. She just liked us around. Felt more secure, like.'

'We'll need to send an urgent message to the rest of her security entourage,' I demanded. 'Do you know where they're staying?'

'They'll be here this afternoon. Word was sent to her place in the country as soon as her body was found. Truth be told, there's been some almighty cock-up somewhere along the line. Some of the other boys will be feeling a bit sheepish.'

'You don't say,' I grunted.

'If only I'd known she was coming to the city,' he replied. 'Could have gone to fetch her and escort her. Or at least get the place ready.'

'So no news had been sent in advance of her arrival?'

'Nothing. First I knew about it was . . . well, when it was a bit too late.'

'Normally she sends this kind of information in advance, I take it.'

'She lets us know her movements all the time – she's very methodical.'

There was the potential that one of her guards could have killed her. 'We're going to take a look inside,' I said. 'Can you lead the way?'

'Of course, of course.' He scrambled to guide us along the path.

'It's like a god-sized yurt,' Sulma Tan commented, and I agreed. For a rich woman, there wasn't much wealth on display. Many of the items appeared to be the kind of thing that you would expect in the usual yurts of tribal leaders, which could occasionally be seen in Koton.

But to the educated eye the rugs, throws and few ornaments were of sublime quality, with incredibly ornate stitching and some very exclusive designs. There was a simplicity to her artistic appreciation, but she did not skimp on the details. This could be seen in the old-style frescos – boring, by modern standards, but incredibly elegant geometric designs that only a skilled artist could create on drying plaster. *Now* I could see why Sulma Tan might have admired a place like this. Her home was full of authenticity and good taste, without showing off.

A small brass statue of a bull stood in one corner of the house, and I was reminded of what Priest Damsak had said about the primitive, older gods. There was another such statue in the kitchen and one in a small sunlit quarter of the garden. I remarked on these to Sulma Tan.

'Curious,' she replied. 'One does not see so many examples of this these days.'

'Did she worship the older gods?'

Sulma Tan shrugged. 'What does it matter which deity we pray to? She was certainly one for the old ways. A traditionalist, people have said, but she kept herself to herself so I cannot vouch for these rumours. She did not like money to be wasted on frivolous matters. She even petitioned the queen not to waste money and resources on the census.'

The craftsmanship displayed in the house was not to be sniffed at – with large, robust fireplaces with immense logs ready to be burned, and thick timber beams stretched across high ceilings. Everything was very well put together. The tone of the colours continuing through the building was of a sombre crimson shade, with a few gold-trim highlights that drew the eye. Each of the many bedrooms, too, shared this tone and simplicity.

Lydia Marinus may well have been one of the richest people in Koton, but unlike someone in Detrata she didn't flaunt it.

'It seems a large house for someone who doesn't spend much time in the city,' I commented to the guard.

'Her country place is much bigger,' he muttered. 'This was small to her.'

'But still, there's a lot of unused space here.'

'It wasn't just a house, like.' An uneasiness grew about his manner and he started shifting his weight from foot to foot, glancing at the floor.

'Tell me more,' I demanded.

'Now and then she'd bring poor children in for classes. Even owned one of the orphanages. Gave a lot of money to help out. Not just the poor, but those kids who might otherwise find themselves picking pockets in the marketplaces. She wanted to reform them. Give them an opportunity in life. Use her money for good. It ain't common knowledge and that's the way she wanted it.'

'Why keep a nice thing quiet?'

'She said it would make her look soft to the men she dealt with. Said they were all former military types who loved posturing. Said they'd use the knowledge against her. Make her weak in business deals, like.'

'Understandable . . . Where would the children stay?'

'There's a dormitory on the other side of the garden, and a large room where they'd take their lessons. She'd pay for one of the speakers from the nice schools to come here and talk history or rhetoric, though she was hardly here to see it all. Like to think I learned a bit while I was on duty, heh.'

Sulma Tan wore a puzzled expression.

'Is something the matter?' I asked.

'There was no declaration of this in the records,' she said. 'This is one of the biggest buildings in the city and it is registered as a dwelling not a school.'

'She didn't want folk to know,' the guard stressed once again. 'Though I never got to speak with her privately, since she was a bit of a recluse, from talking with the other guards who've heard her, they say she felt guilty about her good fortune in life and wanted to help others. Maybe she felt guilty about her own family, I dunno. But she didn't want folk knowing about it, certainly not any competitors. They'd say it was a weakness of character, something like that. I'm not the sort who gets involved in business.'

'How long had the house been used this way?' Sulma Tan asked.

The man shrugged. 'At least as long as I've been here, and that's six summers. That wasn't all she did. She would go out into the city in disguise, giving alms to the poor. Used to have us guards shadow her from a distance to make sure she came to no harm.'

Yet again the murder victim was someone who did good work for the community of Koton, though this time it was someone whose kind acts were done in private. A private act for a private woman. Just how much did she keep to herself?

'Were there ever any gatherings here apart from that?' I asked. 'Celebrations, business meetings, that sort of thing.'

The guard smiled dryly. 'Never. You hear of some guards else-where getting lucky at things like parties. Lady of good standing wants someone a bit rough when their husband is out of the city. Sometimes they get with someone like me at a gathering.' His face soured a little and he smiled grimly. 'Not a chance here, though. No one ever came to visit. No fine ladies. Most of our time was spent staring at the herbs or listening to the sound of children's voices echoing along the corridors.'

'That's not a bad way of passing time,' I said. 'Did you ever have any trouble here while you were on duty? Thieves looking to take some trinket in the middle of the night? Strange people loitering in the gardens?'

He shook his head. 'What trinkets? You've seen the place. There's not much to steal unless you know what you're looking for, and thieves are rarely that discerning. Nah, we never had any trouble. The walls are high enough to stop most people from getting into the gardens anyway. This was a quiet patch and I liked it that way. A lot of private guards get rough deals, but I suppose this was a good job all right.'

I turned to Sulma Tan. 'How common is private protection in Koton?'

'Very,' she replied. 'There is a thriving industry for those who used to be in the military. We ask our soldiers to commit to ten years before they are free to do as they please – a tradition of sorts. It is not a national service, however. Without wars, there are many soldiers who get to the end of that decade as trained warriors and are looking for work. There's enough money from trade to pay for such luxuries, too.'

'And people like Lydia Marinus would be happy to oblige.'

Contemplating the limited findings so far, I tried to build a coherent picture of the person who perpetrated these crimes. Yet *another* member of the highest level of Kotonese society had been murdered. Whoever had perpetrated these crimes had a good working knowledge of the movement of the victims in high social circles. In the case of Lydia, they knew how to get her into the city when she did not often spend time here.

Grendor and Lydia were close to the queen. Had they been conspiring in a plot? Sulma Tan had already shown some attempts at influence by Lydia over the census. I put that question to her.

'It is . . . certainly possible. Though I confess, I do not know of any such plots. They were on good terms with the queen, so why would they seek to remove her?'

'Other clans or family leaders might have put them up to it.'

'Lydia is too wealthy to have her favours bought.'

'She might have sought the crown herself. The woman had everything but that.'

Her expression, once again, gave nothing away. If the queen had been killing off rivals, it was unlikely that Sulma Tan would accompany me on the case – unless it was to ensure I knew too little.

'It is just as likely,' Sulma Tan speculated, 'that Detratan spies might have put Lydia and Grendor up to corrupting the throne somehow. But you might know more about that than I do.'

'Let us leave a coup as a potential theory, but one with little evidence.'

Nothing about this sat right in my mind. What's more, the lack of clear purpose or motive behind the killings was becoming increasingly frustrating – not that I would ever show this to Sulma Tan.

'One object, at the moment, connects at least two of the victims. So would it perhaps connect the third?'

'Evum,' Sulma Tan confirmed.

'Lydia Marinus could possess evum at any of her properties,

if it is not upon her body. We must organize a systematic search to find out.'

A clamour came from somewhere outside — the sound of hooves on cobbles, soon followed by voices calling through the long corridors.

'That'll be the others.' The guard hastily led us back the way we had come.

Return of the Guard

Presently we were confronted by seven men, each one wearing a similar leather breastplate with a scaled leaf pattern, and a long green cloak. They were of mixed ages, but a thickset man in his late forties, with a few scars on his face and two-day-long stubble, came forward demanding to know who we were.

Sulma Tan stopped him in his tracks and revealed her title, before introducing me as the man investigating the murder of Lydia Marinus.

He grimaced and looked towards the wall of the corridor. There was a sudden sense of shame about the men and they couldn't seem to look anywhere but their own feet. One of them made a circular movement around his chest, and then reversed the direction of his hand – a gesture I believe was associated with the two gods Astran and Nastra.

'And,' Sulma Tan finished, 'we will require a full account of Lydia's final movements. You should have been protecting her, should you not?'

'Yeah,' he sighed loudly. There was nothing but abject failure in his expression. He had failed to protect his mistress. He had failed at his one duty, and he knew it. 'Yeah, we should have done better. We should have. But we weren't to know she was heading off, were we? She never goes anywhere without us. Never.'

'What's your name?'

'Santhan Brak, formerly Captain of the Horse Guards.'

'How long have you worked for Lydia?'

'Nine years, head of her personal protection for the past two.'

'Tell us what happened then, Santhan.'

'A messenger came bearing a tube from the city,' he began in a measured and precise manner. 'Actually, he had three messages. Nothing new there, of course, it happens all the time. Lady Marinus is – *was* – a busy lady, and she would often be sending letters to various people about business details. This time there was a different message. Don't know what was in it, but it was different. I remember the occasion very distinctly – as sometimes I'm permitted in her private quarters. When she read the letter, this look came over her face . . .'

'How do you mean?' I asked.

'She turned white. Had a distant look. For a moment I thought someone in her family had died, but then I realized that she's got no one left, so it couldn't have been. Then I thought maybe a business failure, one of the mines had collapsed or something, but it wasn't that.'

'So what was it?'

'She didn't tell me. Didn't tell anyone. When I asked she merely rolled up the message and put it up her sleeve. She maintained a sense of dignity though – made out that there was nothing amiss. Did a lot of that. Hid her feelings.' Santhan paused for a moment, searching for the right thing to tell me. 'You know, I served her for all those years and got to see her more than anyone else. There was no family, of course. Despite that, despite my familiarity, sometimes I felt as if I barely knew her.'

There was no reason to dispute what he was saying. 'But you

have no idea what that message could have been, or where it came from?'

'Well, it came from the city. You see the messenger brought it in a bundle and said he'd come directly from Kuvash.'

'The messenger has gone?'

'Oh yeah, long left. Headed up along the coast with more deliveries to make – chap like that could be gone for days before he returns, not that I'd got his name at the time – they only show their medal of identification.'

'Did he look like the other messengers? There was nothing unusual about him?'

'Seemed fairly standard to me.'

'There's a good chance Lydia might have brought the message back with her to the city,' I muttered to Sulma Tan.

As if reading my thoughts she replied, 'There wasn't a note found on her body or anywhere nearby. There were no private possessions at all, come to think of it, merely the clothes that covered her wounds.'

That was frustrating, but at least the fact of the message's existence and its origins confirmed to me that the killers were still operating in Kuvash. They had not fled. That led to the speculation of how many more people would end up being killed before we found the persons responsible.

'Precisely when was the last time you saw Lydia?'

'Lady Marinus?' Santhan puffed up his cheeks and let out a long sigh. His fellow soldiers remained rigid by his side. 'Two days ago,' he said at last. 'In the morning.'

'It took you this long to get here,' Sulma Tan commented. 'And you were her *protection*?'

Santhan shot her an angry glare and snapped, 'I'll not take comments on soldiering from a woman, especially one who sits behind a desk all day.'

Sulma Tan curled up her lips and leant into him, uttering the words quietly. '*This* woman would have placed a report on your performance into the hands of the queen. *That* woman would, if she thought it appropriate, have you and your men executed for betraying a good friend, or whatever reason took her fancy. So keep your tongue firmly in your head, before you lose the latter.'

Though his expression was full of anger, Santhan lowered his head. 'Aye, lady. I forget my station.'

Sulma Tan remained impassive and for a moment nobody spoke, as if waiting for the tension to drift out of the open doors.

It struck me how Sulma Tan did not get visibly angry about such things – but spoke in a cool, if somewhat vicious manner in reply. But there was the slip of the tongue: *whatever reason took her fancy* could get a person executed. It reaffirmed the suspicion I had had since I'd arrived in Koton. That the queen possibly ruled in some royal dictatorship, without any real assistance from a council or senate, without any accountability to her people. If there was a political coup in the making, it was easy to see where the motivation lay. Royals were meant to rule along with democratically elected officials in exchange for the benefits of trade from being in the Vispasian Royal Union. It was a two-hundred-year-old agreement that did not appear to be fulfilled. I would remember to mention this in a report to the Sun Chamber later on. And, in the event that some of my messages were being read, I would write that information in code.

'It was two mornings ago,' I said, bringing the conversation back on track. 'How did she leave you if she normally has you by her side all the time?'

'She asked me to bring our horses around the front and to wait for her in the dining room, before she headed to her private baths. That is the one moment of the day where she remains alone. She has no bath attendants, nothing like that. I think she liked the privacy – it was just her and the water.'

'What was she like at that time?'

'There were no more signs that she was disturbed by the message, if that's what you mean. As I say, she has a good face for hiding her feelings. Lady in her position needs to be like that. So she carried on as normal.'

'And you were . . . ?'

'Waiting in the dining room. The opposite side to her house to where I'd taken the horses. Time passes and one of the other lads came to ask me why she's taking so long. We head to the bath where there's no noise, no splashes. Eventually we go inside and find it empty. Search the whole house. In the end there's nothing to be found and when Varn here,' he nodded to a short but muscular individual, 'took a look out front, we saw that her horse had gone. Couldn't even see her in the surrounding hills.'

'What was your next course of action?' Sulma Tan asked, in a much more friendly tone than before.

'I sent a few men in different directions, leaving one back just in case she returned. It was clear she'd taken the horse to go somewhere, so there seemed no point in looking around the house. Hours later and we'd seen nothing. We gave it another night, waiting for her to return, and waited for patrols to get back and then we got word from the city about what had happened. So we set out last night to get here as quick as we could. There the story ends.'

'Has she ever left you alone before, for any length of time?' I asked.

'Never. Absolutely not. I wouldn't say she was paranoid, but she paid us for protection and safety.'

'Had you ever had any trouble previously?'

'No more than what you'd expect in the world of business. If things got heated then we were there to calm things down, a lady who lives alone like that, and who has so much to lose, needs a few spare hands if things get rough.'

'She *deliberately* left you because she didn't want you to follow,' I concluded. 'For the first time in her life, she went somewhere without telling you. All of this came immediately after a message arrived from the city, a message she brought with her and which was presumably taken from her during her murder. Whatever was in that message would reveal, of course, what we're dealing with, but that's not available to us.'

'Could it be a business rival?' Santhan asked.

'Were there really any serious rivals to someone of such power?' I asked in return. 'You should know.'

'Guess not. But maybe there were those who wanted what she had.'

'Again, were you aware of any?'

He shrugged and shook his head.

'Besides, the killer has not taken anything . . . No. All they've taken is her life and that's probably all they wanted.'

'You have a theory forming, am I correct?' Sulma Tan said.

'Not really. For a while now I've believed the past to be behind the deaths of Bishop Tahn Valin and Grendor of the Cape. And Lydia's death also leads me along this same road. A message that came out of the blue, enticing her to the city. Something from the past. A secret that she wanted no one to know about . . . These three people were killed the same way for a reason. Somehow, by looking at these three lives, we'll find out what has connected them all.'

Santhan was listening eagerly and clearly wanted to know what to do. His mistress was the one who gave the orders, and now there were none. He rested a hand on the wall and looked at me expectantly.

'Santhan,' I said, 'you will lead us to Lydia's country residence tomorrow evening, after the games. Along the way you will tell me absolutely everything you know about her life. You may know more than anyone. What you say may help me to discover a vicious killer.'

'Aye, sir.'

'Good. We'll meet you here. Don't stray too far in case we need you.'

With that, Santhan took his men back through the corridor and outside, leaving Sulma Tan and me to linger in the calm of the house. We moved to one of the lighter rooms, overlooking the gardens towards the front.

As my gaze drifted across the herbs there, I reflected on the direction of the case. Sulma Tan, too, remained quiet – though she couldn't hide the fact that she was unsettled.

'Have recent developments given you reason for concern?' I asked.

'He was right.' She gave a deep breath and tilted back her head.

'Who, Santhan?'

'He said I spend too much time behind a desk.'

'I must confess, it is not the life for me. As much as my life has its problems, I love being among people out in the world. Seeing different landscapes.'

'I envy you,' she said. 'Seeing so much of the world the way you do.'

'The other option always seems more attractive,' I replied.

'No. I genuinely envy you.'

'There are always opportunities to come and work in the Sun Chamber,' I said. 'I'm sure they'd welcome your ferocious intelligence.'

'I don't know if that is the life for me. My place is here with my queen.'

'I must confess, I'm deeply glad to have such intelligence to hand. We're going to need both our minds if we're going to solve these crimes.'

Catching Up

Allius Golt was waiting for me on the street corner by the front gate of the palace compound. He was standing there in somewhat more ceremonial garb – a fine, dark-leather breastplate and highly polished boots glinting in the afternoon sunlight. He stood a little taller and looked into the distance, as if I was his commanding officer.

I introduced him to Sulma Tan and she explained how she could permit him access inside the palace – or wherever he was required to work. After we went inside and the guards searched him, we saw to it that he was issued with passwords for the next three days, for morning and night, which he silently mouthed a few times until they were committed to his memory.

We walked the long corridors and were granted access to increasingly off-limits sections of the palace, until eventually we reached our quarters. There, Allius turned his back to the wall and took his position on duty.

Inside, Leana and Nambu had returned from their interview with Grendor's friends. They were currently working through yet another set of sword techniques, though this had been of a gentler and more instructive nature. They both turned to face us on our arrival, and we sat down to exchange information.

First I mentioned Allius Golt, the man on the door, telling them of the reason for extra protection.

Leana was quick to understand the need for more help, which was a relief. It was important she understood that I was not questioning her abilities. One of Leana's admirable qualities was that, despite her competitiveness, despite her desire to be better at fighting or learning fluent Detratan, she would never think of her own pride first.

'How did it go with Grendor's friends?' I asked.

'Spirits save me, at first they would not speak to me.'

'Why was that?' Sulma Tan asked.

'Because of the colour of my skin,' came the nonchalant reply.

'Oh.' Sulma Tan looked embarrassed.

'It is not your fault.' Leana shrugged. 'I am used to this. I am merely thankful that I am not as pale as northern people. They suffer so badly under the sun. Not even the slave dealers will trade them.'

'That may be so,' Sulma Tan said, 'but in this prefecture we pride ourselves on being a welcoming people. We believe in the latest thinking, in dignity and politeness, and not hostility. The queen once wrote a pamphlet demanding that a certain level of decorum be shown to visitors.'

'Perhaps,' Leana said, 'the people we saw have yet to read it. But eventually from these men I managed to discover . . . very little. We met up with three of them individually, and another two who were brothers that shared a house. Each of them reacted similarly, apart from the two brothers. They were very odd – to the extent that I thought they might have been lovers as well as brothers.'

Nambu's reaction clearly demonstrated that her mind was revisiting her disgust.

'But when I presented the queen's seal,' Leana said, 'each of them more or less cowered into the corner of the room and was only too willing to give any information, what little use it was.'

'I rather enjoyed it,' Nambu added with a grin.

'Seeing them individually helped verify their accounts,' Leana continued. 'They all said exactly the same thing, though I did not think they had rehearsed it. According to them there was nothing strange about his behaviour. He had spoken warmly of future events – both the next day and the following years. He was in good spirits, joking and laughing. He left alone, having consumed only a small amount of wine – because he never liked returning drunk to his wife. There is nothing here of use.'

'I wouldn't say that,' I replied. 'Someone who does not expect trouble, someone who shows no signs of worry, is either a very good actor, or they *genuinely* have no reason to feel worried. Grendor was currently living a happy life. This, again, suggests to me that the reason for his murder was because of something that happened in the past.'

'We assume much.' Sulma Tan sounded mildly annoyed.

'That is the nature of our work,' I replied. 'The facts do not present themselves easily. Patterns must be observed. Similarities established. Even the differences could tell us something. We have three victims of a similar age, all killed within the prefecture, all having been murdered in a way that suggests a kind of brutal revenge. Grendor had nothing to worry about in his current life. Lydia Marinus receives a letter, which she shares with no one and which forces her to act out of character. All the victims have been on display in public, in one way or another. And they are all linked.'

At that moment I discussed the connection with Grendor's

Naval Exports, with Lydia's mining operations, and the evum that potentially connected them all. I lifted out the bishop's ring again. 'This is something to do with the murders. It connects all three victims in some way.' I stepped over to Sulma Tan and finished softly: 'So do not despair. We have some direction.'

The Census

An uneventful evening passed, bringing a much-needed period of deep rest and regeneration of the soul. Even my dreams were peaceful, visions of sipping wine under the shade of an olive tree, with not a soul for miles.

It was Allius Golt who eventually summoned me back to the land of the living, by knocking harshly on the door.

'I brought a small sand timer with me, given you said how dark it was down here.' He spoke through the gap in the partly open door, showing no signs of tiredness from having spent the entire evening on guard. In one hand he held out an ornate instrument, which he placed back in his satchel. 'Six rotations of this make up one hour. I gave it forty-two rotations before deciding to wake you. Somewhere out there, by my reckoning, the dawn light should be showing.'

'Excellent thinking.' I was impressed at his preparation and dedication.

'You might think this was purely for your benefit, but it helps keep a man sane on watches like this. It's routine that you start to crave after a while, familiar things, reassurances.'

'Were there any disturbances during the night?'

'No one came close to me . . . though it wasn't easy to tell if I'm honest. If it's possible, it would be prudent to see that this corridor can be lit throughout. At the moment, I'm standing by a cresset – I might as well have a target painted on my chest, for all the good it does.'

'I see your point. I'll see if we can get that changed.'

'Much appreciated, sir. But as I say, I don't think anyone came down here. You get to hear the odd shuffle, rats most likely, but in these long corridors, looking out into the dark for seven hours, sounds can trick the mind. Best not to let paranoia get the better of you.'

'You're free to head home, of course,' I said. 'You have access for the next few days so by all means come down here by dusk – no need to wait for me outside. And I, myself, might not always be here. But that doesn't mean you won't go without coin for your efforts.'

'Understood.' With a sharp nod, he turned and marched along the passageway, into the darkness.

I headed back into the room to light more candles. Removing my shirt, I examined my abdomen in the warm light: nearly all the bruises had now vanished. There were no cuts, no scars, and very few blemishes. Just a few patches of discoloration to indicate that I had been on the receiving end of sustained violence. It was remarkable, really, that the healing had been so rapid. Just a few days and the transformation was one of thirty days' worth of healing.

I reached for the ring in my pocket and examined it under the light.

Until she spoke I didn't notice that Leana was standing there watching me. 'You are questioning its properties again, are you not?'

Her gaze was fixed on the ring and it felt like a good time to reveal the thoughts that had been haunting me. 'Leana, in spite of forgetting to take the tisane I've not experienced a single seizure – not since this ring has been in my possession.'

Leana was indifferent to the notion, but she was definitely not dismissive of what I had said. 'Your rate of healing is like nothing I have seen before. And I have seen you scarred and beaten up many times, but you take an age to get over it, and keep reminding me about it. Yet, spirits save us, you have healed in an unnatural way. This is obvious.'

'But is it the ring, though?' I said, holding it out. To me, it could have been a life-changer. Though I had grown used to them, to not have seizures would have been beyond relief. 'Is it this *evum*?'

Her eyes glanced to the ring and back to mine. 'You have not had a single seizure, so you say. Not even a small one?'

'Not so much as a mental flicker. Not even a headache.' The lack of suffering made me wonder if the gods had finally relinquished whatever hold they had over me. If this ring possessed properties, it seemed like a true gift from the gods. But I reminded myself that it was evidence in a case; it was not mine to own.

Leana nodded. 'The longest I have known you go without one in your sleep is ten days or so. We may be early in our assumptions. You say you have stopped taking the apothecary's herbs that we acquired in Tryum?'

'I have some left, but I have not had time to make a tisane.'

'I have told you to do so twice before I exercised.'

'I know, I'm sorry.'

'Is Nambu asleep still?'

'I believe she is. I will wake her up for practice. This should be a good opportunity for training, as in the real world we do not always get to choose the time of a fight.'

Leana picked up another sword and headed into Nambu's room.

A while later there was a disgruntled young voice, a strict, firm reply, and a half-hearted clash of swords.

'Not good enough!' Leana shouted.

I smiled slightly. Leana often said the same thing about me.

The Koton Games were to be held from mid-morning through to the late afternoon, once there had been ample opportunity for Sulma Tan to present her census summary to Queen Dokuz in the palace.

Since she realized that I was keen on speaking with the queen once again, Sulma Tan had asked if I would like to attend court in order to see her present her findings. Truth be told, now that the queen had left her daughter with us, I was surprised that our company had not been sought by her majesty more often. It felt like a good idea to remind her of the fact that she had asked me to help her, not to mention to give details of Nambu's time with us, so I happily accepted the offer.

To some people, that early morning discussion might have come across as rather dull, but to me it was an opportunity to glimpse into the dynamics of Koton.

The announcements were to take place in what was laughingly referred to as the Kotonese Parliament. It was a beautifully ornate hall crafted from grey stone, marbled floors, with tall, narrow archways and large lead-framed windows, which let in a spectacular amount of morning light.

Wearing a shimmering blue gown, which appeared to change its hue as she moved, Queen Dokuz was seated on her immense throne. A modest silver crown was perched on her head, but today she seemed to suffer the weight of it. Her eunuch stood behind her chair with an air of amusement, if not complete indifference to the occasion. Around the two of them, garbed in green, blue and red robes, clerics, advisors and counsellors circled like hawks, until the queen dispersed the flock with a single outstretched arm. They soon took their positions seated on the floor around her, very much beneath her gaze.

Others were seated further away from the queen's enclave of officials, but even this large group of a hundred or so people appeared to be anything but average. Rich silks, flamboyant hats, large gemstones – though no evum, I noted – were on display.

Sulma Tan was talking to an old man, whom she'd previously pointed out to me as the queen's first secretary, Bren Dellears, a man who was hoping to retire very soon. He had reached the age of seventy-six summers, and desired to spend more time with his family. For a scholar he had a fine posture, and in his youth had taken to a routine of exercises to preserve himself – something he encouraged Sulma Tan to do herself. His departure meant that within the year Sulma Tan would become the first secretary. As part of her rite of passage, today she would announce the results of the five-year census to the queen and her court. She would then be questioned by anyone within the queen's first circle on any of the details, and be expected to discuss the issues at length.

Sulma Tan stood only a few paces from the queen, ready to address only her.

The plan was that she would continue reading from pieces of parchment handed to her by Bren Dellears, moving through the themes of the nation – population facts, agriculture, industry, arts and so on. Before she began, however, the queen spotted me standing at the back of the hall and beckoned me forward.

I hastened through a gap between the seated guests and stood alongside Sulma Tan.

'Before we go through the details,' the queen announced, her voice resonating far down the hall, 'I wish to know of your progress in solving the vile murders.'

'We are getting closer with each new day,' I said.

'You do not seem yourself convinced,' she replied.

'I am, but it is a rather troubling and sophisticated case.'

'That may be so. Everyone within this hall is frightened for their lives. How many more of our circle must die needlessly?'

'As I say, my lady, we get closer with each day and I am confident that we will find whoever did this.'

She simply stared at me, and it was almost impossible to read her expression. It was a well-honed royal gaze, one that had been crafted to inspire fear and awe in the recipient. She then asked much more quietly, 'Discreetly – how is the princess getting on?'

There and then I wanted to reply with a dozen other questions. Why was someone trying to kidnap her? What is it you fear? Why aren't you telling me about Nambu? But here, in front of this audience, it was not the appropriate time.

'She is getting on splendidly,' I whispered. 'We are teaching her the arts of self-defence and the investigative methods of the Sun Chamber. She has a fine inquisitive mind.'

'Of course she has, being of the Sorghatan lineage.'

'It goes without saying, majesty. But I wonder, could we perhaps have a moment in private – when it suits you – to speak about her. I have a few questions not fit for the ears of those outside of immediate family.'

'You may. I will see to it you have the time.' Her expression remained cold and unreadable. 'You may now be seated.'

I gave a slight bow and took a few steps back, finding a spot on the floor from which to watch Sulma Tan's presentation.

For the next hour, as the morning sun grew in intensity, and the bright light behind her gave her the appearance that she had been granted god-like powers, she spoke at length about the state of the country: from an estimate of the number of children who had died that year, to discussing a community of septuagenarians living on their own island; from the number of farms to the

number of private clan castles. Ores that had been mined, building projects, major discoveries, population movements, it was
one of the most comprehensive speeches I'd ever heard. Curiously
she had mentioned the same discrepancies in population numbers
that I had read about in the manuscript hall, though this time she
had narrowed them down to younger age ranges. I wondered if
this had anything to do with Lydia Marinus' orphanage work
– that she had taken young people out of the official system in
some way.

I was fascinated to learn about the important tribal lineages,
and how much of Kotonese society was ultimately built around
a handful of large, powerful clans – the Yenui, Tahtar and the
Rukrid. Many of these names mentioned I had overheard in the
context of the Senate. No doubt some of these had been awarded
ceremonial positions as a gesture of peace, to prevent the need
for a coup. I suspected that those around me now had achieved
their favour in the court because of their passivity over the years.
It was no wonder everyone sat around like sycophants, delighting
in the details, applauding as the tax revenues were announced,
and making the appropriate noises when discussing the passing
of certain well-respected members of society.

Scanning the crowd, I hoped to discern whether or not anyone appeared visibly worried about their safety. Perhaps someone
might have shown nervousness or was peering over their shoulder
to see if anyone might strike. But no, it was not to be.

The queen appeared neither pleased nor displeased. She merely
absorbed what was revealed, and no one but she questioned Sulma
Tan. Whether or not that was out of fear of interrupting the
queen was anyone's guess.

The Koton Games

No matter what day it was, it could be guaranteed that some-where in the Vispasian Royal Union there would be festivities taking place. Nearly always, either in a large city square or tucked away in a warren-like cave settlement, there would be various events held in honour of the gods, or in celebration of some profound moment in history.

Here on the outskirts of the city of Kuvash, there was a regular event held every thirty days in honour of Astran and Nastra, in which the finest archers, riders, sword fighters and wrestlers competed. Only now did I realize just how deeply held religious beliefs were in Koton. There were religious symbols carried on banners, depictions of the gods in horse and fish form to denote their presence on land and in the sea, and numerous priests intoned the words of their gods to the various groups who would pause to listen.

Surprisingly, the event was not held for the plentiful citizens of the city, but rather for those in the wealthier Sorghatan Prefecture. It didn't stop huge crowds gathering along the sides of the roads, however, following the passage of the four dozen participants as if they were members of some victorious army.

In Sun Chamber circles, such events were very well thought of — they were an outlet for the combative nature of people, quenching a thirst for war without any of the harsh realities of conflict. I suspected that financial aid was occasionally redirected via Sun Chamber assistance to ensure that games like this were a regular occurrence, in order that peace be maintained between nations, though I had not seen any evidence of the matter.

The combatants and the authorized spectators, all of whom were dressed in their fineries, with garlanded hair and bright dye on their faces, made their way along the road leading east from the city under the brilliant sunlight. The sharp hills shimmered in the distance and the river cut through the landscape undulating its way towards them. Grassland, grazed by thousands of animals, dominated the mile or two surrounding the city.

There was definitely an air of festivity among the gathered throng. Leana and I rode a little distance behind the queen who, to my surprise, did not opt for a carriage. She rode a resplendent black mare, without a saddle, and was dressed in relatively modest clothing for a royal — a sumptuously decorated leather breastplate fitted on top of a purple tunic. For this afternoon, Nambu would be required to ride alongside her mother, rather than be in the so-called safety of our company.

Our jubilant mass proceeded east at a leisurely pace.

The site of the games was in fact a series of large, well-kept circular green fields, bordered with tidy hedges as if these were manicured gardens rather than arenas in which people would fight. Little coloured flags marked boundaries, which became more defined as the crowds filed in. There was a central small stand constructed from stone, which could probably accommodate three or four hundred people. The blue banners of Koton, bound to several poles, snapped and rattled in the strong westerly breeze. Their colours were bold against the bright sky.

The stand paled in comparison to the massive Stadium of Lentus in Tryum, but it was a pleasant enough place for many to watch the proceedings. We were permitted into the royal enclave, while many of the others – people of good standing in the city – milled around the low hedgerows, taking their places in the small garden arenas to watch the events. We stood approximately twenty feet away from where the queen, Nambu, Sulma Tan, eunuchs, guards and various servants, looked down upon the afternoon's unfolding events. Food was brought to many of the attendees on small silver plates. Soldiers chatted with insouciance as sword fighters began their battles, arrows thudded into targets, and wrestlers took their bizarre angular stances.

It was all very prim and proper. Polite ripples of applause filtered out across the fields as the participants began to assemble. The day only got warmer. A constant yet gentle hum of chatter echoed in the grounds. This was all very *civilized*. However, to me it was a waste of valuable time, which could be better spent on the investigation.

Now and then the crowd would rise as finalists for various skills moved before the main stand, and the queen and her daughter would file through the throng in order to exchange pleasantries. That aspect was very informal – such a thing would never happen at the Stadium of Lentus, unless under very special circumstances. The fact that the king would have been standing some distance from the chariot racers, and would have seen himself as a different level of being entirely, would have prevented that. The queen appeared to thrive on *being seen* as someone at one with her people – though admittedly it was simply a large inner circle of her people. When I asked Sulma Tan if there were any politicians present, she pointed out the Rukrid clan's senators down below, alongside those of the Tahtar family. Both clans were garbed in resplendent silks of blue, red and purple, but the Rukrids' clothing featured the family crest of a sickle and star. They were completely at ease with the day and their position below the queen. If there were any rivalries, they were not on display today. Perhaps that was the whole point of the games – to show that all was well with society.

'Sulma Tan – in your census speech, something came to mind concerning Lydia Marinus. I have read elsewhere of discrepancies in population information.'

For a moment her usual calm countenance felt fragile. 'My census gatherings are accurate.'

'Oh, I'm not questioning how robust they are. Something piqued my curiosity. Do you think the discrepancies could be because of things like Lydia Marinus' orphanage work? She must have taken many children out of official statistics, educating them and perhaps resettling them.'

Sulma Tan leaned in close to reply. 'I have communicated with the operators of the orphanage, and they confirm well over a thousand children passed through Lydia's unofficial channels over the years. Lydia donated handsomely to the orphanages.'

'Grendor did too, if I recall.'

We gave each other a knowing look as another connection was confirmed. 'A thousand children or more were bettered. The orphanages, which were happy that their capacity was expanded thanks to Lydia, suggest many became workers for her operations abroad as she sought to grow her businesses. The queen requested that the orphanage be set up two decades ago. She wanted to get children off the streets and looked after. Well, it seems that Lydia helped them even further by educating and reforming many of them.'

'Lydia thought the census was a waste of resources,' I remarked. 'I would wager one reason was so that attention was not drawn to her reform work. It seems so strange that such honourable deeds are concealed.'

Sulma Tan merely gazed through the sun across the heads of the elite of Kotonese society. I remained unconvinced as to the discrepancies in the population. There remained many more who were unaccounted for.

While people drifted in and out of the garden areas, their hazy shadows began to lengthen. Men and women fought; some lost, some won, but there never seemed to be a loss of dignity. The aromas of foods caught my senses when the wind remained calm and I considered getting something to eat.

I was about to ask Leana if she, too, would like a snack, but paused upon seeing her expression of intense focus as she looked to her left, across the hundreds of faces in the stand.

'Is everything all right?' I asked.

'No. There is a man, approximately your height and build, though of a slightly paler complexion, moving ever-closer to Nambu. He has been watching her for some time – though I cannot say for how long precisely. Long enough that I have noticed, and I can confirm he does not look trustworthy.'

'I can't quite make him out . . .' I tried to follow her gaze, but she quite rightly did not want to point at him in case he spotted us.

'He is standing under the banner pole nearest the lower step, looking away from the events.'

'Oh yes, there he is.' The man was tall with blond hair, and a gaunt face, wearing what looked to be a fitted leather breastplate and a black cloak.

'We should probably get a bit closer.'

No sooner had I spoken, when the crowd all rose and applauded as another pair of finalists – two bare-chested and enormous wrestlers – moved before the stand and stomped their feet into the grassy mud opposite each other.

'Go quickly,' I urged, and we shoved our way through the great and good of Koton, apologizing as we went.

We were nearing the banner pole where we had seen the man, but he had now moved.

'He is higher up,' Leana said, 'nearer the queen.'

'No, the queen is further down there.' I pointed to where she was speaking with the wrestlers. 'He's going after Nambu.'

We changed course and headed right for him, but he was using the opportunity of the moment to move quickly up the steps of the stand, right towards where Nambu was seated and to where the queen was returning.

Leana vanished amid the throng as she sprinted nimbly towards him, leaving me to continue ungracefully pushing my way there.

I caught a glimpse of his leap towards Nambu.

Leana intercepted him and engaged in close-quarter combat. A scream came from the crowd. People turned their attention to the two individuals fighting on the upper step of the stand, pushing each other against the waist-high stone wall that was between them and a forty-foot drop.

I reached Nambu just as the eunuch, Brell, ushered her to safety.

First Leana disabled the attacker's knife arm by smacking his wrists repeatedly against the wall until the blade fell over the side. Then, while pinning down his wrist, she stamped sideways into his stomach before slamming his head upwards with her knee. Still he attempted to fight back, losing all sense of control now as he flailed his arms. The crowd watched, curiously silent, as Leana finished him off with blows to his legs.

As if realizing that he would be captured, he leapt head first over the side of the stand. With a collective shriek, the crowd, myself among their mass, surged towards the wall and peered over to see if he had survived.

The man's body lay sprawled and broken on the stone below.

If he had landed on the grass a few feet to one side, he might have survived, but a trickle of blood began to emerge, suggesting his head had connected with the hard surface.

Leana moved next to me, breathless and regaining her composure, sweat glistening on her brow. There was a small cut to her hand, but aside from that she looked well, and soon she had regained her breath.

'Are you hurt?'

'No,' she replied. 'He was very good though. I am sorry if he is dead. I tried not to kill him. Though at least it is not my fault this time, no?'

Down below, a few spectators had moved to the side of the body, crouching down and gesturing over it.

'We should get down there and take a look,' I said, 'before that lot mess with him too much.'

'It will take us just as long to get down there as it did to get across the stand,' Leana replied, indicating the thick mass of bodies that stood before us. 'Is it not interesting that, despite all the civilized competitions that have been going on today, this lot are still far more interested in the sight of a corpse.'

'Who is this man?'

'You saved my daughter's life,' the queen announced.

I hadn't noticed the queen approaching until she spoke to us. There was a renewed firmness in her voice and only now did I realize how tall she was, how much presence she possessed within a group of people. That others bowed at her arrival only added to her lustre of a goddess among them.

The sun was almost ready to set now and an orange light washed across the scene. Leana, Sulma Tan and myself were kneeling by the sprawled body of the attacker. The crowd were separated from us by a ring of twenty soldiers in the blue and black of the equestrian regiments. Surrounded by a coterie of eunuchs in red gowns, Nambu was standing between two soldiers. Her expression was one of embarrassment, though she had no reason to feel that way. Perhaps, with youthful pride, she felt that she could defend herself now thanks to Leana's lessons in swordplay. Still, at least she had witnessed just how talented Leana could be in combat.

'It was my duty.' Leana never liked a fuss being made over her, but she was probably going to have to put up with what was coming.

'You are a hero of this nation,' the queen declared, loud enough for anyone nearby to hear. 'You have protected the Sorghatan lineage. I knew it was wise to leave her in your skilled hands.'

'Again,' Leana bowed her head, 'please think nothing of it. You entrusted your daughter to our care. This is our job.'

'You shall be rewarded,' the queen declared. There was no getting out of it. But, as if the previous conversation had not happened, she snapped her fingers at the corpse. 'Who is this man?'

'I hoped you might be able to shed some light on the matter.' The words escaped my mouth before I had a chance to think. Even Leana looked surprised.

'Why?' the queen glared at me. 'Do you think I *know* him?'

There was a tension thickening the air between us. Though I represented the Sun Chamber, I knew I had to be respectful before a royal – especially one who clearly did not suffer fools, or challenges to her authority.

But it was Nambu, surprisingly, who came to my assistance, pushing forward from her eunuch escort into the parted circle. 'He means, Mother, that he's not *stupid*.'

'Do not speak to me like that, girl.'

'You don't just hand me over to strangers without being seriously worried for my safety in the palace. He knows that. We both know that. If he thinks there might be more to this, he's entitled to know.'

The crowd were utterly silent. Birds shrieked from the nearby treetops and the banners could be heard snapping in the wind. The queen's gaze moved repeatedly between her daughter and myself. I was anxious to see how a subtle tyrant queen might react to her daughter's indiscretion.

She gave a command for the soldiers to widen the circle and to disperse the crowd. They held aloft their glaives and the crowd, naturally fearful, stepped back. The horses began to canter clockwise, edging out more and more until the nearest person was a good hundred paces away.

'Now that any spies are out of earshot . . .'

Or rather, I thought, now anyone else at all was out of earshot.

The queen now stood in a noble pose, her head tilted up, her face stern. Her make-up was cracking slightly. 'First you should realize this: I know very little about the attack, the attacker, or indeed why Nambu is being targeted. I am the queen and yet I remain in the dark – this is not something I am accustomed to. You will notice I have very few servants compared with many other rulers – this is not representative of how we are as a people. Indeed, as a result of my father taking over Koton by military might, to make a show of his power he possessed hundreds of servants, many of whom were barely more than unsanctioned slaves. No, the reason I surround myself by so few is because I trust so few people. A guard may slip a knife into one's back with remarkable ease.'

Though I never spoke the thought, it did occur to me that her father had claimed the throne with a military coup, and that he may well have passed on his paranoia to his daughter. 'And you fear that would happen to Nambu – that one of your guards would hold some grudge against your family?'

She remained perfectly still as she regarded me. 'I do not know what others think. I can judge only on what I see. But what I do know is this: there have been moves in the past, within the palace, to take Nambu. To take her from under my eye. Two men we caught previously were both killed while trying to escape. One cut his throat before my guards could get to him.'

A silence fell upon the scene, and I contemplated the efforts to claim Nambu. It did not seem prudent to divulge that there had been another attempt recently. The queen did not need to know such things at the moment.

'Do you know of any schemes to end your lineage?' I asked.

The queen laughed. 'I suspect schemes are being planned all the time,' she replied. 'But it is nearly always talk cooked up in taverns known for their political discussions.'

'People wish for more say in the affairs of state?' I asked.

'What good would it do? They would only derail our nation's progress with their own trivial desires. They would seek to re-distribute wealth among their own kind and say it is for the good of people. Petty men with petty ideals make up my government. They are ill-suited to *lead* and to bring about progress. They would have the women of our nation at home weaving again, instead of being my secretary,' she gestured to the quiet Sulma Tan, 'or a future queen' – a gesture to her daughter. 'No, old feuds coming to the fore are the usual reason for talk against me. But as I say, this is only talk. But there is action to take a young girl and do Nastra-knows what to her. That is why I wanted her to go with you, so she would not follow the predictable rituals of state. So whoever it is who has repeatedly breached my court will not have an easy opportunity.'

She steered me back towards the corpse. All of us stood in a circle, staring down at the attacker. Leana knelt down and turned him over.

'I do not recognize him,' the queen said.

'Is it possible he comes from some secret organization?' Leana asked.

'A religious group maybe?' I added. 'Or fanatical cult?'

'Sometimes,' Leana muttered, 'I find it hard to understand the difference between such things in Vispasia.'

There was a smile on the queen's lips. 'This is why we have only the one major religion in Koton.'

'It could well be a professional assassination attempt on the princess.'

Nambu looked at me, her wide eyes betraying little. She shrugged. 'I don't know what all the fuss is about.'

'Quite,' the queen snapped, lifting her chin, 'and we've enough to worry about as it is with good friends and powerful people being murdered, let alone a further conspiracy. Astran's mercy . . .'

'With greatest respect – and I ask only to aid my investigation – what happens if neither yourself nor Nambu are on the throne? To whom does power devolve?'

'An interim government would be formed, much like in Detrata,' the queen replied without hesitation. 'The next in line will be sought and that could mean either of two of my cousins, one of whom is a lay preacher in the community of Astran and Nastra, and the other is confined to a faraway temple – because she is a leper. The preacher wouldn't be permitted to rule since we have a separation of the temple from the affairs of the state – unless he chose to forgo his religious calling.'

'They are not exactly challengers to the throne then,' I added.

She looked down at the body one last time. 'Not exactly, no. We will hang this one's corpse as a warning.' Then, to her daughter, she said, 'Come.' For the first time there was something resembling normal affection – a gentle hand on her shoulder as she was led away. Sulma Tan followed while Leana and I knelt beside the corpse, staring hopelessly at its resting form as the sun dipped below the horizon.

Within a minute guards came to take the body away.

'Search his possessions thoroughly,' I said to them, but judging by the haphazard way they tried to lift him, I doubted their job would be anything like thorough.

Evening Discussions

Once again I studied the papers taken from the premises of Naval Exports, hoping that something new might materialize. The word *evum* still stuck out, calling to me from the page, but there was little more that could be made of what was presented.

The candles flickered and burned down low. Somewhere beyond the closed door, Allius Golt stood on guard.

Leana was taking Nambu through some of her stretches. When we had arrived back in these quarters, there had been a gem-studded bracelet waiting for Leana as reward for her service earlier in the day. The item was wonderfully ornamental, and the emeralds in it were worth a year's wages. Leana was totally indifferent to the trinket, and merely shoved it in her belongings.

There was an extra level of determination in the young princess's face now, as if she had been unsettled by the events earlier in the day. Perhaps it was a point of honour, to want to defend herself rather than have others protect her.

Talking about it might help her process things so, after they had finished, I put that thought to her and wondered what she would make of it.

Exhausted from some dynamic moves, the young girl perched

on the end of the bed and untied her hair. Leana slumped across the couch, and I turned fully from the desk to give the princess all my attention.

'I want to be prepared in case it happens again.' She dabbed the perspiration on her forehead with her sleeve.

'And you think there will be another attack?' I asked.

'I want to be prepared,' she repeated. 'For whatever happens to me. I do not want to have to be saved again.'

I shot a brief smile at Leana. 'You heard her – next time let the attacker claim her.'

'That's not what I mean,' she replied. 'Leana, thank you so very much . . .'

Leana dismissed her thanks with a wave of her hand. 'Think nothing of it. The amount of times I have saved his skin . . .'

'Well, I'm grateful,' Nambu continued. 'I just don't want to have to be a burden to anyone. I want to be able to look after myself. I have led such a protected life. I'm old enough now to know better than that.'

She was still young, of course, but when was a bad age to learn the arts of defence?

'Do you think you could cope,' Leana asked, 'with your blade above a man's heart, your hand poised to press down and end his life – do you think you could do that?'

'Yes,' she replied, somewhat hesitantly.

'The moment you do will end your childhood.'

'I'm not a child,' Nambu snapped. 'I'm older than a child.'

'The path to adulthood is not through a numbered gate.' Leana leaned up in the chair. 'Many are still children though they are twice your age. They live their lives cushioned from the realities of the world. They are infantile. They have had everything done for them. They have earned nothing. They have the souls of children, but they live in grown-up bodies.'

'Are you saying I'm cushioned?' Nambu asked, before looking glumly at the floor. 'It isn't easy, you know.'

Leana sighed. 'When I was your age, my family had all the money I could wish for. Spirits save me, we had a palace as grand as this. We wore clothes of such fine weaving. We were surrounded by art. Atrewen culture, at its height, would have eclipsed anything that Vispasia could offer. One day I was walking along polished onyx floors, through gold arches that glittered in soft sunlight. The very next day, the civil wars broke out in our district.'

A natural pause developed, and I felt I did not wish the conversation to end. In a few sentences Leana had muttered more about her past than I had really known. She talked very little about those days.

'Then what?' Nambu asked bluntly.

'I had been sheltered from the war,' Leana continued. 'I led that soft existence. I knew very little about why we were fighting – even who we were fighting. But it was my mother who made me eventually watch. She said it would be for my own good. Standing there in my precious silk gown I looked from our balcony as fires took the forests surrounding the palace. We could hear the screams of the villagers as they were cut down before they had the chance to get out of bed in the morning. The soldiers protecting our compound stood in their brilliant white tunics, their shields glimmering in the morning sun. I remember them being so neat – those crisp white lines. The walls of our compound soon gave way to the assault. The gate collapsed. The walls were scaled. We were besieged. As those fine soldiers protected us, being slaughtered so that we could live on, some of my family ushered a few of us through tunnels until we emerged in the cliffs, then dropped down by rope to the shore and escaped on ships. That was the moment I stopped being a child. Within a year I had learned the skills of a warrior, for there was no other choice. I watched as my own father was beheaded in battle. My mother was stabbed through the stomach trying to defend his corpse. Later I led rebel forces in retaliation, and we had some success. Men and women would have died for me.'

'Oh my.'

'Think on that responsibility, young Nambu, for it will be yours one day . . . But the wars became more violent. My people were wiped out because of their spiritual preferences or simply because they were associated with my family. The rest of my kin I saw killed, spirits save them. My husband — for I married when I was just a little older than you are now — was killed in front of me. Eventually I became the last in my bloodline to survive. I met Lucan here amidst an ocean of corpses — corpses that were there on my behalf, trying to restore my family's name to the throne of Atrewe. It is quite a responsibility for a young woman to bear, I can assure you.'

After a profound silence, Nambu asked, 'How old were you?'

'When the wars began, a mere eleven summers. When I mastered the basic arts of being a warrior, twelve. When I became advanced enough to lead a unit of my people, fourteen. When I married, fifteen. When I became, as you say in your cultures, a widow, seventeen. I met Lucan not long after that, a few years ago now.'

'That was not much of a childhood,' Nambu muttered, transfixed by Leana's tale.

This wasn't precisely how I remembered those events upon my arrival in Atrewe all those years ago, when I had first met Leana. The situation was more complex — the wars that involved her family also involved securing minerals for trading with the Vispasian Royal Union, a lucrative venture for whoever won, and I had certain suspicions that soldiers had been sent from the nation of Venyn in order to arm the rebels in the first place.

I could never prove this and, of course, there was no point in raising the issue now.

Silence came and I had nothing to add to the matter, for I had led something of a privileged life. My Detratan summers, growing up, were long and uneventful. I played games in our large gardens, and received tuition from incredibly fine minds. There was never a day where there was a shortage of food for our table. With my friends – sons and daughters of the senatorial class – we were taken on short journeys to see some of the wonders of our nation. Thanks to the close protection of the Civil Cohorts, there were very few visits by thieves.

Indeed, I had led rather an idyllic childhood. No events came, save the early death of my mother, to corrupt my view of the world. No horrific killings were enacted before my eyes. Leana had experienced far greater luxuries and endured far greater evils within a few years than most people would ever know existed.

I viewed Leana and Nambu in a very different light. They had both been denied a normal existence – Leana through atrocities, Nambu through being sheltered to the point of being a prisoner.

Suddenly it occurred to me that it was simply a basic right for a child to be allowed to play in the sun without a care in the world, if only for a while.

The world was full of struggle but surely that was due to striving to achieve growth and prosperity, leaving a legacy of fine arts and technology, all ultimately for the next generation? We look after them, we give them food to survive and flourish, to see that they are happy.

At least being an Officer of the Sun Chamber, I could do something no matter how small to ensure that children had that opportunity to . . . play. Unfortunately, right now my business was protecting people who were decades older and who lived a very comfortable life. Who would be next to fall foul of our murderer?

'What's your plan tomorrow?' Nambu asked.

Only then did I realize how much time had passed, and how deep the silence had been, since Leana had told us her story. We each must have been lost in our own private worlds for some time.

'At daybreak,' I said, 'we travel to Lydia Marinus' country house to see if it offers any more clues than her city dwelling. I put in a request with Sulma Tan for a small armed escort – not that I think there will be trouble, but we can conduct a more thorough search of the house. She'll also ensure that members of Lydia Marinus' private guard can lead the way.'

'Such a shame that Lydia has gone too,' Nambu said.

'You knew her?' Only then had it occurred to me that a 'friend' of her mother's could have brought them in contact with one another.

'I met her twice.' Nambu yawned. 'She was very kind to me. But everyone has to be kind to the heir to the throne.'

'*We* don't have to be kind,' I commented.

'No,' Nambu replied. 'And that's why I like your company.'

I prodded Leana's boot with the tip of my own. 'You hear that? You're clearly not working her hard enough if she still likes us.'

A Sprawling Villa

Our horses, Kinder and Manthwe, were waiting for us in the palace courtyard courtesy of the farrier Sojun, who had since left the premises. Nambu had given the order for her own majestic white animal to be brought round and moments later Sulma Tan arrived on horseback with a dozen soldiers in the blue and black colours of the equestrian regiments, each one with a hunting bow strung across their shoulders and a quiver full of arrows at the waist. Four of Lydia Marinus' own private guard arrived a moment later, their faces glum.

Leana leapt onto her horse without the use of stirrups or saddle. As if shamed by the fact that she had not been brought up in the same way, or wishing to emulate it herself, Nambu requested for her own equipment to be removed while I helped her up.

However, I was not to be intimidated by them and was more than happy to sit in a saddle. We had a six-hour ride ahead of us through this unfamiliar landscape and comfort would be very welcome.

Dawn had only just broken. In a pale, blue light we passed along the main thoroughfares to the gate of the prefecture. The few people who were around at this hour looked up curious as to what the fuss was about, but soon returned to their routines.

We exited and continued through the second prefecture at a fair pace, our noise preceding us and clearing the route out of the city. Nambu rode beside Leana, dressed plainly again in a brown tunic and black cloak, her hair tied back in a simple fashion.

The sun was still barely touching the hills, the buildings sparser, the road muddier, the road clearer, and with haste we rode through the country.

About an hour into our journey, I became alarmed.

Leana pointed them out: in the distance were three bright banners and a few hundred cavalrymen riding across the grassland. From here they seemed to trickle down the land like a mudslide, but the colours were of the Kotonese military — equestrian regiments and archers. Further beyond, just about visible, was another unit of soldiers — this time on foot, advancing far more slowly, but probably with no less determination. They were moving in a different direction to ours, but it was clear that they were headed towards the border with Detrata. All in all there must have been two thousand soldiers on the move. If it had been raining, we'd probably not have seen them. As it was, the clear skies allowed nothing to hide from view.

I moved my horse forward so that it was next to Sulma Tan. 'What news from the border?' I said, and gestured to the troop movements across the far slopes.

'Our military is dispersed around the country,' she replied. 'Sometimes we have large-scale exercises in order to keep them well trained, and to show other nations that we are used to armed conflict.'

'By other nations, I take it you mean Detrata?'

'Yes.'

'We are all fools when it comes to armed conflict within Vispasia,' I said. 'It is peace that has allowed all nations to flourish. A war will benefit no one.'

'This is true,' she replied. 'But we are not the ones who are beating war drums. I am surprised that Detrata wishes to act like this, considering the queen has been heavily influenced by their art and science. But we have to defend our lands. They have been given to our people, and they will remain for our people.'

'I can find out through my correspondence what is happening,' I said, 'but it will be quicker to ask you outright. What have you heard of Detrata's movements and why are you moving so many soldiers?'

'You are Detratan,' she replied. 'Is it fair to discuss this? You understand,' she tilted her head to indicate the soldier riding alongside, 'that I must ask such questions.'

'I am an Officer of the Sun Chamber,' I snapped, rather zealously so the soldier would understand that she was doing me no favours. 'My duty lies with Koton every bit as much as Detrata.'

'Well, there is no harm in sharing what is becoming public knowledge, and which you would find out in due course.'

I indicated for her to go on, now that this pretence was over.

'There are currently around fourteen thousand Detratan soldiers massing between two settlements a mere five miles from the border. Luckily we are a nation of few large cities, so there is nowhere within their reach at the moment. But an advancing army could very easily march across the border to be in such a position.'

'Have they made threats?'

'Yes, yes — there are siege engines in their ranks.'

'And diplomacy?'

'We have heard nothing. Ambassadors have been sent to Tryum in the past five days, but as yet we have heard nothing in response.'

'Why did you not say anything sooner?'

'You didn't ask,' she replied. 'And besides, I did not realize it was in your power to do anything. Presumably this is business of the Sun Chamber and you have people already looking into this. Astran knows, we have sent enough messages to Free State.'

'Then I am sure the matter is in hand.'

I did not fully believe my own words. Tensions between states had been known in the past, of course, and those had been settled in a court made up of a magistrate and senior clerics from all Vispasian nations.

But these tensions were usually because of smaller matters such as trading disputes, unfair revenue redistribution and occasion-ally localized violence over something like the death of an am-bassador. I was not wholly convinced the Sun Chamber had ever addressed the issue of such a threatening military formation on this scale. The Sun Legion was tens of thousands strong, of course, and was occasionally used to protect the peace – but those thousands were distributed across Vispasia and would take some time to bring together and make the fourteen thousand troops think again.

Lydia Marinus' estate was about a mile long according to the map and contained a walled villa, large gardens and long rectangular lakes, tombs, statues, a theatre and grottos. At the centre was a large square residence, around a hundred yards long on all sides and designed in the best Vispasian architecture of the Old Detratan Empire. The main site was tucked into the bottom of a gentle valley surrounded by poplars on one side, and what looked like farmland on the other. A few people could be seen moving between the buildings. Two members of her private guard were out stalking the perimeter and already two riders were on their way up the hill to greet us and see what we wanted.

Presumably such a settlement did not stand still immediately when the owner died. I'd known servants to continue working long after their employer's death, until the money had run out. Gardens still needed maintaining. Stone floors still needed cleaning. And here, farmland still needed tending to.

It occurred to me that, confronted with so many private soldiers, no murderer would seriously think they would be able to kill Lydia Marinus *here*. No, it would be far easier to lure Lydia away before killing her, which is exactly what they had done. Instead, a messenger breached these defences on someone else's behalf.

'Lydia did not build it herself,' Sulma Tan said. 'This site is four hundred years old and used to belong to one of the old Detratan kings. She restored everything to its former glory.'

'This seems fit for royal habitation,' I declared. 'It's breathtaking.'

'And yet it is of no use to her now she is dead,' Leana muttered.

'Very true,' I replied.

The two riders coming to meet us were dressed identically to those from Lydia's private guard who were with us – in a dark, decorative leather breastplate, blue tunic and long green cloak.

Santhan Brak, the man I had spoken to at Lydia's house in Kuvash, nudged his horse forward and began a terse conversation with them, while I regarded the villa. At first I thought it would have been a breathtaking place to live, to be able to walk among the pools and statues, smelling herbs from the gardens, being away from the hubbub.

Living here, I thought, I would always speculate at the number of places an assassin could hide. But she did have her own guard to protect her. In fact, on closer inspection, there were stables and an area that looked like a barracks of sorts. At least another four of these guard were walking across a courtyard. There were more military personnel milling about behind the gardens. Some were sprawling on benches, their swords no longer fixed to their waists.

Yes, it was a safe place. It was a haven. The reasons for staying away from the city were obvious, but . . . why abandon this? She had essentially run away from her own guard, and from the safety of her property. Surely, if it had been a business meeting of some importance, she could have arranged for it to have taken place here? What could have been so serious to make her leave on her own?

Santhan Brak had negotiated our way inside and, after a brief exchange of words with those who had come to meet us, we guided our horses down the track and towards the villa.

Everyone gathered in the main residential quarters of the villa. Standing in the atrium amid old-style frescos and glorious scenes of Detratan history, I felt as if I had suddenly been transported back to my old country. It was curious, though probably not an important point, that Lydia had opted to restore a villa that had links to Detrata, a country where we had both been born. It was possible she could never quite let go of her roots, that she never felt a full part of Kotonese society.

Standing on a small stool, to raise myself above the gathered ranks of guards, servants and soldiers, I cleared my throat, ready to issue the day's orders.

'Days ago Lydia Marinus was found dead not far from her home in Kuvash,' I began. 'Her body was covered in hundreds of wounds and she probably suffered in terrible pain before her throat was cut.' I examined the glum faces, many of which visibly showed they were disturbed by the details. 'She left this property without telling anyone. She took her horse and rode to the city alone. The next time she was seen, she was dead. My name is

Officer Lucan Drakenfeld of the Sun Chamber, and I am overseeing the investigation into Lydia's death. There have been other, similar murders that we suspect are connected to hers. Those people also died in a similar, grim manner. With the full cooperation of Santhan Brak, who many of you will know, I have brought with me a number of people from Kuvash and we have come to search the property, and you can help us. We are to scrutinize every room and every building. Santhan Brak will direct you into various quarters. You are to open every drawer and cupboard, and look in every pot. This is not a permit to pillage her belongings – we will conduct searches when people leave. Sulma Tan here,' I gestured to her with an outstretched hand, 'will see to it that you spend an evening in gaol if you so much as take a scrap of cloth. However, there will be financial rewards for anybody who produces beneficial evidence.

'You *must* report anything that stands out as strange, but I am particularly keen on two things. The first was a note brought to Lydia by messenger on the day of her disappearance. I strongly believe that whatever was in that note was directly responsible for her leaving the property without telling anyone. That note led to her death, and that note has not been found. Secondly, there is a . . . type of *ruby*, which I believe links these cases, so any items of jewellery – especially if it is found in a concealed location – must be reported to us instantly. As I say, rewards for such a discovery will be significant. Finally, I would be very grateful if any journals, ledgers or papers could be brought to my attention, no matter how incidental you think they may be. Should anyone need to find me, I will be ensconced in Lydia's living quarters for the next couple of hours. If the search yields nothing today, we will stay the night and continue through to the next day.'

There was a discernible groan from some of them, and I could well understand the sentiment. It wasn't as if I wanted to remain here all that time myself. Everyone filtered out until the room was empty, and the search of this enormous property began in earnest.

Leana, Nambu and myself were shown into Lydia's private bedroom, while Sulma Tan told us that she would investigate the adjoining study and examine the papers.

I opened ornate wooden shutters to allow the sun inside and terracotta and blue colours soon filled my vision. Sparsely furnished, the space was large enough for forty or fifty people to sit comfortably. Even the bed, under another set of shutters, was big enough to accommodate four. The shutters opened up onto a delightful garden, a warm suntrap with vines growing around the property and the slow trickle of a fountain just out of sight. I imagined how peaceful this would have been for Lydia to wake up to, or even to still her mind at night while remaining on top of her businesses. A tranquil haven indeed, and not the sort of place one would willingly want to leave.

Inside the bedroom there was little else of notice – a chair, a desk on which stood a silver-rimmed mirror, as well as several items of make-up in a closed wooden box and the peeling of a wax seal. Had this been where she read her final message, the one sent from Kuvash to lure her away from her well-protected villa? There were no markings, no obvious lettering in the wax, nothing to distinguish it from a hundred other letters that may have passed through her hands.

Everything around us, as expected, showed superb craftsmanship. Again Lydia's wealth did not reveal itself in garish ornamentation, but in the details. Even rebuilding something that had fallen into disrepair as opposed to building something new showed a reverence for traditional skills.

I stood directly in the centre of the room, trying to get a better impression of who Lydia was and wondering what could possibly have made her a target. What could a neat, tasteful mature woman have done to warrant such a painful death? What could someone who spent so much of her time away from the rest of the world have managed to do that matched Bishop Tahn Valin and Grendor?

While Leana searched for hidden compartments around the walls and under the bed, Nambu opened the drawers of the desk one by one, rooting around inside and making general noises of dissatisfaction. Eventually she called me over, whereupon she presented me with several items of jewellery in her outstretched palms. There were golden necklaces set with emeralds, a diamond ring in an onyx box, a sapphire brooch, and a bracelet in the shape of a serpent.

'Are these any use?' she asked.

By which she meant, presumably, are any of these potentially the red stone I had labelled as evum?

'This is a good find, Nambu, but sadly none of these seem to be what we're hoping to find.'

She had a look of determination on her face as she placed the items back in the drawer. There was a wonderful focus to the princess, a desire to be helpful, to be more than a shadow.

Leana called from beside the bed: 'This might be what we are looking for.'

She was crouching over a tile that she had prised open with her sword, which was now on one side. A small pile of items lay on the other side.

'What have you got?' I asked.

'Personal items. One of which is a ring and, spirits save me, it is very much like the bishop's . . .'

As she held it up to me, my heart skipped a beat.

The stone was much larger than the bishop's, and was fixed

within a gold four-claw setting that formed the teeth of a serpent. The body of the serpent formed the ring itself. The craftsmanship of the piece was sublime. It was a heavy item, far more so than the bishop's, which I pulled out of my pocket to compare. Kneeling on the bed, I moved the rings into the direct light of the window. The gemstones possessed the same strange sheen and cloudy colour as each other. There was no doubt in my mind that they were the same material and I asked Leana to verify this for me.

The discovery of this ring could certainly confirm a link between all three murders. Whatever evum was, people were definitely being killed because it was in their property or upon their person. The question lingered as to why Lydia had not taken it with her when she'd left for the city alone.

'Looks the same,' Leana said eventually.

'I think so too. Though Lydia's shows far greater effort has gone into the design of the ring. I wonder why that is?'

'The bishop could not afford the same jeweller to do the work?'

'Yes. But what does that say – Nambu, what do you think?'

I knew the answer but the princess lit up at being brought back into the process. 'It says that they had to get the stones set themselves.'

'Absolutely. The bishop opted for a cheaper, more austere rendering – Lydia could afford something notably better. Grendor of the Cape decided to have his set in an amulet instead.'

'What is the significance of that?' Leana shrugged.

I did not have a clear answer for that question, but thought that it had something to do with the secrecy of the material. Using different jewellers meant that no single person would become intimate with the material or ask too many questions. Alternatively it could mean that the stones were so rare that a jeweller had given up his business, even passed away, before he had the chance to work on the same stone.

The whole case was frustrating me. We were always one step behind a killing, never really having the opportunity to discover *why* this was happening. The fact that there were multiple bodies helped and hindered – it was like we were being set a puzzle, deliberately and consciously.

'Again, this was hidden close to the bed,' Leana said. 'I wonder if this is simply a convenient hiding place to hide things within sleeping distance?'

She might have kept it there to make the most of the properties of the material, I wanted to say. To use the stone's life-affirming powers.

Each time I had to keep myself from confessing these fanciful thoughts. Among us all, only I had experienced the effects of the stone, but people would start to think I was insane for believing this, like some gibbering old hermit who thinks he's a god.

'Who can say,' I replied. 'No one else has access to her room, so no one else could stumble across it by accident. We should remember that she did not have the problem that the bishop did.'

'What was that?' Nambu asked.

'The bishop did not wear such decorations. It was frowned upon in the temple.' I gestured to the items that Nambu had found. 'As you see, Lydia was able to wear jewellery without there being reason to upset any gods – or priests. That makes this doubly curious that she had hidden it. Whereas the bishop had good reason, Lydia – on the surface – did not. Yet she wanted to *hide* it. She did not wish it to be *known*.'

'She was worried about it being seen,' Leana declared. 'Maybe that's the real reason the bishop did not wear it too. Nothing to do with decorations.'

'I think that might be the case. And let's not forget that Grendor of the Cape had worn an amulet featuring this gemstone, but he had worn it underneath his shirt. He, too, did not make it public.' I got off the bed and paced about the room. 'Let us continue with this theme, then, that the stone was something known only to a few people.'

'Yet,' Leana added, 'precious enough that people kept it nearby at all times. Worn close to their chest, or kept close to where they slept. Yet what I do not understand is why not fashion it to wear in the open? A skilled goldsmith could have made a container for it.'

'I suppose it's pretty clear what happens if this ring is known publicly. If it's the reason they're all dead, then there's a very sensible explanation for not wanting it to be known. It seems unlikely that they knew they were going to be killed for wearing it. Which makes me suspect that wearing the stone came with shame and fear.'

'Were they really murdered simply because they wore a stone?' Leana asked.

'Hmm. It's hardly plausible that they would be butchered for the simple act of wearing it,' I replied. 'No. The rings, the stones, they represent something else entirely. There was a connection, certainly. An organization? A corporation? And how far back does it go, because these victims – none of them were young. There's history here, something that has gone on for a very long time, and all we have to show for it so far are two items of jewellery. But it's more than we had before. We just need to get to the heart of these stones. Why does no one know about them, other than the victims? Not even the jeweller had seen it before.'

Sighing, I put the rings in my pocket, sat on the edge of the bed and gestured at the scrap of paper that Leana had pulled out from the floor. 'What does the letter say?'

Though it was unlikely, perhaps there was a chance it was the message that had lured her to the city.

Leana unfolded it and scanned down the page. 'A love note. She was in a relationship with a woman back in Detrata, someone called Leyanda.' A pause, her tone changing to one of surprise. 'The daughter of Senator Chastra. Bitter old man. They speak of hidden desires, the inability to express their true feelings ... the usual kind of nonsense. How you Detratans have the luxury to worry about such matters.'

Leana handed me the note and I glanced over it briefly. It told us little about the case. It was indeed just a note that Lydia had wanted kept out of anyone's hands – possibly more for the other woman's sake than her own. Chastra, as I remembered, was a truly embittered man with a vicious tongue. No doubt he had chosen a suitor for the woman already, another business proposition to further himself in the world.

In the rest of the pile of items that Leana had drawn up, there was nothing else important to the case, at least, not that I could see. A dried flower, a silver chain, a seashell, all of which could have been tokens from Leyanda, memories from a particular day, a treasure to keep close at hand when the sentiments became overwhelming.

While I contemplated the ring further, the search continued.

Now and then one of the guards would bring a box of items for me to sift through – various personal letters, all of which were very businesslike. There were relatively few other trinkets. Usually people of such wealth had no problem in showing it off, yet Lydia clearly was not cut from quite the same cloth as others. Did it mean anything? Was she like a puritanical priest and expecting death at any moment – so did not clutter up her life with trinkets that couldn't be taken with her into the afterlife?

As the sun dipped towards the horizon, it was becoming painfully obvious that we would not find anything to help the case. With each passing hour, my frustrations grew.

That was until Sulma Tan called me into the adjoining study.

The List

We entered a small room by a discreet oak door, which had been painted the same terracotta shade as the walls. It was the kind of entrance one might easily pass without noticing. Next to the door were shelves bearing ornaments and small busts of old Detratan kings, which only added to the reasons not to notice this door.

The room had a remarkable iron-framed window that overlooked one of the kitchen gardens. Even from here I could see it was rich in herbs. Beyond stood a small fountain, and the garden was smothered in several beautiful arrays of rose bushes. The study was wood-panelled in a way that reminded me of a fine room in a monastery rather than a Detratan-styled villa. Evidently this had been added on at a later stage, perhaps to satisfy Lydia's need for discretion. It was a narrow room, too, no more than eight paces wide with bare floorboards, a desk, various writing implements and four heavy shelves of ledgers.

With an extra air of confidence, Sulma Tan directed me to sit at the desk, and pointed out a piece of paper that glowed warmly in the evening sunlight.

'What am I looking at?' I asked.

'It is a list of names I found within an otherwise empty ledger, written in a very archaic form of the language. What do you think is strange about these names?'

I glanced over the list but was unable to decipher the script. I asked Sulma Tan if she could read it out. 'Well, the important names on this list are Grendor of the Cape, Bishop Tahn Valin . . . And a little further down, Lydia Marinus. There are four other names though.'

'Do you know who these people are?'

She scanned the list once again. 'This couple are bankers, for the most part, but they own an armoury, which the queen uses to supply our own military. I can't recall their names. The two others, Han and Lunus Saul Kahn . . . I can't recall their roles . . . But I would think these four people should be very worried for their safety.'

'I agree. What is the list's purpose?'

'I believe it to be a notification of access to . . . just a moment.' Sulma Tan reached over to one of the nearby shelves to retrieve a map, and laid it out flat across the desk. 'This is the Kotonese coast and islands. And now things get *very* interesting. The access list, or perhaps a list of passengers, is for this little island here. Evum. I have never seen it before.'

'Evum,' I repeated. 'So it's not the stone, but an island?'

'Yes, yes. Well, according to this anyway, and it lies a hundred miles north-east of our coast. I have just conducted the greatest survey of our nation and its properties – yet I, too, have never heard of it. But it exists. Simply not on any of our maps.'

'How could it be missed?' I asked.

'Also of interest is that Grendor, being a naval officer, conducted cartographical surveys – or arranged for them to be conducted – of the sea and coastline.'

'And he somehow missed off an island.' I could not believe what I was hearing. 'Let me get this quite clear. This list – which we can assume to be a list of victims – involves *passengers* to the island of Evum, a hitherto unknown place. Evum isn't the stone – but perhaps the location where the stone was mined.'

Sulma Tan nodded. 'That was where my thoughts were taking me.'

'By Polla . . .' I breathed, and looked back at the list of names. The only script I could understand was the date, which was for a period over two years ago. Was that the last time the journey to Evum had been carried out?

'What's this place?' I pointed to the almost illegible word. 'Brutahn. I recognize that from your maps, I think.'

Sulma Tan peered over, her eyes narrowing. 'It is a port town at the mouth of the estuary, the next settlement up from Kuvash. It must be where they sailed from, as it was discreet enough. What do we do now?'

Leaning back in the chair and staring out of the window, I contemplated this question. The sun finally lowered itself over the far hills.

'We protect the others on the list. We put them on watch – in secrecy, though, since there is a very good chance we can capture the murderers in mid act.' I looked up at Sulma Tan. 'Is that possible? To shadow these people but not have anyone know about it?'

Without hesitation she replied, 'We can do this immediately upon our return.'

'Presently I would like to look further into the matter of this new island.'

'Yes, so would I,' Sulma Tan sighed.

I sent word out to round up as many of those on the premises as possible. After they had gathered in the atrium, I informed them that the search could carry on, but that some of us would be returning to Kuvash immediately.

An hour later we were riding back. Evening light glimmered in hilltop pools that I had not noticed on the way, and now and then we passed through a meadow of flowers emptying their delightful scent into the air. The mild climate and the tang of smoke from burning fires in yurts made for a pleasant journey, one that possessed a calming silence. It enabled me to contemplate what we had found, and I wondered if we were making one too many assumptions.

Sometimes supposition, trying to tease out the correct way of thinking, or in this case attempting to get into the minds of the murderers, was all I had to go on. It was not much, admittedly, and it often went against my more logical, Polla-based instincts.

Why had an entire island been kept off maps by Grendor? The obvious answer was that he did not want anyone finding the place, but what was on the island worth protecting? If this was the precious mineral I had mistakenly called evum, then the group of people on Lydia's list had been involved with its extraction. That was all well and good, but I still could not link it to the murders. Mining precious stones is not worthy of murder, unless someone else was after it?

But even then, there were more subtle ways to go about it. These murders were violent and very ritualistic incidents. If someone had wanted to take over the island, for example, then the obvious deaths of individuals in Kuvash would attract attention.

No, whatever that mineral was, I did not think it the reason for the murders. It was on Evum that we would find answers, perhaps, and I was determined to go there after we protected the others on the list. However, hours later, as we arrived back in the Sorghatan

Prefecture back in Kuvash, it soon became apparent that we were already too late.

Two more people on the list had been found dead.

All Tied Up

Tagg Drennar and his wife Meruwa had been found in the centre of a market square sitting back-to-back on the floor. The husband's intestines had been wrapped around them both, as if it was a rope that bonded them. Their bodies appeared to sag, their heads lolling to the same side. They were covered in blood from the open torso.

This was the only difference to the other murders. Otherwise the two of them bore the same wounds. Numerous lacerations, which were the probable cause of death, their tongues removed, and knife entries in the eye sockets. As Tagg had been slit horizontally, his skin was peeled back to reveal his glistening innards. This was a unique twist in the series of murders. Was it a new addition to a ritual, or was this a different killer?

A mesmerizing, rapid fluttering of bats came and went with the wind. Soldiers had sealed off the cobbled square, but it had not stopped people from leaning out of their windows to see what was going on. Even at this late hour many a lantern-silhouetted form peered into the gloom. All of those inquisitive faces were asking to be interrogated, so methodically, over the next two hours, I had soldiers from the City Watch head round to all the properties in order to take any statements. Every single apartment, every terraced dwelling, every drunk passing by was investigated by the military and asked if they had seen anything. Though I did not speak it out loud, I assumed the people of Koton would be used to such bold intrusion by soldiers, and their compliance in the matter confirmed this. Given the elusive nature of the crimes so far, I was not optimistic that these interviews would prove successful and as time slid by, when all that came forward were fanciful meanderings of the eccentric, accounts that involved many-limbed monsters and ghosts, it was confirmed.

To add to the eeriness, a soldier made a minor confession, away from his comrades. A slender man with a long nose, his manner was nervous. 'Funny thing, sir. Only, when we first found the bodies, they were arranged slightly differently. Truth be told we only turned our backs for a minute, like. No more. Two at the most. And in that time . . . well, their heads seemed to droop the other way. And a leg had been bent.'

'Are you quite sure?' I said.

'Aye. I mean, it could have been one of the lads playing a joke with us I guess.' He nodded as if reassuring himself. 'That's likely. But thought you ought to know, being Sun Chamber and all that.'

'Thanks for telling me.'

He gave me a salute and marched back to his position. A joke, a coincidence, a bad witness – or something more sinister. All of the bodies had, in some way, not remained still. All of them had something to do with evum.

With regards to the murder itself, all we knew was that no one had seen a thing. It was absurd that the killers were able to act in such a way. When I enquired about the routines of the plaza, soldiers simply told me that it was a market square that would have packed up earlier in the evening. A heavy traffic of horses and carts would have been here a while before. One of them suggested it was possible the murderers could have brought the corpses here in a cart, blending in with all the others, and then be the last to leave in the darkness.

Despite her protests to remain, I had asked that Nambu return with Leana so that she could get some sleep. Tomorrow would be another busy day and I was tired myself. I wondered whether or not it was wise to take her along to Evum. Perhaps I was taking liberties in dragging the young girl from place to place, forgetting that she was of royal lineage. I did not want to be accused of treating her poorly, so would dragging her to a potentially dangerous island be wise?

With my hands in my pockets I turned to regard the dead couple bound in their final moments. It had been a ghastly way to die. A civic cleaner – a scrawny, elderly fellow – had found the two of them while he was sweeping the square for the morning's trading, and he reported it to the authorities instantly. No one had so far come forward with information. Admittedly this public square was low on passers-by at that hour, but it said a lot about the skill of our murderer that they had not yet been seen.

This took the body count to five now and for each of the preceding incidents nothing had been noticed, despite the very public locations in which the victims had been found.

'The cut was sloppy.' Sulma Tan was still crouching by the side of Tagg Drennar, examining his wound rigorously. 'I doubt these are skilled people, for there are less messy ways of peeling back folds of skin.'

'Who were these two?' I asked.

'The Drennars were small-scale merchant bankers. They were obscure. They held no public stalls, and no building had been registered in their name, so few people will have heard of them. In fact, they maintained a very low profile in general, though I recognize them from their occasional meetings with the queen due to them owning an armoury. But they did not discuss those matters in front of me.'

'Which makes their appearance here all the more surprising.'

'Yes.' She rose and stood by my side.

'Was any royal money held in their bank?' I asked.

Sulma Tan betrayed herself with her expression, but I admired her pride. 'No. They dealt with select individuals in other nations as well as ours.' At least her obviousness when she was lying confirmed how frequently she had been telling the truth. I did not hold it against her that she was protecting her sovereign.

'What should we next do?' she asked.

'The remaining two names on the list – are they based in the city?'

'We are already investigating. I despatched a messenger to one of my administrators.'

'When you find out if they're living in Kuvash, you should have them watched immediately.' I gestured to the deceased couple. 'There is a good chance they will end up like this. But more importantly I will now want to talk to them to get some answers.'

She nodded. 'These soldiers will help remove the bodies and take them back to the palace when you are done with them.'

'Thank you.'

Sulma Tan walked with speed into the distance, her cloak flailing, and faded into the night.

Meanwhile, for the second time that night I moved across the cobbles to inspect the bodies. At my indication, a soldier came over with a torch to cast light upon them, and blood glistened in its light.

The Drennars were in their fifties, which was an age consistent with the other victims. Tagg had shoulder-length grey hair, while

Meruwa's was still blonde and came down to her waist. They were heavily built individuals and what clothes remained on them were clearly once resplendent. Curiously, Meruwa's boots were on the wrong feet – that indicated a level of haste about the act. It was as if the killer had been forced to act quickly: after having made the many cuts up and down her body, they struggled to remember which boot went on which foot.

However, something else struck me as very odd. Not about the individual incident itself, nor about the physical evidence before me.

But the fact that there were *two* victims.

How was it possible for *one* killer, working alone, to have managed to accomplish such an act? It didn't seem likely that one person would have been able to overpower two heavy people, at least not without great difficulty. And though it seems strange to say it, there did not seem to be – at least from this initial glance – signs of a severe struggle. If these were like the other victims, then the wounds would have been inflicted once they had been incapacitated in some way. I noticed rope marks on their wrists, where they had so clearly been bound, perhaps in some backstreet workshop.

Other than the initial note, which was not solid grounds for evidence on the matter, it became more apparent that there were two killers; maybe even a gang operating in a calculated, organized manner.

There was no note upon either of their persons, and nothing else to go on. I informed the nearest soldiers that I had finished and that they could take the bodies.

'Try not to sever the innards,' I said. 'Keep them as intact as you possibly can. I realize that might not be a particularly easy job.'

With insouciance the soldiers moved over to the bodies to contemplate how they would carry out the act of separation.

I made my way alone back through the long streets feeling incredibly weary yet eager to press on. The search was successful – we had a list, we had a new direction in which to steer our investigation, and it felt as if the mosaic of ideas and observations was beginning to form a much grander picture.

A few elements were still obscured, but I couldn't help thinking of the size of the revelation already: a hitherto unknown island had suddenly appeared on the map. What would that mean for the nation of Koton? Would it have implications across the contin-ent? I needed to keep all of these ideas relatively fresh to despatch another message to my superiors in Free State first thing in the morning. It was important to rest my head, though. Tomorrow was going to be a long day.

The Final Names

With the clarity of a new morning, I found myself excited, and even had something of a plan at the back of my mind. But even that was to change.

After some brief administrative work involving writing my letter to the Sun Chamber to update them on recent events, Sulma Tan sent over a messenger. He carried details of the final two members on the list of names taken from Lydia Marinus' house.

Her letter was brief yet revealing. These final two were living within the Sorghatan Prefecture – and very much alive. Four soldiers had been despatched in civilian clothing, though armed discreetly, to visit their house and offer protection against any potential attacks. They were to keep a low profile so the murderer – or murderers – would not realize how far we had come in our understanding of the crimes.

The names of the individuals were Han and Lunus Saul Kahn.

The Kahns, according to Sulma Tan's message, and much to my surprise, were two eccentric brothers. Twins, in fact. It occurred to me that they might have been the same curious brothers who dined with Grendor the night before he was killed, the ones to which Nambu took a dislike and whom Leana had interviewed. They had massed a sizeable amount of wealth together through business, but mostly trading with Detrata, and neither of them had married.

In addition to this Sulma Tan had requested that the physician Carlon conduct an examination of the Drennars' bodies, and he had free time this afternoon when he could dedicate himself to the grim task.

I sent an oral reply back via the messenger and told him we would join Sulma Tan at the front entrance to the palace within an hour, and then we would proceed to the dwelling of Han and Lunus Saul Kahn.

Leana, Nambu, Sulma Tan and I left as the sun was starting to rise. The long shadows were retreating like ghosts and the morning became sharp and clear. The air as ever was rich with the smell of woodsmoke, and I knew the heat would come soon enough, today with some intensity.

In all of the past few days I had never felt so energized. Here we were, finally, with the opportunity to get to the bottom of the mystery, to get some understanding of what had happened in the past.

Potential questions bubbled through my mind: about how I would go about steering these two brothers to giving honest and open answers. If I was to glean anything from them, they needed to feel able to discuss the past. To do that it might be prudent if they felt scared. I would not threaten them, but the best approach would be to make them aware of what had happened to the other names on the list, and that it was in their best interests to tell me what had gone on.

Their house was a three-storey, whitewashed structure in the wealthier end of the prefecture, and situated in the corner of an elegant courtyard. As with many other buildings in this small quarter, bamboo had been used in its construction, in the guttering and for decorative details, lending the building a different style.

A soldier in civic dress leant insouciantly against the wall. He nodded to Sulma Tan upon our arrival. It didn't seem as if anyone else was following us — if we were being watched, it was from the shadows, or through the slit of a window.

One knock on the door and another guard opened it from inside. We were ushered in quickly; discreetly we filed in.

The house was very pleasant — modest, yet with the occasional bust or fresco that denoted these people were by no means poor. The kitchen took up much of the lowest floor, with a thick wooden table at the centre and a floor composed of dulled terracotta tiles. There was a lovely, small sculpture of Astran and Nastra in a small walled garden to the rear of the property and it was in that minuscule, tranquil spot, with the scent of rosemary and lavender thick in the air, that we conducted the questioning.

The two brothers were not identical twins, but they looked phenomenally similar. Both tall and skinny, their purple and black tunics hung off their bodies rather than fitting well. Each had short-cropped grey hair and tired eyes that constantly regarded the distance. They had difficulty making eye contact, though this didn't seem to be guilt, more a life-long habit of preferring to be alone. At first I thought they had both been drinking, but I could not smell any wine upon their breath. They perched together on an ornamental stone bench, in the shade of a small pear tree. Everyone else stood around them in a semicircle, but if the sight was intimidating in any way, the brothers did not show it.

'This list contains several names,' I began, holding up the paper. 'We found it at the villa of Lydia Marinus. At the time, she was the latest victim in our investigation; but several others had been killed before that. Upon returning to the city, we found two more of these people had been murdered. You may have heard of the method of their killing.' I confess to adding some drama to the moment, drawing on my performances over the years in courts. 'They were probably long and deliberately painful deaths. Hundreds of tiny cuts were found on their bodies. The wounds were probably not enough to kill them at first. Bishop Tahn Valin had been cut up into pieces, but others were — if I may use the expression — luckier in their ends. However, the latest two victims, man and wife, were bound together by the innards of the husband.'

I paused to notice their faces had creased up in disgust. Staring at the floor, they held each other's hands nervously.

'At the moment,' I stressed, 'you are quite safe. You have protection, but we cannot vouch for how long we can offer these men.'

'Resources are tight,' Sulma Tan added. 'They may have to leave with us.'

'Given the trade in ex-soldiers in Koton,' I continued to the brothers, 'you might find it necessary to invest in some protection yourself.'

They nodded in unison.

'The reason I am here, however, is not to guarantee your safety. Should the pair of you die, it will merely add another dimension to this investigation.'

One of them opened his mouth as if to say something, but thought better of it. If these were arrogant individuals before, there were certainly no signs any more.

'But you have some use to me while you're both still alive, and that is why we are all here. You have the choice to make your existence easier. It could mean the difference between living a normal life and spending the rest of it looking over your shoulder to see if someone will seize you and butcher you. Do we understand each other?'

Another nod.

'Before we get to business, what can you tell me of the night of Grendor's murder?'

'We already told your assistants,' one replied. 'We remained with the group when Grendor left. We do not often get out much, but when we do we tend to . . . enjoy ourselves as much as possible. We left the evening in good spirits.'

I took a calculated risk, and made the statement bluntly: 'This affair all started a very long time ago, didn't it?'

They appeared startled by my assertion, yet didn't say anything else.

'It's probably best if you give the specifics now,' I sighed, wanting them to think I possessed a certain level of information.

'We do not know what you mean,' came the reply from Lunus.

'Grendor of the Cape, Bishop Tahn Valin, Lydia Marinus . . . you've been involved together for many years. Indeed, we *know*.'

'Then why are you here?'

This was going to be harder than I hoped. It was better when people spoke at length, for they soon betrayed themselves or gave away an awkward fact. These two, however, were clearly comfortable in silence. The advantage was with them: in the eyes of the law they had committed no crime, they had done nothing wrong. There was no *need* to speak.

'Can you tell us what Evum is like?'

Clear surprise came on Han's face. He looked to his brother and then back to me again. 'We never went there.'

With that statement he confirmed the island's existence. 'We've got a document that says you travelled there with the others who are now dead.'

'We remained on the ship.'

'You travelled all the way to an island that doesn't appear on any common map – and you did not disembark?'

'No.' This was a firm answer, a wish for the questioning to end.

'How long does it take to get there?' I asked.

'Not long. Depends on the wind. Most of a day.'

'What is on the island?'

'We simply do not know,' Han sighed. 'We never left the ship.'

'So why did you travel there in the first place?'

No answer was forthcoming. They were hiding something.

'It seems rather unreasonable,' I continued, 'that you travelled for a day on a ship to an unknown island, returned on that ship, and never once left it.'

'We were sick. We do not travel well. This was our first time on a boat.'

It was a sentiment with which I could sympathize. 'So, I will repeat the question: why did you travel there?'

After a drawn-out hesitation, it was Han who spoke. 'We were looking into options to trade.'

I didn't believe him for a moment. I reached into my pocket, in which I had kept both Lydia's and the bishop's rings, and held them out for the brothers to see. 'Trading in gemstones like these, you mean.'

Lunus was firmer than his brother, who appeared exasperated by even delicate questioning. He flatly denied knowing what the stones were, but I could tell by his brother's pathetic expression that he'd had enough of this.

'I'd like to interview the two of you separately.'

'We won't speak apart,' Lunus declared, more of an instruction to his brother than information to me. 'We will maintain our silence.'

An uneasy tension came between the two of them. This charade continued for some time – me speculating at what they might have done, them saying nothing. My frustrations increased, but in a way they had already told me much of what I needed to know. The existence of Evum had been confirmed. The fact that they denied ever having set foot on the place made me realize that I would have to visit the island. The mystery would finally be solved there, I felt, but there was one more thing that I could use them for. And, of course, we still needed Carlon's reports on the bodies of last night's couple – he might have something useful to tell us in addition to what happened to the other bodies. He might even have recovered another gemstone.

'Well, if there's nothing you have to say for yourselves, then there's nothing we can do to help you.' I moved to Sulma Tan and whispered in her ear to dismiss the soldiers, but have them observe the property continually, from a good distance.

The killers would come for them and I was happy to use them as bait.

As the soldiers filed out one by one, the brothers' expressions clearly displayed their fear. Sulma Tan stepped back through the house, leaving just Leana, Nambu and myself in their opulent dwelling.

Leana stood behind me with her arms folded, as I paced one last time before the brothers. Their green eyes, bright in the sunlight, lingered on Nambu, and I wondered if they recognized her, that a princess of the nation was standing in their small garden. A songbird skittered around between a bush and the wall. The sounds of the city drifted by in the distance.

'Please, can you leave soldiers here?'

In the end all I did was smile without giving an answer before we, too, left the property.

'Do you think that was useful?' Nambu asked outside their house. The four of us had moved some way down the street and I could only spot one of the soldiers within the vicinity of the house.

'I do,' I replied. 'Whatever they've done in the past, it's too much for them to open up today.'

'I suggest we torture them,' Leana muttered.

'Why? They have done nothing wrong. They have broken no laws.'

'But we need to know more.'

'I don't think stretching them out and pressing hot irons against their skin is likely to yield any more than we have now. And, the two of them are far more useful to us in good condition. No, these two would rather take whatever their secret is to their graves.'

'Then they might have to do exactly that,' Leana added.

'True, but we have some very valuable information.' I placed my hand on Leana's shoulder with enthusiasm. 'Evum is a confirmed reality and we must go there.' I looked across to Sulma Tan but she pre-empted my speech.

Sulma Tan said, 'This morning I have seen to it that we can be allocated three naval ships for our use. It was important we investigate this island even without any confirmation. The crews are preparing the vessels already, so we can start our journey whenever you are ready.'

Nambu looked up excitedly. 'When will we leave?'

'I'm not exactly sure,' I replied. I still was not certain we should take Nambu with us.

'Lucan does not appreciate the sea,' Leana declared. 'He often cowers below deck nursing his stomach.'

'Thank you, Leana,' I replied. 'But no, that isn't the reason for my hesitation this time. We have some work to do here and we need to do it soon. Well, I say work . . . we have some *waiting* to do.'

'Waiting for what?' Nambu sighed.

'For the fish to take our bait.'

Bait

A day and a night passed. A violent storm washed across the city bringing sudden and ferocious rains, before vanishing as quickly as it came, leaving the morning to be clearer, crisper and far more fragrant. But despite the drastic events in the skies, there was no movement down on the ground, especially around the house of the Saul Kahn brothers. They remained confined within their own house. I had extended an offer to them that they could despatch a messenger to my quarters should they wish to reconsider their silence on certain matters, but nothing had arrived.

Carlon's report from the Drennar couple proved consistent with the other deaths. The lacerations had been identical; there were rope marks around their wrists, suggesting they had been restrained perhaps to a chair or a bench as wounds were inflicted upon them. The only difference between their end and that of the others was simply that the innards had been used to bind them in death. It was a public spectacle, one designed to cause maximum publicity and humiliation. Carlon speculated that our murderers were now starting to enjoy the ritual killings.

We had not found any jewellery, and an investigation of their surprisingly modest and almost spiritually austere home proved useless. Their dwelling was littered with frescos and artworks all depicting death, and a discreet painting related to the cult of Hymound. That the old gods were involved somehow seemed a curious link.

There was a skull on their bedside table, and I wondered what kind of mentality desired to be surrounded by such things. I'd heard of certain scholars wanting to be reminded of death as it spurred them on to make the most of the day, but a reminder was one thing – theirs was an obsession.

'At least now they have got the best reminder of all,' Leana had commented at the time.

The city was beginning to display signs of a frightened culture. Trade had diminished so rapidly from the marketplaces that the queen was, according to Sulma Tan, beginning to panic. This lack of trade meant that what military resources there were went to the public squares in order to inspire confidence. It struck me that all it did was show how much of a militaristic, centrally dictated state Koton was in reality. No politicians had debated this, Sulma Tan said, annoyed that precious resources were being redirected from the potential border conflict with Detrata. It was simply an order from the queen, and one that didn't work. It could be seen in the faces of all those passing by the lines of soldiers – glum faces, fearful expressions. Those who had not heard of the numerous murders in the city would be confronted with almost an invasion force in their own lives. It was the sign of a frightened queen, not one in control and certainly not one looking after her people.

Meanwhile, Sulma Tan had seen to it that twenty soldiers took different shifts watching the house of the Kahns. They stationed themselves in secluded alleyways around the property, some taking on the guise of the homeless, others that of traders going about their business, and – much to the Kahns' relief – a number with full military weaponry inside their house.

The Kahns would not have felt completely safe given that they were aware of being targets for murder, but they would be protected. Two lives would be saved, at the very least, and that was something to take from all of the carnage that we had seen.

I had instructed the brothers to go about their routines as normal, for it was *routines* that the murderers had always seemed to understand. From Bishop Tahn Valin to Lydia Marinus there was a clear understanding of the victims' movements.

In this relative calm while we waited for an attempt on the Kahns' lives, I speculated who could know the routines of these people. Who could have access to all levels of society, from a simple priest to the wealthiest woman in the land? Something did not sit right with me on that issue. Not even Sulma Tan knew of such matters, and she perhaps had access to more information than most people. She theorized that perhaps there was a network of murderers, where they were able to exchange information with ease, and that thought was consistent with my own, that it required multiple people to be able to capture, torture and kill a couple. Did it have anything to do with the number of private guards available in the city? Had a powerful network formed with access to intimate secrets?

If that was the case, what was the point in all of these murders, and what had any of it to do with the island of Evum?

To her credit, Sulma Tan had not yet let on to the queen that she knew about an island previously unmapped. That in itself was brave, because it would be part of the queen's territories and she would want to know about it.

Sulma Tan had spent several hours in the city's library, browsing the rolls of paper that ought to have shown the whereabouts of Evum. She paced back and forth, and consulted numerous administrators – again without letting on that the island existed – in order to find every map and chart that had ever been constructed. It transpired that several charts were missing, though no one had ever really checked for the better part of twenty years. The maps that were there were newer, with official seals and no Evum marked. Sulma Tan could only conclude that the official records had been altered, and if Evum had been on any map, those maps had been removed.

This made my desire to see the island all the more potent.

I considered that we would have to go very soon, and leave the two brothers to the mercy of the military. They would have to make their own decisions. Perhaps I could lend them Allius Golt to keep an eye on the property while we were at sea – then, should anyone attempt to gain entry to their house, they would meet a formidable opponent.

But it turned out that we did not have to wait long.

On the second night, as I spoke with Sulma Tan in her office in preparation for leaving for Evum, we received an urgent message.

There has been an attempt on the lives of the brothers. An individual has been captured.

In quiet haste, I fetched Leana and left Nambu to her sleep. In front of the door to our quarters the ever-watchful eye of Allius Golt peered into the corridor.

As moonlight glittered in the puddles from the evening shower, the three of us sped across the city.

I Know You

Alarmingly bright-blue eyes stared back at me. They were set within one of the most defiant faces I had ever looked upon. The woman was young, no more than twenty-five summers old. Her long, chestnut hair came down to her waist, though it was held back with several bands. A fitted leather breastplate protected her wiry and muscular frame, and she wore solid boots and plain brown trousers. After acknowledging my presence she settled back on her chair; her hands had been tied behind her back, but she wasn't disgruntled. She now appeared completely serene. Happy, almost.

Nine of us gathered in the Kahn brothers' front parlour. The fire crackled away gently, and added light came from a dozen candles. The open shutters brought in a gentle breeze and the sight of an indigo sky filled with stars.

Two soldiers stood just a step behind her, should she try to escape. This struck me as especially curious – they obviously saw her as a threat, and the black eyes and bloodied noses suggested that she had not exactly given in easily before being captured. Four weapons had been taken from her person, all of them knives of varying length. Two were standard military issue, according to

Sulma Tan, but the others were not – they were sharp hunting knives, crafted exquisitely with various animal motifs and ivory handles.

Despite the number of guards in the neighbourhood, her arrest came when the two brothers were singing quietly to each other in their small enclosed garden. Somehow, and with considerable skill, she had managed to make it to the house without being seen, climbed over the wall and attempted to strike at Han.

But she did not see the soldier sitting quietly just inside the wall. He had leapt up to grab her outstretched arm, and a fight ensued. As the brothers ran inside for help other soldiers came outside and attempted to subdue her.

One of the soldiers had heard movements of a second person outside the wall and, after clambering up to take a better look, saw a single figure running down a passageway. A small unit was despatched to investigate.

All we had was this one young woman, whom the guards did not recognize.

But I did.

When I had visited Sojun, the farrier who looked after our horses, he had later been with this woman. What was it he said? That she trained horses for the military?

As we stood around her, watching her, I decided to keep that information to myself to use at the right moment.

Only I simply could not connect her with the events surrounding the series of murders. Murderers generally *know* their victims. They share a social stratum, for example. They possess a rivalry for a seat of power, or a lover. Generally they are of the same class, made of the same timber. But the people who had been killed were several stages higher up the hierarchy of Koton than someone who served the military. Was she an assassin, hired on behalf of someone else? She didn't seem to fit the mould at all. There was something strange about this case and her polite refusal to answer any questions made it all the more baffling.

'What is your name?' I asked at first, in both Detratan and Kotonese.

Her smile was indifferent.

'Why have you come to attack Han and Lunus?'

She glanced to the floor, the smile fading somewhat, but she did not seem distressed. She was at ease in this awkwardness.

'We can have you tortured if you won't speak now,' I said, an empty gesture for I rarely resorted to such measures.

She rolled her eyes, as if she had been expecting me to say it.

One of the soldiers whispered in my ear, 'We've tried all that, sir. She wouldn't say a thing before. Probably won't now. Tried to rough her up a little, but she just accepted the pain. Closed herself off to it all – seen that before in the field.'

I sighed at the fact that they had resorted to violence so soon. It was never my preferred way of doing things as it was crude and often ineffective. Any answers obtained by such methods were spurious at best. So if they had tried this, the young woman clearly was not going to respond to variations on the theme.

'Clear the house,' I said, my eyes fixed on her.

'Sir?'

'Leave me with her,' I said.

'She's—'

'Just do it,' I snapped.

That got a reaction out of her, but it wasn't much – just a slight surprise, which I counted as a victory of sorts. Any reaction would have done.

Leana exchanged glances with me and she knew that I truly meant to be alone with the woman, but she had seen my various methods by now. She steered a surprised-looking Sulma Tan out of the room, and soon the footsteps and disgruntled voices could be heard outside in the courtyard.

The door closed and it was just the two of us.

Closing the shutters, I looked over my shoulder and spoke quietly to her in Detratan.

'Sojun's a good lad, isn't he? He doesn't say much though. You must have picked up that habit from him.'

In an instant, her countenance had changed. If she had been in control before, she wasn't any longer, now that I had access to information that she didn't want revealed.

'That's right,' I continued. 'You're his . . . lover? Or is anything more formal developing? There's nothing quite like young love, is there? These things don't usually last though. Marriage isn't often about love, is it? You'll find yourself married off before long. Do you—'

'Let me go.' A firm, crisp response. She was used to giving orders no doubt. 'I've not done anything to deserve this.'

Inwardly I smiled, but didn't show it. Right now I wanted reactions from her, and it was working. It was true we'd not caught her doing anything specifically wrong – we had not caught her in the act of murder. But, if she had been responsible for the other deaths, if she had even been involved in some slight way, she must have felt that it was all over now. A sense of relief, of sorts, must have been developing inside her.

'Before the sun rises we will have your home searched,' I said. 'We will want to search the property of anyone who is involved with you. That means Sojun's dwelling as well.'

No response now.

'Was he the one running away earlier, when you were caught?' I asked. 'That was not particularly protective of him, I must say.'

She didn't react to these statements and it wasn't surprising. They were not sophisticated, but I still wanted to explore her state of mind. I was worried we knew too little and that she was someone of control. She had to be liberated of this notion and made to feel vulnerable.

'We will bring him in to answer questions – of that you have my word.' I crouched down before her, once again in awe of the brightness of her eyes. 'You were going to kill Han and Lunus Saul Kahn tonight. You were going to cut them up, slowly, in whatever workshop you have, and then you were going to leave their bodies in a public place. You were going to do this to teach them a lesson. They were the last names on that list, weren't they?'

'List?' She looked up at me. 'I have no idea what you are talking about.'

The list to her would have been a mental one, of course. It was sheer coincidence that our physical list was the same.

'Don't concern yourself with how I know such things,' I continued. 'All you need to do is start telling me the truth. Only then can I begin to help you.'

She snorted derisively.

'You do not think the truth worthwhile?'

No response came, but she was no longer acting smug or complacent. We had crossed a barrier of sorts.

'I know all about Evum.'

There.

A flinch: inner pain.

'I'm going to travel to the island tomorrow morning.'

Her face changed and she glared at me. 'You do not know *the first thing* about Evum.'

I let her stare at me. I gave her the chance to witness my calm expression.

'Then why don't you start telling me about Evum? Talk to me.'

'No.'

'Why not?' My voice was soothing.

'Because you won't believe me,' she snapped.

'You don't know that. I've seen many sights in Vispasia – and beyond – and there are many things that do not fit our common logic.'

'You *still* won't believe me,' she said. 'This country is not what you think.'

'You can tell from my accent that I'm not from Koton,' I replied. 'I don't care what this country is or is not. All I want to know is why so many people have been killed and what they have to do with the island of Evum.'

'If you don't know that, then it proves you know nothing at all.'

'Maybe. But by giving such a response you've proven that you're somehow involved with their deaths. Who else could know of such a connection?'

'Plenty of people.'

'None who I've met,' I replied. This was delicately poised. Perhaps focusing on her initial reaction to the name of the island would reap more benefits.

'What's Evum like?' I asked.

'You're going there,' she grunted. 'Find out for yourself.'

'The place obviously means something to you. Why not let me *help* you?'

She sneered at the comment. 'How can you possibly help?'

I paced the room and reached into the depths of my mind, trying to ascertain why this young woman could possibly have wanted to kill people more than twice her age.

'What exactly did they do to you,' I continued, 'all those years ago?'

When she looked up at me her eyes lacked the lustre they had only moments ago. She possessed a face full of potentially vivid expression and it grew to one of sadness, which changed to anger. Then she regarded the floor once again.

I crouched before her, and stared up. 'You must have been a child, back then. What did they do to you?'

A spatter of laughter came from outside; the soldiers had found something amusing.

'Ask the Kahns,' she sighed.

'They have remained rather silent when questioned. If they're hiding something that you know about, and that you're angry about, then keeping it to yourself will not progress matters any further.'

Again, the silence.

'Do you realize the trouble you are in? You are already likely to be charged with attempting to kill these two men. It may well make you a suspect in the series of recent murders, even without evidence, depending on how the court sees fit. You could be executed.'

She remained in this quiet state for the rest of the evening. I was not certain if I had pushed things too far, but I had certainly opened her up more than before. This was progress.

Decisions

While guards stood watch over her, I took the Kahn brothers into their small garden once again, under the pretence of having them show me her route of attack. I stood upon a stone bench to peer over the wall. A network of small passageways extended in two directions, through which it was possible for anyone to have escaped with relative ease.

Stepping back down, and aware that the others were out of earshot, I asked them some direct questions.

'What did you do all those years ago to make a young woman so angry with you that she came here, in the dead of night, to kill you both?'

Han was clearly taken aback by my question. It even disarmed the usually steady Lunus, who opened his mouth as if to speak and then paused. Eventually he extended his arm and said, 'I have no idea why she is here. She's insane, quite clearly.'

'With effort even the acts of a madwoman can be understood. Did you abuse her as a child?'

'Certainly not!' Han protested. 'Just because I live with my brother, it does not make us wish to commit foul deeds with children. We are sophisticated people. We abhor such sentiments.'

Moonlight glimmered off a window in an adjacent house and caught my eye, reminding me just how late it was.

'I'm going to request that you remain in your property for the next several days.'

'Are we under arrest?'

'No,' I cautioned. 'But for the sake of this investigation, and given the lack of information and clarity, you must remain here until we are satisfied. You are not to move — and we'll keep a guard on your door.'

'How long could it take until you are *satisfied*?' Lunus asked, slipping down to sit on a bench. The despair was clear on his face.

'As long as necessary.'

I marched back through their house and looked at the young woman, who still remained nameless, and who was still on the chair. At that point I realized the world of the Kahns had been kept quite separate from her own. I needed to bring them together, even if for a moment, so I called the brothers back into the room and had them stand in front of her.

They were reluctant to do so and their hesitation betrayed them badly.

The woman spat at their feet, but said no more.

Why wasn't anyone saying anything?

There was a ruckus outside and to my surprise moments later two soldiers smashed back the front door to the property and threw the battered but living body of Sojun into the room. The woman reacted as one might expect of a lover, shocked and concerned, but she adjusted her manner accordingly.

'Elliah,' Sojun muttered, blood dripping from his mouth.

She sighed, disappointed that he had given her name. Sojun would be the weak link in all of this.

One of the soldiers stepped forward. 'We found him around

the side of the property trying to look in to see if this bitch was still alive. He's strong, I'll give him that, but no skilled fighter.'

I nodded my appreciation to the soldiers and walked over to Sojun, looking down at him. I gave an audible sigh. 'I hope you treat my horses better than you do other people.'

I felt that the two prisoners would be beneficial – I would play them off against each other, until we had a confession. 'Let's take these two back for questioning – separate cells. Sulma Tan, can you arrange for your queen's torturers to be woken and brought to the palace. We'll need them tonight.'

'How many?' she asked.

'Just two.' I stared down at a petrified Sojun, and encouraged his fear to deepen. 'Tonight we get answers from these two, or we end up with two more corpses. Unless one talks, in which case freedom for both might be considered.'

Midnight, and deep in the dungeons of the queen's palace, where much older violence was visible in the scuffed and stained brickwork, we commenced our questioning.

It was prudent to let Sojun witness one of the torturers arrive and set up. The torturer was a sickly-looking man in his late fifties, dressed in a simple green tunic, and who carried with him a satchel full of mind-boggling instruments. He greeted me softly before laying out some of his devices on the floor, asking whether or not we had various straps and so forth. One of the guards went away to fetch what was required but, of course, I had no intention of torturing Elliah or Sojun, at least not today.

If they had committed a crime then they would most certainly not be freed, but it was important they did not know what their fate would be.

It must have been midnight by this time and the two of them were now in, for me, a perfect situation. Neither of them would know what the other was going to say. Neither would witness a confession from the other. Neither would be aware if they had been *betrayed* by their lover.

One of them could, of course, tell me everything – and I only needed one of them to do so – but it would be extremely unlikely that both would remain silent. Should that be the case, then I would be forced to have one of them watch the other be tortured. But such were the benefits of having true partners in crime in such a predicament, it seldom came to the breaking of skin.

As I suspected, it was Sojun who told me everything. The torturer had only to pick up a large blade and, in the doorway, mutter 'Ladies first' before walking off. It was his first move in torturing the captive, implying that another such official was in her cell waiting for my word to begin.

Sojun could not let his lover suffer. It was apparent in his pained expression from the moment he had arrived. For a big man, he was certainly soft inside.

'Wait,' he began. 'Before you go to her . . .' Sojun sighed.

'Yes?' I asked.

'Look, this ain't my battle.' Sojun tried to rearrange the chains around his ankles. He took a more upright position on the floor, pressing himself up against the cold, stone wall. Muscles, from hundreds of days hammering in his workshop, were visible underneath his white shirt. His eyes flickered in the light of the cresset. 'I'm not doing any of this for me. Never have. Understand that.'

'You kill people for her?'

'It's not like that,' he replied. 'Isn't that simple.'

'It never is.' I dipped a cloth in a bucket of water and handed it to him, so he could wipe the blood from his face. It was a conscious gesture that I was here to help, that I was on his side.

'I'm only telling you this now, because there's a chance of some good coming from this mess. We've done our work. But you're an outsider. Not part of this nation. You could do something.'

His words had my curiosity piqued. I gestured for him to continue.

'It's her war. Her battle. There are others involved, too. They do the killing, different ones at different times, though most are there to watch. To see it come to an end. I'm just around to help her. Didn't want her to do it alone. If I give you names will you let her go free?'

'That depends on how helpful it is, but yes, that can be considered.' It felt as if I had winced at the lie, but I hoped I was a good enough actor at concealing it.

'I'll want your word before I give names.'

'I can't promise anything, Sojun,' I said softly. 'These are not my laws. These are not my people who have been murdered.'

'She's fighting on behalf of others.'

'Fighting. Is there a war going on?'

'There has been for decades, though no one would know about it. Not all wars require armies. You need to realize that this is all a lot more than revenge. This ain't just getting one back. I'll tell you, and you'll understand. Maybe you'll go easy on her. Maybe you'll help.'

'But it is revenge of a kind, isn't it? For the past.'

He grimaced. 'Twenty years ago, it all happened to her. It's why she's got the scars. She was a kid, Elliah. An orphan. Tough little nut to crack, so she keeps telling me, but I'm not so sure. Her memory is sketchy as to why it happened. But she ended up on an island.'

'Evum.'

He raised his head, acknowledging the fact that I knew more than he originally thought. A glimmer of optimism flashed through his eyes. 'That's right. Evum. There's a mineral there that they mine.'

'Who mines?'

'The children. Kids. They spend all day and night scrambling through the narrowest of tunnels, trying to get the mineral. There're dozens of them there at any one time. I'm sure some must get forgotten about, and die somewhere deep underground. But that's the funny thing about that mine – from what Elliah says, it seems to keep them going. Keeps them living for longer than they should. Of course, that's why the cult has it mined in the first place. For long-lasting life. To stay young. To heal quickly.'

I reached in my pocket and brought out Lydia Marinus' ring. 'This is the mineral, isn't it? This is what everyone is after?'

He squinted in the poor lighting. 'Aye, could be.'

'Who is "everyone"?' I continued.

Another shrug. 'Those who operate the place. I don't know who. Never asked, never wanted to know. Less I knew, the better. I get the idea there's a lot of them, and they're rooted deep in this culture of ours.'

Sojun's words were rather fanciful. The only reason he might have for such an imagination would be to make his own role in the deaths seem somehow less of an event, to give me the impression that there was something more sinister and profound, and that his murderous acts were mere footnotes.

'What was Elliah's role on Evum?' I asked.

'She worked the mines like any other kid. She was five or six summers at the time. She's got vague memories of a mother, but nothing much. She was taken off the streets. They did things to her there – the people, the guards. The rich men and women who came from afar to get a tiny piece of their precious mineral. Sometimes it was merely hitting them. Other times . . . Those kids didn't really stand a chance of having a childhood. There were dozens of them there, same age as her, crawling around, being abused. You know how these things work – a man of the world like yourself. You know how low people can get when they're isolated. You know it isn't pretty.'

'Yet she managed to escape . . .'

'Some of them did. Elliah told me that many tried to swim from the island. Most died at sea from exhaustion or they turned blue if the water was cold. A few – a tiny handful – managed to escape on boats when the wealthy types came to visit, when a ship went back to the mainland. Occasionally, when pirates used the island, kids might flee on board one of their rogue vessels. To a worse fate, who knows? Maybe they became pirates themselves. That'd be a better life at least. Some made it back though. Elliah was one of those – she left after just a couple of years on the island, stowing away on a vessel. When it moored in a cove, at night she jumped overboard and swam ashore. Somehow she scraped by until she was old enough to join the army. She did well there. Never seemed to feel pain. Always had something to prove. Impressed her commanders. Managed to make something of herself in a regiment full of men.'

'How did the two of you meet?'

There was a tenderness now about the way he spoke. The lines of affection were around his mouth and eyes. 'It was years ago, when she'd come to have her horses cared for at our stables. We were both young. You know how these things happen.'

'When did she first suggest killing those connected to the island?'

'She didn't. She was contacted by another survivor. There was a group of them who had got away from Evum. One of them was a little older and remembered her. Got some information. Names, and the likes. Knew who was involved. Knew who shipped things back here. Knew what was going on. They had a network. She told me about it. I'm not a man who fears a little blood. It was justice, wasn't it? Killing them like that.'

'Justice is not yours to decide.'

'Don't talk shit. Who else is going to see these powerful people get punished for what they've done? Soldiers? They'll not touch those higher than them.'

'Give me the names of those involved, Sojun, and this will all be over. There's no opportunity to escape and we will find the others, just like we found you. If you help us – if you speed things up – then we can see about some sort of justice. I will try to help you.'

'Don't care about me, officer,' Sojun grunted. 'See that *Elliah* goes free instead.'

'I will give you my word I will do my very best to argue her case for freedom – that's all you can hope for, given the circumstances. The queen will listen only to her own conscience. But I *will* try.'

'Aye,' he breathed.

Sojun listed four names, only one of which I recognized. Brell the eunuch. The figure who stood beside the queen every day, who shadowed her in her court and offered vague witticisms and scowling expressions. Sojun told me that, because the queen never trusted being surrounded by people who remembered the old days, she preferred the company of the young. Brell had been in her employment for two years. He would have known through his association with the queen when certain people would be in the city and their movements. And he was in a position to acquire addresses. In fact, he would have been the perfect informant. All of this explained just how it was possible to run rings round the authorities, and to capture some of the most important people in the city.

There was simply no single murderer.

I wrote down the names and their potential whereabouts. All of them were to be found in the wealthier prefecture. In hushed tones in the corridor I instructed a soldier to gather together a group of armed guards, with Sulma Tan's permission, and the raids of their properties began in earnest.

'I was the only one in the group who hadn't been affected by whatever went on on that island,' Sojun grunted. 'As I said, wasn't my battle. Did what I did because of Elliah.'

'And what did you do for her? Did you do the torturing? Did you inflict any wounds. Did *you* cut up the bishop?'

'No. I did none of that.' A sigh and a distant gaze. Sojun drew his knees to his chest, rattling his chains. 'We used the cellar underneath the stables, where I did my metal work. And metal work was all I did during the act. Didn't do any killing myself. The stables are out of the way. Noises are to be expected at all hours. We'd get complaints all the time, since it was a good location, but no one would notice a little more activity. The noises I made drowned out whatever screams there were, but those victims were usually unconscious and, as I said, we were in the cellars. It's quiet in there. No one can hear you. Get knocked out and you might never be found until a client wants his horses back. I didn't ask what they did at the time. Didn't really want to know. Not my business. But I understood, right? I knew what those kids had all gone through. Knew what needed to be done. If I could help them do that, help them sort their heads out in this way, then I considered it a good thing. And you never know — by removing this scum from the city, the ringleaders of this kind of operation might prevent more of the same from happening. That was our justice — it was done to help people there. Astran knows that island isn't on any map.'

The question of *why now* still lingered, but the solution was simple enough: 'You only started doing it now because you discovered the bishop would be leaving soon. That's what started it all.'

He gave a nod.

'How come his body had been dismembered, while the others weren't?'

'Have you ever killed a man? Well they hadn't. They were scared. Didn't know what to do. They messed it up.'

'So once you had killed him, that started the momentum. You had to go on.'

'The rest wanted to take 'em out as quickly as possible and then get out of the city. We were all in this as *one* — and weren't going to rest until we'd finished. We had learned movement, behaviours. We conferred. We plotted. You don't do a thing like this on a whim. '

Sojun went on to say that the activity on Evum need not be restricted to the past. It was very likely it was *still* happening and that the Sun Chamber should do something about it.

I had my doubts we could do something. Though unethical, there was nothing within the legal framework to prohibit children from working, no matter how poor the conditions. As for abuse, however, though many of us might be clear on rights and wrongs, the law did not always support the matter. The law was a blunt hammer, not a fine scalpel. Yet again my investigations were taking me deep into uncharted waters.

'How come no one came to the authorities to report what had gone on there,' I said, 'on Evum? It's possible that help could have been found eventually.'

A shake of the head, and his words were not bitter, simply sad. 'You think anyone would give a shit? The island doesn't exist, as far as the authorities are concerned. It isn't on a map. We couldn't get there to free others. You think someone's going to believe people like us against the likes of Grendor of the Cape, or that

Lydia Marinus woman? She was the worst, of course. She stole children through her orphanages. Vanishing them. Bet it still goes on. We heard that she educated children.' He gave an emotionless laugh. 'I wonder if she teaches them about morals? But anyway. You tell a soldier, he doesn't care. You crawl to the politicians, you beg outside of their houses for a moment of their time, and they give you a hollow look. Tell you to stop wasting their time. They're not going to bring change – only action is.'

'What about the queen? Brell, the eunuch – he was close to the queen. I'm sure he could have said something about what was going on there. She might have even listened to him and sent an investigative team?'

'No.' Sojun shook his head and gave a sigh. 'You don't get it, do you? There's ways of justice. Some things have to be done right. Done in person. To release the ghosts that follow Elliah around day and night. Brell wasn't going to tell the queen. He more than any other wanted to bring about its end himself. Ask him how he became a eunuch – and watch his face. That'll tell you far more than I can about what it means to him.'

'This sounds more like revenge than justice.'

'I'm telling you, officer. There was no other way to do what's right by those kids. You might think badly of me, but I know in here,' he thumped his wide chest, 'that I done the right thing.'

The guard slammed the door firmly and slid the bolt across.

'How many soldiers can be spared?' I asked Sulma Tan as we turned our backs on the cells. Cressets lined the corridors, and there was no one else nearby save one guard deeper into the gloom.

'In reality?' she replied. 'None. But we can make allowances.'

'If there's activity on Evum even now, there is likely to be protection. We may need some good warriors.'

'Most of them are reinforcing the borders as we speak. That's why there are so few guards around the palace now.'

'You must have some in the city you can spare?'

It was difficult to read her expression in the dark, but her initial silence felt awkward. 'If I spare some soldiers, what will be my excuse? How will I explain why two dozen men have been taken out of the city?'

'A good point,' I conceded.

'We should now tell the queen everything,' Sulma Tan replied. 'Her eunuch, Brell, is about to be arrested. Though he does not live near her quarters, she will find out about this in the morning. She will have questions of her own as to why he is being taken, yes.'

'If we have time to explain, the morning would be an appropriate moment to tell her.'

'No,' Sulma Tan said. 'Tonight. I will tell her tonight. She should know as soon as possible else we risk angering her.'

'Will you need me there?'

'Not officially. No, go. Go and sleep. I will make the provisions for soldiers to make the journey across to Evum. They will be ready for us to leave first thing in the morning unless you hear otherwise.'

'I'm incredibly grateful for all your help,' I said, pausing to stress the point with sincerity. 'This case would not have been resolved without your assistance. When I report to the Sun Chamber, and to your queen, I will make sure that you receive the credit you deserve.'

There was a look in her eyes that almost reached happiness, but she was too tired to fully commit herself. 'This is merely my job.'

I shook my head. 'You've gone beyond what's required of a station like yours. I've been in several large cities of Vispasia and liaised with dozens of administrators and officials. You have been open, clear, informative and helpful. Others would be lucky to show one of those positive qualities.'

'We have not finished yet. We will have all our answers when we arrive on Evum, and only then. For now, get some rest.'

I continued back through the labyrinthine corridors with Leana. Together we headed back to our quarters, a burning torch lighting our way.

And when we arrived, we saw the sprawled form of Allius Golt.

Allius Golt

Blood had pooled next to his head, but it had not come from a blow to his skull. Instead, what had killed Allius Golt was a cut to his throat. The poor man lay on his back, his eyes closed, his sword to one side out of reach. His chair had been knocked over, and the timer he used to measure the evening's progress had been smashed.

Rightly so, his corpse was not Leana's first concern. She drew her own blade and tentatively moved towards the open door to our temporary living quarters — rooms that very few people were meant to know about. I immediately followed her inside, fearing the worst for Nambu's safety.

There we came across another body.

However it was not the princess's. A man we did not recognize lay face down. Garbed in an all-black outfit, the exact same kind as worn by her other attackers, his brown hair was tied in a tail as long as his arm, and a short sword was protruding from his back.

To one side, sitting on my bed with her knees drawn up to her chest, and with her bright eyes now red with tears, was the young princess. I moved to sit beside her, quickly but without appearing too threatening.

The young girl was clearly disturbed. In fact, she looked as if she was in shock.

'Are you all right?' I asked.

She squirmed a nod, then buried her head behind her arms. She began to heave with sobs, so I leaned in and held her close. Leana, meanwhile, checked the other rooms for intruders, leaving us in darkness. She returned promptly and shook her head. The glow of the torchlight lowered towards the corpse as she scrutinized the body.

The hilt of the blade appeared, from this distance, to have once belonged to Nambu. The position of it in the man's back indicated he had not seen her, because she was probably hiding behind the door as he entered. She had thrust the weapon from a crouching position, upwards into the man's back. Presumably he had not anticipated that the princess had received some training with a sword and unwittingly he had become her first kill.

Nambu, however, was now beginning to realize what it felt like to take a life with one's own hands.

Eventually her heaves diminished and she took control of her emotions.

'I heard a noise outside,' she said. 'If it was a fight it was very quick and after a gurgling scream everything went quiet, so I assumed the worst and thought I'd be attacked again, and so I hid there trying to remember everything Leana had taught me.' She indicated the corner behind the door. 'When the man came in I . . .'

Now was not the time for me to question just how the hell an intruder could have tracked her all the way down here without being caught.

Her face creased up and I thought we were going to lose her momentarily, but she quickly regained her composure. 'I stabbed him, just in his weak spot like you said, Leana.'

'You did good work,' Leana declared.

'How can it be good?' Nambu muttered. 'He's dead. Dead because of what I did to him.'

'Precisely so,' Leana replied. 'If you had not killed him then, spirits save you, he could have killed you. You saved your own life. This is a good thing. Even Lucan could not say otherwise.'

'Leana's correct,' I said. But I was not so sure it was strictly the truth that he had come to kill Nambu. Their previous efforts had seemed to be more about capturing her.

'Remember what this feels like,' I said.

'I'm sorry?' Nambu looked up at me, curious.

'Remember what this feels like, to have killed someone.'

'Why would you say that to me?'

'Because you have done this yourself. Your mother, when she decides to have someone executed, does so at a distance. She is removed from the act of removing a life. These matters are acts of the gods and goddesses, not the business of the mortals. Just remember that, for when it comes to killing someone it is the business of gods you're messing with. It comes with profound implications.'

'You will confuse her,' Leana grunted, before moving away to look over the corpse again.

'It is an important lesson. One day you will rule this nation. You will have the power to send armies to die in your name, perhaps. You will have political prisoners executed. You will be responsible for killing people, but it will never be from your hand. This is what it is like.' I gestured towards the corpse. 'Even though the reason was pure, that was a life you removed.'

'He speaks too much,' Leana said. 'I have killed many people. Hundreds. This is not the business of the gods but real life. I just deal with it, like I would deciding what to eat for supper. It is only profound if you choose for it to be so.'

'We may have come from different backgrounds,' I added, 'in reaching our conclusions on the matter.'

'If you had seen what I had seen,' Leana said, 'you would not think much of this. Now.' Leana marched over to the young princess and gently but firmly hauled her off the bed, and patted her down as if she was plumping up a cushion. 'You need to sleep. We will tell you all about the case tomorrow. But sleep while we clean up this corpse.'

'I'm not sure I can sleep,' Nambu whispered, staring guiltily at the corpse.

'You will,' Leana said. 'I am proud of you. Look at you, a warrior princess. You are like me.'

It wasn't exactly a smile on Nambu's face, but she no longer appeared to be quite as sad. Moments later she shuffled off into her bedroom, and closed the door behind her.

'A warrior princess,' I said, 'just like you.'

'Let us speak no more of the past.'

'Familiar territory, then,' I said. I lit another candle and moved over to the corpse to make a closer inspection. Whoever this was he must have acquired inside information from deep inside the queen's circle to know where to find her. I noticed that the man's black shirt had become untucked in his fall, and that the small of his back was revealed. Something strange there – an unusual shape for clothing – caught my eye. Lifting the material back revealed a small tattoo of the sickle and star.

'Oh,' I muttered.

'What is it?' Leana crouched down alongside me to get a better look.

'This tiny symbol is of the Rukrid clan. Sulma Tan had pointed out their heraldry at the games. He must be a member of that family. We must notify the queen immediately.'

Leana stood up and moved to the door. 'I would not like to be in the Rukrid clan come the morning. I will go back to alert the staff. You stay here and comfort Nambu.'

Deep Blue Waters

All of those involved in the murders had now been caught in the night-time raids conducted by the ruthlessly efficient soldiers of Kuvash. Each of the suspects had been sleeping in their bed, unaware of their fate. Now they were deep within the city's gaols, a secret of the state.

We decided not to take Nambu with us to Evum. It was too dangerous – even though nowhere was safe for the princess. Disappointed not to travel, and to have to spend more time in her old quarters, she appeared to understand the reason. Her maturity impressed me greatly.

'How long do you think it will take?' Nambu asked.

'Sulma Tan said about ten hours, depending on whether or not the wind is behind us, and how easy it is to find the place.'

'Do they know where to find the island though?'

'The map we found is detailed enough, apparently. Our captains suggest we arrive just before dawn tomorrow, when our approach cannot easily be seen. It is best if you remain safe with your mother for the moment. Now, forgive me, princess, for I must sail soon.'

Nambu tilted her head in a way that reminded me of the queen, and acknowledged her understanding.

The sea does not agree with me. I have never enjoyed a journey on a ship, not even a short one. Whatever I have done to offend the gods, it must have been something truly awful. Every time a ship slips from its moorings and into unstable waters, my stomach lurches and I cannot seem to find a solid stance. Often I can be found nursing my woes below deck for the duration of a voyage. Leana would frequently ridicule me – and I think she often enjoyed trips across water simply because she could laugh at me. However, I had grown used to being sick at sea.

But late that morning, as the trireme sailed at speed, the sails snagging tight in the wind and the oars cutting through the deep water, I did not *fully loathe* the experience.

This was indeed a first. My stomach did not lurch. My legs were stable.

This was no coincidence as I knew at once the reason. There, in my pocket, were two rings containing the mineral that had been mined on Evum. The mineral which had, so far, managed to stave off my seizures, and which had hastened my recovery from a thorough beating. I wondered if the mineral's properties had been responsible for the strange behaviour of the bishop's remains, but I put such ridiculous thoughts out of my mind. All I knew was that the mineral had changed me somehow. It had enhanced me.

Even Leana was surprised. 'Lucan, you have not emptied your stomach of its contents yet. Why is this?'

I shrugged, knowing she would quickly dismiss my thoughts. Yet, Sojun had also confirmed the stone's special properties, so I could not be completely insane in possessing such thoughts.

'Perhaps I am finally getting used to the sea,' I called back. 'Spirits save me. That day has finally come.'

For several hours we cut through the sea, the captain confident that we would locate our destination. We had several men on lookout, each of them keenly scrutinizing the distance for signs of the island. Sixty soldiers and whatever crew we had on these ships would, I hoped, be enough. Though I did not know what would await us.

During the trip I wished I could have brought prisoners with me to interview, especially Brell. From what Sulma Tan had told me, Brell was a key figure in the series of murders. He would have been the one to identify the victims' movements. He would have briefed the others on the best way to capture the likes of Lydia Marinus and Grendor of the Cape. But instead everyone remained back in Kuvash, in a cell somewhere in the bowels of the royal palace.

If I had brought any of them with me, would they have been able to guide us around Evum? It might have been possible that their hatred of what went on there, or the journey back to their past, would provoke something. It could be considered cruel to bring them back to their place of childhood desolation – where their innocence had first been lost. They were better off right now out of sight, out of the way of this operation. With them facing execution for their crimes, what I didn't want was for one of them to hurl themselves overboard. I hoped that my instructions for there to be a constant suicide watch were not unheeded.

I felt relief at having brought the murders to a close, yet filled with foreboding about our journey.

As I conversed with Sulma Tan before sunset, gripping the balustrade and looking down to regard the hypnotic rhythm of the oars, it became apparent there was a more pressing issue in her mind.

'When I spoke to her last night,' Sulma Tan said, 'the queen did not seem overly disturbed that children were being used to mine for a mineral — nor that the mineral existed. She was little disturbed by the fact that her eunuch was involved in the killings.'

'What did disturb her then?'

'Mostly three things now. The first being the fact that she has tried to bring enlightenment to Koton and this represents a failure. The old ways still endure.'

'Do you think she was being honest by claiming to know nothing about it?'

'I do — because I, too, knew nothing. If anyone should have heard of such crimes, then it should have been me. She must wait to see what we report back from Evum. Then she'll want me to assess exactly who was caught up in this affair. There will be an internal investigation as to how the queen did not know what went on and why there was an island missing from her maps. She was upset by her lack of control.'

'But not upset with you, surely? You helped bring this to her attention and resolve the issues.'

'This may be so, but a queen cannot know everything, and—'

'This is a queen who likes to know everything.'

'You speak bluntly.' She glanced at me with uncertainty before looking out to sea.

There was something about the water that — in my stable state — I could begin to appreciate. One could clear one's mind by regarding the churn of the waters, the rhythm of the sea.

I shrugged at her comment. 'What was the third issue that disturbed her — the Rukrid clan's attempts on Nambu?'

'Yes. A queen can be mortally wounded by such things, for it erodes that most important quality: trust. Who in her circle was

working with the family? Why were they trying to kill Nambu
– to prevent the family line from continuing? She now has that
to worry about as well. She placed Nambu with you because you
would have no agendas.'

'What does she intend to do?'

'The less you know of that,' Sulma Tan replied, 'the better.'

The Island

Figures rushed about the main deck. Sails had changed direction and the oars had slowed. The weather was calm and the orange sun was starting to dip below the horizon. Our three ships were now drifting through calm waters, though not out of control. Up ahead on the horizon was an island with a series of cliffs.

'What's going on?' I called across the deck.

The captain of our ship, a young, slender man who had spent many days in the open sun, approached us in a sense of urgency. Somehow he had made a naval officer's uniform seem rather scruffy, and I hoped this was no omen for a disastrous mission. 'We think that's the island, sir.'

I looked to Sulma Tan, who looked at me and then back to him. 'Are you certain?'

'If the charts are right and my goddess is smiling on us then aye, that's Evum.'

Was my goddess smiling on me, though? The tension was heavy in the air. The investigation had come this far. Relief was just a short distance away.

'What is your plan, captain?' asked Sulma Tan.

The captain scratched his head. 'Depends how you want to play your hand, my lady,' he grunted. 'Got the cover of darkness to find somewhere to come ashore. I say give it two hours, until it's dark, and make our way there.'

'Sensible suggestions, captain,' she replied, and turned to me. 'Until darkness falls.'

The captain, to his credit, brought no bad omens. True to his word, as soon as the sky was indigo, he gave the orders for the ships to steer towards the island. The wind was loud enough to obscure the sound of the oars breaking the water as we made our way stealthily along the coast.

Evum was no more than a mile long. Unlikely to have been overlooked by naval cartographers, but it was an easy oversight if Grendor maintained any influence over the task. The lack of its existence on any map probably explained why Sojun's embittered gang never returned. It would have been difficult to find. Far easier to take revenge in the city.

Little lights of what looked like cottages could be perceived further inland, and smoke from several chimneys – or some sparking structure of an industrial nature. The island did not appear equipped for defending itself. No battlements stood stark against the stars that glittered up behind. It was possible there were small lookout points nestled into the cliffside, but in the dark it was difficult to know. The captain had tasked several men with scrutinizing the shores though none of them seemed concerned.

By midnight we had found a small bay on the north side of Evum, no more than two hundred feet wide, surrounded by dunes, enough to form a natural shelter. By the luck of the gods we did not strike any rocks as we steered carefully into the small inlet. The captain gave the order for a plank to be lowered and there would be a short walk where we would have to wade through waist-high water.

Soldiers headed out almost simultaneously from the three ships. Their orders were to stay together. Leana, Sulma Tan and myself then waded ashore together, raising our belongings above our heads as we moved though the still-warm waters. On the beach we attempted to dry ourselves.

The surf gently licked along the shoreline and a sharp, vegetative tang filled the air. There were no lights, no shapes against the starlight other than the grasses.

A gibbous moon was directly overhead, making our progress visible to others. But it also illuminated the way as we moved behind the spearhead of soldiers advancing along the beach. Only then did I notice two archers cautiously scanning the shoreline, covering our path.

We ascended the dunes, towards long grasses, and after consulting briefly with the captain the scouting group went on ahead, investigating a passage through a small gorge. I worried that they could be prime targets for snipers up above, but again the place looked to be undefended.

We waited in the shadow of the gorge for an hour, until eventually the call came for us to move onwards. Though we were quite safe surrounded by so many soldiers I was nervous with anticipation.

So far it had all been too easy.

One of the scouts dashed up to me in the gloom. 'Officer Drakenfeld, we've located a primary structure to the east. A quick walk across rocky terrain.'

'Guarded?' I asked, unable to read his expression.

A shake of the head. 'It's unguarded, so far as we can tell.'

'What do you think the place is?'

'It's industrial, possibly a place to process the mineral we think.'

'How many people do you think are there?'

'Hard to say. On a site that size, perhaps in daytime there would be a good thirty or forty workers.'

'If we raided this structure, do you believe there will be little in the way of defence?'

'Fairly confident, sir.'

'Fairly?'

'Fairly.'

That was as good as one could expect from such a situation. 'We'll move on at your command.'

'Very good, sir.'

The scout moved away and gave some orders in Kotonese. Within a heartbeat the rest of the soldiers began to ready their arms and line up in formation. Sulma Tan, Leana and myself were urged to take our places among the soldiers. We all marched through the gorge, the churn of the sea in the distance.

Bones

Our pace slowed up as the building came into sight. A large, rectangular stone construct, with three wide chimneys and surrounded by workshop detritus, it had been built into a small gully, with a river running along the bottom.

But while the soldiers fanned out, with a section moving around the other side of the building, something didn't quite feel right.

The stench.

It was the odour that put me off. 'Leana,' I called, and she froze too. 'Do you smell that?'

She nodded, her eyes widening, and moved to say something, but another of the scouts came to find me again. 'Sir, we've found something,' she announced, her face grim. 'You'd better come this way.'

We trotted behind her, following a narrow path through discarded crates, waste and long grasses, until we arrived at a field at the back of the building.

Because of the bright moon, the tiny, jutting bones could still be perceived.

There must have been two dozen corpses in this field, half-heartedly dug into the ground.

'Bring torches,' I called, and when no one replied I shouted the order again, almost losing my voice.

Light came. Things glistened, but there was no longer any pink flesh here. Charred skin and small, blackened skulls, hollow eyes amidst the stems of rye grass. We were walking among the foetid bones of dead children.

'Spirits save them,' Leana breathed. 'They are all so *young*.'

'Why have they killed them?'

'That is why,' Leana replied, pointing to the corner of the field. There, glinting dully in the moonlight, was a large brass statue of a bull – one similar to statues I had seen at Lydia Marinus' house. Once it had been heated by a huge pyre, which was now a smouldering pile of ash. The statue must have been fifteen feet tall, and at least thirty feet long.

'The old ways,' I remarked.

We moved over quickly, whereupon I instructed a dozen men to look inside the structure. They obliged, first cautiously touching the statue to see if it was still hot.

'It's safe to touch, but hasn't long gone out,' someone said. 'Seems a hasty business.'

Rope was tossed up and, when it had hooked securely, three soldiers climbed to the top of the statue. One by one they peered inside. One of them collapsed off the side, falling into the long grass. Another retched the contents of his stomach down the side of the statue. The reaction was enough to confirm the worst.

More torches were brought to the scene.

'Describe what you can see inside,' I called up.

The man peered over the edge once again but said nothing.

'What can you see?' I called again.

'B-bodies, sir,' he replied. Then, more firmly, 'Two of them. Remains. Children's remains.'

'By Polla ...' I breathed, rubbing my eyes. 'What have we stumbled onto?'

'It's hideous,' Sulma Tan replied. There were tears in her eyes. There were probably some in my own, too.

'Child sacrifice,' Leana muttered. 'Such desperation to please the old gods.'

I grabbed one of the torches from a soldier, who stood agape, and wandered off into the field of broken young bodies.

Some of these could have been no older than two or three summers. Others were perhaps in their teenage years, but it did not detract from the crime. Even if these were adults, I would have been horrified, but to kill them at such a young age and on such a scale.

And for what reason? Were these not the workers?

Some of the corpses were very fresh – and had not been burned, though their naked bodies displayed ritualistic torture – icons had been burned into their skin, and there were cuts across their wrists and throats. The nearest one that had not been charred, whose throat had been cut, still had its eyes open to the world.

I moved the torch over his face and looked into that lifeless gaze – two blue eyes regarded me, very much dead, but still with the power to move me.

Dawn broke across the field, gradually illuminating the full extent of the horrors. I counted forty-three in all, but guessed there were many more underground elsewhere. This was a graveyard for burned and broken lives. Many had clearly been sacrificed, according to the old ways. But in all my years I had never known victims to be so young. Everyone had heard tales from thousands of years ago, when cultures would conduct such barbaric practices to appease deities. Parents would even offer up their own children for favours. It had not so much been immoral then, as amoral.

These beliefs were outside of our way of thinking. To see such an atrocity in our age, however, was chilling.

The command had been given for the soldiers to move on to see if there was anyone still alive, workers or children.

The rest of us simply stood in an adjacent field, trying to piece together what might have gone on, wondering how it was possible that so many young people could be eliminated. How many future craftsmen, artists, bakers, dancers, chariot racers – just how many of these children had been turned completely or partly to ash?

Later, much later, as the sun reached its zenith, there was a sign from a small pocket of soldiers. A signal came down from a grassy hillside that they had caught several men.

About an hour later, these prisoners were being marched down the slope where they were forced to kneel in front of the large stone building, their hands on their heads, facing the wall.

Satisfied these prisoners were under control, two of the soldiers dressed in blue and black approached me.

'Found them in a small shack on the other side of the island, sir,' said a tall officer. 'There's a bigger operation down there – just the mineral, though. Rock processing. There's a small jetty where the mineral is shipped from.'

'Are there any documents? Is there any evidence?'

'Burned.'

'They must have seen our ship coming,' I replied, 'and tried to conceal what was here.'

'Aye. They smell of fires, the lot of them. Most likely they burned these kids too so we couldn't find them.'

'Do you have any idea how long it takes to burn a body?' I said. 'Those children were burned before we turned up. It takes a lot more people to do it, too. No doubt there are more hiding on the island somewhere. Find them. Leave these ones here.'

'Sir.'

The soldiers followed my orders. I nodded to Leana and we both walked around the front, facing the eight men, who were a range of ages. The youngest no more than twenty summers, the oldest in his fifties, and each looked well fed. Their faces had been blackened by soot, and their clothing was stained beyond recognition. They held their heads low.

Barely able to hide my anger at the lack of humanity, I eventually composed myself and addressed them all.

'My name,' I began, shouting loudly above the wind, 'is Lucan Drakenfeld. I am an Officer of the Sun Chamber, the highest legal authority in the Vispasian Royal Union.'

I repeated the statement in Kotonese.

'You are all to be arrested and taken back to the mainland. Your crimes, if you are found responsible, will lead to your execution. I cannot guarantee it will be a quick death. You are likely to be subjected to a painful and humiliating end.'

Again, I repeated myself in the other language.

'I will take you one by one to the adjacent field where so many bodies lie in various states of decomposition. You will have the opportunity to prove your innocence. By explaining what has gone on here, and who is responsible, there is a slender opportunity for mercy. I am not an unreasonable man.' I gave a brief pause. 'However, my assistant here is not so kind.' Leana drew her sword, the blade glimmering in the morning sun. 'Should you be . . . unhelpful in any way, I cannot guarantee any of the laws of this continent will be adhered to, nor that your pain will be minimal. Having seen what's happened here, I can't say I care all that much. The choice, gentlemen, is yours.'

I pointed at the oldest man in the group. The soldiers dragged him into the field indelicately before they kicked him in the ribs.

Another soldier brought forward my travel case, containing paper and ink, and followed me into the field. There I set up my operation and began the afternoon-long process to find out the truth of what had happened here on Evum.

Answers

The raw emotional state of these men meant that the answers came swiftly. Confessions were muttered through tear-soaked lips, the relief of their being caught all too clear.

I tried not to speculate on the morality of these men. I had seen people do strange things when enough coin could line their pockets. Standards could vanish in the blink of an eye when a group was left to establish its own rules, far removed from the guiding lines of common society. I was not here to judge, not yet, just looking for answers.

And they came soon enough.

Every month for decades, ever since the island had been in operation, children had been killed to please the ancient god Hymound, the 'King of the Multitudes'. The cult out here was extreme, a faction based on a much older and debased form of the religion, one which thrived with less violent elements on the mainland. Those involved took their faith every bit as seriously as I did with Polla.

The cult was deeply connected to the land, and concerned itself with blood and renewal. Omens were to be found in the passage of birds. The weather was scrutinized for signs and animal entrails were studied assiduously. Entrails offered guidance – and out here human intestines were more reliable. The youngest member of our current cohort of prisoners was a former child labourer, and attributed his position of authority to his dedication to Hymound.

Throughout the painstaking interviews the men spoke with passion. There were outbursts amid the mumbled, often contradictory, pieces of evidence. When pressed on what Hymound offered them, the response was always the same. Immortality. The opportunity to endure.

A special child was burned ceremonially every month in the brass bull. Or, more specifically, they forced children to burn their *kin*. The chosen one's ashes rose into the sky to be welcomed by Hymound – it was an honour, the captives claimed, and many children were glad to be relieved of their lives in the mines. As these offerings lived on in the heavens, it was assumed their sacrifice would hasten the discovery of more evum on the island.

Children were taken, over the years, out of the orphanages and brought on ships in the dead of night. Many of the men did not know who was responsible for acquiring or transporting the children – they just arrived – but I could guess who might be involved. It was even said that one of the wealthy donors offered up their own son in an effort to satisfy the gods so that they could be rewarded with their evum much sooner – such was their desperation, such was the difficulty in finding pockets of evum on this island.

The lengths people would go to in order to extend their lives.

I pushed for names. In the heat of the moment, I felt I had no reservations about inflicting any torture upon them – there was no civilization out here, and all my standard rules were irrelevant.

However, the threat of Leana's blade was enough with these dejected men.

The names came forth.

Lydia Marinus. Grendor of the Cape. Bishop Tahn Valin. The Kahn brothers. They had all been part of the scheme. They were all abusing children and using them for material and metaphysical gain. But there were far more names. Presumably the killers could not have known them all and had murdered those they could get to. Other individuals involved in this island's despicable operation might have tried hard to keep their influence to a minimum. Either way these names would be issued to Sulma Tan and the queen. Their investigation would have to continue into the furthest reaches of their culture.

The operation existed to harvest the mineral known by several names. Evumite. Redstone. Bloodstone. Life-giver. There were local names, too. This, combined with some of the strange word-hybrids in their syntax, indicated that people had been isolated here for so long that their language had evolved. I had no doubt that those in charge of the operation would have gone to any lengths to keep the workers here for ever. It would have been too much of a risk to take them back to the mainland.

Evumite, they claimed, was able to extend life and grant special powers at times; when pressed on what these powers were, they could not say. As they spoke I wondered if such powers had been the reason why the bodies of those murdered on the mainland had stirred in some way – that there was still some strange form of life within them.

The precious mineral was available in incredibly rare quantities, located in isolated pockets buried deep underground. Very little ever made it to the mainland. Everyone who worked here, who was no longer a child, and who had proved themselves during five years of service, was permitted a small lump of evumite as payment for their trouble. A charitable gesture, the captives claimed. The longer those people served, the more evumite they might be given. The man I thought was in his fifties said he was eighty-four years old and had worked here since he was eleven.

Children had been shipped to the island simply to work the mines. They were small enough to fit through the tiny tunnels that formed a vast system underground. Those who made it to adulthood were either disappeared or employed to inflict torture on others. Evumite was so difficult to find that the operation perhaps produced a fistful a year at first, but the more sacrifices that were made, the more successful the mines had become. These offerings to the gods, no matter how shocking, were *working* according to the needs of the island. The captives before me could not even contemplate that the success might have been purely coincidental.

What happened on Evum was not just the workings of the ancient cult of Hymound, as I had first thought. It was also a self-sustaining business operation organized by some of the wealthiest people in Koton – largely traditionalists and people who secretly worshipped the old gods. Money and donations came to fund it in exchange for evumite, and the chance to live forever. Lydia Marinus had been the backbone of the operation, donating a great deal of mining equipment.

Sulma Tan was shocked as she read the names I had taken down, and confirmed their position high up in Kotonese society. She had no doubt the queen would want them purged. We could only speculate on how many of these stones had made their way throughout Vispasia over the years.

Later I sat slumped against a wall as grasses stirred in the breeze and the evening sun began to fade from the skies. In the distance was the sound of the sea, calming and rhythmic. Leana remained quietly beside me, neither of us wanting to engage in much conversation. For the first time in weeks I felt at peace, though I suspected I was in some state of disbelief, or simply too numb to process what I had seen.

'We like to think we're not primitive people, we Kotonese,' one soldier remarked to me as he passed by, 'but look at us. We still use human blood for pleasing the gods. We're still barbarians.' His crestfallen expression, which was shared by others here, suggested that they felt the burden of the discovery. It had been a betrayal of their own nation, of everything they had stood for. He reached under the neckline of his tunic and produced a Nastran symbol upon a chain. 'Don't think bad of us, sir. Not everyone worships Hymound.'

A simple nod, thin-lipped, was all I could muster as he walked away. Contemplating the legality of the matter, I began to pen an urgent missive to the Sun Chamber in Free State, which I would deliver as soon as we were back on the mainland.

Such practices as human sacrifice had been outlawed at the creation of the Vispasian Royal Union, two centuries ago. Indeed, it was written into the constitution of each member nation and, for as long as anyone could remember, only animals could be used in blood offerings on altars across the continent.

Children, though.

Not just humans, but lives terminated before they had the chance to blossom into something great.

As I questioned the men, soldiers continued to round up prisoners from various pockets of the island. I saw them returning with more figures chained in a line, their hands raised above their heads. At first I felt that these could be interrogated in the morning, but something struck me as odd, so I walked over to meet them.

'Where are the children?' I demanded of the soldiers. 'They couldn't have all been burned.'

'We've not found any, sir,' one replied. Behind him the line of prisoners was being marched to the side of the building alongside the others. 'This lot said they've all been put down. Burnt.'

'They're lying. Go back and find them.'

'It's getting dark, sir. An hour of light left at the most.'

'Go back,' I repeated. 'Take torches to light and go back. Search every building on the island. Go underground – that's where some of them will be. We're not leaving this island until we have secured their freedom. They've suffered long enough. Any survivors will be taken back to the mainland.'

He stared at me blankly.

'Do it!'

'Sir.'

Dispiritedly, they reorganized themselves. After hearing me, another eight men volunteered their services and a moment later they all marched off with unlit torches.

Back in our makeshift camp, someone had lit a large fire away from the prisoners. The smell of cooking drifted towards me and I trudged over to the others without much of an appetite.

'Do you honestly think they will find any of them?' Sulma Tan asked, rising to greet me.

'I do not think anything,' I replied. 'This is simply the right thing to do. For far too long on this island there has been a shortage of this sentiment.'

Glowing in the light of the fire, her tired, worn gaze met my own. Respectfully, she added, 'I am not so sure I could be in the Sun Chamber, if this is what you have to deal with all the time.'

'It isn't always this bad.'

'I am horrified,' she said. 'The queen will be horrified, too. Everything she has been trying to build in her country has been undermined by the people closest to her. This is not how it was meant to be.'

'Then the queen needs to choose better friends in future,' was all I could manage in response.

The Return

Twenty-three children came with us on the journey back to the mainland.

Just twenty-three.

There may well have been more survivors and I prayed to Polla that those children were able to tap some hitherto undiscovered vein of evumite in order to stay alive. It might prolong their existence just a little longer, enough to keep them going until another force could be sent to investigate the operations on the island thoroughly.

We made sure the rescued children were fed well. They were, understandably, very silent and unwilling to say much, no matter what language I tried. Aboard the other two ships we kept our prisoners in chains below deck, feeding them meagre rations for the day — which was, probably, more than they would receive when we got back to the palace gaols.

Now that the investigation had been concluded, I used the opportunity to write down my discoveries in full so that I could present them to the queen and send an urgent messenger to brief the Sun Chamber on the entire affair.

It had been a curious journey from discovering the severed and discarded pieces of Bishop Tahn Valin, before finding Grendor of the Cape, Lydia Marinus and Tagg and Meruwa Drennar – highly influential people within the nation – dead in a public place, their bodies dumped. Originally it had looked like their lives were not connected but all of them were, in fact, bound together by this vile operation.

I thought again of those who had committed the murders, who had been victims and had escaped, bided their time, and taken revenge when the opportunity came. If I had gone through the experiences they had endured, if I had suffered the same daily privations as them – being made to crawl through tunnels, being beaten and worse – would I have been able to let those experiences go?

Murder was murder, however, no matter how justifiable. To remove a life from this world is the decision of the gods, and the gods only.

For now, though, the difficult choice of what to do with these people was not mine to make. All I could do was simply inform the rulers and lawmakers of what had gone on, and let them come to their own conclusions, no matter how uncomfortable they were. It was for nation states to enforce their own justice, and not the will of the Sun Chamber.

We were meant to sift through the debris and present the case as we saw it. Should we operate any differently, should we demand that nations behave in a certain way then that would create a very different Vispasia, one not too far removed from being an empire. That was not what the Sun Chamber was about. Besides, it was unlikely that any royal would want to submit to a higher authority – other than their gods.

During the afternoon I leaned over the balustrade observing the distance, lost in my own thoughts, my cloak flapping in the breeze. Leana approached me with her welcoming insouciance, her boots heavy on the deck.

'No sickness still?' she asked.

'None.'

'No seizures?'

'Nothing for many days now.'

'This evumite – you claimed it had properties. This whole mining operation has claimed that too. The reason for our being here is based on the realization that this rock has properties.'

'What are you getting at?'

'Spirits save me. You have not taken the ring out of your pocket since you realized what it could do. It obviously helps you. Will you keep it?'

It was true that I had recovered swiftly from my injuries when I had been beaten, and that my seizures and sickness were no longer a concern. There was no denying that owning such a thing would enhance my life in numerous ways. Not only would my seizures be a thing of the past, but my work might improve if I could recover from the unavoidable skirmishes that came from being an Officer of the Sun Chamber.

'It could,' she added, 'make both our lives a lot more simple, could it not?'

'If I *take* this for my own gain, Leana, then am I any better than those men and women who made children suffer in dark tunnels, simply to enhance the pleasure of their own existence?'

'We cannot know if it was pleasure. The people who owned it had much to gain by remaining alive – land and wealth and status. Therefore they had much to lose in death.'

'Either way, this stone has the blood of children all over it. It has the history of an operation that is unspeakably sinister, that has destroyed the lives of the most innocent of our world.'

'You are still stupid if you do not take it. Your life was a challenge with your seizures and now it is not.'

'That may be so. However, we managed to cope with the problem, more or less. If my seizures have gone away, then more problems will come to fill in the void and occupy my mind. But the issue remains that the stones are not only evidence in this case, but it would be improper if I left here with one in my pocket. It would be a theft – not only of a trinket, but my morals would forever be gone.'

I expected more admonishment from Leana, but none came. Instead she nodded. 'Good. I expected you would say that, so I am pleased that you have not disappointed me.'

'Nice to know that you're checking up on me.'

'You are not the only one who understands morals,' she replied. 'I have read the same books as you, albeit in more refined languages.'

'And probably in better bindings,' I added, a nod to her once-fantastic wealth – something else that I had learned so recently.

Leana did not respond to my comment. Instead she laid a firm hand on my shoulder before marching back across the deck, leaving me alone with the blue vista, the cool breeze and the repetitive sound of oars cutting through the water.

Blockade

Our arrival back at the docks in Kuvash revealed a bad sign. There was next to no activity in the water. The ships that would once drift along the river to the estuary and beyond were still firmly roped to their moorings. The busy activity of trade had ceased. Instead, a single vessel with a raised naval flag indicated a military closure. No ships were permitted in or out, by orders of the queen.

Sulma Tan was clearly vexed, though her cool, stern expression betrayed little emotion. As we neared the bank, she began to walk the deck impatiently.

'If you have other business,' I said, 'go to the queen. Make clear my command to your soldiers and I'll handle the rest.'

She scanned my eyes for any hint of speaking between the lines. I was only a little insulted that, after all I had done for her nation, she found hesitation in doing so.

'Have everyone converge at the palace. The children can be looked after in comfort by the staff there. You know where to take the prisoners. I'll ask the captain of our ship to accompany your entourage there.' She untwisted a gold signet ring from her thumb and handed it to me. It bore the markings of the nation, a raised stag set in a blue stone. The craftsmanship was exquisite, the detailing crisp. 'Should you have any trouble, show this and it will ensure that whatever instructions you have will be carried out.'

'You're most kind.' I indicated the vacant waters and the strange sense of quiet. 'What do you think it is?'

'I think we are at war, Lucan. My nation and yours have probably come to conflict. Detrata was our biggest trading partner – now look. The only people who will make money now are those in the weapons trade.'

Sulma Tan rode on ahead, while the rest of us marched behind on foot.

We received no bother on our way through the city. Armed escorts ensured no trouble came from the prisoners. The captured men trudged in a line, their faces reddened by the sun, their clothing filthy. A few passers-by gave us curious glances as we led twenty-three glum-looking children through the streets, but other than that our passage was without incident.

This was late afternoon and the city should have been thriving. As it was, a handful of carts were led away from empty marketplaces. Awnings offered shelter to no one. A handful of people regarded us from open windows, to see if we brought news with us; but they soon looked away.

The prisoners were taken to the palace gaols, the children to a guest room usually reserved for ambassadors or visiting dignitaries. They were brought good food as well as new clothing and, in the briefest possible terms, I explained to the members of staff nearby just what an ordeal they had been through. My firm words were enough to see them treated like royalty.

And then Leana and I simply waited to present our findings to Queen Dokuz Sorghatan.

*

By the time Sulma Tan came to find us it was early evening. She brought information that a member of the Sun Chamber had arrived, a man named Dorval. I hadn't heard of him.

The two of us were brought together and left alone in a private chamber. The warm light of several cressets showed him to be of good physique. Athletic and with a noble bearing, he stood a shade shorter than myself. He was roughly the same age, and with keen, green eyes and chestnut hair. A diffident fellow, he had a likeable demeanour.

Our first sentences were spoken in code, as we explored just what level of clearance we each had, and when we came to a satisfactory conclusion we wandered out of earshot of gossiping administrators lingering in the doorway, or guards who could have been spies.

'There are not many agents left in these parts,' I said, now speaking standard Detratan.

'Oh we're still to be found here and there,' he said and smiled. 'We're just not as obvious as rumour makes us out to be.' Dorval's tone grew more serious. 'And we only make ourselves known when strictly necessary.'

'How long have you been in Kuvash?' I asked.

'I arrived a few hours after you set off on your trip, so I remained here for the night. Not a bad city really. Successful mission?'

I wondered how much he knew. 'A success in terms of completion of my investigation. However, it was something of a failure for the soul and a belief in human dignity.'

'It gets to you, being an officer, doesn't it?' he said. 'Still, it's not much better being an agent, but I mustn't complain too much – things are about to get a lot worse.'

'The border conflict?'

'You could put it like that. I'd prefer to call it jingoistic war-mongering in very poor disguise.'

'Who's at fault?'

'Who do you think?' Dorval muttered. 'The new Detratan republic is on the warpath. Ambassadors are fleeing or being killed outright, and Koton will likely fall very soon. Friend, I give it ten days. Ten days before ten thousand men march into the city, and they won't be wearing Kotonese colours.'

'This place isn't exactly kitted out for a siege.'

'Which is why Koton will easily fall under the advance of Detrata.'

'And nothing can be done about it?'

'The Sun Legions are on standby, having so recently been sent out of Detrata to Maristan, but I'm not sure they'll intervene in the matter. Not now things are this serious, anyway. They normally like to add pressure or help provide force to settle small disputes. Getting involved in a conflict this size would mean they had to pick sides. That act, simple though it may seem, would result in the Sun Chamber breaking up the Vispasian Royal Union. It is unthinkable.'

'Shouldn't they do that? Should they not simply protect Koton from their aggressor?'

'Well said, for a Detratan boy, but these things are not for us to decide. Besides, much blood will be spilled, friend. It may be that if Koton surrenders quickly, many lives will be spared and the Sun Chamber can attempt to negotiate a reconciliation afterwards. Maybe they'll redraw the borders slightly and that will be enough to see that Detrata's thirst for conquest is quenched.'

'Do you honestly think a few yards of land will satisfy them?' I asked.

'Not a chance.' He grinned. 'I'm ever the optimist.'

For a moment it felt as if he had more to tell me on the subject, some subtle nuance on the art of war or on the prevention of bloodshed. Instead an easy silence fell between us.

'Why are you here?' I asked.

'To connect with you in the first instance. To inform the queen of the military manoeuvres and advise where she should organize her defences.'

'And you think she will take advice from outside her nation?'

'She has the choice to ignore me,' he added. 'Anyway, I'm really here to get the royals across the border when the time comes, though she doesn't know it yet. Koton will fall. Kuvash will be taken. Queen Dokuz can either hang around to greet the invading army or perhaps I can tempt her to safety. She'll be more valuable alive in the long run.'

'She's a proud woman,' I replied. 'I've no idea what she'll say.'

'I can be charming when I need to.' There was a flash in his eyes as he spoke.

'Do you need any help getting them out?'

He shook his head. 'We've people ready throughout the city on standby. Besides, my friend, you have other orders. You're to return to Free State.'

'Is my investigation here known?' I asked.

'Partially. You'll have a chance to report fully in person, in the Free City. All officers from the northern and western nations are being recalled right now. There's a conclave the likes of which we've not seen in years.'

'This situation must indeed be serious.'

'Only time will tell, friend,' he replied coolly.

'I need to make my final report to the queen and send through my messages to the Sun Chamber ahead of me. It's urgent that I do so, given the nature of the investigation and what I discovered.' I informed him, in a concise manner, of what had been going on here and on Evum. Dorval listened without comment to the horrors I described, his gaze occasionally flickering to the door-way as someone passed along the corridor outside.

When I finished he rolled his lips and nodded thoughtfully. 'You did well. The Drakenfelds are certainly thorough. They were right about you – you're like your father in his prime.'

As long as I wasn't like him in later life . . .

'So be it,' Dorval continued. 'Present your findings to the queen. Make your farewells and we'll have you out first thing in the morning.'

'What action do you think will be taken here when I'm gone?'

'If you'd have asked me a year ago, then that would have been simple enough to decide. As it is . . . with war about to flare up, we may need to keep some of your findings secret. Can you imagine what such a mineral might mean during wartime?'

He had a point. Though I did not work for the Sun Chamber for glory, I had hoped for some recognition. He must have seen my expression, for he added, 'But don't worry – the commissioner, so they say, is already impressed with you. This will enhance your standing in the right circles, ones that will see you amply rewarded.'

'So long as justice is served.'

Dorval shrugged and guided me back to the others. 'The continent is now at war, friend. Justice will have a new meaning.'

In a private court session I gave my findings to the queen. The only other people present were Princess Nambu Sorghatan, Sulma Tan, Leana and myself. Guards had been sent from the room. The hall remained almost empty, the queen's throne suddenly so isolated and vulnerable.

Using my notes, I spoke at length. For over an hour the queen listened to my unintentional humiliation of her nation. My words reverberated around the chamber, even though I spoke with quiet consideration. She nodded here and there in my speech, and asked me to expand upon points, but generally she let me continue without interruption. When it came to physical evidence, I laid out the two rings containing evumite on a purple cushion provided by Sulma Tan.

After I concluded the case, the queen's expression remained blank for some time. Nambu was visibly aghast, and had remained so since I began my description of the events on the island.

After a profound silence, the queen spoke considered words. 'Given all things remain the same with the current political tensions, what would be your suggestions for further steps to take with this case?'

'Sulma Tan would, I'm sure, be able to handle any further investigation required. That is acting upon the names provided by the prisoners, and rounding up everyone else who was involved. This operation probably runs deep in your society and there are still many questions to be answered. From what I understand, the network of those who conducted the operation is spread wide. It was built up over the years, with core ringleaders. I suggest you start your investigations with the Kahn brothers . . .'

The queen gave a silent nod and I could only imagine the suffering those two men would soon undergo.

'There is still the separate matter of the original murders, of course, and of those responsible. Brell being among their number.'

'Quite. This is most embarrassing.' The queen's gaze lingered on me. I could not help but notice her eyes glazed with tears she might soon allow to flow. 'And do you think they should receive justice, given that their lives had been so brutally abused at a young age?'

'That is not for me to say, your majesty,' I breathed, wary of interfering with justice and wary of what her response would be.

'Astran's mercy,' she snapped. 'I am asking you what you *think*.'

A sigh, as I searched my soul for an answer. 'I believe murder is murder, your majesty. What they did was horrific even if the victims deserved punishment. Their past gives reason to the murder, but I do not believe it provides an excuse for killing. These are my own quiet reflections, based purely on my desire to see less blood being spilt across our continent.' At that moment I recalled how I had given my word to Sojun that I would argue the case for Elliah, yet I could not overstep the line of interference. 'I will add one thing, and that is we are dealing with exceptional circumstances. The minds of the young would have been changed excessively by what deeds were enacted on that island. Elliah, Sojun and Brell — we may call them murderers. But in their own way they, too, are victims. Evil deeds breed only more evil. Would we have done any differently? However, such talk stretches my duties too far. I am here merely to facilitate the law. To decide upon who should live and die is the business of the gods only. '

A knowing smile came to her lips. 'And this is where the matter remains a difficulty, for we royals are sanctioned by the gods, are we not? We are their messengers. We are the will of the gods.'

'I do not envy you, your majesty.'

'They will be executed alongside those taken from this new island of mine. They will all receive punishment for, as you say, interfering in the business of the gods.'

'But Mother,' Nambu interrupted. 'Would you not be the same in their position?'

'Silence, child. They had the choice to inform us. They chose their own peculiar ways of justice.'

'Maybe,' Nambu pressed, 'they thought if Lydia and Grendor were involved then you might be too? And that bringing it up might have meant their heads were cut off?'

I held back a smile. The girl had a point. Besides, I knew from interviewing Sojun that the killers had wanted to do this their own way. Punishment had to come from their hands, no matter what the law said.

The queen turned to me. 'Will you inform the Sun Chamber of these events?'

'I'm afraid I must, as with all my work. They will want to know, but it will remain confidential amongst my peers.'

'Our reputation will suffer.' The queen's expression grew to one of anguish. 'Since my father's death, and despite the best efforts of other clans, I have worked to prove we Kotonese are the equals of any other Vispasian nation. Look at us. We are savages after all. It is in our *blood*. For pity's sake, they worshipped Hymound! I knew he was a dark god, but really . . .'

'I have witnessed nothing but an advanced society, the equal of any in this continent, and I have worked with people as skilled and as intelligent as Sulma Tan. Whenever I speak of Koton, I will make sure that its true reputation is known.'

'Spoken with the confidence of a Detratan,' she sighed.

I decided to continue with my boldness, now I had paid her nation a compliment. 'Might I enquire as to what will happen to the Rukrid family? Before we left for Evum, we discovered that they had been behind the attempts to kill or capture Nambu.'

'Yes.' She gave a bitter laugh. 'It is amazing what news torture brings. They wanted to stop *my lineage*, would you believe? The issues with Detrata forced their hand sooner. They thought I was weak in the face of such rampant imperialism. I, who have sent most of my troops to the border, who risk my own security by moving soldiers away, and they think *I* am weak? They have been trying for years to get to me. So they thought they would get to my daughter instead, and made repeated efforts to ensure I was the last of my line. At first they paid for assassins and then, able to trust no one else, they trained their own family members to commit the crime.'

'I trust you responded accordingly.' As I spoke I glanced at Nambu and could see the pain in her face, knowing what her mother had done.

'The Rukrid family is no longer a concern, Drakenfeld.'

'Have they been forced to flee?' I recalled there had been a good dozen of the Rukrid clan present at the Kotonese Games, young and old, and I imagined them scampering across the border in fear after what happened.

A cruel smile came to her lips, the sign of the savage queen materializing for just an instant.

'You misunderstand me,' she said. 'The Rukrid family is no more.'

That was that. Leana and I had done our job, and I had resisted interfering in the matter more than was necessary. We headed to our quarters to pack up our belongings, though I was in no hurry to leave for Free State. A long journey lay ahead of us, and would take a good few weeks of travelling. Once we arrived, who knew how long we would remain there?

Sulma Tan knocked on the open door and I casually beckoned her in, glad to be seeing her one last time before we were to leave. She was wearing a vibrant green dress, styled like a long tunic, but considerably more ornate, and her boots were well polished.

'I have a message from Nambu,' she said. 'Well, more specifically, the message is for Leana.'

'Can she not come here in person?' Leana asked.

'Her mother wants her by her side as she begins to understand the coming conflict. It will apparently be good for her and I can appreciate the sentiment. I think what you did was a good thing in helping the young princess. The queen was even quietly impressed that her daughter killed a man.'

'It is understandable,' Leana muttered. 'What does Nambu say?'

'She wishes for you to write with further instructions on how to carry on her training from time to time. Mere direction, perhaps techniques she can seek out from local tutors.'

Leana gave a smile of a kind I had rarely seen. 'I will insist on a punishing regime from afar.'

As if aware of some desire for Sulma Tan and myself to be alone, Leana strolled into the adjacent room, where Nambu had spent her stay with us.

'That was not completely the reason why I came,' Sulma Tan confessed.

'No?' I moved tentatively to the other side of the bed.

'I wanted to give you this.' From her pocket she produced a small purple velvet purse. 'But please, you must open it on the road.'

'I will,' I replied, and firmly placed the item within the pocket of my tunic.

'Thank you for your help,' I offered. 'Without it we would have been truly floundering.'

'It was mostly your work.'

'Our work,' I replied. 'You used the census information. You helped with so much of the research.'

'If you ever visit Koton again,' she whispered, 'please, come to Kuvash. I will see you are welcome here.'

And with that she smiled and walked away, soon leaving only the sound of her footsteps.

Departure

In the pink light of dawn Dorval saw us off from the stables, a wry smile on his face that could have been taken to mean any number of things.

It was difficult not to imagine what scenes might have gone on here at the stables, where the murder victims had been taken. Even now the military had closed down Sojun's workshop, with just one yawning soldier standing outside the door, rubbing his hands in the morning chill. If I knew Sulma Tan at all, later in the day there would be an operation being conducted down below.

I was sad to never get a chance to speak to Sojun and Elliah again, or even Brell. There was much that I could have uncovered, so much more I wanted to ask about the details, but events were conspiring against me and it was important that the affair was concluded with local powers at the helm. I had carried out my orders – to investigate the murders.

The lanes of the prefecture began to become busy again: traders trundling out with carts to the marketplaces, various coloured awnings being extended over pole-strung meats. By the time we passed through the prefecture gates, the sounds of prices being chanted could already be heard. A priest began to sprinkle white petals along the road behind us.

It would be some time before we arrived in Free City, where we were scheduled to liaise at the conclave of officers from the Sun Chamber. There we would discover our instructions as to where to go next, no doubt, but once again we moved our lives on, never settling, never putting down roots. And this is how we would exist indefinitely.

We rode through the poorer prefecture where, after being in the Sorghatan section for so long, everything was so crammed in and haphazardly constructed. Presently, as we continued on our way, the buildings became lower, cruder and spaced further apart. The city began to return to something more ancient, and a true representation of who these people were: a nomadic culture that had tried to settle. This was the real Koton, the one the queen tried to hide in her own prefecture.

Two or three miles away from the city and yurts appeared on the open horizon. A warm wind rippled through the grassland, which extended as far as the eye could see.

'You did not hand back the ring,' Leana pointed out.

'Yes, I did,' I replied. 'I placed them both on the cushion for the queen as evidence. You saw me do it.'

Leana shook her head. 'I meant Sulma Tan's ring, the one she gave you for access and command.'

'Oh.' I reached into my inner pocket and there it was.

'You will feel obliged to return it to her one day,' Leana said, 'if I know you at all. Your sense of duty will conveniently strike.'

'We will just have to see if Koton is still standing. But this reminds me . . .' I reached into my tunic and pulled out the purse. 'She gave me this before I left and told me to open it on the road.'

'Well, we are now on the road.'

After untying the string knot I emptied out the contents into my palm. There was a note, and inside the fold of paper was a ring. In fact, it was Bishop Tahn Valin's ring, polished, and on a golden chain.

'What does the note say?'

I read it out as we made our way.

Officer Drakenfeld, I have observed that you have felt benefits from this stone. Despite its history, such benefits deserve to be felt by one so . . . caring. Such a stone would be far better in your hands than in our nation, highlighting our guilt. We have enough of that as it is and the queen wishes them no longer in her sight. It is a burden to us and it would be a further duty for you to take it on our behalf. If you feel that you cannot wear it then please use it as a token to think about the preciousness of life or that you are helping us personally. Many lives have been sacrificed for something so powerful. To let it go to waste would sadden an already sour affair.

'She knew your seizures had stopped,' Leana muttered.

Lost for words, I placed the chain around my neck and tucked the stone securely inside my shirt.

'So you have a mysterious ring as a souvenir. I take it,' Leana said, 'that I am to mention its properties to no one?'

'Even if you did,' I replied, 'I'm not sure anyone would believe you.'

Clouds began to roll in across the region, eventually bringing drizzle. Leana retrieved her wax coat from her baggage and I followed suit, and soon the rain intensified. Large muddy puddles formed in the road and the distant hills became lost. As we rode out along the main road past the last village, I peered back towards the distant city of Kuvash. A group of seven children were chasing each other excitedly, oblivious to the rain.

One of them, a black-haired lad in a brown shirt, suddenly slipped in the mud by the side of the road and his head struck a tree stump. His friends clustered around him. We could hear a few shrieks.

Leana and I dismounted and walked over to see if he was OK. He must have been only ten years old at the most, and had cracked open his skull on a sharp protrusion from the stump. Trickles of blood came down his broad cheeks, to mix with his tears and the rain. His fists clenched and unclenched repeatedly as throbs of pain passed through his body. The other six looked up to us for guidance, and a girl with short-cropped hair asked in Kotonese if we could help.

Perhaps this was a sign or a test from Polla, but as Leana began to bandage the injured child's head with a strip of torn cloth, I had no hesitation in reaching into my shirt and retrieving the ring that Sulma Tan had given me. I made a double loop of the chain, and draped it over the child's wounded head so that the ring fell just beneath his ragged collar. As his friends were still looking on, I whispered in a serious tone that the ring was magic, that it would help him, and that he was to tell no one. He squirmed a nod, fighting through the pain of his injury. Whether or not he believed me, I could not say.

We ordered the boy's friends to help him walk home, to make sure he rested and drank plenty of water. With that, Leana and I mounted our horses once again.

'Not a word,' I said to Leana, as we edged forwards. I could see she was thinking how stupid I had been to give away the ring, but I felt an awful lot lighter for it no longer being upon my conscience.

'You would not listen to me anyway,' Leana muttered.

As our horses crested the hill, the rain easing off a little, I glanced back at the group of children. The injured boy was being helped along by two others, whose arms were around his shoulders. They had smiles on their faces and their raucous laughter travelled some distance. Whether or not it was all bravado, the boy seemed to be shrugging off his injury as all seven of the children entered a large wooden hut.

They had their whole lives ahead of them.